MAGGY

BOOK TWO OF THE BRIDES OF CLAN MACDOUGALL, A SWEET SERIES

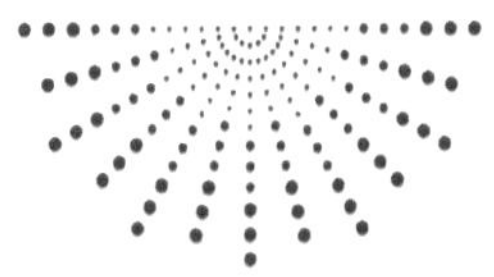

SUZAN TISDALE

ISBN: 978-1-943244-59-1

ALSO BY SUZAN TISDALE

The Clan MacDougall Series

Laiden's Daughter

Findley's Lass

Wee William's Woman

McKenna's Honor

The Clan MacDougall Boxed Set

The Clan Graham Series

Rowan's Lady

Frederick's Queen

The Mackintoshes and McLarens Series

Ian's Rose

The Bowie Bride

Rodrick the Bold

Brogan's Promise

The Clan McDunnah Series

A Murmur of Providence

A Whisper of Fate

A Breath of Promise

The Clan McDunnah Boxed Set

Moirra's Heart Series

Stealing Moirra's Heart

Saving Moirra's Heart

Stand Alone Novels

Isle of the Blessed

Forever Her Champion

The Edge of Forever

Arriving 2018

The MacAllens and Randalls Series:

Secrets of the Heart

Arriving in 2019:

Black Richard's Heart

Kiss of the Red Scorpion

The Daughters of Moirra Dundotter Series:

Mariote

Esa

Muriale

Orabilis

The Brides of the Clan MacDougall

(A Sweet Series)

Aishlinn

Maggy

Nora

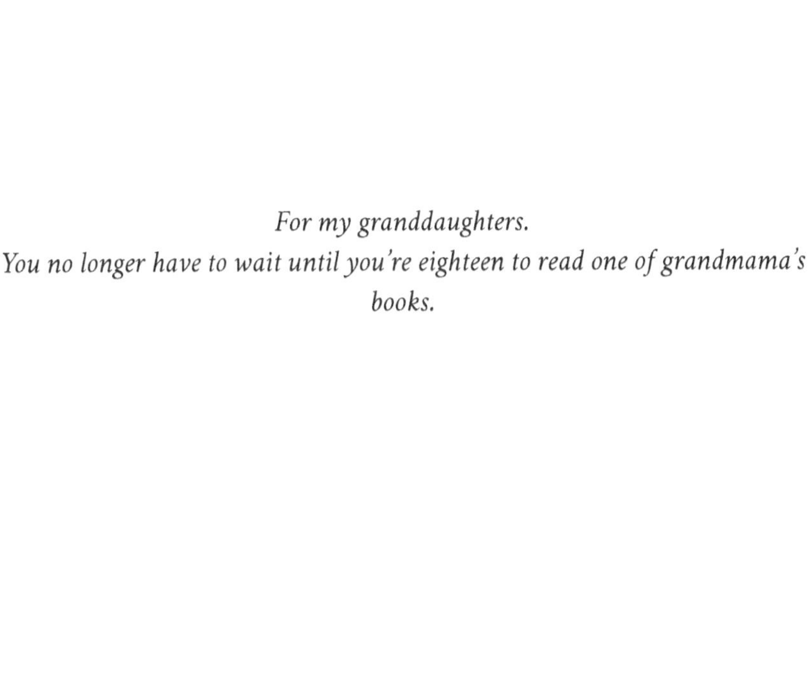

For my granddaughters.
You no longer have to wait until you're eighteen to read one of grandmama's books.

LIFE

"Life is inherently risky. There is only one big risk you should avoid at all costs, and that is the risk of doing nothing."
– Denis Waitley

PROLOGUE

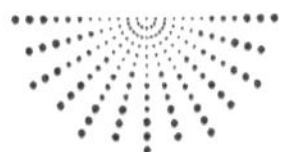

They were just children. Five boys, ranging in age from eight to ten and two, and not one of them had any sense of direction. But what they lacked in that regard, they certainly made up with fierce determination and tenacity. And rock throwing skills.

At first, Findley was certain the boys were nothing more than a ruse to keep suspicion away from some group of men, cowards more likely than not, who had actually stolen the thirty head of cattle. Who would hang a group of lads that young for stealing cattle? Let the lads take the blame, and mayhap a beating, instead of placing guilt where it should really lie.

But the more Findley, his younger brother Richard, and their good friends Gowan and Tall Thomas interrogated the thieves, the more Findley believed their story: They had stolen the cattle, not only to feed their people, but also to prove to their mum they were indeed fine warriors. The only thing the lads would admit to was the fact that four of them were orphans who had been adopted by a fine woman named Maggy and that their clan had been wiped out by a pox years before. They refused to divulge much else.

Now Findley and his men were leading the boys and the cattle down the small hill toward their home. Findley shook his head, pitied with the sight before him. One hut made of mud with a thatch roof surrounded by a few tents -- all of which had seen much better days -- sat between a meandering river and a dense forest.

A small garden sat near the edge of the forest to the south of the home. Chickens pecked away at the dirt. Not far off stood a small, fenced area that apparently housed the three plow horses the reivers had managed to use in their theft of Angus McKenna's cattle.

Although the small farm was not nearly as grand as the castle that Findley and his men called home, it was still clean and tidy in appearance.

Several very auld women sat around a long trestle table, chatting away as they appeared to be mending clothing. The smile on the oldest looking woman—if such a thing were possible, as they were all rather ancient looking—disappeared as she saw the men and boys approaching on horseback. Her wrinkled face, brown from years of exposure to the sun, looked more like a dried apple with tiny eyes attached to it. If looks were arrows, Findley and his men would have died instantly from the glare she shot at them. Within moments, the other women who sat with her followed suit with glares of their own. Clearly, Findley and his men were not welcome here.

The chickens squawked their contempt and displeasure as Findley and his men disturbed their late morning feast. They went scattering about as the group walked their horses through the yard. The boys sat tense and nervous on their mounts, casting each other looks of despair and dread. Findley supposed they were anxious about seeing their mum and owning up to their transgression.

As they drew nearer, one of the auld women left the table and disappeared inside the hut. Moments later, the door flew open with a loud bang, and the most beautiful auburn-haired lass Findley had ever seen came running out. His mouth suddenly felt quite dry, and his heart thrummed rapidly for several long moments.

She stopped dead in her tracks at the sight before her. Four large Highlanders sat atop massive steeds, and they had her boys. Her stomach tightened as her emotions bounced from relief at seeing her sons alive to anger that they'd left their home without a word to anyone.

The Highlanders alarmed her. Reflexively, she slowly dropped her hands to her sides to make certain her *sgian dubh* was still in her pocket. Her first inclination was to demand they let her boys go. If that didn't work, she was not above thrusting her knife into each man's heart.

She eyed Findley and his men suspiciously as she stood motionless some twenty feet away.

"I take it these reivers belong to ye, lass?" Richard asked as he dismounted. He flashed a smile that normally made young lasses giggle and twitter, for he was considered a very handsome man. His smile apparently had no such effect on the woman standing before them. Her face had turned to stone as she continued to stare.

The two youngest boys, each of whom had been riding with an older brother, slipped down from the horses. They went running toward her, happily crying out "Mum!" as they flung themselves around her waist. She hugged them closely, never once taking her eyes off the men.

"Who are ye?" she asked, her voice catching slightly as she fought back her burgeoning fear. Strange men coming to her home was never a good thing.

"I be Findley McKenna," Findley said, finally finding his voice as he dismounted. "This be me brother Richard," he said with a nod in Richard's direction. "And they be Gowan and Tall Thomas," he said with a nod toward his friends. Gowan smiled and bowed slightly at the waist before he, too, dismounted.

The three older boys quietly slid down and stood by their horses. "Mum," said the oldest before realizing he didn't quite know how to explain the chain of events that led to this moment.

"Robert," she said, still clinging to the smaller boys. "Ye are well?"

"Aye, we are well. They've done us no harm," he said, looking first at the men then down at his bare feet. He and his brothers stood side-by-side, hands shaking as they waited for the skelping to begin.

"Collin? Andrew? Does he speak the truth?"

The boys nodded and muttered, "Aye."

She took a deep breath before speaking. "Come here," she told them.

Solemnly, as if their feet were encased in stone, the boys went and stood in front of her. She eyed each of them for a moment before opening her arms and pulling them to her. Tears began to stream down her face, and she trembled as she held them. The boys' shoulders finally relaxed, and they returned her embrace.

After a few moments, she let them loose and wiped the tears from her eyes with the backs of her hands. "I swear if ye ever do that to me again, I'll skin each of ye alive!" she seethed. "What on earth possessed ye to leave in the middle of the night like that?"

Each of the boys took a few steps away as she thrust her hands to her hips and glared at them. "Do ye have any idea the fright ye put me through?" Her voice rose, angrier than she could ever remember being with them. "Do ye have any idea how we have all worried over ye? Nae knowin' if ye be dead or hurt or kidnapped?"

She began pacing in front of them, and the more she yelled, the more the boys' shoulders sagged. They kept their gaze firmly planted on the ground as their mother continued to chastise them.

"Of all the foolish things to do! And for what purpose? Where on earth have ye been, and what have ye been doin'?" She aimed her last question at her oldest son, Robert.

He cleared his throat before answering. "We went to get a cow."

Maggy stared at him, quite baffled. "What?"

"We went to get us a cow."

Her brow furrowed into a deep crease. "A cow? And how did ye plan on buyin' a cow when ye've nae a coin to yer name?"

Robert started to speak but thought better of it.

"Speak the truth, Robert, do nae stroll around it," she said bluntly. "Ye went to *steal* a cow."

Robert stood upright, squared his shoulders and looked his mum straight in the eye. "Aye, we did."

Maggy eyed him for a moment, hands once again resting on her hips. "I have taught ye all better than that."

"Aye, ye have, Mum. But --"

She wouldn't allow him to finish. "But? There be no *but*. Stealin' is wrong, and ye ken it! There be no reason on God's earth to be stealin'!"

Robert found the courage then to speak his mind. "Aye, stealin' is wrong, but 'twas more wrong listenin' to me brothers' and me family's stomachs growl all the time from hunger! I could no longer stand to listen to it!"

"So ye took it upon yerself to go steal a cow?" she demanded. Aye, she understood well enough how he felt, for it angered and saddened her to no end to listen to the hungry stomachs of all those entrusted to her care. But that didn't mean she could allow her sons to steal.

Robert decided it would do him no good to continue to speak on the matter. His mum's mind was made up, and there would be no explaining it to her.

Maggy looked at Findley. "If ye plan on hangin' me sons, I would ask that ye hang me instead."

Her sons gasped and began to protest at her offer to take their places. Findley and his men, however, threw their heads back and laughed. "Nay, lass, we do nae plan on hangin' *any* of ye!" Findley said after he got his laughter under some semblance of control.

Maggy was not amused. "Whatever ye plan on doin' to me sons, I ask that ye let me take their places. Whether it be a skelpin' or other form of punishment."

Findley shook his head, unable to to stop smiling at the beautiful young woman, before it finally occurred to him that she was quite serious. Apparently, she had dealt with men less kind, less honorable than he. "Lass," he said as he walked toward her. "I would never beat a child or a woman, no matter what their transgressions might be."

He could tell from the fear that flashed in her eyes that she did not believe him. He also took note that she had slipped her hand into the pocket of her dress. "I would have done the same to feed me own family, if the circumstances were the same." He stopped just a few feet from her and crossed his arms over his chest with his feet spread apart.

One only had to look at the scrawny forms of the boys and the gaunt faces of the auld people around him to sum up the situation. This was a disparate group of poor people, thrown together under less than desirable circumstances. And the beautiful woman standing before him was doing her best to take care of them and teach the lads right from wrong.

"I ask that *ye* show yer lads a bit of compassion, lass, fer they were only tryin' to take care of their family, like good men do."

Maggy Boyle wasn't sure what to make of his impassioned speech. But there was something in those brown eyes of his that told her he meant what he said. There was something there, in that thoughtful smile of his that held a promise, an assurance that she hadn't felt in a good number of years. Mayhap this man could be trusted.

CHAPTER ONE

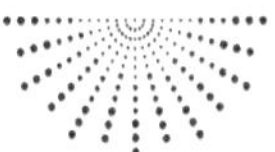

The Highlands, Autumn 1344

'Twas not long after the heather had bloomed that Findley McKenna and three of his men left Castle Gregor on their journey northeast. Had they been on horseback and not driving heavy wagons, they could have arrived at their destination in three short days instead of the five it was taking them.

The sun shone brightly in the blue autumn sky. A whisper-soft breeze caressed the deep crimson, gold, and purple trees that spread across the Highlands. No other season was as beautiful as autumn in the Highlands, well, other than winter, spring and summer.

Although there was plenty of time before winter would arrive, Findley was quite eager to get to the reiver camp before the fall rains set in. It was difficult enough making their way across the lands by wagon in good weather, and he had no desire to travel through mud and muck with wagons hopefully full of people.

For days now, he had been quietly mulling over in his mind what he would say to Maggy. He needed to convince her, and what remained of her clan, to return to Castle Gregor with him. He prayed that she and her people would be glad for the offer of a safe and permanent home.

It had taken very little effort to convince his chief and the clan council that this small band of people was in serious need of assistance. Findley had appealed to the chief's strong sense of honor and duty toward the less fortunate, but he had personal reasons for wanting to bring them back. He was quite certain that he had fallen in love with the beautiful mother of five. That, or he had lost his mind altogether.

At the moment, he was leaning more toward insanity, for how could a person fall so hopelessly in love with someone after only a few hours together? It had not, by any stretch of the imagination, been a romantic interlude they had shared. Nay, 'twas far from that, for most of the time had been spent with Maggy scolding her sons for stealing, for skulking away in the dark of night and terrifying her beyond measure. She had admitted to Findley that day that her biggest fear was the boys had either been kidnapped for ransom or taken as slaves. Either way, she would not have had the means necessary to procure their freedom.

She had apologized repeatedly to Findley and his men for her sons' stupidity and apparent lack of morals. Between apologizing and scolding her sons, there had been little time for anything even remotely resembling romance. There was just something about the woman that, even as she scolded her sons, he found intriguing. He could not have told anyone what that something was, only that he felt drawn to her.

At some point after leaving the reivers and their beautiful mother, the image of Maggy's dark auburn hair and bright green eyes began to creep into his thoughts. If he thought about it long enough, he would surmise that those thoughts began to creep in approximately one minute after saying good-bye. It was all downhill from there. For some God-forsaken reason, he was consumed by her.

Even when he had taken a dirk to his side in a battle against the English in the summer, his thoughts had been of Maggy. As he lay on the bloodied battleground, clinging to life, his last thought before losing consciousness had been of her. He fought death as fiercely as he had fought any battle in his life just so that he might live to see her again.

Findley and his men, Richard, Patrick and Wee William, drove the wagons as fast as the rocky terrain would allow. As far as Findley was concerned, they couldn't go fast enough. The longer they rode, the more anxious he became, and he could only pray that Maggy and her people would listen to reason and agree to his offer.

It was early afternoon when they crested the small hill near the River Clyde that Maggy's clan called home. Something was wrong. Very wrong.

Death lingered in the air. He and his men caught the distinct odor and instantly drew their broadswords. As they pulled rein and stopped the horses, their eyes scanned the sight before them. Findley's heart pounded with fear and dread as he threw on the wagon brake and leapt down from his seat. Destruction and death lay before them.

Nothing remained of the hut where the auld women had at one time slept, save for the charred wooden frame and three bodies burned beyond recognition. Bile rose in the back of Findley's throat as the anger simmered.

Wee William stood beside him shaking his head, while Richard and Patrick searched through the remains.

"I would say it happened at least two days ago. Maybe three," Wee William said in a hushed, reverent tone.

Findley could only nod his head as his mind raced, and he stared at the dead bodies at his feet. He could only pray that they wouldn't find Maggy or her boys among the dead.

Patrick and Richard walked toward the river and found two more of the auld women lying dead along the bank. Findley and Wee William soon joined them. The final death toll was put at seven. There was no sign of Maggy or her boys anywhere.

It was Richard who finally asked the question that Findley couldn't. "Where be Maggy and the lads?"

Findley couldn't respond; his heart wouldn't allow him to go there, to think of the possibilities of where Maggy and the lads could be. He bent and studied the tracks left in the mud and judged there had been at least ten on horseback. The tracks led in from the east and apparently left in the same direction they had arrived.

"Who ye think coulda done this?" Wee William asked to no one in particular.

Just then, a gust of wind swept down from the hills, scattering bits of dust and leaves. A small scrap of cloth landed on Wee William's foot. It was as if God Himself had answered the question. Wee William picked up the cloth and studied it closely for a moment. His jaw set as anger filled his eyes, for he'd recognize that bit of plaid anywhere. He handed it to Findley for his inspection. It took only a moment for him to come to the same conclusion.

"Buchannans." A chill slid down his spine at saying the name.

CHAPTER TWO

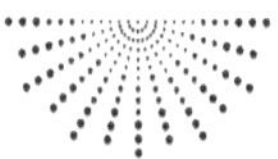

"Only evil men would kill the auld and leave the bodies for the wolves and scavengers." It was Wee William's gravely voice, lined with contempt, that broke through the silence.

Findley McKenna gripped the piece of bloodied plaid until his knuckles turned white. Time seemed to suspend interminably before his heart beat again. 'Twas even longer before he could draw a breath. Rage as hot as a blacksmith's forge pounded through his veins. His eyes turned to dark slits as he surveyed the death and destruction that surrounded him.

Findley drew his lips into a thin, hard line and fought to speak over the knot that had formed in his throat. "Aye," he muttered.

While his feelings for Maggy Boyle had been unspoken, his men had well surmised that he had more than a strong affection for the auburn-haired beauty. They had not traveled these many days just to bring supplies and an offer to foster the five young lads she called her sons. Maggy had inexplicably won Findley's heart.

"Search again," he ordered his men. While each man was certain a second search would yield the same results as the first, they searched without question. His men would follow him through the bowels of hell if he asked them to.

Findley tore through the blackened tents and the charred remains of Maggy's hut. He lifted the trestle table and tossed it aside as if it weighed no more than the bloodied fabric clenched between his fingers. With unrestrained rage, he ripped through the carnage in search of her.

As a warrior, Findley had fought in too many battles to number. Never in all the times that he had come close to death had he felt this kind of fear. It clawed and slashed at his soul, shredding it into inestimable pieces. *Please,* he prayed, *dunnae let me find her. Nae here, nae like this.*

"Findley." The sound of Richard's voice broke through the madness that was tearing at his mind.

Findley stopped and turned toward his younger brother. Drenched in sweat and with his heart filled with dread, he dared ask the question. "Have ye found her?"

He was was afraid he would not survive beyond the next minute if Richard answered in the affirmative.

"Nay," Richard answered. "They be not here, Findley."

"The Buchannans have her." Wee William was the only one brave enough to put to voice what the rest of them knew without question.

The reality of the situation tore through Findley's heart with as much force as an enemy sword. Maggy was alive, but she was in the hands of a man he was certain had no soul. More likely than not, the man had imprisoned her for his own purposes. Or worse yet, he was taking her to the slave traders in the high north. He could not shake the image of Maggy being stripped, thrown into chains and put on display to be sold to the man with the most coin.

A pox had wiped out nearly every member of Maggy's clan. For three years she had managed to hold the small clan together. Maggy, a handful of auld people, and five young boys were all that remained of a once proud and growing clan. While she had birthed only one of the five boys who called her mum, she loved them all with a fierceness and maturity that belied her young age.

She had survived all the hard and lean years only to be taken by a coldblooded killer.

Findley studied the faces of the three men who had taken this journey with him. He hadn't planned on finding the auld dead and Maggy and her boys missing. Nor had he planned for battle. The Buchannan clan's numbers had been rapidly increasing of late, and latest estimates put them at well over a hundred. Logic dictated the four of them could not lay siege to more than a hundred men. His heart, however, did not give a damn about what logic might have to say on the matter.

He turned his attention to the bit of plaid still clenched in his hand. Its crimson, green, and goldenrod colors were now soaked with the blood of innocents. He took in a slow breath before stuffing the cloth into the folds of his tunic.

"Unhitch the wagons. We be goin' after Maggy and her boys."

His voice was as cold as the steel blade of a broadsword and just as deadly. It warned each of the men who surrounded him that there would be no discussion on the matter. He turned and headed toward the wagons. His younger brother Richard followed after him.

"Findley," Richard said, "do nae let yer heart cloud yer good judgment." If any other man had spoken those words to Findley, he would have gutted him without any thought to the matter.

"Maggy and the boys are out there somewhere, Richard," Findley tossed over his shoulder. "With or without ye, I'll get them back."

"I never said ye'd be doin' it without me, brother," Richard told him as they approached one of the wagons. "I simply be askin' ye to think through the matter for a moment. We will be needin' the supplies on these wagons, Findley." He made no attempt to help his older brother, who was angrily working the chains and tethers of the harnesses.

"We will travel faster without them!" Findley was angry. Any patience he may have owned was left in the rubble of what remained of Maggy's home.

"Aye, we could," Richard answered as he rubbed a hand across his bearded face. "Renfrew be but a day's ride from here, with the wagons. We can be there in time for the midday meal on the morrow. The Buchannan keep be at least a sennight from here."

Findley stopped abruptly and looked at his brother curiously. "And what be yer point?"

"I say we take the wagons to Renfrew. Trade them in for fresh horses and purchase the aid of a few men. Then we head for the Buchannan keep."

Findley blinked as he ran the idea through his mind. He did not want to waste precious time trading wagons or trying to purchase the fealty of other men. His only concern was to get to Maggy. Who knew what harm might already have been done to her, or what might yet come.

"Think of it, brother," Richard went on. "There be only four of us. While yer thirst for revenge may be strong at the moment, and there be not another man I would want on the fields of battle with me, we cannae go against a hundred men with just the four of us. Let us go to Renfrew, sell the wagons, and buy a few men, men good with a sword. We can send a messenger back to Dunshire and beg Angus for more help."

His brother was right, as much as he hated admitting to it. Wee William and Patrick were now standing with them, and by the solemn expressions they wore on their faces, they appeared to agree with the idea.

Hatred and anger had seized control of his heart, which made thinking clearly next to impossible. He knew Richard's idea made good sense. No matter how much bloodlust ran through Findley's veins nor how badly his heart burned with wanting to rescue Maggy, they did need more men to go against the Buchannan clan.

"To Renfrew then," Findley said through clenched teeth as he began to reattach the harness. "But the first time it appears the wagons slow us, I'll not think twice of leaving ye to them."

<hr>

THEY HAD RIDDEN until long after the sun had set. With no moon to help guide them, it was far too risky to proceed through the pitch-black night pulling heavy wagons.

Findley slept restlessly, unable to clear his mind of the worry over where Maggy might be and what she might be going through. While she was a strong woman who had managed to keep her small clan together, it was an altogether different matter to be held as a prisoner or slave. He swore by all that was holy, truthful, and right that he would kill any man who brought her harm.

He tried to make sense of why the Buchannan had attacked Maggy's home. Aye, Malcolm Buchannan was as tetched as they came. By anyone's standards the man was insane. His reputation was the thing ghost stories were made of, and that reputation had cast a pall across all of Scotland.

Findley had never met the man, but he did know a few who had. If the current stories floating around the Highlands were true, Malcolm Buchannan never acted unless there was something to be gained from it.

What could he possibly gain from Maggy Boyle?

He rose before the first light of day, rolling from under the wagon where he had tossed and turned most of the night. With a heavy heart and racing mind, he grabbed water from the back of the wagon and splashed it across his face and neck. His trews and tunic were filthy and travel-worn, but that was of no import at the time. He doubted Maggy would give one whit what he might look like as long as he was able to save her from the Buchannans.

Trying to push thoughts of Maggy from his mind was as easy as pushing a boulder up a mountain. He took the bit of plaid from his tunic and stared at it for a long time. He could only pray that the blood that soaked it did not belong to Maggy or any of her boys. As he stood in the light of dawn of early morning, running his thumb over the small bit of fabric, his emotions ran from despair to anger and back again. He had to find her. No matter what had happened to her, no matter what tortures Malcolm Buchannan might thrust upon her, Findley knew that he would spend the rest of his life trying to make it up to her.

Most people, he thought, would not understand the guilt that battered at his heart, the guilt that often kept him awake at night. Just as he had let his family down years ago, he had let Maggy and her family down as well. He had done it by not arriving sooner. He had let them all down by not being there to defend them against the Buchannans.

Irritably, he tucked the plaid back into his shirt and looked toward the horizon. Maggy was out there, somewhere, and God only knew what was happening to her now.

Anger would be his catalyst for moving forward, revenge the thing that kept him from falling apart altogether. He would not rest until he found her.

One by one, his men began to wake. After breaking their fast over bannocks and dried beef, they headed toward Renfrew just as the sun began to break. The beautiful morning, with its purple and azure sky, was in direct contrast to the bleakness lying heavy in his heart. Findley doubted he would ever enjoy another sunrise until he had Maggy safely in his arms.

Had they not been low on coin, he would have deserted the wagons the day before and set out on horseback. The battle taking place between what his heart said (leave the wagons and ride fast) and what his mind said (he needed more men than he currently had at his disposal) was causing his head to throb incessantly.

They traveled in silence and as fast as the rough terrain would allow. They'd ridden for only a few hours when a wheel on one of the wagons became lodged between two large rocks. An hour of daylight was lost when they had to unhitch horses from the other wagons to help dislodge it. Findley set forth with a burst of heated blasphemies, growing angrier with each wasted moment that passed. His men quickly caught on to his foul mood and left him alone with it.

Later in the morning, Patrick asked for a brief respite to stretch his legs and empty his bladder. Findley unhappily agreed to the small rest.

As he stood behind a tree answering nature's call, Patrick heard a slight rustling of leaves coming from his left. He pretended not to hear it as he strained his ears to listen. He was certain neither Findley nor Wee William had followed him in to the woods.

As he laced up his trews, he began to whistle softly while surreptitiously scanning the woods. He heard the faint sound again. Whoever was hiding nearby was doing a terrible job at being quiet.

Patrick feigned a yawn, stretched his arms out wide and began to walk in the direction of the noise. He had taken but a few short steps when he heard the blood curdling sound of a battle cry, which was quickly followed by something quite hard hitting him in the side of his head!

He let out a loud curse as stars began to explode in front of his eyes, and an intense jolt of pain shot down the side of his head to his elbow. Momentarily stunned, Patrick reached for his dirk, and through a dizzying amount of pain, he began to look around for the person who had hit him. His vision had blurred, and before he could get a good grip on the situation at hand, he heard a voice yell out, "Go to hell, ye dirty bastard!"

Patrick couldn't have sworn to it at that moment, what with his ringing ears, blurred vision, and the goose egg throbbing on his temple, but he thought the voice sounded rather young.

He whirled around toward the source of the voice, only to be hit in the chest with another stone, this one the size of a chicken egg. Before he knew it, all manner of rocks were being thrown his way, and a litany of curses and blasphemies were being shouted at him. In a matter of moments, he was besieged and felled to the ground by stones and rocks and was quickly surrounded by a band of lads who began kicking at him while they cursed.

"Bloody Buchannan!" the smallest of the lads shouted as he landed a kick to the side of Patrick's stomach.

Another boy, not much older than the first, spat at him and yelled, "Ye can burn in hell ye hedge-born eejit!" The boy evidently felt it quite necessary then to kick Patrick in his ribs.

The largest of the four boys had a look of anger that Patrick had seen before only in the eyes of a warrior. The lad held a rather ominous-looking rock, a small boulder really, in both his hands and had raised it over his head, fully prepared to send it crashing into Patrick's skull.

Funny, but Patrick had always thought that he would die on the battlefield in some fiery, brave, final act of heroism. He'd never imagined himself being pummeled to death with rocks thrown by a group of small boys.

Just as the lad was ready to send his small boulder crashing down, a much larger hand swooped in and grabbed it from behind whilst another grabbed the back of his tunic and jerked him violently away from Patrick. As the lad let loose with curses, more men and hands appeared and began pulling the boys off Patrick.

"Filthy rotten Buchannans!" The boys were cursing and screaming in protest.

Wee William's voice boomed through the forest, sending birds to flight and other animals scurrying to safety. "Settle yerselves down now, ye heathens!" he shouted.

Flailing arms and legs stopped mid flail, mouths hung open, and all eyes turned to the giant before them. Patrick was certain that had he been any one of those boys at whom Wee William had just yelled, more likely than not he would have pissed his pants.

"We will have no more of it, ye beasties!" William added for good measure, giving each of the boys an angry glare as he tossed the large rock over his shoulder. It landed with a dull thud on the ground behind him.

Apparently, there was not much on this earth that frightened the oldest of the boys, for he returned Wee William's glare with one of his own. "Shove it up yer arse, ye filthy dog of a Buchannan scum!"

Patrick had known Wee William for most of his life and never in all that time had he ever seen the man blink when an insult had been hurled his way. But Wee William did just that.

Truth be told, what had surprised William the most was that he had never met someone who had not been intimidated by his size or the mere sound of his deep, gravelly voice. It threw him completely off guard, but only for a fleeting moment.

"Haud yer wheest, ye little heathen! I be no more a Buchannan than ye are!" William's response seemed to surprise the boy into a momentary bout of silence. The lad began to look about at the men before him. He could not hide his relief when he recognized Richard and Findley.

"Aye," Findley said when he saw the flicker of recognition in the lad's eyes. Findley was holding a young boy under one arm and another by the scruff of his tunic. "'Tis me, Findley, and me brother Richard. Ye remember us, don't ye lads?"

The lad's jaw set to stone as he nodded his head. "Aye." His face was awash with distrust and anger.

"Might I ask why ye felt the need to attack me man Patrick, here?" Findley asked as he eyed each of the boys. Patrick lay still on the ground trying to catch his breath. The boy Findley held under his arm began to wriggle as he spoke. "We thought ye was Buchannans."

Findley rolled his eyes. "Apparently."

"And we hate them dirty dogs!" The boy wriggled again, fighting to be set free. Findley adjusted the lad and squeezed him tighter.

"Settle down, ye hellion!" he warned. He recognized the boy as Maggy's youngest, Liam. "Elst I'll let Wee William skelp ye!"

The boy lifted his head, took one look at Wee William's angry glare and settled down immediately. He may have felt brave enough to pelt a man to death with rocks, but he wasn't stupid. The giant standing just a few feet away, holding his oldest brother up with one hand as if he were showing the group a large fish he'd just caught, could easily kill him with one blow. Liam decided it best not to chance raising the man's ire.

Findley and his men gave the boys a moment to settle themselves down before loosening their grasps and freeing them. Wee William disgustedly shoved the oldest boy to the center of the group, clearly not happy with the lad's stubbornness.

An overwhelming sense of relief had washed over Findley the moment he had seen the boys, even if they had been pelting Patrick with rocks. At least they were alive! Now if the same could be said of Maggy, his heart might begin to beat again.

"Where be yer mum?" Findley asked as he extended a hand and pulled Patrick to his feet. Findley would have sworn the knot on Patrick's head was growing with each throb of his pulse.

Patrick shook his head, took a deep breath, and turned to look at the boys. "Can I skelp these little hellions, Findley?" he asked with another shake of his head. He looked determined to do just that, with or without Findley's permission.

"Nay," Findley answered. "Nae until we find out where Maggy is." He glowered at the boys. "I'll ask ye again. Where be yer mum?"

Each boy clamped his mouth shut and shook his head, refusing to divulge Maggy's whereabouts. Findley's nostrils flared as he took in another deep breath in an attempt to ward off the strong urge to throttle each of their scrawny necks.

He studied each of them more closely and noticed they had lost weight since the last time he'd seen them. Their clothes were torn and frayed at the edges. The oldest appeared to be wearing clothes made for someone twice his size. The sleeves of the boy's tunic had been rolled up several times, yet they still fell to his wrists. Only two of the boys were blessed with a pair of boots.

He imagined it had been some time since any of them had bathed or eaten a good meal. Terrified yet determined eyes, lined with dark circles, stared back at him.

"Lads, we are here to help, and we need to know where yer mum is." Findley spoke in an even tone and tried to hide his worry.

"Go to hell," the oldest boy said. "Ye can skin me, poke me eyes with sticks, and pull me fingernails off! I ain't tellin' ye nothin'! Ye cannae have her!" The fierceness in his eyes promised each of the men standing before him that he meant exactly what he said.

Wee William took one broad step, grabbed the lad by his dirty tunic, and lifted him off the ground. He held the boy close to his own face. "Let's test that theory!" Wee William seethed.

Not a flinch, not even a flash of fear could be seen in the lad's face. Findley and his men were stunned. Apparently, Wee William had finally met his match, and it was in a lad half his height and a fraction of his weight. The lad was going to make one hell of a warrior someday. That is, if he could ever get his temper under control. It was his fearlessness that caused Findley concern. A man without fear would often make reckless decisions.

As Wee William threatened the oldest lad, the youngest, Liam, rushed toward Wee William and kicked him in the leg. Wee William batted the child away with his free hand as if he were nothing more than a pesky gnat. He kept his eyes locked on the lad before him.

"Put me brother down!" Liam yelled as Richard swooped in and pulled him away from Wee William.

Findley had reached the limit of his patience. "I have had enough!" he boomed. "We are here to help, ye fools!"

All eyes turned to him as he continued, his voice laced with anger and frustration. "We ken the Buchannans attacked yer camp. 'Tis why we are here! We hate the filthy curs as much as ye do! And I swear, if ye do nae tell me where yer mum is right this very moment, I'll skelp each and every one of ye!" He paused long enough to take a breath.

"Now, do ye wanna leave yer mum with no children and break her heart and risk the chance of the Buchannans findin' her, or do ye want to do the intelligent thing and tell us where she is so that we can help?"

The boys looked to each other, silently searching for direction and approval. The boy who appeared to be nearest in size and age to the eldest finally spoke. "Do ye promise ye'll nae harm her?" There was much worry and distrust in the lad's bright blue eyes.

It dawned on Findley that he knew all too well what the lads were going through. He had been just ten and one when his family was murdered. Their deaths had taken a hard toll on Findley, and it was many years before he could learn to trust anyone again.

It had been but a few days since the Buchannans had raided the lads' home, and it was not going to be easy to convince them that Findley and his men could be trusted. Findley was asking them to put their faith in a nearly complete stranger.

He let out a long, heavy breath and began to chew on the inside of his cheek. "Lads," he searched for the right words. "I ken ye be afeared ye cannae trust us, and I cannae blame ye fer it." He rubbed the back of his neck as he put a hand on his hip. "Ye're just wantin' to protect yer mum, and 'tis verra noble. A good warrior protects his family to his own death. Ye be doin' the right thing." He would have done the very same thing had he been in their shoes.

Pride flickered momentarily in the eyes of the oldest boy, but only for the briefest of moments before it was replaced with a look of suspicion. He stared at Findley for a long while, searching for any sign that he was being disingenuous. He then turned to Wee William. "Can I talk to me brothers fer a moment?" he asked.

Gone from his face was the hatred and repugnance. Replacing it was a look of solemnity far beyond his years. He should be enjoying his youth. Instead, he had been thrust into the role of a man, a leader and protector.

Wee William nodded thoughtfully and set the boy down. The four boys huddled together and spoke in hushed tones for quite some time. Occasionally, one of them would look up at Wee William as if he were trying to size him up, before drawing back into the conversation.

Findley and his men came together, giving the boys the time and space they needed.

"Do ye think Maggy is well?" Richard whispered as he dusted dirt from the legs of his trews.

Findley gave a quick glance at each of the boys before answering. "I believe she is. And I believe they be protectin' her. They ken where she is." He looked thoughtfully at his brother. "Ye ken as well as I, brother, how hard it is to trust someone, especially a man, when ye've lost all that ye have."

Richard nodded his head and turned to look at the boys. He had been nine when he lost his family, along with their entire village. Although the man responsible for those deaths was now dead, Richard still fought with nightmares. He believed that evil would always exist in this world. Evil men were like bugs: ye squash one, and there were a hundred more ready to takes its place.

"Aye, I do." He understood it all too well.

Richard realized then that one of the boys, the one who looked very much like Liam, was missing. "Do ye think the other small lad be with Maggy?" he asked, bringing it to Findley's attention.

"I would hope so, Richard." Perhaps they'd left the lad with Maggy as her guard and protector. A smile came to Findley's face at thinking of these five young boys who were protecting their mum with all that they had in them. Aye, they'd make fine warriors indeed someday. He was glad they were on his side, for they would undeniably be formidable adversaries.

***

THE BOYS HAD APPARENTLY COME to some decisions. They formed a line, crossed their arms over their chests, and put stern looks upon their faces as they faced Findley and his men. They'd let the eldest do the talking.

"I be Robert," the oldest lad said by way of an introduction. "These are me brothers, Andrew, Collin, and Liam." Each boy gave a curt nod of his head at the mention of his name.

"Ye seen what the Buchannans did," Robert said.

Findley detected a slight catch to the boy's voice. It was the first time he showed any sign of weakness.

Findley and his men remained quiet and gave slight nods of their heads. Aye, they'd seen it, and it would be forever burned in Findley's memory.

"The Buchannan wants our mum fer his wife. 'Tis why they raided our home." Robert cleared his throat and stood taller.

Findley's stomach lurched at the thought of Maggy being forced to wed the Buchannan. He'd kill the coward before he allowed that to happen. He began to chew on the inside of his cheek again and kept his thoughts to himself.

"But our mum does nae want to marry him," Andrew offered. The boy was nearly as tall as Robert but was in sharp contrast to Robert's blond hair and green eyes. Andrew had a thick mop of red hair, a freckled face, and vivid blue eyes. He could have easily passed for Patrick's younger brother. "She dunnae like the man."

"And we dunnae like him either," Liam offered as he swiped a hand across his sweaty forehead. "The Buchannan's a rotten, filthy, evil man," he said as he spat at the ground. The boy had tenacity even if he severely lacked good manners.

"Do ye kiss yer mum with that filthy mouth of yers, lad?" Wee William asked. Liam's face turned crimson.

"I would never talk like that in front of me mum!" he told him.

"'Tis good to know it," Wee William said. "I'll thank ye kindly to watch yer language at all times, lad." He shot a warning look toward the boy but said nothing more. The boy didn't realize it, but it was his first lesson in being a gentleman as well as a warrior: control your temper and, at all times, behave honorably.

They turned their attentions back to Robert. "They burned ye out 'cause the Buchannan wants yer mum fer his wife?" Patrick asked for the sake of clarity.

Robert nodded his head. "Aye, they did."

The men pondered the information for a moment. While Findley could imagine why any number of men would take a fancy to Maggy, what with her auburn hair, bright green eyes, and beautiful face. But to kill innocent people for her? Nay, that wasn't done to impress or woo her into marriage; 'twas done to scare her into it.

"How did ye escape them?" Richard asked.

"We were nae there when they came. The lads and I was huntin' rabbits. Mum was lookin' for herbs to help break Ian's fever. We heard the ruckus and hid 'til the bast—" Robert stopped himself as he cast an apologetic look toward Wee William, "—'til the eejits left."

Wee William gave the lad an approving smile. "And yer mum and Ian?" Wee William asked.

Robert looked at his brothers, and his expression turned sorrowful. "Mum is well. But Ian..." his voice trailed off, and his eyes began to water.

"What of Ian?" Findley asked, knowing he wasn't going to like the lad's answer.

"The Buchannans got him."

CHAPTER THREE

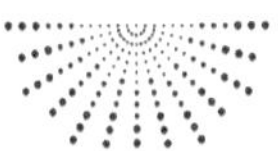

The Buchannans had Ian. He was just a boy, no more than eight years. Findley's stomach tightened with thinking how terrified the boy must be -- if he still lived. His only hope at the moment was that the Buchannan was keeping the lad alive in order to force Maggy into marrying him.

Patrick shook his head as he stared at the boys. "Ye're sure of it?"

Robert nodded his head slowly. "Aye. We were hidin' in the woods when we heard Ian screamin' something fierce. We hid at the edge of the woods when the Buchannans rode off with him."

Robert turned away from the men to wipe the tears from his eyes. Only bairns cry, he admonished himself for acting so childishly. Cryin' won't get Ian back.

Findley's jaw clenched as he took a deep breath in an attempt to settle his apprehension. "Where's yer mum?" he asked. His firm voice held a warning that no one should try his patience further by keeping her whereabouts secret.

"She be safe and nae far from here," Andrew offered. "But we wanna talk to ye first before we take ye to her." There was a sense of urgency to his voice.

Findley would give them no more than another minute before he would insist they take him to Maggy. "What is it?" he asked impatiently.

Andrew looked at Robert and cleared his throat. "Do ye beat yer women where yer from?" he asked, turning to look at Wee William.

Aghast, Findley and his men answered in unison, "Nay!" While they knew of men who thought nothing of beating their wives and children, such actions were not just frowned upon among their clan, they were grounds for expulsion.

"How many in yer clan?" Andrew asked.

"More than four hundred," Patrick offered.

Andrew nodded his head in approval. "How many are warriors?"

Patrick was perplexed by the question and wondered where it was leading. "Well more than half."

The lads looked to be impressed with the numbers. They all turned to look at Wee William. "How many look like him?" Andrew asked as he motioned his head at Wee William.

Patrick and Richard laughed aloud while Wee William smiled wryly.

"I can assure ye lads, there isn't another man as big as our Wee William in all of Scotland," Richard told them.

If there had been, they would most assuredly have met the man on the battlefield or heard tales at some point, for Wee William was a giant of a man. He stood nearly seven feet tall, with arms the size of tree trunks, massive legs, and a very broad chest. He had the strength of at least five men. He was a man and a warrior of unparalleled proportions.

The boys looked a bit disappointed with learning there was none other like Wee William. "Are ye married?" Andrew asked.

A look of utter surprise came to the faces of each of the men before they burst forth in a fit of laughter. Wee William married? Och! Wee William scared most men near to shaking. Unfortunately, he had the same effect on women.

It would take an act of divine intervention to find a woman who would not tremble with fright at his immense girth and gravelly voice. She'd have to have a very strong constitution and be braver than most men to see beyond that, as well as his full beard, his unruly hair, and many scars.

"Nay!" Richard choked on his laughter. "Wee William be not married."

Findley was not nearly as amused as his men. They were wasting precious time. "Why do ye ask, lads?" His voice was calm as he tried to mask his impatience.

'Twas Robert who answered. "We need to find our mum a husband. If she be married, then the Buchannan will leave her be and give us back our Ian." He didn't take his eyes from Wee William. "She needs a man who can protect her. Keep the Buchannan away from her. A man who wilna beat her."

The sudden awareness that the lads meant for their mum to marry Wee William hit each of the men like a bucket of cold water. "Ye want yer mum to marry Wee William?" Patrick asked. He was astounded by the suggestion.

Wee William shot his friend a hard look. "And what be wrong with that?" he asked as he crossed his arms over his chest. "Aside from the fact that I ain't lookin' to get married any time in the near future, do ye think I would nae make a good husband?"

Patrick bit his lip to keep from laughing further. "Nay! Ye'd make a fine husband." He was doing his best to hold his laughter in. "If yer wife be blind and six and a half feet tall!"

Wee William's face turned to dark. He scowled as he started toward his friend. "Ye little shite!"

Patrick was laughing too hard to move or defend himself from Wee William's wrath. He doubled over and did not worry much that his friend might be tempted to strangle him. They'd been needling each other for years, and he was confident Wee William knew it was all in jest.

Findley had reached his limits. "Gentlemen!" he shouted. "We have no time for nonsense!"

He turned to look at the boys. "Lads, while I am sure ye mean well, do ye nae think ye might want to take yer mum's feelings into consideration before marryin' her off?" Besides, he thought to himself, I plan on askin' her fer that pleasure.

He had to admit that the boys were doing their best to be brave and take a firm hold of the situation in order to protect their mum. But there had to be a better way than having her marry Wee William.

Robert looked at Findley as if he had spiders crawling out his ears. "She be a woman. She dunnae get a say in the matter, do she?"

Unfortunately, that was often the case. Marriages were oftentimes the result of men trying to better their own purses, increase their lands or holdings, or to stop war. Seldom were the feelings of either party brought into the decision-making process. But this situation was different. Maggy was a widow, the mother of five boys, and 'twas the boys trying to foster a union for her. And if she were to marry anyone, it would be Findley.

Findley had to quash a smile. "Aye, lad, she does get a say in the matter." He'd take the time later to explain to the boys that a woman's feeling should always be considered.

Robert looked as though he did not believe Findley. "It matters not. He's big," he said, nodding his head toward Wee William. "The biggest man I ever seen. Surely he can scare the Buchannan into leavin' mum alone and givin' us back our Ian."

The mention of Ian brought them all back to the here and now. It would definitely take more than a terrifying Wee William to get the Buchannan to return the boy. It would take an all-out assault.

MAGGY HAD GROWN worried over her boys. They'd been gone far too long. She began to chastise herself for allowing them to leave to hunt for a rabbit or a pheasant for their dinner. She should have kept them nearby or insisted she go along with them. As it was, she had been digging for roots to roast along with whatever the lads might be able to catch.

Her mind began to race with thoughts that mayhap the Buchannans had found them and now held all of her boys as captives. The thought sickened her. It was bad enough they had Ian. To think for a moment that the Buchannan could get his hands on her other boys was nearly more than her heart could bear.

She had to keep herself together, for all of their sakes. She had to get to her brother in Dundee. And if not him, then her other brother in Aberdeen. If she could get herself and the boys to one of them, then she could call on the rest of her brothers for help in procuring Ian's safe return. Her brothers were her only hope at the moment.

They'd been walking for days now, heading toward Renfrew. No blankets, no food, and not a supply or belonging to their names. It was all beginning to take its toll on her heart as well as her body.

She paced around their makeshift camp for a time, cursing under her breath all the while praying for her boys to return safely. She had let them go hunting only because they were growing weary of eating roasted roots and drinking bark tea.

Too much time had passed for her liking, and she simply could not bear waiting any longer. She pulled the roots from the coals, covered them with leaves, and set out in search of her boys.

IAN. He had to be alive. If he weren't, no Buchannan would be safe from Findley's wrath.

They would gather up Maggy and the boys and head for Renfrew. Once there, he'd send a messenger back to Dunshire and beg Angus for more men. While the boys might be good rock throwers, they weren't exactly the kind of warriors he needed at the moment.

Findley looked at the bedraggled and near starving lads before him: covered with dirt, grungy from days without bathing, and scrawny from lack of good meals. They were just children.

How many other children, he wondered, could have gone through what these lads had and still manage to maintain the determination, strength, and dignity of the boys now standing before him? They reminded Findley very much of himself at that age.

"Lads," Findley began. "We will worry about marryin' yer mum off later. For now, we have to get ye to Renfrew. Then we will send ye to our keep in Dunshire. Ye'll be safe there. We will get Ian back."

Robert's expression turned to stone. "Nay," he said, crossing his arms over his chest, standing firm and resolute. "We will nae hide like cowards."

Findley took a deep breath. Robert was a very stubborn young man. "Lad, we ken ye want yer brother back and that ye want to help. But ye cannae go up against the Buchannans with rocks." He meant no insult, but he wasn't about to treat the boy like a bairn.

Liam chimed in. "We coulda gone agin the bloody Buchannans if we had swords." His little face twisted into a scowl as he looked to his oldest brother.

Robert gave the lad a smile, a nod, and ran his fingers through the mop of curly dark hair. Robert's gesture was one of a lad far older and more mature than his actual years. Findley could see great things in Robert's future, if only he could learn to control his temper and listen to wisdom.

"I am sure ye would have, lad," Wee William offered. "And ye've done a fine job of protectin' yer mum." Wee William walked toward the small boy and put his hand on his shoulder.

Wee William was well known for having a soft spot the size of Scotland in his heart for bairns and children. He then turned and studied Robert for a long moment, sizing the lad up. "Ye'll do well as a warrior."

Robert's chest puffed out a bit at the compliment even though he did his best to hide his pride. "So, ye'll marry our mum then?" Robert asked. He wasn't about to let the question go unanswered. "She be a bonny woman. And right smart too."

Wee William chuckled. "I am sure she is, lad. But I be nae the marryin' kind. And Findley be right. Ye need to let yer mum decide such things. And there be other ways of protectin' her."

"Like what?" Robert asked with a crease forming on his brow.

"Like killin' the evil men responsible."

Robert apparently liked the idea. His lips curved upward ever so slightly, and he gave a quick nod of his head in approval. "Aye. But cannae we do both?"

Wee William shook his head. "Lad, listen to me well. We are wastin' time now. The longer we stand here makin' plans fer yer mum's future, the longer the Buchannan has yer brother." Wee William let Robert think on that for a moment. "Now, would ye rather we argue over yer mum's future or hie off and get the bloody curs?"

Robert didn't need to think on it very long. "Hie off and get the bloody curs."

Wee William reached out and grabbed the boy's shoulder and gave it an approving squeeze. As Wee William gave the boy a favorable smile, a faint swooshing sound filled the air, and a moment later something hit Wee William's temple and sent him crashing to the ground.

In the small amount of time it took Findley and his men to get their bearings and draw swords, an inordinate number of rocks began to fly in from behind Findley. They were being pelted with stones, and whoever was doing the pelting had perfect aim.

The boys stood frozen for a brief moment before Patrick and Richard scooped up the smallest boys, grabbed the other two by their arms, and headed for cover. Unfortunately, they had to leave their fallen friend behind, for there were far too many rocks and stones barraging them.

Findley crouched low and let out a curse as one of the stones hit him in the shoulder. Although he was unable to see the attacker, he had a sneaky suspicion who it was.

He dove into the trees behind him while his men scattered about on the other side of the clearing. He took a moment to get a bearing on where the assault was being launched. Keeping low, he noiselessly made his way through the brambles in search of the rock thrower.

She had hidden herself quite well in the thick underbrush and had amassed a good number of stones that were piled on the ground to her right. She was able to throw two at a time, one in each hand, quite easily. She would squat down long enough to grab more stones before popping up again to throw them.

Maggy had grabbed two more stones and popped up, ready to throw more stones at the men who had her sons. She paused briefly when she realized they no longer stood stunned in the middle of the clearing but had instead taken cover. Cursing under her breath, she knelt to gather the stones, hurriedly tossing them into her apron, unaware that someone lurked nearby.

Findley had stealthily made his way toward her and stood just a few short steps away as she loaded her apron. He could not speak for he was so relieved to see her, even if she was assaulting them.

From his close vantage point, he could tell she had lost weight over the past few months. She had been more curvaceous when he first met her. Now her tattered and dirty brown dress hung loosely on her shrinking frame. His heart sank with the realization that she and her boys were dwindling away from lack of food. They were starving, gaunt, and far too thin.

He would soon rectify that. Once he got them back to his keep, they'd never want for food, shelter or clothing ever again. He would see to it that the boys were raised up to be good Highland warriors. They would have proper educations. He would make sure they traveled the world to enjoy all the wonders it offered.

And he would wrap Maggy in the finest of fabrics. Never again would she wear torn, rough and threadbare clothing. He would dress her in the finest silks, damasks and velvets. Emeralds, rubies and diamonds would drape from her delicate ears and beautiful, long neck. He would give her the world.

He forced his mind back to the here and now. His heart pounded mercilessly in his chest as he watched her gathering more ammunition.

Maggy had taken a few steps away before Findley found his voice. "Maggy!" His voice cracked.

Startled, she let loose of her apron, and all the stones spilled onto the ground before her feet. All but one. Without thinking, she hurled that stone toward the voice, and it skimmed along the hairline of his forehead.

A shock of white light flashed in his eyes as pain thundered in his skull and brought forth a momentary sensation of wooziness. He stumbled backwards a step or two, angry with himself for not being prepared for her response. The pain hammering in his skull hurt worse than the dirk he had taken to his side in the summer.

She did not realize until it was too late that it was Findley who had called her name. She watched him stumble backwards and saw the blood begin to trickle down his face. A momentary sense of guilt filled her stomach before her good senses took hold. While she remembered him as the kind man who had returned her sons to her that past spring, too much had taken place in her life since. He was still a stranger, and she could not risk trusting that he was still kind.

There was no time to waste learning what his intentions were. Hastily, she scooped up a few rocks and tore off through the woods. She cursed herself repeatedly for allowing the boys to go hunting without her. What she wouldn't give to have a few dirks or even a sword instead of the blasted stones! Her only thoughts were how she could get her boys away from these men.

She had hoped to cause enough of a distraction so that the boys could flee. But that had not worked. Instead, the men had grabbed her boys and now cowered in the woods. She would need a much better plan and better weapons in order to free them.

Maggy raced through the woods, ignoring the pinecones and sticks that tore through her old, worn shoes. Ducking under low-lying branches and limbs, she searched for a means of escape or, at the least, a place to hide.

If she could hide herself well enough, it might buy her some time to come up with a new plan. Mayhap these men would give up the search for her and hie off to wherever it was they were intending to go. She could follow at a safe distance and wait for a better time for another attack in which to free her sons.

It had taken several moments before the wooziness left, and the pain subsided enough for Findley to stand upright. The blood rushing in his head made it quite difficult to hear anything around him. Breathing heavily, he scanned the area surrounding him for some sign of Maggy. He realized the sweat he was wiping from his brow was in fact blood, and he let loose with a curse. He needed to find her and quickly, before she wreaked even more havoc on his men.

He took a few unsteady steps forward and caught a glimpse of movement a good fifty yards or more ahead and to his left. The lass had the speed of a red deer! He shook the cobwebs from his head and ran after her.

She was zigzagging through the woods at a very rapid pace. Smart girl, he thought. He imagined most women would have gone running in fear, screaming at the tops of their lungs. He thought of what Robert had said earlier, about his mum being "right smart". The lad's description had been accurate.

Occasionally he could see the flash of her auburn hair as she ran swiftly and nearly soundlessly through the scrub and brushwood. She was running deeper into the woods, which would make it far more difficult to find her. He was growing frustrated with the game of cat and mouse. While he could understand she would be fearful, pummeling him or his men to death with stones for something the Buchannans had done was down right iniquitous!

He had run for a good distance when he realized he had lost sight of her. He stopped abruptly, his eyes cautiously looking for any sign of her. He had reached the limit of his patience.

"Maggy!" he shouted, hoping his voice would carry through the thick forest. "I mean ye no harm! We are here to help!"

His breathing was labored, and the pain in his skull was increasing at a rapid pace.

"We ken what the Buchannans did! We will nae hurt yer lads, Maggy, I promise!" He strained his ears to listen for the sound of her voice or even the faint rustle of leaves. If she had heard him, she was apparently choosing to ignore him.

Damn stubborn woman! They were wasting precious time. They needed to get to Renfrew before dark and at the pace they were going the chances of succeeding were next to nil.

"Maggy!" He decided to make another attempt at appealing to her good sense. "We wanna take ye and yer boys to Renfrew! Ye'll be safe there, lass! Then we will work at getting Ian back fer ye!"

He took another deep breath. "Please, Maggy," he spoke those pleading words, had not yelled them. "Let me help."

He stood under a large oak tree and skimmed the landscape for any sign of her whereabouts. He felt his heart sinking with each silent, unanswered moment that passed. She was undoubtedly lying low and probably planning another way of attack. He could not rightly blame her.

The wooziness had returned, and he wasn't sure if it was from the growing knot on his head or from dread and worry over Maggy. He leaned against the tree and slid down it where he rested his head in his hands. The flow of blood had slowed down a bit and was beginning to feel sticky against his hands.

His head throbbed, and his stomach felt sick with worry. He was beginning to wonder if Maggy hadn't lumped him in with the same lot of cowards as the Buchannans. The thought gnawed at him, for he knew nothing could be further from the truth. But he wouldn't be able to prove that to her if he couldn't find her.

He sat alone, lost in his thoughts. He had to get back to his men and the boys. Mayhap the boys would have a better chance at weeding their mum out than he had. As he was getting ready to stand, he heard the most beautiful voice in the world speak his name.

"Findley."

The relief at seeing her was indescribable. Then he caught sight of the stones she held in her hands. He dared not move for fear she would fling the stones at him, and she'd already proven she had very good aim.

"Maggy," he managed to scratch out.

She stood some ten feet away. Close enough that should she feel the need to pelt him again, she could, yet far enough away that should the need to run arise, she would have a good head start. He was afraid to move for fear she would hit him and take off running again.

"Did ye speak the truth about helping me to get Ian?" she asked him, studying him closely.

"Aye, I did."

She was turning the stones in her hands, rubbing them with her thumbs as if she wasn't sure she should believe him. "Why?"

If he told her he thought she had captivated his heart and taken his soul prisoner, he'd be a dead man in the blink of an eye. He would have loved nothing more than to tell her just that. He decided however, that honesty was probably not the best route to take at the moment.

"We came to bring ye supplies and an offer to foster yer sons. That's how we came upon yer camp or what was left of it. We ken it be the Buchannans that done it." It wasn't the complete truth, but it would do.

Maggy eyed him suspiciously. "Why?"

Findley blinked. "Why what?" The knot on his head was pounding ruthlessly, and he felt as though an impenetrable fog was descending upon his thoughts.

Maggy rolled her eyes at him. "Why did ye bring supplies and an offer to foster me boys?"

She continued to rub the stones with her thumbs. Maggy had learned very early in life that men never did anything without expecting something in return. What had Findley expected by bringing supplies? What was in it for him to offer to foster her sons?

"Because ye needed the help." That much was true.

"And what do ye be expectin' in return for your good deeds?" The crease in her brow deepened.

"Nothin'." It was a complete lie. What he hoped for and what he expected were two entirely different matters. He hoped for a chance to win her heart as she had unknowingly won his. He wanted to pull her into his arms and begin kissing her from the top of her head to the tips of her toes, and he wanted a lifetime in which to accomplish it in. He expected her to kill him dead where he sat if he breathed a word of his thoughts aloud.

Maggy snorted. She had seen through his lie. "Men dunnae give anythin' without expectin' somethin' in return, Findley." She had all but called him a liar, and even though she was right, it still wounded his pride.

"As much as ye might not wanna believe me, lass, there are some good men out there who do try to do what is right and what is honorable."

He took in a deep breath before pushing himself to his feet. The movement caused his head to spin, and he nearly fell over. Maggy didn't rush to offer him any help, which was probably the right course of action. For if she had, he would have scooped her up, thrown her over his shoulder and carried her back to his men and her sons. That is, if he could have gotten his head to quit spinning. What he wouldn't give for a sip of the chief's best right now.

Instead, she took a few cautious steps backwards, never taking her eyes from him. He remained where he was, putting his hand on the trunk of the tree for balance.

"I ken ye dunnae believe me, and I cannae blame ye fer it. But do nae go lumpin' me or my men in with the Buchannan scum." He hadn't meant to sound so angry, but the pain and his frustration were quickly taking over his good senses.

"We came to offer ye help, to take ye all back to Dunshire with us, if ye'd accept such an offer. And if not, we had supplies to leave ye, to help get ye through the winter."

That much was true. Although he would not admit to anyone that had she turned down his offer to return to Dunshire with him, it would have taken a lifetime to get over the hurt.

"Now," he said, straightening his back and resting his hands on his hips. "We can argue it all the day long if ye wish. But we be wastin' precious time. Me men and I are goin' to Renfrew -- with or without ye, it does nae matter to me."

It was another lie, for there would be no way on this earth that he'd leave her or the boys out here alone. He would drag her kicking and screaming all the way to Renfrew if he had to.

"Once we make it to Renfrew, we are tradin' the wagons in fer horses and men." He shook the fog from his head and began walking away.

Maggy stood with her mouth open. Did he really mean to leave her and the boys here? Alone? With God only knew how many Buchannans roaming the countryside looking for them? Certainly, it was a ruse to get her to follow him, and it was working. Before she realized it, her feet were moving to catch up to him.

"And then what, Findley?" she demanded.

He spun around, his face hard and angry. Maggy stopped dead in her tracks, fully prepared to hurl more stones at him if necessary. "And then I plan on gettin' Ian."

CHAPTER FOUR

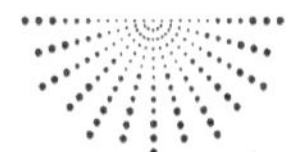

Avoice in the back of her mind reminded her that men did nothing purely for the sake of goodness. There was always a price, always strings attached. Men were not mysterious creatures. They were beastly things. They wielded their power over others with no thought to anything but how they could increase their riches, their wealth, and obtain more power.

Her own husband had married her for those same reasons. It garnered him more wealth, and he had wanted nothing else from their marriage.

It wasn't that Maggy brought any lands, titles, or holdings to their marriage. Nay, she'd been as poor as dirt from the day she was born. And she could never figure out how her mother had been able to broker a marriage between the two of them. For reasons she was never privy to, Gawter's uncle had promised to double Gawter's holdings if only he'd agree to marry Maggy. Being the greedy man that he was, Gawter could not turn down such an offer.

Maggy knew she had not brought Gawter any amount of true happiness, for that had not been his goal. Nay, he found his happiness in the arms of other women, not in Maggy's. Their marriage had been a means to an end and nothing more. There had been no romance, no kind words, no handholding or long walks across their lands. It had been void of anything remotely heartfelt or sincere. It had been empty.

She had learned long ago that women were nothing more than chattel. They were traded like sheep or horses. A woman had no voice in any matter, and her opinions were of no import to anyone.

At the moment however, her heart was speaking louder than her mind. It was booming in her chest, as loud as a hundred Scottish drums, to listen, to hope.

Mayhap Findley was different. Mayhap he spoke the truth. Mayhap he was a good man who wanted only to help. Her life experiences taught her that those men were as rare as two-headed pigs.

Her heart ached with missing her son Ian, and it begged her to listen to Findley. He had turned away from her and was walking, albeit a bit wobbly thanks to her true aim, back toward the clearing.

"Findley," she called after him.

He came to a stop, hung his head, and placed his hands on his hips. It wasn't easy to tamp down the myriad of thoughts and feelings swarming in his mind and heart. He was angry with the Buchannans for burning out Maggy's home, for killing the auld, and for taking Ian. He was angry at Maggy for being so stubborn and for lumping him in with the filthy Buchannans and for causing the growing knot on his forehead.

But most of all, he was angry with himself for not having arrived weeks ago to take Maggy and her family back to Dunshire. Had he not been stabbed by an English soldier's dirk this past summer, he would have been here sooner, and this whole disaster could have been avoided. And he'd be well on his way to winning her heart.

He took a deep breath and turned to face her. There was a good deal of fear and distrust simmering in those bright green eyes of hers. More anger toward the Buchannans began to boil up in his stomach, for it had been they who had made her afraid.

Findley knew the only way to rid her of her trepidation was to rescue Ian. He knew that Maggy would not rest nor would she shed the mantle of fear draped around her heart until she had her son back in her arms. Findley would go to the ends of the earth to bring Ian back to her.

When he saw her eyes brimming with tears, what was left of his heart shattered. "Maggy," he spoke softly. "I ken yer afraid, and rightly so. And I ken I ask a great deal of ye, to put yer trust into the hands of a stranger."

He studied her for a moment. Her auburn braid had come loose; the long tendrils tumbled down her back. The gentle breeze ran through it like fingers, and he wished it were his fingers that touched it.

"Tell me why I should believe ye," she said quietly. Give me one reason to trust you.

Findley let out a short breath. "Lass, I dunnae ken what I can say other than ask ye to trust me. I mean neither ye nor yers any harm; I only want to help."

"But why?" She had to know the reasons behind his offer to help, elst she'd not be able to trust him.

"Because it be the right and honorable thing to do." Had he not been fearful that she would either throw another rock to his head or turn and run like a skittish deer, he would have told her more. He would have told her of his feelings for her. Before he realized it, however, more words tumbled from his mouth. "And I be searchin' for redemption."

Her expression turned from fear to curiosity. Redemption? What on earth could Findley McKenna have done in his life that required redemption? The question itself was the answer. If her heart asked what he could have done that needed redeeming, she fully believed that it was God's way of telling her she could trust him. At least for now.

"Ye truly want to help me get me son back?" She would let the subject of redemption alone for now.

"Aye, I do."

There was something fleeting in those dark brown eyes of his. Something that pleaded with her to believe him.

She swallowed hard before taking a deep breath. "I'll take yer offer of help."

His shoulders relaxed as he let out a sigh of relief. A wry smile came to his face. "Will ye be puttin' down yer weapons now?" he asked, staring at the stones she still held in her hands.

She fought the urge to return his captivating smile. "Nay," she told him as she tucked the stones into the pocket of her apron. "I may need them yet."

Findley took her words as a warning. She'd trust him only in so far as he'd not bring physical harm to her or her boys. Her trust was only temporary.

She maintained a safe distance as they walked back toward the clearing. Findley allowed her the space she needed, understanding she held a good deal of reservation about him. He could not say that he blamed her for being unable to trust men.

As they stepped into the clearing, Findley whistled, a clear signal to his men that all was well. Moments later, his men stepped forward, peering cautiously at Findley and Maggy. The boys raced toward her and smothered her with hugs.

When Wee William caught a glimpse of Maggy for the first time, he came to a dead stop at the edge of the clearing. The most peculiar look had come to his face. His eyes grew wide, and his mouth fell open. Patrick came and stood beside his friend who at the moment appeared to be made of stone.

"What be the matter, Wee William?" he asked as he followed Wee William's gaze. His own eyes fell to Maggy then. A bonny woman, aye, but her beauty didn't have the same effect on Patrick as it had on William.

"Wee William?" Patrick asked, nudging the man from his trance with an elbow to his ribs.

Wee William swallowed hard and whispered. "I would shave me beard and cut me hair if she asked me to."

CHAPTER FIVE

"Nay," Findley said firmly. "Ye'll go to our keep in Dunshire. Ye'll not be going against the Buchannans with us."

Five sets of very determined and angry eyes glared at him. Findley could well understand their desire to do whatever they could to get Ian back. However, four young lads and a woman weren't the kind of help he needed to lay siege to the Buchannan keep.

"Findley," Maggy began. "Ian is me son. I'll not sit idly by whilst ye and yer men attempt to rescue him."

Insulted, Findley's eyes turned to dark slits. "Attempt?" he asked. "Do ye nae think I can get him back?"

Maggy took a deep breath. "I dinna say that." She stared back at him. "I am sayin' ye'll not do it without me."

Under different circumstances he might well have found her stubbornness appealing and attractive. As it was, they were wasting valuable time arguing the point. If they would just get in the wagons, they could discuss the matter as they rode to Renfrew. But nay, Maggy and her boys refused to board the wagons until they had his promise that they would be allowed to assist in retrieving Ian.

"Maggy, I ken ye want yer son back."

She drew her lips into a firm line as she stared back at him. "Aye. I do," she told him.

"If ye'll just get into the wagon, we can discuss it on our way to Renfrew."

"Not until I have yer promise ye'll not try to send me to yer keep."

If he had arrived days ago, days before the Buchannans had attacked, she may well have been tempted to accept his offer to foster her sons and live amongst his clan. But now everything had changed, and she could no longer afford the luxury of pretending she and her sons could ever live out a normal existence. She wondered just how much Findley knew about her or Liam. She also wondered if he knew the real reasons behind the attack.

His patience had been stretched thin. He realized that logic would not play into any decision she might make this day.

"Fine. I promise I'll nae try to send ye back to my keep," he told her. It didn't mean he wouldn't leave her safely in Renfrew.

"Ye promise?" she asked, eyeing him suspiciously.

He grunted. "Maggy!" He was growing more frustrated by the moment. "I promise I'll nae send ye to me keep! Now please," he lowered his voice, doing his best not to yell, but his patience was wearing thin. "Get into the wagons."

She had been married to a master liar and manipulator for five years. She saw right through Findley's lie. Deciding she wanted nothing more than to move forward, she would, for now, allow him this one lie. While he might keep his promise not to send her to Dunshire, more likely than not he would skirt the issue and leave her and her boys either in Renfrew or some other place along the way.

"Fine," she said. "We will go to Renfrew." But she had no intentions of remaining there.

Findley let out a relieved breath and nodded to his men while Maggy gave a curt nod to her boys and headed toward the wagons.

"Robert," Wee William called to the boy. "Have ye ever driven a wagon?"

Robert raced up to stand before Wee William. "Nay, but I imagine I can learn."

Wee William gave the boy an approving nod and Robert scurried up the wagon. Wee William gave him a few quick instructions before untying the leads from the brake and handing them to him.

Liam had appeared at Wee William's side. "What will ye have me do?" the boy asked eagerly.

Wee William smiled down at the boy. "Ye've the most important job of all, lad," he said as he lifted the boy up and sat him next to Robert.

"Ye have to keep yer eyes open and be lookin' fer any signs of trouble."

Liam would take his role seriously. "Aye," he said as he looked out at the horizon. "Do I get a broadsword or a dirk?" He asked.

Wee William stifled a chuckle. "Nay, lad, nae yet."

Liam looked disappointed. "I'll teach ye the proper use of a broadsword soon enough," Wee William told him. "But fer now, I need ye to be on the look out for Buchannans, or anyone else for that matter."

Patrick called after Andrew and Collin. "Andrew," he said. "How old be ye?"

"Ten and two," he answered, looking up at the man who could very well have passed for his older brother.

"I be almost ten and one!" Collin told him, looking quite eager to help.

Patrick nodded, "That'll do. The two of ye will drive this wagon," he told them. "Ye stay between Findley's wagon and Robert's."

Richard would lead the way while Wee William and Patrick followed up the rear on their mounts. With any luck, they'd reach Renfrew by month's end. Wee William knew it was too much to hope for to reach it by nightfall.

MAGGY WAS NOT HAPPY, not happy at all. She sat as far from Findley as the wagon seat would allow and refused to partake in any small talk. After Findley's lie, she doubted she could trust the man beyond getting her to Renfrew. She was certain that once there, he would slip out at one point or another and leave without her.

Half an hour had passed since Findley had given up his attempts at conversation. He could not figure out why Maggy was angry. Shouldn't she be happy that he and his men had found her and her boys before the Buchannans did?

He could stand the silence no longer. "Do ye mind tellin' me why ye're so angry?"

Maggy rolled her eyes and shook her head. It puzzled her to no end as to how men, stupid beasts really, had managed to control the earth. If women were in charge, well, life would certainly be different. She imagined that if women held the power that men did, there'd be no more wars, no more political firestorms, and definitely no more arranged marriages. There would finally be peace on this earth.

But men did have all the power. And they certainly hadn't gained it using any mental intellect. They'd gotten it through sheer brute strength.

Findley took a deep breath. "Maggy, I cannae fix the problem if I dunnae ken what I have done wrong."

Maggy mulled it over for a moment. She needed the ride to Renfrew. Did he make his offer to get Ian back for noble reasons? Or did he know more than he was letting on? Was that why he was so adamant about getting to Renfrew and the reason behind his blatant lie? She wished she knew him better.

Mayhap his reasons were noble, and he truly had no clue what was really going on with the Buchannan. But what would happen once he learned the truth behind Ian's abduction? All men were, after all, the same -- simple-minded beasts. She decided it was far too much to hope that Findley would be any different.

Chances were he would respond in the same fashion as the Buchannan. Aye, he might not use brutal tactics to get what he wanted. The problem was that he would want what she could offer, and she had no desire to give it to anyone.

"Ye'll be leavin' us in Renfrew, won't ye?"

Blunt and to the point, yet another trait he might enjoy in a woman if the circumstances were different. "What leads ye to believe that?" he asked, keeping his eyes on the horizon.

"I was married fer a time, Findley. I be not an innocent lass who cannae tell when she is bein' lied to." She looked at him out of the corner of her eye.

He wasn't sure how to respond. He had told the truth earlier, that he would not send her to his keep in Dunshire. She was apparently smart enough to figure out he planned on leaving her in Renfrew.

"Maggy," he began as he tried to find a way back to her good side. "I have only yer safety in mind. I dunnae want any harm to come to ye or yer boys."

"And why do ye care about me safety or that of me boys?" She folded her hands in her lap and looked at him.

Findley chewed his tongue for a moment before answering. "I have told ye before. 'Tis the right thing to do, to help those that need it." He prayed she would accept his answer and not drag it out further.

She caught the flicker of something as it flashed across his face. He had said earlier that he sought redemption and spoke of honor. There was more to it than what he was sharing.

"Why do ye seek redemption?" If she caught him in another lie, she would be glad for him to leave her in Renfrew.

He felt the color drain from his face as his stomach tightened. He rarely spoke of what had happened to his family and how he had failed them. He came to the sudden realization that there was a very strong chance he'd not be able to gain her affections. And once she learned why he sought redemption, would she look at him with shame?

Better she learned the truth now and be done with it. He felt all hope at winning her heart fall away with what he was about to tell her.

He took a deep breath and let it out very slowly. "I failed me family. Because of it, they be dead."

Her expression wasn't what he had expected. Instead of looking at him with disgust and shame, she looked puzzled. "How did ye fail them?"

His jaw hardened. "Does it matter?" he asked. "They be dead, and it be me fault."

"Aye, it does matter."

It was his turn to look puzzled.

"Findley," she said before taking a short breath in. "If I am to entrust the safety of meself and me boys to ye, then I have a right to ken."

Maggy knew there were many ways in which a man could fail his family. Some were far worse than others.

"I was nae there to protect them. There was an attack on our village." He cleared his throat before going on. "Because I was nae there, the entire village was destroyed, including me own family."

The images of his own burned and destroyed village began to blend with what had happened to Maggy's. His stomach tightened further, and his heart began to pound with guilt. He had failed them all.

"Where were ye when it happened?" she asked softly.

"I was off with me friends," he answered, "fishin'."

"Did ye ken an attack was comin'?"

He thought it a ridiculous question. "Of course not. Had I ken it, I would nae have been fishin'."

"Then why blame yerself?" She could see the guilt etched on his face, and her heart began to break for him.

"If I had been there, I could have helped." In Findley's mind, it made perfectly good sense. Many people over the years had tried to tell him not to blame himself. But those people simply did not understand how he could not relinquish the guilt. He carried it with him, wherever he went. He wore it like a second skin.

Maggy could well understand his guilt. Had she been at home, instead of in the forest, she could have protected her small clan from the Buchannans.

But everything would have ended differently had she been there. She and her boys would either be dead, or she would have been forced to marry the Buchannan in order to save them all. The thought of marrying Malcolm Buchannan sickened her.

She had refused the Buchannan chief's proposal each and every time he had made it over the past several months. There had been numerous reasons why she had refused him. The man was as disgusting as he was cruel. He apparently disliked bathing, for he stunk to the high heavens, and his teeth were yellow. The thought of being married to someone who was that cruel and that filthy was revolting. She could not imagine anyone who would willingly lie with the man, let alone bear his child. She simply could not bring herself to agree to marry him.

Once the Buchannan got what he wanted, Maggy and her sons would have no longer held any value to him. They were simply a means to an end.

No matter how well she understood the circumstances, she still could not rid herself of the guilt. She would never be able to forgive herself for the deaths of her people or for Ian's abduction.

She suddenly realized that she and Findley had much in common. Both felt they had failed those they loved the most.

"I be truly sorry fer yer loss, Findley," she said, resisting the urge to reach out and touch his hand. "I understand yer grief and guilt."

Findley had been carrying around the guilt for far too many years. He did not believe anyone, least of all Maggy, could either understand it or forgive him. "What do ye ken of it?" he snorted.

His words stung as much as if he had slapped her. "I feel the same way, ye fool. I was nae there for me people or me son, and now look where I be." She gritted her teeth and looked away.

I be an eejit. He swallowed hard, feeling like a complete fool. "Lass," he began, "I be sorry. I sometimes forget I be nae the only one bad things have happened to."

'Tis because yer a man. Ye cannae think beyond yerself.

THEY RODE in silence for quite some time. Maggy was not as angry with Findley as she had been. Now she was simply disappointed in him. For a moment she had allowed herself to believe he might be different, that he might not be an idiot like most of the men she knew. He had proved her wrong.

Findley studied her from the corner of his eye. She was the most beautiful woman he had ever had the pleasure of laying eyes to. She had an oval-shaped face that held a straight nose, full pink lips and bright green eyes, nearly the color of spring grass. And all that was surrounded by thick masses of deep auburn hair tied into a beautiful braid that fell over her shoulder and across an ample bosom.

For a moment, he pictured himself there, with her arms wrapped around him and his head resting gently upon her chest. 'Twould be heaven and home to be with her in such an intimate manner.

He had become smitten with her months ago, and she had no idea how he felt about her. His original plan had been to take her and her clan back to Castle Gregor, and from there he would woo her and get to know her better.

In his mind's eye, the scenarios were always perfect. They would have shared walks along the loch and long rides across Clan MacDougall's lands. He would have impressed her with his skills on the practice fields. He would have wooed her and won her heart, and she would be his forever.

His daydream of Maggy falling into his arms and professing her undying love and devotion to him, and he to her, were broken when Wee William appeared beside their wagon.

"Have ye told the lassie yet, Findley?" Wee William asked from Maggy's side of the wagon.

There was a twinkling of something in Wee William's eye that did not settle well with Findley.

"Told me what?" Maggy asked as she smiled up at Wee William.

Findley eyed his friend suspiciously, uncertain as to what he spoke of.

There was a devious grin on Wee William's lips. "Yer boys be wantin' ye to marry me."

Maggy's mouth literally fell open while Findley's confused face instantly turned to a deep, hard scowl. "Be gone with ye, William," he ordered.

"Nay," Maggy said, looking first to Findley then back to Wee William.

"Pray, tell me. What is it me boys have done?"

Wee William chuckled. "They be tryin' to forge a bargain for ye."

Maggy's brow creased as she pursed her lips together. She had done her best to teach her sons that arranged marriages were not a good idea in any situation. She prayed her boys held tightly to their secret. "They are, are they?"

Wee William nodded his head and continued to smile. "Aye, that they are, lassie." He leaned forward on his mount to get a better look at Findley. Wee William was thoroughly enjoying the sour look that his leader's face currently held.

"And have they told ye why they want us to marry?" she asked, quietly praying her secret was still safe.

Wee William's lips curved upward as he continued to look at the lovely lass sitting beside Findley. "Aye. They think I can protect ye from the Buchannan. They believe that if ye're married, the Buchannan will leave ye be."

He sat taller in his saddle as his smile broadened. "Ye see, lassie, they appear to be impressed with me size and stature." He looked rather proud of himself at the moment.

"Wee William," Findley began before he was interrupted by Maggy.

"I can see why," she said, ignoring Findley. "Ye be a mountain of a man, Wee William. I doubt there are many who are nae impressed with ye. Especially the lasses."

A breath caught in Findley's throat, as a wave of something akin to panic flashed over him. Certainly, she could not be impressed with the giant riding alongside her. Certainly, she could not be considering the prospect of marrying Wee William.

Wee William raised an eyebrow and continued to smile at Maggy. "I have to beat them off with a stick, lass."

Maggy giggled. 'Twas the first time Findley had heard such sweetness come from her, and he was angry that he hadn't been the one to make her laugh. He tightened his grip on the reins and bit his tongue. Things were not going as he had planned.

"I would imagine so, William." She continued to smile up at him. "And I imagine me boys have nothin' but good intentions in mind. But I could nae marry a man who had to constantly beat the women away with a stick."

"Aye. I imagine 'twould be a difficult cross to bear, lassie."

"'Twould be indeed. And I thank ye fer yer offer, but I'll have to decline it."

Wee William winked at her, and then cast a devilish smile at Findley before turning back to Maggy. "I would have shaved me beard fer ye, lass. And there be not a woman in all of Scotland that ever made me think such a thing."

He bowed his head to her, pulled rein, and rode back to Robert's wagon.

Findley's gums began to ache from clenching his teeth. He had not appreciated the little tete-a-tete that Wee William had shared with Maggy. The man knew how Findley felt about the auburn-haired beauty. And still, he had openly flirted with her, right in front of him!

His knuckles had turned white, and his face burned crimson with anger. He was mad at himself for not putting his best foot forward when it came to the beautiful lass sitting beside him. He was angry with Wee William for charming a laugh from her. And he was very upset that Maggy had apparently been impressed with the giant fool.

Part of him wanted nothing more than to take her into his arms and tell her why he had come for her. The illogical, thickheaded part of him said to let Wee William have her if that was what she wanted.

"What be the matter, Findley?" Maggy asked, looking confused.

Suddenly he found himself wanting to consume vast amounts of ale. He snapped the reins and shouted at the horses to move faster. The horses lurched forward, rattling harness and wagon alike. The quick movement caused Maggy to jerk and fall into him. Instinctively, she threw her arms around his waist and held tight.

A wave of something quite peculiar and unknown washed over her the moment she was pressed against him. 'Twas a sensation that she had never felt in all her twenty and four years on this earth. The tingling had started in her stomach and radiated out toward her fingers and toes. She was not sure at the moment, but she thought the feeling might be one of delight.

She cursed under her breath and did her best to convince herself that the feeling was simply fear of nearly being thrown from the wagon. 'Twas all Findley's blasted fault!

"Findley!" she squeaked at him. "Hold care!"

"We need to make Renfrew before nightfall," he told her, keeping his eyes on the land before him. He was doing his best to ignore how wonderful it felt to have her pressed so closely to him.

She finally righted herself and clung to the seat with trembling hands. Doing her best to regain her composure, she put a stern look to her face.

"Aye, and I would like to arrive in one piece!"

Findley rolled his eyes and urged the horses faster. "I promised ye a ride to Renfrew. I did nae promise 'twould be filled with roses and rainbows."

Maggy cocked her head at him. What on earth had come over him?

"And I be not asking fer such things, especially from the likes of ye," she fumed at him.

"And I would nae give 'em to ye if ye asked!" he threw back at her.

"But I do ask that ye at least take me sons into consideration! Neither has ever driven a wagon before, Findley! I imagine they'd be hard pressed to keep up with a madman!"

Findley drew in a fast breath, ground his teeth together, and pulled the reins to slow the horses. He cast a glance over his shoulder to find that his men had not attempted to keep up with them. They were often smarter than he gave them credit for.

He took a moment to look at her full on. God's teeth, the woman was beautiful, even if she did possess the look of a very angry if not fearful woman at the moment.

"I be sorry for frightening ye, lass," he offered.

Her face burned with anger and her eyes darkened. She'd not allow him the pleasure of knowing she had been quite frightened, but for reasons he was not aware of.

"Foolish man!"

"Blast it, woman!" His voice was thick with frustration. "I did nae travel all these many days only to fight with ye!"

She was taken aback by his statement and not sure what he meant by it. "Why did ye then?"

He swallowed hard and started to speak.

"And dunnae say it be fer redemption. Or for honorable reasons. No man be that humble or honorable."

She could not trust him outright, not yet. She needed to know just what he knew about her, Liam, and her clan. Logic dictated that he did know the truth. No man, no matter how honorable and noble, would put his life on the line for someone he did not know.

Somewhere deep within her, she allowed herself to hope, however, that he did not know. She wanted very much to believe that not all men were selfish idiots. She wanted to believe in him.

Findley was far too angry and frustrated at the moment to speak, let alone speak the truth. He suddenly felt quite foolish for allowing his heart to control his life. He was a warrior, for the sake of Christ! Give him an opponent on the battlefield, and he was unstoppable, brave and fierce.

Make him look into those bright green eyes, and he was reduced to a babbling idiot who could not find his way out of a room with ten doors.

He breathed in slowly, through his nose, and out again before trying to answer her question. "There be all manner of reasons. One, it is the right thing to do. Two, I do seek redemption." He stopped suddenly, unable to will his mouth to move forward.

"And three?" she asked, growing more frustrated by the moment. He was hiding something, she was sure of it.

"And three, I care about what happens to ye and yer boys," he blurted.

She had no good response. I care could mean all manner of things. He could care as a brother does for a sister, or as a father does for a daughter. Or as friend cares for a friend. She would not allow her mind to go any further than friend.

She tried to appear unmoved by his statement. "Thank ye, then," she murmured.

He could only nod his head and move the horses forward. He wondered if there would ever come a time when he could simply tell her what was in his heart.

CHAPTER SIX

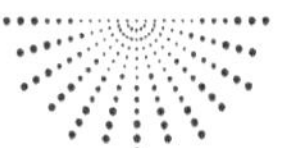

Ian wrapped his arms around his knees and did his best to be brave. He stared at the scratch marks on the wall of the room where he was being held. If he was correct, it had been five days since the men attacked his home. He had been in this dark, cold and dirty room for the past two days.

The back of his head still smarted where one of the guards had smacked him that morning. Ian had refused to answer the very large and smelly man's question.

"Are ye ascared, brat?" the man had asked. Ian would not give him the satisfaction of an answer. He simply stared up at him from his dirty pallet. When he continued to remain silent, even after the man had repeated his question, the man smacked him hard. But Ian refused to allow him the satisfaction of seeing him cry.

The truth was he was scared. Still, he refused to allow the man to see it. Ian was positive that none of his other brothers would cower in fear if it were one of them here in this cold and dirty castle. Nay, they'd be brave. And they wouldn't cry – not one of them. So, Ian did his best to maintain the outward appearance of calm, even when he felt like throwing up.

His stomach growled, loudly voicing dissatisfaction at not having had a thing to eat all day. The guard who had hit him earlier that morning had promised he'd not allow him to eat until Ian answered his question.

The more his stomach rumbled and protested, the more Ian began to wish he had simply answered. But the man was a dirty Buchannan. Ian would starve before he'd allow any of them to see his fear.

Ian began to think of his brothers and his mum. Both his mums, actually. His real mum had died three years past. Sometimes he missed her, but only because he thought he should. Deep down, however, he was glad that Maggy was his mum now. She did a much better job of it than his real mum had.

Oh, he knew his real mum had loved him in her own odd way. But she wasn't as fierce at it as Maggy. His real mum was quite busy with her own life and had very little time to share with him. She didn't tell him stories, didn't make sure he ate his vegetables, and didn't insist he bathe thrice weekly like Maggy did.

She also didn't tell him to watch his manners or mind his tongue. Nay, she didn't remind him to say his prayers or thank the Good Lord above before each meal like Maggy.

Where his mum would just smile and tousle his hair before leaving for days on end, Maggy would appear genuinely grieved to to see him leave when his mum finally returned. Maggy would hug him with tears in her eyes, a sure sign she cared enough to miss him.

Aye, there were many differences between the two women. Very often he wondered if it were wrong to love Maggy more. He finally concluded that perhaps it had been a mistake to begin with, that he had been born to the wrong woman. Mayhap he should have been born to Maggy to begin with.

The sun was beginning to lower itself when he heard the latch to the door being lifted. He prayed it wasn't the same mean guard from the morning, for he was so hungry now, he doubted he had the resolve to maintain his dignity. If asked again, he was certain his hunger would win out, and he'd answer any question, just for a few bites of food.

The door pushed open and a man he had not seen before stepped into the room. His eyes scanned the dark room until they fell upon Ian.

"There ye are, ye beasty," he said with a devious smile. "Up with ye now," he ordered. He reached Ian in three quick steps and yanked him up by one arm.

"Yer future step-sire wishes to see ye," he said as he dragged Ian from the pallet and out the door.

Ian was not stupid and knew exactly to whom the guard referred. The chief of the Clan Buchannan wanted to see him. Ian knew that fact did not bode well for him.

Mayhap the Buchannan had heard he was not being cooperative with the guards. Or mayhap he wanted to torture him into telling him where his mum and brothers might be.

Ian knew exactly where his mum and brothers would head to, for the plan had been pounded into his head ever since he could remember. Until the Buchannans had showed up and burned out their home, Ian could never understand why such a plan was necessary. Until that day, they'd all lived perfectly happy lives, and escape plans seemed silly to him. While he still didn't understand why the Buchannan wanted to marry his mum so badly that he'd kill for her hand, he felt better knowing help would eventually arrive.

And help would arrive in the form of Maggy's brothers. She had seven of them, and every last one of them would drop what they were doing in order to help her. At least that's what Maggy had told Ian and his brothers. Ian knew she'd try to reach the nearest brother first, the one who lived in Dundee.

He'd take that secret to the grave.

Ian swallowed hard as he stared up at the man. He had seen with his own eyes how evil the Buchannan men could be. They had forced Ian to watch as they cut Audra's throat when she refused to tell them where Maggy was. Audra had been like a grand-mum to him. The Buchannan men had laughed maliciously when they had set the tents on fire and destroyed Ian's home.

The men had taunted him, smacked him about his head, and

kicked dirt into his face on the three-day journey back to the Buchannan keep. For two days they had kept him locked in the dark room, coming in occasionally to taunt him further or to bring him his porridge and bread.

Now the Buchannan himself had sent for him. Fear shot through to his toes, and he tried hard not to pee his pants. Out of respect for his brothers and his mum, he'd not show his fear.

Robert had explained it to them many times over the years. Robert's words were engraved in his brain: warriors aren't afraid of anything, and we are warriors. We protect our own.

He kept Robert's words at the forefront of his mind now as he was led down the staircase and into the large gathering room. We protect our own. We be nae afraid of anythin'.

The more he heard Robert's voice, the braver he felt. The tall man dragged him through the gathering room, their steps kicking up fetid smells of old food and dog poop that intermingled with the rotten rushes. Ian told himself that if he lived through this ordeal, and God blessed him into manhood, he'd never let his own home become so filthy or in such disrepair.

The man pulled him down a long, dank hallway where they paused outside a heavy door. Before knocking on the door, the man cleared his throat and cast a disgusted look down at Ian. *Warriors be not afraid of anythin'.*

A voice from within bid them to enter. The man opened the door and pulled Ian inside. *We protect our own. We be not afraid of anythin'.*

Ian's courage was instantly replaced with fear. More fear than he had felt when the man had run his blade across Audra's throat.

He felt his heart and stomach plummet to his toes and the color drain from his own skin when he came face to face with the madman sitting behind the large, dark desk.

Two evil-looking eyes stared back at him. One was a dull brown, the other colorless and milky looking. A large scar ran down the entire right side of the man's face, across his eyebrow, his white eye, his cheek, and his beard before it disappeared somewhere under his filthy shirt.

The madman continued to stare at Ian, all the while maintaining an insidious smile on his lips. His teeth were yellow with bits of food stuck to them. There was a festering sore on his upper lip. Grimy, slick-looking hair the color of dirt framed his filthy face. 'Twas difficult to ascertain the true color of his skin, for it was so dark and greasy.

Ian felt his legs turn to jelly, and he was glad the man next to him held such a firm grip on his arm. If the man let go, Ian was certain he'd not be able to stand on his own two feet.

Ian had heard stories of the Buchannan before. All of the stories held the same vein, that the Buchannan was a ruthless, greedy, and insane man. Aye, he had heard of the scars and how ugly the man was, but nothing could have prepared him for witnessing it with his own eyes.

They were silent for several long moments whilst the Buchannan seemed to stare right into Ian's very soul. Ian's breathing began to increase from sheer fright as he looked at the sight before him.

After a very long time, the man slowly leaned forward across the desk, never taking his dull eye from Ian's. He kept his palms flat as he spread them out across the dirty wood.

"Bah!" the Buchannan suddenly shouted.

Ian sucked in a deep breath as the room began to spin all around him. In an instant, everything turned black.

———

THE BUCHANNAN WASN'T INSULTED by the fact that the boy fainted. His skin had grown quite thick over the years. He had grown used to the stares, the faces that turned away from his hideous scars and terrifying eyes. Such responses to his ghastly appearance no longer bothered him.

Aye, in the beginning, it had bothered him. Each time someone turned his head away from him, it was as if the cold blade of a dirk was being twisted into his heart.

Even his beautiful Cairen, with a heart of gold, could not abide his grotesqueness. The fact that she could not look beyond the scars had been his undoing. The day she had informed him that she could not marry him had been the day of his ruin. Malcolm was never the same after that.

He hadn't always been this way – ruthless, insane, and greedy. Nay, in his younger days he had been a handsome fellow, braw, strong and honest. He owned a heart back then. He cared for the sick and the poor, grieved for men and friends lost on the battlefield. And he had loved.

He had loved Cairen deeply, passionately and without restriction. Cairen had been his world. Until fate intervened and destroyed his face and his life along with it.

The fact that the boy fainted was nothing new for the Buchannan. What had shocked him to his nettles was the fact that he felt sorry for the lad. The Buchannan hadn't felt pity for anyone or anything in a very long time. He hadn't felt anything but anger and hatred toward his fellow man in more than a decade.

But the fear in the little boy's bright green eyes right before they fluttered shut and he fell to the floor? It chilled him to the bone. The child's reaction had been exactly what he wanted: terrified. But something else had happened, something that Malcolm Buchannan wasn't prepared for. It was the flutter of a memory of a feeling he had no desire to feel. Compassion.

Aye, that was what had angered him to the point that he ran his arm across his desk, flinging the contents to the floor.

The three men standing in the room did not flinch. They were used to such outbursts from their leader.

"Take him back to his room!" Malcolm ordered.

The man who had brought Ian in scooped him up and headed toward the door.

Malcolm called after him, "And see to it that he is fed!"

The man nodded. "Aye, m'laird." He waited a moment for any further instructions. When he saw none forthcoming, he turned away again and resisted the urge to shake his head.

"And for the sake of Christ, give the brat a bath! He stinks worse than me!" Malcolm shouted.

The man halted for only a moment and was glad his back was turned to his chief. His leader could not then see the quizzical look upon his face. It was as he and the other men had feared. Their laird had finally lost what little of his mind he had left.

CHAPTER SEVEN

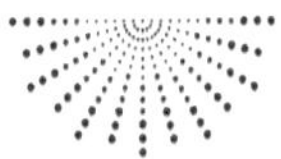

The sight of Renfrew in the distance brought a great sense of relief to Findley, Maggy, and the rest of their ragtag band. Even though it was a mere dot off in the horizon, the relief was palpable. They would enter the town under the cover of darkness.

Neither he nor Maggy had uttered a word to each other in the past hour.

"Is that Renfrew?" Maggy asked, finally breaking the silence.

"Aye, 'tis," Findley answered, glad to hear the sound of her voice.

"What be yer plan here, Findley?" she asked, keeping her gaze straight ahead. She began to grow fearful over the possibility of being seen by someone from her past.

"'Tis late in the day. We will seek rooms at the Bent Arrow Inn. In the morning we will trade our wagons for fresh horses and more men to help us. I'll also send a messenger back to Dunshire seeking more help."

Maggy took the chance to look at him. "And what of me and me boys?"

He had decided hours ago that he could not leave her in Renfrew. However, he had also decided he'd not let her go against the Buchannan clan with him. They would travel together as far as Stirling. He was not sure what he would do with them then and was glad he had a few days to think it over.

His plan, if Angus would agree to it, was to have more men meet him in Aberdeen. While he did not like the idea of leaving her alone in Stirling, he did not see where he had much choice in the matter. He needed to keep her as far away from Malcolm Buchannan and his men as he could.

"I'll not be leavin' ye in Renfrew," he answered. He would not share his entire plan with her, for he did not want to argue with her further.

"I thank ye fer that, Findley," she told him. "Do ye plan on launching our attack from Aberdeen?" she asked. Aberdeen made the most sense, as it was the closest city to the Buchannan keep.

"Aye, I do," he answered.

"I have a brother in Aberdeen," she told him. "He will be more than willin' to help us. It will be good to see him again." Maggy knew her brother would be more than simply surprised to see her.

While it was good to know she had a brother who might be willing to help, he had no intentions of allowing her to get that close to the Buchannans.

Maggy took note of his furrowed brow, and instinct told her he was holding back.

"Does that not fit with yer plans?" she asked, reading his face like an open book.

For a moment Findley began to wonder if the woman wasn't a witch or sorceress of some sort, with the ability of reading a man's mind. He studied her for a moment and decided perhaps she wasn't a witch but simply a very astute young woman.

"Nay," he said. "It does no'."

"But me brother can help us, Findley. Surely ye see the logic in it." The chances of being recognized in Aberdeen were immense. But it was a risk she was willing to take in order to get Ian back.

She wondered for a moment how much more she should share with him. Should she tell him of her brother in Dundee or the one in Perth? Both would be more than willing to help.

"Maggy, do not fly into another rage, for I swear I'll lose me mind if ye do! If ye've a brother in Aberdeen ye wish to stay with, then I'll take ye there." He would take her anywhere she wished to go as long as it was not the Buchannan keep.

What she didn't catch was the fact he hadn't said when he'd take her there. When the whole ordeal was over, he would take her anywhere she wished to go. He prayed, however, that she would wish to stay with him.

He watched as her shoulders relax in relief.

"I mean not to be a bother to ye, Findley," she said after a moment. "I ken ye mean well. And don't be thinkin' I am not grateful to ye, fer I truly am." She knew that, without Findley, her chances of reaching Renfrew alive and in one piece would have been next to none.

The question of why the Buchannans had attacked her clan still gnawed at him. The boys had said the Buchannan wanted to marry her. Maggy was the most beautiful woman he had ever known, and he could well understand any man's desire to marry her. Och! Even Wee William was willing to shave his beard for her.

But for Malcolm Buchannan to attack and kill her people made no sense. What could the man gain from it? Aye, she had turned down his offer of marriage, but was that enough to drive the man to kill? Instinct told Findley that the attack wasn't simply the workings of a madman. There had to be more to it.

"Maggy," he asked. "Why did the Buchannan attack yer home?"

"Who kens what makes a man do anythin'?" she mumbled.

He had caught a glimmer of fear and worry flash over her face in the instant before she answered.

"Maggy, if there is more to it, let me ken now. I can nae help if I dunnae ken the whole truth."

He could only hope she heard the sincerity in his voice, for she couldn't see it on his face. She was keeping her eyes glued to the horizon. He knew she was holding back and assumed it was fear that kept her from telling him.

"Maggy, I be nothin' like the Buchannan or any of his men. I truly do want to help. But I need to ken the truth of it."

She could not muster the courage to tell him. If she told him, then he would look at her and Liam differently. Not with compassion and care, but with hungry, greedy eyes. Though she didn't understand why, she simply couldn't bear the thought of him looking at her that way.

"Findley, I cannae say why the Buchannan attacked." She could not tell him the truth just yet.

"Do ye nae mean ye refuse to tell me?" he gritted his teeth. Why could she not trust him?

"If I promise to tell ye someday, will ye leave me be?" She had no intentions of telling him anything in the immediate future.

He knew someday could mean anything, for he had bade her the same promise of taking her to Aberdeen.

"And can ye give me an idea of when someday might be, lass?"

She finally turned to look at him. Her eyes were filled with a combination of anger and weariness. "Please, Findley, leave it be."

"I am only tryin' to help ye, ye stubborn woman!"

"And I thanked ye fer it, ye fool!"

Findley growled. "I swear ye'll be the death of me someday! Ye're the most stubborn woman I have ever met!"

"And ye be a pig-headed lummox!"

His eyes drew into angry slits. "I have a mind to leave ye in Renfrew after all."

Maggy's eyes instantly mirrored his. "'Twould be fine with me! I'll walk to the Buchannan's keep if I have to. I'll even marry him if I must!"

His breath hitched at the thought of it. "Ye'll do no such thing!"

She threw her shoulders back and put her hands on her hips. "And just who do ye think ye be to tell me what I can and cannae do?"

She had him there. He had no more a right to tell her what to do than she him. But it would be over his dead body that he would allow her to marry Malcolm Buchannan. Or anyone else for that matter, for no matter how much she irritated and frustrated him, he was still hopelessly in love with her. He was beginning to wonder if he wasn't as insane as the Buchannan chief.

"I be the man who traveled for days to bring ye supplies and an offer of a new home! And I ask for nothin' in return! I be the man who bade ye a promise to get yer son back!" He felt ashamed for raising his voice, but he had to get his point across somehow.

She had done a good job over the past days at keeping the tears at bay, at least while in the presence of her boys. She had succeeded in hiding her fear and dread from them, knowing she could not burden them any further than she already had.

But the wall began to break and as much as she tried, she could not hold the tears at bay any longer. "I am afraid for Ian, Findley," she said as tears trailed down her cheeks.

Aye, give him a battlefield full of men hell-bent on taking his life from him. Give him a broadsword or a dirk and he could fight any man and win. But make him stare into those bright green eyes filled with tears, and he was done. The anger and frustration he had felt only moments ago disappeared in the blink of a teary green eye.

"Wheest, lass," he spoke quietly, trying to reassure her. He wrapped an arm around her shoulder and drew her in to his chest. "All will be well. We will get yer Ian back. I swear it."

He sent a silent prayer up to God that it would be a promise he could keep.

Night had fallen when they reached the outskirts of Renfrew. It suddenly dawned on Findley that they would have problems securing rooms. While he, his men, and the lads would have no troubles, Maggy would be a different story.

"Lass," he said suddenly. "Do ye have something with which to cover yer hair?"

"Aye, it's among me other satchels and trunks ye have in the back of yer wagon," she answered sarcastically, shooting him a look that said she thought he was daft.

Findley let out an exasperated sigh. "Lass, forgive me. But ye'll need to cover yer hair here."

The only thing she had to cover her hair was her shawl. She cursed under her breath. It mattered not that she was a widow. Traveling with four men without the aid of a chaperone would be enough to have her branded a harlot. Not that she planned on staying in Renfrew long enough to worry over her reputation.

She pulled her shawl up over her head and grasped it under her chin. She would save her argument against such customs for a later time. All she wished for at the moment was to be off the hard wagon seat, to soak in a hot bath, and slip into a warm bed.

"And lass, ye'll have to pretend to be me wife fer the night." He braced himself for the protest he was certain would come.

"I beg yer pardon?" she asked, shocked that he would suggest such a thing.

"Lass, they'll nae give a room to a single woman, widowed or no', without a proper chaperone. Ye ken it as well as I."

She did know it, and she didn't like it. "If we pretend we be married, it means we will be sharin' a room," she murmured.

She looked at him closely for a moment. He was a very braw man. His dark brown hair hung well past his shoulders with braids that framed a more-than-handsome face. His deep, dark brown eyes and thick eyelashes could melt the heart of many a young woman. Hers included, if she were to allow such a thing to happen.

His broad shoulders and muscles seemed to be chiseled from stone. She had felt them when she had grabbed on to him earlier. For a brief moment she imagined resting her head in a very intimate fashion on his wide and masculine chest.

Under different circumstances, she might well have liked the thought of sharing a room with him. She shook the thoughts aside and castigated herself for allowing her mind to roam to thoughts no self-respecting mother of five should have.

"Aye, lass, that we will," he tried to hide the pleasure such a thought brought to his heart.

"Findley, I—" she tried to find the right words to explain what she was thinking. Then she realized she could not share such thoughts with him.

He sensed her apprehension and took it to mean she would rather not share a room with him. "Would ye rather pretend Wee William was yer husband?" he asked, gritting his teeth together.

She did not need to think on it. She knew sharing a room with Wee William would just fuel her sons' plans for the two of them to marry. That in itself was a battle she did not wish to wage.

"Nay," she told him.

"Richard or Patrick then?"

She shook her head. "Nay."

"Would ye prefer to sleep in the wagons?" He sensed an undercurrent of something and dared not hope it meant anything other than her having a proper sense of right and wrong.

"Nay. I wish for a hot bath and a warm meal. And if it means pretending to be yer wife fer a night, then so be it," she told him. She was tired, worn, and hungry.

"But dunnae be gettin' no ideas, Findley. It'll be a marriage in name only."

He could not stifle a chuckle. "But, lass, it be our weddin' night!" He feigned hurt feelings and smiled at her. She returned his smile as she shook her head.

He was very glad he had finally managed to bring a smile to her face.

***

THERE WERE ONLY three inns from which to choose. Two of them Findley would not have set foot in without at least ten more men to watch his back.

The Bent Arrow Inn sat at the edge of town. While still filled with nefarious sorts, it was the least dangerous of their options. They pulled the wagons in and parked near the stables. Two young lads came out to greet them and take charge of the horses. Findley recognized them as the innkeeper's youngest sons.

Patrick gave a coin to each lad with instructions to keep a close eye on the wagons.

"If the wagons still be here in the morn," he began, "and nothin' be stolen or lost, I'll give ye each another piece of silver."

Wide smiles erupted on the boys' freckled faces.

"Aye!" the tallest of the lads said. "We will sleep in the wagons if we have to!"

Findley had known the innkeeper and his wife for several years. Beyton and Fiona Lindsey were well into their forties. They, or more specifically Fiona, ran their inn with an iron fist.

It was commonly known that Beyton, who was short compared to most men, was the brains and Fiona, who was several inches taller than her husband, was the brawn. She had no qualms about hitting an unruly visitor over the head with a broom, chamber pot, or whatever else might be within reach. She had hauled enough men out of her inn over the years that most knew not to try her patience.

Fiona was quite happy to learn that Findley had finally found his good sense and married. She showed her approval with a hard slap to Findley's back and a warm embrace for Maggy. Beyton however, cast a pitiful look at Findley as if to say, "Enjoy the honeymoon. It be all downhill from here."

Beyton and Fiona were quite shocked to learn the young lass before them was the mother of the four young boys. Findley took only a moment to explain they weren't all hers. Uncertain if Malcolm Buchannan had any men in Renfrew, he kept as many details as he could to himself.

They procured three rooms. Two for his men and the boys, and the third he would share with Maggy.

Fiona refused to tote multiple tubs and water up the two flights of stairs, so it was decided that Findley, his men, and the boys would bathe in a room just off the kitchen. First, however, she enlisted their help in toting a tub upstairs for Maggy.

Fiona led the group through the crowded barroom, ordering men to part and hold their tongues for a lady was present. The sea of men parted and remained sullenly quiet while the tired and worn group pushed through.

Maggy kept her shawl drawn tightly around her face while holding tightly to Liam's hand. She avoided all eye contact with the patrons. It had been years since she had stepped foot in any village or town. She had no desire for her true identity to be revealed by the off-chance meeting of someone from her past.

Fiona led them to their respective rooms. The men and lads would have two rooms in the middle while Maggy and Findley's room was at the end of the dark hallway.

To say the room was small would be an understatement. A small bed, barely big enough to sleep one person, sat against one wall with a fireplace directly opposite. A small fur covered the only window in the room.

There was barely enough room for the bed, let alone a tub, but somehow they managed to squeeze one in. Maggy was more than happy to make do with their meager accommodations in exchange for a hot bath and a warm, soft place to sleep.

When she made an attempt to leave to assist with readying her sons' baths, Fiona clucked her tongue. "Och! Lass, I have had nine bairns, seven of which were lads. I'll make sure they wash themselves properly."

Fiona gave her a reassuring smile. "Besides, 'tis yer weddin' night! Even though ye be a mum, ye are first a bride this night. Ye enjoy yer bath and ready yerself fer yer husband!" She giggled and gave Maggy a wink before leaving the room.

Maggy was glad that Findley and the rest of his little band of warriors were below stairs busy filling buckets and not within earshot. She felt the heat rise in her cheeks when her mind began to wander to points she knew well it shouldn't. Thoughts of Findley and what he might look like soaking in a tub with water cascading down a bare chest that she was certain was firm and well-muscled made her toes tingle.

'Twas true that Findley was a very braw and well-built man. If her current predicament were different, she might well welcome the thoughts. She might even have entertained the idea of an illicit encounter with him.

She shook the mental images from her mind as she sat patiently on the bed waiting for the men and boys to fetch water. *I am a mother, for goodness sake! Findley could nae possibly be interested in a widowed mum with five lads. 'Twould be too large a responsibility for any man to undertake. And to have such thoughts outside of marriage? Sinful, just sinful.* She took a few moments to pray for forgiveness. Then she prayed for strength to fight against her wicked mind.

She began to wonder again why Findley was offering to help her get Ian back. As much as she wanted to believe he and his men were helping out of the goodness of their hearts, she could not let go of the possibility that he might have ulterior motives.

He certainly had not let on that he knew the truth. Could he be that good at deception?

Soon the men returned with buckets of hot water. Maggy scooted further back onto the soft mattress and watched.

The small room could only hold two of the men comfortably – to fit more would have been next to impossible. So, the men lined up, with Findley at the lead as they passed the buckets along.

From her place on the bed, she could not see into the hallway. She listened intently but could not hear her sons. Her boys were never quiet unless they were eating, sleeping, or hiding. She grew uncomfortable at not being able to hear or see them.

"Where are me boys, Findley?"

"They be below stairs, lass. Fiona's makin' them bathe," he said as he emptied another bucket into the tub.

"Alone?" she asked unable to mask her worry.

"Nay, Fiona's with them. Beyton as well."

"But what if there be Buchannans about?" She felt anger creeping in. How could they leave her boys alone? She knew the Buchannans would be neither swayed nor frightened by Fiona or Beyton. If they wanted the boys, they could easily take them.

Findley emptied another bucket into the tub. "Lass, they be fine." He was not worried, for Beyton and Fiona's two older sons worked the inn with them. Findley had one of them stationed at the entrance to the inn, the other at the rear.

"But Findley, ye cannae leave me boys alone! What if the Buchannans followed us, and now they be simply waitin' for a chance to take them?" The panic was rising in her voice.

Findley sighed heavily as he poured in the last of the water. Wee William and Patrick had already left to go guard the lads after handing their buckets up to Richard.

Findley turned in time to see Maggy scurrying off the bed.

"Lass!" he said loudly. "Yer boys be fine!" He shook his head as he watched Richard smile and head for the stairs.

"But Findley!" she began protesting as her feet hit the floor, and she headed toward the door.

"Maggy," he said, lowering his voice. He reached out and stopped her with a hand to her shoulder. "Wee William and Patrick are below stairs by now and guarding your boys with their lives. Ye needn't worry so!"

Maggy spun around, her brow creased and her eyes filled with anger. "I be their mum, Findley! Ye dunnae understand it, ye fool! I ken the Buchannan and what he can do. Me boys are all I have left in this world!"

She shoved his hand off her shoulder. She had to see for herself that her boys were well.

Findley drew his shoulders back. Through clenched teeth he said, "I do understand it, Maggy, and I be no fool." He took a deep breath in. "And mayhap if ye were to tell me the truth of why the man wants ye badly enough to kill fer ye, I could do better to protect all of ye!"

He was doing his best to be patient with her. The last few days had been a living hell for her. He reminded himself of how he had felt all those years ago when his family had been murdered. Richard had been all he had left in the world. For years after, Findley had protected him fervently. To this very day, he'd lay down his own life in order to save his brother's.

"Then how can ye leave them unattended?" she asked rather coolly and ignoring his last statement altogether.

"I did nae leave them unattended! I left them in good care. 'Tis nae as if I told them to go run up and down the street shouting 'We are here! Go tell the Buchannans!'"

Mayhap it was the exhaustion, the bone-weariness and worry that made her so angry. Mayhap it was the hunger or the days of dust and grime that seemed to weigh her down and make her feel so sad.

Or mayhap it was the rightfully felt fear that she had whenever the boys were not within eyesight that caused her to want to scream and cry at the same time.

Her eyes welled with tears as she folded her arms across her stomach. This wasn't how she normally behaved. In all the years she had been married to her cheating, lying, poor excuse of a husband, she had never carried on like a shrew or a fishwife. She had never nagged or cried or asked him for anything. Maggy had always been the dutiful, quiet wife who allowed her husband his dalliances as well as his temper tantrums.

But since his death, she had gained an independence that she had grown to enjoy. She had provided for her clan and her children and kept them safe and healthy. But the last months had been more difficult and trying. And the past days had been a living hell. Her emotions were getting the better of her, and that angered her more than anything else. She was losing control of her good senses.

Findley's shoulders sagged when he saw the tears brimming in her eyes again. He imagined men could get on better in this world if their women didn't cry with such frequency.

"Maggy," he began. "I promise, we will protect yer sons." As much as he wanted to reach out and pull her to his chest, he felt certain she'd scratch his eyes out if he did.

"Ye be tired and hungry," he said. "Would ye like me to go check on yer boys whilst ye take yer bath?"

"Aye," she said with a quick nod of her head. She brushed the tears away with her fingertips.

Findley looked down at her with a thoughtful smile. "Fine then. I will go see them and report back shortly. Lock the door after me, and dunnae let anyone in but me."

"How will I ken it's ye?" she asked, taking in a deep breath.

"I'll knock twice, then thrice," he offered.

Maggy nodded and shut the door behind him. She turned back,

and her eyes fell on the tub and then the bed. She wasn't sure which she wanted more at the moment: to bathe or to sleep.

Then it hit her like a wall of cold water. Where will Findley sleep this night? Did he intend on sharing the bed with her?

Mayhap after the tub was removed, he could sprawl out on the floor. A sudden wave of guilt washed over her. How could she make him sleep on the floor while she took the bed? He'd already done much more than anyone else would have under the same circumstances. And he was intent on getting Ian back for her.

Nay, she could not in good conscience ask him to sleep on the floor. She would take the floor, and he could have the bed. It was the least she could do by way of a thank you. Mayhap someday she would be able to repay him for all that he had done and was planning to do.

She sighed. "If he does get Ian back, I could live a thousand lifetimes and not be able to repay him."

CHAPTER EIGHT

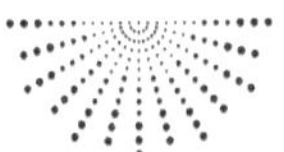

They had argued for nearly a quarter of an hour over who would take the bed. Findley won only because he was bigger and stronger.

After he had returned to tell Maggy that her boys were fine and well, he left again for a much-needed bath of his own. When he had returned an hour later, he had found Maggy wrapped in nothing but a blanket. It took a monumental effort on his part not to lift her into his arms and kiss every square inch of her body.

She had been sitting by the fire, drying her hair, the blanket drawn tightly around her body. Findley could see her slender ankles and a bit of her bare shoulders, and his breath caught in his throat. God's teeth, she was beautiful.

Maggy had washed her clothes out in the tub after taking her bath. The worn dress and shift hung on hooks over the hearth to dry. He found himself envious of the lucky blanket that was keeping her warm and wished it were his arms that were wrapped around her.

Fiona had sent up a tray of bread, cheese, and venison along with two tankards of ale. Maggy sat on the stool while she ate, and Findley sat on the floor, his long legs stretched out in front of him as he leaned against the wall.

'Twas difficult for Maggy to not stare at his well-muscled legs, for his leather trews fit over them rather magnificently. As they ate in silence, Maggy realized she was staring at his chest. And when he smiled at her, as if he knew what she was thinking, she felt her face burn with embarrassment.

Frequently she would poke out a hand from under her blanket and test the dryness of her shift. Findley had to bite his tongue to keep from laughing at her apparent nervousness. He thought of asking her why she was so nervous, but he was afraid it would lead to another argument. He was enjoying the silence. And the fact that she was completely naked under the blanket helped improve his mood. Why spoil such a lovely evening?

The silence, however, did not last as long as he would have liked. She had insisted on taking the floor because she had no other way of thanking him. He could have thought of countless other ways to express her gratitude, but his honor kept him from putting a voice to such notions.

No self-respecting man would allow a woman to sleep on the hard floor whilst he took the bed. He had grown weary of arguing his point. He reached her in two strides, scooped her up in his arms, and plunked her down on the bed.

"I'll hear no more of it, lass," he had told her with a devious grin.

He then covered her with a fur, his knuckles inadvertently brushing against the soft skin of her shoulders. He wasn't sure, but he thought he heard her gasp when he touched her. She looked confused, as well as a bit terrified, and appeared to be bracing herself for something.

"Good sleep to ye, lass," he said before turning away. He gave her no time to argue as he put out the flame of the tallow with his fingers. The low-burning embers in the fireplace cast a soft, warm glow into the room.

In the near dark, he unfastened his plaid and spread it out on the floor in front of the hearth. He told himself he could rest comfortably knowing that Wee William was keeping the first watch in the hallway and that Maggy was safe now.

But sleep did not come. To know she was just a step away and naked was maddening.

Fiona had given Maggy lilac-scented soap with which to bathe. The scent of it hung in the air, blending with the smoke from the fire, and it left him feeling intoxicated. He did his best to tamp down the lustful thoughts coursing through his mind. He wasn't sure he could survive too many more nights with her but a step away, especially if she slept each night like she was now.

One large question still hung in the air. Why had the Buchannan attacked her home? What could Malcolm Buchannan gain from marrying Maggy? Anyone with a bit of common sense could see that she and her clan were impoverished. They were peasants barely scraping by. There could be no monetary gain from such a union.

Mayhap it all boiled down to the fact that Malcolm Buchannan was simply mad. His inner voice told him there had to be more to it than the machinations of a mad man. Maggy was keeping something from him, he was sure of it. But what?

She did not trust him, and he wondered if she ever would.

Findley slipped his fingers into his tunic and pulled out the bloodied plaid. He had kept it as a reminder of what the Buchannan had done to Maggy and her family. Now that he had her in the care of himself and his men, he no longer needed it as a reminder of what had happened. He was half tempted to toss the fabric into the embers and let it burn. He couldn't do that just yet and would not have been able to explain the why of it to anyone. Instead, he slipped it back into his tunic and rolled over and tried to sleep.

He lay in the dark listening to the sounds of her steady breathing over the occasional crackle of embers. He wondered how many heart-beats he would survive if he climbed into the bed with her. Not many, he thought. Sweet talk and poetic words would not win him her heart, nor would they gain her trust. Nay, Maggy was the kind of woman to whom a man needed to prove his worth with actions, not pretty words.

Mayhap once he retrieved Ian, Maggy would find it in her heart to trust him. He would do his best to prove to her that she could.

SLEEP DID NOT COME any easier for Maggy. She worried over Ian. Had his fever worsened? How were the Buchannan men treating him? Was he warm? Were they feeding him?

Soft tears escaped and left trails down the sides of her face as she feigned sleep. She cursed Malcolm Buchannan and his men. If they let any harm come to her son, she would chase the animals to the ends of the earth if she had to. She'd have no problem killing any of them.

She cursed her husband and his family for putting her in this position to begin with. Had Gawter's family been honorable or the least bit kind, she would have had no problem remaining with them. But they were neither of those things, and his uncle was the worst of the entire lot. As it was, she had been forced to take Liam away from his home and birthright in order to protect him.

Maggy knew that had Gawter survived the pox, her life would be completely different. He would not have let her raise the four boys she now considered her sons. She would not have regained the independence of her youth that she had given up the day she married the cold man. But more likely than not, he would have eventually succeeded at taking her life. He had, after all, tried more than once.

She had felt a great deal of relief when Gawter died. She had not pined away for him, had not thrown herself on his dead body begging God to take her life so that she could be with her husband. She had not grieved at losing him.

While she did feel sorrow over the fact that her son was without a father, she knew that they were both much better off without him. Without Gawter there to influence Liam, Maggy could see to it that he grew to be a fine, honest and honorable man. Liam would be everything his father wasn't.

Maggy knew, however, that all of her boys needed a father. They needed a strong, honest role model. But what man in his right mind would be willing to take on a widowed mother of five? There would be plenty of men to line up and make the offer if Maggy and Liam's true identities were discovered.

She also knew that if she were to accept any offers of marriage, there would be no guarantee that her new husband would allow her to keep all of her boys. In the end she would be forced to say goodbye to all but Liam. Her fervent prayer was that she would have some say in where they went and who would care for them.

Mayhap that was the best thing. Was she being selfish for keeping them all with her? How much had she asked them to sacrifice so that she could remain independent and free? Mayhap she should allow them to go, to be fostered and educated. But the thought of being away from her boys for any length of time tore at her heart. They were her sons. They needed her as much as she needed them.

It was a very long time before she finally succumbed to exhaustion. Her last thoughts before falling asleep were of her boys and the happy moments they had shared over the past few years.

FINDLEY WOKE BEFORE DAWN. He had slept, but not as soundly or as comfortably as he would have liked. He was careful not to wake Maggy, for he had heard her tossing and turning most of the night. He decided that what she needed most was uninterrupted sleep.

He stared at her while he quietly donned his plaid. She was curled into a little ball in the middle of the bed and had the blankets pulled tightly around her chin. Her auburn hair was loose and tumbled out over the pillows. The smell of lilacs still hung in the air. He took in a deep breath and held it as a smile came to his face. What he wouldn't give to wake up beside her each morning.

He quietly stepped from the room and closed the door carefully. Patrick had traded places with Wee William in the middle of the night and now sat in a chair between the doors of the lads' rooms.

"How did the lads sleep?" Findley whispered.

Patrick stretched and stood. "Liam woke a few times from bad dreams, but all in all I would say it went well."

Findley gave him an approving nod. He imagined it would be quite some time before any of them would sleep soundly.

"We have much to do this day," Findley told him.

"Aye. Richard is below stairs breaking his fast. Should we let the lads sleep a bit longer?"

"Aye," Findley agreed. "And Maggy as well. Richard and I will see to trading the supplies. We will wake the lads when we return." He turned to leave when Patrick stopped him.

"Findley," he began. "I have not much coin, but I would like to buy the lads a pair of boots. They cannae get too far with bare feet or boots with holes in 'em."

Findley agreed. They made plans to take the boys for new boots. Findley knew that clothes for the boys had been packed in the wagons. He'd remove those as well as anything else they might need for the days ahead before trading the rest for coin. He made a mental list of all the things that would need to be done as he headed down the back staircase and into the kitchen.

Richard was sitting at a small table eating eggs, ham, and fresh bread. Fiona's daughter-in-law, a very comely lass around the age of ten and eight, Findley guessed, offered him the same breakfast.

"How was yer weddin' night?" Richard asked with a wry grin.

Findley nearly choked on his eggs. He shot his brother a look of warning. The lass brought him a mug of ale and smiled down at him before returning to the basins.

"Was it everythin' ye hoped it would be?" Richard needled.

"My weddin' night be none of yer business, brother," Findley answered before taking a pull of the ale.

"Aye. A gentleman does nae kiss an' tell." Richard grinned.

Findley made a silent promise to pummel his brother senseless once they were away from the inn.

Before they were finished eating, Beyton entered the kitchen from the back door. Close behind him were one of his older sons and a son-in-law. Findley saw the advantage of having many sons; there were plenty of hands and strong backs to help when needed.

"I have yer messengers fer ye, Findley," Beyton said with a proud smile. "They can be in Dunshire within four days."

Findley studied the two young men. Beyton's son took after his mother, for he was tall and fair. The son-in-law was a bit shorter, but just as well built, and both looked as though they could hold their own if needed.

The young lass brought Findley a parchment and quill, and within a quarter hour he had his request written and the messengers on their way. He prayed the weather would hold and that Angus would send the help he so desperately needed.

It wasn't long before Patrick and Wee William came down the stairs with four hungry young boys in tow. So much for letting the boys sleep in. The lads devoured their breakfast with a fervor that resembled scavengers on the carcass of a dead mule deer. Though Findley realized having many sons had its advantages, he wondered as he watched them eat how on earth anyone could afford to feed them on a regular basis.

Liam was the first to finish eating. He excitedly jumped up and came to Findley. He pulled on Findley's sleeve and motioned with his finger for him to bend so that he could whisper in his ear.

"Are we goin' after Ian now?" he asked.

The lad looked positively forlorn when Findley shook his head nay. "But dunnae worrit, lad. We will be spendin' our day preparin' for our battle against the Buchannans."

That seemed to lift the lad's spirits. He was ready to do whatever he must in order to get his brother back.

"What do we do first?" he asked anxiously.

Findley smiled. "First, we must get ye into proper battle gear," he said as he glanced down at the lad's bare feet.

"We will need to get ye boots and some new clothes."

Liam nodded his head and crossed his arms over his chest. "Aye," he said very seriously. "I dunnae suppose it would do to go into battle with bare feet." He thought on it for a moment before adding, "Do I get a hauberk and broadsword as well?"

Findley had to bite his tongue to keep from laughing. He had to admire the young boy's tenacity and eagerness.

"I dunnae think there is time to have a hauberk made to fit ye, lad, but we will see about a *sgian dubh*."

A *sgian dubh* might not be as grand as a sword in the eyes of a small boy. But knowing he was trusted enough to have a weapon at all was enough to bring a smile of pride to his face.

"But ye'll have to keep it secret from yer mum," Findley told him. While he didn't like the idea of keeping secrets from the lad's mother, he knew Maggy would have a fit if she found out Findley was actually arming her sons.

Under different circumstances he would not have considered anything other than a wooden sword for such a small boy. But desperate times often call for desperate measures. Without knowing what lie in store for them over the next days, he would feel better knowing each of the lads had some way of defending himself if the need arose.

When the rest of his men and the lads were finished breaking their fast, Findley led them out of doors and to the stables. Once it was determined the stables were free of any unwanted eyes or ears, they huddled together and made plans for the morning.

In order to keep from drawing any unnecessary attention, each man would be partnered with a lad. For the remainder of their journey, each would be considered father and son. Their journey would take them to towns and cities, and Findley knew that the larger the group the more attention it would draw.

At first, each of the lads wanted Wee William to act as their da and guardian. They were impressed not only by the man's size but his personality as well. Wee William had apparently entertained the lads to tears the night before with stories filled with battles well fought intermingled with winning the hearts of more than a few fair lasses. While the younger lads weren't quite as anxious to win the heart of any lass, they were all quite eager to learn how to be as fierce a warrior as Wee William.

Wee William would stand out in any crowd. Not wanting to disappoint the lads any further, they decided that Wee William would act as uncle to each.

Patrick and Andrew were paired together, for they looked the most alike. Richard would be father to Collin and Findley would be father to both Robert and Liam.

"Can I call ye Da then, Findley?" Liam asked.

A breath caught in Findley's throat. "Aye," he answered with a nod.

If the truth were told, Findley would have liked to be a father to all the lads. His thoughts turned to the beautiful woman who was sleeping peacefully in a small, warm bed on the third floor of the inn. He wished that they were truly married and that he were lying in the bed with her instead of making plans for laying siege to a castle.

"Da," Robert tested the word a time or two. At first he felt guilty for saying it. His parents had been good, decent people. The pox had taken them, along with his two younger brothers and baby sister, and he missed all of them more than he would ever care to admit.

It had taken Robert more than a year after losing them before he could begin to think of calling Maggy Mum. He dealt with the guilt by understanding that his mum and Maggy had been friends. Under the circumstances, he doubted his mother would have been angry over it.

But to call another man Da? That would take some getting used to. He decided that because he was only pretending in order to keep their identities safe and to get their Ian back, he could muddle through it for now. But once their mission was complete, he'd go back to calling the man Findley.

Once the temporary fatherhood was established and missions assigned, fathers and sons stepped out of the stables. Wee William would stay behind to guard over Maggy.

"We will meet back here within an hour's time," Findley told Wee William.

"If there be any trouble, I'll send one of Beyton's sons to fetch ye," Wee William said.

"Let's pray there isn't any," Richard said.

With that, the new fathers left with their new sons. It could be said that none was more proud at the moment than Findley. Even if it be for a short time. *Mayhap I can prove to Maggy that I would make a good father to her lads. She might begin to see me in a different light then.*

CHAPTER NINE

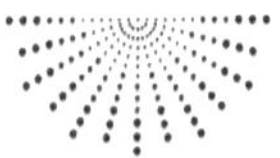

Maggy woke to the sound of stifled chuckles and whispers. She knew those sounds well, and she tried to suppress a smile. What were her boys up to now?

She feigned sleep, pulled the fur over her head and burrowed deeper into the soft bed. She knew her boys were up to something. The sweet giggles and wheests led her to believe her lads were trying to surprise her with something.

"Mum," Liam whispered as he climbed onto the bed and over her.

She felt the weight of someone else sitting at the foot of the bed. Very slowly she opened her eyes and smiled. She found the room filled not only with her sons, but with Findley and his men as well.

This must be what pickles in a barrel feel like, all crammed in together, she thought to herself. The room seemed infinitely smaller with all the men and boys crowded in.

"What is this?" she asked as she tried to sit. Suddenly she was grateful that the weight of the boys on her fur kept her from doing just that, for she remembered that she was naked underneath it.

They were all smiling at her, even the men. Her brow creased quizzically. It felt very strange to have so many men staring and smiling. A sudden bout of dread washed over her. They be probably tryin' to marry me off to one of them again.

"We have presents fer ye!" Liam said proudly. Oh, how she loved that boy's smile!

"Presents?" she asked. "What kind of presents?"

She imagined they must be flowers and pretty stones and the like, for her boys didn't have a coin to their names.

Robert came forward first and held out his hand. Not expecting anything other than some small token he had found out of doors, she smiled and held her hand out.

She was delighted to tears when he placed a tortoise shell comb into the palm of her hand. It was exquisite! It seemed an eternity had passed since she had owned anything so fine.

"Where on earth did ye find it?" she asked breathlessly. Instantly she began to worry that her sons, who had proven in the past they weren't beyond reiving something in order to impress her, might have obtained the comb through less than honest means.

"We bought it." Robert's beaming smile perplexed her.

"How? Ye've no coin!" she eyed them all suspiciously.

"Dunnae worrit, mum," Robert said. "We did nae steal it! We earned the money mucking stalls fer Beyton and Fiona."

Maggy's shoulders fell and she felt guilty for assuming the worst. "Och!" she whispered. "Ye shoulda spent yer hard-earned coin on yerselves, lads!"

There were so many things that her sons needed that she could not give them. Her guilt increased tenfold with the thought, for her sons needed boots, clothes, and food. She had no clue how she'd be able to provide those things for them.

They had mucked stalls to earn coin and then spent it on her instead of something they needed. Tears formed in her eyes as she stared down at the beautiful comb. It was a small thing, just a comb, but the sentiment behind it was immeasurable.

"Lass, why do ye cry?" Findley asked, his voice laced with confusion.

Maggy wiped a tear from her cheek. "Because me boys need boots and clothes more than I need a comb!"

She tried to hand the comb back to Robert. "Son, ye need to return it and get yer coin back. We will be needin' that to get ye some boots!"

She yanked on the fur and was able to gain enough to cover herself and sit.

Robert shook his head. "Nay! We have new boots!" he smiled down at her as he lifted a foot up and sat it on the edge of the bed.

"See?" he said. "We all have new boots, thanks to Findley." Robert had a very proud smile on his face.

"And we have new tunics and trews!" Collin offered as he held his arms out as wide as he could in the cramped quarters. The other lads followed suit.

Maggy studied each of her boys. She had not noticed their new clothing before. "Findley!" she said as she cast him a confused look. "Ye should nae have done that!"

A broad smile came to Findley's face. "Dunnae worry yerself over it, lass! We had most of the clothes in the wagons. They be used, but clean and in good repair."

"But the boots be new!" Andrew said. "I have never had a pair of new boots before. They feel odd, but good."

"That's because they fit ye," Robert told him.

Andrew nodded his head in agreement as he wiggled his toes inside the boots.

"We have more gifts fer ye, mum," Liam said excitedly. "Collin, give her yers and Andrew's!"

Collin had been sitting at the end of the bed. He reached behind his back and pulled out a pair of new boots for Maggy.

Her hand flew to her mouth as she gasped. "Boots fer me too?"

Collin and Andrew nodded in unison.

Maggy doubted the boys earned enough coin mucking stalls to purchase both a comb and a new pair of boots for her. She started to say something when Findley stepped forward and bent down to whisper in her ear.

"Maggy," he said as his warm breath brushed over her ear. "Allow yer sons this moment."

He pulled away and gave her a pleading look. Maggy looked into his brown eyes and understood. She then turned to look at the proud faces of her sons. This moment meant as much to them as it did to her, mayhap more. She nodded her head and decided to keep her protests to herself.

"I could nae be more proud of ye boys. I thank ye all. No mum was ever blessed with finer sons!"

"There be more, lass," Richard said as he stepped forward and handed her a bundle. "This be from me and Patrick."

Maggy didn't know if her heart could withstand many more acts of kindness and generosity. "Och! Lads, ye should nae be doin' this!" she protested as she took the bundle and began to unfold it.

It was a new dress made of fine green wool! She could not suppress the smile. "Och!" she exclaimed, her heart overflowing with joy and gratitude.

Wee William stepped forward next and presented her with a new gray cloak made of warm wool. "This'll keep ye warm fer a long time, lass," he said as he stepped away.

It wasn't the gifts that overwhelmed her heart with joy. It was the thought and kindness that had gone into each one.

Liam could no longer contain his excitement. He smiled as he crawled onto her lap and thrust two ribbons into her hand. One was green, the other made from a fine fabric the color of ice.

"These are from me and Ian. I ken he woulda wanted to get ye one too, so I picked one out fer him."

Large tears formed in her eyes and trailed down her cheeks. Ian. Oh, how she wished he were here! His smile would have been as bright as Liam's, and he would have held the same bright twinkle in his green eyes. He would have enjoyed presenting a gift to her.

Liam wrapped his arms around her neck, and she buried her face into his hair.

"Wheest, Mum," he whispered. "We will get him back, I promise." He patted her back gently. "I did nae mean to make ye cry."

Maggy shook her head. "Do nae worry it, Liam. I ken we will get him back soon."

She righted herself and forced a smile to her face. "Thank ye fer thinkin' of yer brother. That was a fine thing to do!"

He scurried off her lap and sat next to her.

"We saved the best fer last," Collin said as he looked to Findley. "Close yer eyes!" Collin told her.

Maggy shook her head, let out a happy sigh and closed her eyes.

Findley smiled as he stepped forward and placed the item on her lap. "Ye can open them now," he instructed her.

A gasp caught in her throat when she opened her eyes. It was a magnificent gown, made of fine silk damask. It was ice blue with silver embroidery around the sleeves and bodice. There wasn't an ounce of practicality to it, but that mattered not. It was beautiful! She could not imagine ever having a place or time in which to wear it.

Findley bent to whisper in her ear again. "When yer sons saw that in the dressmaker's window, they refused to buy new boots. They insisted on gettin' it fer ye." He stood back a bit so that she could see his smile. "We had to buy it, elst they would have gone all winter with bare feet!"

Maggy shook her head in disbelief as she held the dress to her bosom. "Now, where on earth do ye suppose I wear this? Whilst I be makin' yer supper?" she asked with a raised eyebrow and a smile.

Everyone laughed along with her.

"If it makes ye happy, ye may!" Robert said.

As she started to fold the dress, she noticed a fine headpiece lying next to her. The white linen cap was lined with silver studs and had a long, soft white veil. It would go beautifully with the blue gown.

Findley clapped his hands together to gain everyone's attention.

"Lads," he began, "ye've things to attend to now."

The men and boys nodded their heads in agreement. Each of the boys gave Maggy a hug as they left the room with the men, and soon Maggy was alone with Findley.

She sat still, taken aback by the mountain of gifts that were piled around her. There had been a time in her life when she had worn the finest of silks, velvets, and damasks. Emeralds, diamonds, and rubies had once adorned her neck, fingers, and ears. But none of those things meant as much to her as the gifts that had been given to her this day.

Findley shut the door and lifted up a bag he had set next to the small table by the bed.

"Maggy," he said. "I have something else fer ye." He reached inside his leather bag and pulled out a fine silk chemise. "I did nae want to give ye this in front of the lads," he said as he held it out for her.

She was not sure what to make of his gift, and she was not ready yet to accept it.

"I have a few foster sisters," he smiled. "I ken ye lasses like fine things like this. I ken it be a bit intimate a topic in nature."

Maggy eyed him cautiously for a moment before taking the chemise. It was delicate, fine, and as soft as the skin of a new babe. It had been quite some time since she had worn anything like it. For a moment, she wondered how on earth Findley could have afforded all the gifts that were given to her.

"Findley, I..." She tried searching for the right words.

His face lit with a broad smile. "Think nothin' of it, lass. I saw the shape yer other clothes were in. I imagine 'tis been a time since ye've been able to have anythin' new. Every lass needs a pretty thing or two."

She took a deep breath. Never in all the years she had been married to Gawter had he presented her with any gift. The jewels she had worn had belonged to his mother, and it had been his uncle who had given them to her. It had also been his uncle who made certain she had been provided with clothing appropriate for her new station.

"Thank ye, Findley," she said with a suddenly dry mouth. "'Twas very nice of ye. But really, I think it all be too much. Mayhap we should take back some of these things and put the coin to better use."

Findley shook his head and crossed his arms over his chest. "Lass, dunnae worry. We earned enough coin sellin' the supplies in our wagons. And we still have enough left. I'll nae be havin' ye argue it further."

Maggy started to protest when he stopped her with a wave of his hand. "Lass, yer boys would be sorely disappointed if ye took any of it back. And ye cannae say ye dunnae need the things we gave ye."

While it was true that she did need the boots, green dress, and cloak, the same couldn't be said for the beautiful blue gown and headpiece. "Ye think this," she said holding up a sleeve of the blue damask, "is a need?"

His lips curved into a wry smile. "Aye, 'tis."

"And how, pray tell, is this a need?"

"Yer boys need to see ye wearin' it," he told her. To himself he added, *I need to see ye wearin' it as well.*

There was a strange expression to his face, one that she could not decipher. It caused her skin to grow warm and her palms to sweat. For a fleeting moment, her stomach began to tingle, just as it had when she had held on to him on the wagon the night before. Was it fear or something else? She hadn't anything in her life experience to compare it to.

As she tried to shake the feeling away, there came a knock at the door. Findley stared into her eyes for a moment before turning to see who was at the door.

His hand instantly went to the broadsword that hung at his side. His men knew to knock twice, then thrice. Whoever stood on the other side had only knocked three times.

"Aye?" Findley called out.

"I have a meal fer yer bride," came the muffled voice of Fiona from the other side.

Findley kept his hand on the hilt of the broadsword before carefully opening the door. He gave a quick glance of the space beyond Fiona before allowing her to enter.

"Good day to ye, lass!" Fiona said to Maggy as she walked into the room. "Ye nearly slept yer day away! Ye must have had one grand weddin' night to keep ye in bed this late!"

Fiona smiled as she set the tray on the table beside the bed. She eyed the clothing that was piled around Maggy. "Och! I see yer husband has been shoppin' fer ye." She placed one hand on her hip as her smile grew. "Aye, it must have been one grand weddin' night indeed to be plied with such gifts!"

Maggy felt her face flush at Fiona's insinuation. As hard as she tried, she could not find an appropriate response.

Fiona let loose with a loud laugh. "Och! Such an innocent thing ye are! A mum of four boys and ye still blush like a girl!"

Fiona shook her head and clucked her tongue. "Ye must be hungry. I have brought ye stew, bread, and some dried figs. Ale as well. Let me ken if ye need anythin' else." She gave Maggy a wink and turned to leave the room.

On her way out, she gave Findley a wink and a grin. "I think it's a fine lass ye chose fer yer wife, Findley," she told him before she left the room.

Findley turned his lips inward to keep from laughing at Maggy's horrified expression.

"Lass! Ye look as though ye've swallowed a bug!"

Maggy's expression quickly turned to one of indifference. "Nay! I was merely caught off guard by Fiona's bluntness."

Findley laughed at her as he began to fold her garments. "Fiona is right. Ye blush like a young girl."

Maggy's brow creased. "Do ye mean to say that I am old?"

"Nay, lass. I dunnae think ye to be old!" he shook his head as he grabbed the tray from the table. "'Twas meant to compliment ye, lass. Ye're blushin' makes ye even more beautiful."

The words were out of his mouth before he could do anything to stop them. He paused, holding the tray, unable to move. His face burned with embarrassment. He stared down at her waiting for her to say something.

Maggy blinked, startled by his comment. She could tell by the expression on his face that he had not meant to say the words out loud.

Her father was the last man she could remember calling her beautiful, and that had been years ago, when she was just a little girl. An exciting chill ran up and down her spine as she looked into Findley's brown eyes. She would never admit to anyone that she found herself enjoying that exciting sensation.

Findley cleared his throat before setting the tray upon her lap. Mayhap he should pretend he had not said anything. "I'll leave ye to eat," he choked out, before giving a quick nod of his head as he left the room in a hurried fashion.

Maggy's eyes followed him out the door. *He thinks me beautiful?* She shook the thought from her mind. *Nay. 'Tis more likely than not something he says to all women.*

FINDLEY WAS NOT sure if he was relieved to have said the words or not. He had done nothing but think of Maggy for months. He had traveled for days to offer her a home. And at some point in the future, he knew he would have to share his feelings with her.

He had hoped, however, that the first time he would have told her he thought her beautiful would have been under more romantic circumstances. Nay, things were not going as he had planned. Everything was upside down and backwards.

Cursing under his breath, he stomped down the stairs and headed out of doors. He blamed everyone from the English to the Buchannan for his current lot.

He had tried to live a good, clean, honorable life. He helped those in need, prayed faithfully every day, and tried to live as God would have him do. But fate seemed to be interfering with his plans at every conceivable turn.

In the spring he had been on a simple mission to retrieve the thirty cattle stolen from his clan. That was when fate stepped in the first time.

Days into their journey they had stumbled upon a lass in serious need of help and protection. While his friends Duncan, Manghus, and Rowan had seen the lass to the safe arms of their clan, Findley, Richard, Gowan, and Tall Thomas had been sent to scout for any signs of the English soldiers whom they expected were searching for her.

With no sign of English soldiers anywhere to be found, they had decided to return to Dunshire. Either by accident, fate, or divine intervention, they had come across the reivers they had originally been searching for.

He and his men were surprised to find that the reivers weren't a band of thieving men but instead five young boys who wanted only to prove to their mum and clan that they were fine warriors who could take care of them. They had stolen the cattle to prove their worth and to feed their very hungry people.

While some men might have skelped the boys and left them for dead for stealing, Findley and his men returned them to their mum. That was how he met Maggy.

Fate stepped in weeks later when he and Richard had gone to Dunblane to obtain supplies to take to Maggy and her clan. They had been in a tavern enjoying an ale when they learned the English were indeed looking for the fair Aishlinn, the lass they had rescued earlier.

Had Aishlinn not decided to take matters into her own hands and turn herself over to the English, Findley would not now be wandering aimlessly around Renfrew. But she had done just that. And when he volunteered to help get her back, fate stepped in yet again.

During the battle to free Aishlinn, who had been married to Duncan for but a day, Findley had taken a blade to his side. He nearly died from it. The only things that kept him from succumbing to death were his thoughts of Maggy.

When he was finally healed enough to sit atop a horse without falling from it, he set off with a plan and a heart bursting with hope. That hope was shattered the moment he saw the death and destruction meted out at the hands of the Buchannan clan.

Was it fate intervening or God telling him he could not have Maggy because he had let down so many people all those years before?

Or was God telling him he could not have her unless he fought for her? Was she too grand a prize for the Lord to just hand her to him without working for it?

His heart could not bear the former, so he decided to lean toward the latter.

Fate be damned.

While he would not want to attempt to know what God might be thinking, he knew he must do his Father's bidding.

She was a treasure, one he would fight for and cherish all of his days, if she'd allow it. One he would protect from all harm. He could not imagine God wanting Maggy to be married to the likes of Malcolm Buchannan. Nay, if she were a treasure, then she deserved better than that.

Findley paced around the rear of the stables. *If the good Lord wants me to prove me worth, so be it. I'll fight fer the lass. I'll keep her safe to me last breath.*

CHAPTER TEN

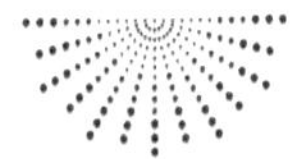

Being a prisoner had only one merit; it made a man's soul burn with an intense hatred that could be used as a catalyst for moving forward and keeping him alive. This prisoner had refused to succumb to the sweet release that death might bring. He chose instead to live.

Vengeance would someday be his, and the man who had deserted him, the man he had once called his friend, would feel the wrath of that hatred.

Deceived and betrayed, he had been imprisoned by the English. Beaten and tortured, he, along with countless others—many of whom had died along the way—had been forced to build fortresses, walls and barricades for the English. It sickened him to know that he had been forced to help defend the English against his own people, his fellow Scots.

And for what? For an unscrupulous woman who thought only of herself and her own gain. Bewitchingly beautiful, with a silver tongue that could get any man to believe anything that she wanted. And she wanted much, very much. Much more than he could ever have hoped to give her. But he hadn't seen the truth of it until it was far too late.

He was not sure which was worse – his friend's betrayal or his wife's.

The prisoner knew his wife would not have waited too long in mourning before she had her legs wrapped around his former best friend, professing her eternal love and devotion to the fool. She was good at lies and good at bedding men and good at little else. The prisoner had made very few mistakes in his life. Trusting the woman he married had been the first. Trusting his best friend had been his second.

There was another force that kept his heart beating and that was his son. As much as he hated his wife and friend, he loved his son a hundred times more. His anger bubbled to the point of insanity knowing that the lad would not even recognize him now.

His son had been just a wean when events and betrayals unfolded and changed his life, heart, and soul forever. He doubted his wife would have done much to keep his memory alive in the eyes and heart of their son. He felt certain the boy didn't even know he existed. By now, the boy probably believed another man was his sire.

The hatred that had kept him alive all these years had proven quite useful in his escape. With his bare hands, he had managed to kill three of the guards before taking their weapons and killing four more of the blasted fools. The whole event had taken just moments to accomplish before he was able to crawl through the stones he had left loose in the outer wall of the fortress.

He had run for days on foot before coming to a small farm where he stole a horse. Years ago, he had been an honorable man who would never have done such a thing. He had left his honor at the gates of the prison years past. Now he was a desperate man, wanting only his freedom and to exact vengeance on those people who had deceived him. Stealing a horse seemed small in comparison to what lie behind him and what lie ahead.

Somehow, he had managed to evade capture as he made his way to Edinburgh. Dirty, hungry and exhausted, with no coin to his name, he had arrived in the dark of night. Edinburgh would be the launching point for his great plan. He would get even with those whose lies had made him a prisoner to begin with.

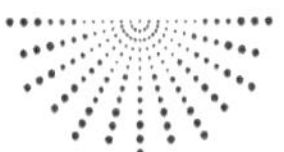

CHAPTER ELEVEN

Well rested, with full stomachs and fresh horses, Findley's band of warriors and reivers set out before dawn. The two older boys were given mounts of their own. Liam would ride with Richard and Collin with Patrick.

Maggy rode with Findley. While it felt good to have her pressed so closely to his back, it was also quite a distraction. He needed to keep his mind sharp and his focus on the task at hand. The last thing he wanted was to be caught off guard by any of the Buchannan clan that might be lurking about.

Earlier that morning, while Maggy was busy readying the lads for their journey, Findley had met with his men. If the weather held and they could keep the stops to a minimum, it was possible they could reach Stirling in two days.

They had discussed the few choices available to them. Hire men and pray they could trust the fealty they had purchased or beg for safe harbor from the monks at the Abbey of St. Mary. They all agreed it was better to put their faith in the men of God. And with God's blessing Findley and his men would reach Aberdeen in less than a fortnight.

The message he had sent to Angus begged for him to send as many men as he could and to meet them in Aberdeen. If all went well, they would arrive just a few days before their reinforcements.

If Angus was as generous as Findley hoped, he would have at least fifty men with which to lay siege to the Buchannan keep. It was Findley's hope to have Ian rescued and back in his mother's arms within a month's time. And God willing, Maggy would be so overjoyed with having her son returned unharmed that she might consider the proposal he intended to offer her.

If the weather held.

If Angus is generous.

If God would just grant him these small requests.

If fate would leave him be for a time.

If Maggy would cooperate and see the right of it and stay in St. Mary, he would be able to fight without worry. And if he could keep his mind off the lass whose arms were now wrapped tightly around his waist, he might just survive this whole ordeal.

There were far too many "ifs" for his liking. He knew that even the best-laid plans could not account for every circumstance. Life was oftentimes fraught with the unexpected. He knew his biggest obstacle would be Maggy's relentless insistence that she help retrieve her son. If he had to lock her in a cell to keep her safe and out of harm's way, then so be it.

They rode for several hours before stopping to rest. Maggy was glad to be off the horse. It had been too many years since she had ridden, and her rump and legs were reminding her of that fact. The bottom of her feet stung when she slid from the back of Findley's horse. Her back and legs begged her to sit in the grass and not move for at least a week's time, but she knew that would only make remounting near impossible.

She stretched her arms and back for a moment before daring to take a few steps, then noticed her sons chatting happily away with Wee William and the rest of the men. The boys seemed unfazed by the journey thus far. Och! To be that young again, with endless energy and hope!

Lost in her thoughts, she did not notice Findley standing behind her until she felt his hot breath on her neck.

"Are ye well, lass?" he asked.

His close proximity startled her, and she jumped and gasped.

Findley's lips curved into a smile. "I did nae mean to startle ye!"

Curse him for being so insufferably handsome! she thought as her heart began to beat faster. *I'll burn in hell fer certain fer the lustful thoughts I am havin'.*

"Next time warn me that ye mean to sneak up on me!"

Findley could not resist the urge to smile. "Now, if I warned ye, it would nae be a surprise, would it?"

She let out a frustrated sigh. Men.

"Ye look verra nice in yer new dress, Maggy," he told her.

I could get lost in his sparkling brown eyes. She swallowed and pushed the thoughts aside.

"Thank ye kindly," she said. Her hands went immediately to her skirts as she made an attempt to smooth out some of the wrinkles. She was wearing the practical green dress. She was saving the blue for a special occasion, although she couldn't imagine any in the near future.

His eyes seem to twinkle more than usual this morn. They brought a flutter of excitement to her stomach, so she forced herself to look away and pretended to look at the beautiful scenery that surrounded them.

Part of her wanted to think there was more to his compliment than polite small talk. Hadn't she lost that youthful, innocent part of herself years ago? Widowed mums of five should not be having such feelings, should they?

Time was not a luxury. They did not linger long as they ate the bread, cheese, and apples that Fiona had graciously packed for them. Soon enough they were mounted again and headed towards Stirling.

"When do ye think we will arrive in Stirling, Findley?" Maggy asked as they rode.

"If all goes well, we shall be there late tomorrow," he answered over his shoulder.

"Do ye think yer chief will send the men ye requested?"

Findley thought on the best way to answer her. While Angus was a fine man with a great sense of honor and duty, Findley could not be certain his chief would answer his plea for help. He could only pray that Angus would send the men he needed.

"Angus is a good man," Findley responded.

"But good enough that he would be willin' to sacrifice men for people he does nae ken?" That had been one of the many questions gnawing at her since yesterday.

"Lass, ye dunnae ken Angus McKenna," Findley answered, and prayed she would drop the subject.

There were many questions running through Maggy's mind as well as her heart. "How well do ye ken him?"

She thought it a very reasonable question. She knew that Findley had lost his family and entire village and carried much guilt over it. She wondered how long he had been a member of Angus' clan. Mayhap Findley was putting too much faith in a man he had not known long.

"I ken him verra well. He is me uncle."

She was surprised to learn that. Maggy could only hope that Findley's family ties were stronger than what she had witnessed in Gawter's family. Gawter's family had been filled with people interested only in furthering their individual wants and desires. There had been no strong bonds of family honor. Maggy was convinced it was ice water and greed that ran through their veins, not blood.

"Are ye close to yer uncle then?"

"Aye," Findley answered. She was asking for reassurance.

"Is he as honorable as ye?"

"Aye, he is." That was the truth.

"Did ye ever find the men responsible for killin' yer family?" She regretted the question as soon as she asked it. She could feel him grow tense and uneasy and wished that she could withdraw the question.

Findley took in a deep breath. "Aye, we did."

She wanted to know more, but she didn't have the heart to ask. She could feel his uneasiness and apprehension.

"I am sorry, Findley," she told him as she laid her head against his back. It felt good to be holding him. She could feel the strength of his muscles as she held on tightly. But there was more than a physical strength to this man. There was a deep, inner strength that seemed to radiate from within him.

"I did nae mean to bring ye any pain. I simply wanted to ken more of the man I am puttin' so much of me faith in."

He could not fault her for that. "Dunnae worrit," he said. "I suppose there is much we each want to ken of the other."

Maggy was losing herself in the moment. It had been years since she felt protected and cared for. Findley reminded her a bit of her da and her brothers. They were honorable men, much like Findley and his men. Her da and brothers would often put the needs of others ahead of their own.

Her heart ached with missing her father. Had he not died so young then mayhap she wouldn't have been forced into the marriage with Gawter.

Her mother had done her best with raising Maggy and her seven brothers alone. When her mum had agreed to the marriage between Gawter and Maggy, it had, at that time, seemed like the answer to many prayers. While sons were perfectly capable of making their own path in life, such was not the case for daughters.

Lila Boyle had done her best to provide a safe life for Maggy. Had Lila been blessed with seeing the future, she might not have been so agreeable to the marriage of her only daughter to a man with no heart.

"I lost me da when I was eight," she murmured, unsure why she chose to share that bit of her past with him. "I miss him verra much."

Findley felt his heart tighten in his chest when he heard the sadness in Maggy's voice. "I was ten and one," he confessed.

Maggy sat upright, certain she had misunderstood him. "Ten and one?"

"Aye," Findley said with a nod of his head.

Maggy was beyond perplexed. "Ten and one?" she repeated, wanting to make sure she had heard him correctly. She had assumed he had been much older when he lost his family, for his guilt was so intense.

"Aye," he answered again, not understanding her confusion.

"Findley, ye were just a boy when ye lost yer family," she said. "How can ye be consumed with such guilt when ye were but a child?"

And there it was. The same question he'd been asked a hundred times over the years. He had yet to meet anyone who could understand how he felt.

"It matters not that I was but ten and one. I was nae there to protect them."

A sudden realization hit her like a wall of water. "Ye dunnae feel guilty that ye weren't there to protect them," she said quietly. "Ye feel guilty that ye did nae die with them."

Findley pulled rein and brought his horse to a rapid stop, and Maggy had to tighten her hold to keep from falling off. He twisted himself as best he could but could not see her face completely. He was instantly angered by her statement. "Ye're daft!"

"Nay, I am nae daft! I speak the truth, and ye refuse to hear it," she threw back at him, loosening her grip once the horse settled.

"Get down," he told her. When she shook her head nay and refused to dismount, he tossed his leg over the neck of his horse and slid down to the ground.

"Ye cannae understand it!" he said through clenched teeth.

"I can understand it well enough, Findley." She was doing her best to remain calm and not lose her temper.

"Ye're a daft woman, Maggy! Ye cannae understand how I feel. It matters not that I was a boy. I was nae there for me family. I was nae there to help fight against the English who invaded our village! I was nae there to save me sister, or me da and mum!"

"And what could ye have done at ten and one?" Maggy asked him pointedly. "Look at Andrew, Findley! He is not much older than ye were at the time. Look at him!" Her voice was rising, frustrated with wanting him to see reason.

His men and the boys had drawn their horses together and stood a good distance from Findley and Maggy. Findley refused to look at Andrew.

"Ye're afraid to look at him," Maggy said. "Ye're afraid to see the right of it. Ye're afraid to face the truth, Findley. Ye've been carryin' around yer guilt fer so long ye dunnae ken how to live without it." Maggy lowered her voice.

"Findley," she whispered. "Ye were just a boy. There was nothin' ye could have done to protect any of them. Ye would have died along with the rest of them, and that is what ye feel guilty over. Nae that ye could nae protect them, but that ye did nae suffer as they did."

No one had ever spoken so bluntly to him before. His whole life, people had tiptoed around the subject. Even his own uncle had failed to see the real reasons behind Findley's guilt.

Where others had failed to see the truth of it, Maggy was able to see it in a matter of moments. His anger continued to burn. What right did she have to speak so bluntly, to be so forward?

"I'll thank ye kindly to keep yer thoughts on the matter to yerself," he said through gritted teeth.

"Nay," Maggy said.

Findley shot her a look of warning. "Lass, I'll give ye one warnin', and only one. Ye be treadin' where ye've no right to go."

It mattered not that she spoke the truth. She had no problems speaking candidly about his secrets, yet she refused to share hers with him.

She knew he was right. She had no right to speak to him in such a forward manner. But to see a man suffer so and to do nothing to help purge the guilt from his heart was something she could not do.

Uncertain if it were motherly instincts or those of a woman who wanted to, at the least, be this man's friend that urged her on, she refused to give up. Whatever the force was that bade her to want to help him as much as he wanted to help her to get her son back, it was far too strong to deny.

"Findley, I mean nae to make ye angry or to pain ye. I mean only to help ye see it so ye can shed these many years of guilt. Ye needn't rid yerself of all of it, fer that would be near impossible. But at the very least, ye need to quit blamin' yerself fer not dyin' that day."

Findley ran a hand through his hair. He was ready to pull her off the horse and let her ride with someone else. He did not want to discuss it further. But women were peculiar things. They put more stock into feelings and thoughts than men did.

"Findley," she said softly. "Had ye died that day, ye'd nae be here to help me and me sons." If he could not see that God had a greater plan for him than dyin' at a young age, she'd make him see it.

He looked up at her with a befuddled expression. "Can ye nae see that?" she asked him.

How many times had he prayed for answers? How many hours had he spent in chapel asking God why? Why had God spared him? Why had God taken his family?

"God has a plan fer ye, Findley. There is somethin' he wants of ye and fer ye. And it was nae to die that day." Maggy swallowed hard and took a deep breath.

She had no doubt that God had a special plan for Findley. What she did doubt was Findley's ability to see it for himself.

***

FINDLEY AND MAGGY rode in silence the rest of the day. He could not put his anger and frustration aside, and Maggy refused to beg for his forgiveness.

They made camp just before sunset, nestling themselves into a copse of tall pine trees. Maggy was used to hard work, but riding a horse for an entire day was exhausting. Her muscles ached, her back hurt, and her bottom was beyond numb.

Were they not considerably low on coin and racing against time, Findley would have taken a path less tiring and acquired rooms at an inn. Although he was still quite upset with Maggy, he didn't like the thought of her sleeping on the cold, hard ground. She deserved better.

While the men in their group felt the tension between Maggy and Findley, the lads were blissfully unaware. The lads understood the gravity of the situation, but they still possessed a youthful excitement about the journey they were on. They chattered endlessly through their simple dinner of bread, fruit, and dried meat. They spoke of how, if they were armed with swords, they would run each of the Buchannan men through.

Maggy was too tired and sore to fight sleep. She slept near the fire with her boys around her. Each of the men took turns keeping watch over them.

The next morning, she found herself in a bit of a grumpy mood. She had slept fitfully, her dreams filled with worry and dread over Ian.

Sleep had apparently done nothing to improve Findley's foul mood either. He spoke in short, curt sentences while they packed camp and mounted their steeds.

As far as Maggy was concerned, Findley could remain as surly and rude as he wanted. She knew she had been right the day before, and she was not about to beg forgiveness in order to have him speak to her again. Deep down though, she wished that he would return to behaving like the sweet, gentle Findley she was growing quite fond of.

The ride to Stirling remained blessedly uneventful. It was nightfall when they saw the city in the distance. Thankfully the moon shone brightly and allowed them to continue riding.

"Will I be yer wife again this night, Findley?" Maggy asked as she tried to remain awake. She was far too tired to remain angry with him.

"Aye," was his curt response.

A sudden sense of dread came over her. Was he so angry that he might leave her in Stirling and refuse to help her get Ian back? As much as she hated to admit it, she did not like having that worry. She not only needed his help, she found herself wanting it.

Doing her best imitation of a Highland warrior, Maggy said, "Dunnae worrit, Findley. It will be in name only. Yer virtue will be safe with me, lad."

He was silent for a long time, and she wasn't sure if he found her remark in the good humor she had intended. Och! Such a stubborn man!

"I thank ye fer that, m'lady. Me virtue and reputation are of the utmost importance to me. I have no desire to be a ruint man," he said.

"Nay, we would nae want to ruin yer chances of gainin' a wife, would we? No woman wants to marry a wanton of a man!" she giggled.

"'Tis true. Every woman wants an inexperienced man fer a husband. One who is virtuous, pure, and innocent," he chuckled.

"Ye be quite right, Findley. Women expect their men to nae know anythin' about the pleasures she can bring him in their marital bed."

"Aye, true, true. And, pray tell m'lady, what pleasures could ye bring me? Or is it a wanton and sinful thing of me to ask?"

"Och! Lad, if I told ye the pleasures I could bring ye, ye'd blush fer certain!"

Maggy was merely repeating things other married women had told her over the years, about the bragging ways of their men. She definitely had no personal experience in such matters. Gawter was merely an efficient seed layer and nothing more. There'd been no warmth, no giggling in the dark, and no tenderness to their joining. It was simply a means to an end.

"Would ye be gentle with me though?" Findley asked.

"Aye," she answered playfully. "At first. But ye must ken that a husband never denies a wife in their marital bed. Ye've a duty, ye see, as a husband."

"A duty ye say?" he said, feigning shock. "If it be a duty such as cookin' yer meals and cleanin' yer home, then mayhap I would nae find pleasure in it."

Maggy's giggle turned to a full-blown laugh. How long had it been since she had laughed so easily and so whole-heartedly?

Findley felt defenseless against the sound of her full and carefree laughter. He found himself falling in love with her all over again and his anger rapidly dissipating.

"Och! I would be certain ye had pleasure in it, husband! Ye cannae get ta breedin' without it!"

The women of her clan had told her that a woman could not get with child if her husband was unable to please her. Maggy knew from her own experience that that was an old wives' tale. Gawter's seed had firmly implanted itself within her womb after only four attempts, and she had not experienced any of the pleasure her clanswomen had spoken of.

"Am I to assume then, wife, that we'd have to keep tryin' until ye got the matter right?"

"Aye," she said. "But ye need nae worrit much. I be a Highlander, and if there is but one thing a Highlander is good at, it be that, lad!"

"Such braggin' ye do! I dunnae believe ye. I fear ye'd have to prove it, lass."

Maggy rested her head against his back again. Her cheeks were beginning to ache from smiling so much. She let out a happy sigh and closed her eyes. This is how it should be, she thought to herself. If it had been like this with Gawter, she would not have minded being his wife.

Her laughter was having a physical effect on his person, and he was glad she sat behind him. The effect only increased when his mind began to wander to licentious yet delightful thoughts of how he'd like to bring her more contented sighs.

They were pulled from their quiet thoughts by the sound of Wee William's voice. "Glad to see yer lover's quarrel is at an end!"

Findley adjusted himself in his saddle and felt Maggy grow tense.

"Be gone with ye, William," Findley said firmly. He didn't want the happy moment with Maggy to be spoiled by his interloping friend.

Wee William chuckled. "Me apologies fer interruptin'," he said as Richard, Patrick, and the lads pulled alongside them.

"But we could nae help but hear the laughter comin' from the two of ye," Wee William said.

"Aye," Richard spoke up. "'Tis nice to see the newly wedded gettin' along so well."

Findley's jaw tightened, and he could feel Maggy's grip around his waist loosen. "Be gone with ye," Findley said through clenched teeth.

"Me thinks the couple are desirin' time alone," Richard said with a devilish smile.

"We have lost him fer certain, lads!" Patrick chimed in. "'Tis what happens when a man marries. He fergets his friends, his companions."

"Can ye blame him, lads?" Richard asked. "Would ye rather be surrounded by the likes of us, or seek the pleasures of a such a bonny wife as Maggy?"

"Ew!" Collin said with a sour look upon his face. "I would rather be with me men than with a wife!"

"Me too," Liam agreed. "A wife tells ye what to do. And she makes ye bathe!"

"That's because women dunnae like smelly things, ye eejit!" Robert offered with an air of experience.

"Men are supposed to smell like men," Liam told him.

"Ye'll never get ye a wife if ye smell like horse dung," Robert told him.

"Good! 'Cause I dunnae want one. I'll keep meself smellin' like horse dung if that keeps women away."

The men laughed at Liam's statement. "Och!" Richard said. "Ye dunnae ken what ye're missin' there, Liam!"

Liam's face twisted into a combined look of disbelief and curiosity. "Missin'?"

"Aye," Richard said with a smile. "A woman is a most wondrous creature, lad. Ye'll discover that when ye're a bit older and wiser. Women be soft, warm, and delightful things."

"'Tis true, Liam," Patrick told him. "If it were nae fer women, we Highlanders would be lonely and untamed beasts."

"I would rather be untamed," Andrew offered. "Ye can come and go as ye please with no one to answer to."

"That might be true, lad," Richard said. "But it be a lonely existence. And there'd be no Highlanders left were it not for the comforts of a woman."

Liam shook his head. "What comfort can a woman bring a man?" he asked, rather disgusted by the whole conversation.

Each man broke into a fit of laughter at his innocent statement. Maggy cringed inwardly, not liking at all the path their conversation was taking.

"Well, ye see, lad," Wee William began.

Maggy stopped him before he could go further. "Food!" she nearly shouted. "A woman brings ye the comfort of food, Liam."

Her son was just eight, and she wasn't prepared to have that particular conversation with him just yet. She prayed the men would realize her discomfort and drop the subject altogether.

Wee William cleared his throat. "Yer mum is right, lad. A woman brings ye the comfort of food. Delicious, hot, remarkable sustenance." He looked rather content at the moment, as if he were lost in a fond memory.

Maggy shot each of the men a look of warning.

Liam shook his head again. "I would rather cook fer meself," he told Wee William.

The men broke into another round of raucous laughter. Maggy shook her head and let loose a frustrated sigh. Liam and Collin cast confused looks at the group.

Collin leaned closer to Ian. "Dunnae worrit, Liam. I would rather cook meself too."

"Aye," Liam said. "Women are nae worth the bathin'."

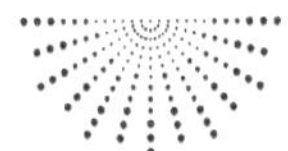

CHAPTER TWELVE

"Why does yer mum refuse to marry me?"

Malcolm Buchannan stared across the table at the small boy. He was beginning to question his own sanity. Perhaps the rumors he had heard about himself were true. They had to be, for what other explanation could there be for asking an eight-year-old lad for advice on women?

But who better to ask than the woman's own son? The boy could surely offer some insight to what Malcolm might need to do to get Maggy to agree to his proposal of marriage.

Malcolm was torn. A large part of him wanted nothing more than to find the wench and force her into marriage. But there was another part of him, something he thought he had lost long ago, that begged him to try a gentler approach. But if the gentle approach failed, he was not above dragging her by the hair and implanting his seed deep within her womb, thus forcing a marriage between them.

Ian stared up at the mad man. He was completely confused, for what did an eight-year-old boy such as himself know about women?

"Ye ken yer mum well, lad. Tell me why she refuses me offer of marriage."

Ian was terrified at speaking the truth. He worried that if he said what he was really thinking, Malcolm would run him through with his broadsword.

They stared at each other for a very long time. The fear in the young boy's eyes was quite evident.

"If I promise not to harm ye in any way, will ye tell me?"

Instinct and common sense warned Ian not to believe a word the man told him.

Malcolm ran a hand across his bearded chin. "I ken ye be afraid of me, lad," he said. "As well ye should be! But I am a man of me word. I promise I'll hold nothin' ye say agin ye."

Ian continued to stare at Malcolm, and his silence began to frustrate Malcolm. "If ye do nae tell me, lad, I'll cut yer wanker off with me sword."

Buchannans didn't make idle threats. 'Twas the only time their word held any value. Mayhap if he gave the man a few answers, he'd leave him be.

"She does nae like yer beard," he offered.

Malcolm touched his long beard and cast a look of disbelief at the boy. "Ye're sayin' me beard be the only reason she wilna marry me?" There had to be more to it than that.

Ian shook his head. "Nay, there be others." Mentally he ticked off the reasons his mum had voiced over the past months for declining the Buchannan's offer. He wouldn't tell him though, not even if he had a hundred warriors standing beside him.

"What else?"

Ian shifted uncomfortably in the chair. "She does nae like bad smells."

Malcolm could not contain his laughter. "She thinks I smell badly, does she?"

Ian nodded his head. "Me mum has a fondness fer bathin'. She makes me and me brothers bathe thrice weekly. More often in the summer."

"So ye're telling me that if I shave me beard and bathe, she would agree to marryin' me?"

Ian blinked. He knew it would take more than a bath and shave to get his mum to agree to such a thing. It would take divine intervention.

"Tell me, lad," Malcolm said drawing his chair closer to the boy, "be there more?"

Ian swallowed hard and thought for a moment. He worried he was tempting fate.

As Ian sat in quiet contemplation, one of the Buchannan's men brought out two trenchers of venison stew and warm bread. Ian's mouth instantly watered. The man set both trenchers in front of Malcolm. The boy's wide eyes and grumbling stomach did not go unnoticed by Malcolm.

"Are ye hungry, lad?"

Ian nodded his head slowly. He imagined he could eat both trenchers and still remain hungry. Silently, he hoped he was not being a coward or betraying his family by admitting to the weakness of hunger.

Malcolm slowly slid one of the trenchers across the table. He smacked the back of Ian's hand when the boy started to lift the spoon to take a bite.

"Ye may eat when ye answer me questions," Malcolm told him.

Ian's heart sank. He prayed that the Buchannan would not ask him to reveal the whereabouts of his mum. Ian knew well where his mum would be heading. Maggy had told them long ago what they would do in the event of an attack.

"So," Malcolm said as he dipped his bread into the warm stew. "Yer mum does nae like me beard or the way I smell."

Ian's stomach growled as the aroma from the stew hit his nostrils. He nodded his head and watched as the Buchannan stuffed his mouth full of bread.

"What else might there be lad, that I could do to win yer mum's heart?" Malcolm asked with a mouth full of food.

Ian's defenses were waning. "Ye might think of cleanin' yer keep."

Malcolm's brow creased. "Cleanin' the keep?"

"Aye. Mum likes a verra clean home. She does nae like messes."

Malcolm shoveled a bite of stew into his mouth and waited.

"Ye might want to lay down new rushes." Ian offered as he watched the Buchannan take another bite. "Mayhap ye'd want clean clothes as well."

Malcolm smiled inwardly. While he no longer had a handsome face, mayhap a bit of charm and cleanliness would help to sway Maggy his way.

Ian watched every bite the Buchannan took. His stomach hurt, and he was tired of cold porridge. The hunger pangs began to loosen his tongue. He'd give Malcolm just enough information in exchange for food. But he made a solemn vow not to disclose too much. Just enough to keep Malcolm happy. "Mayhap have yer men to bathe, too."

Malcolm laughed loudly at that bit of advice. He could well imagine the uproar that little scenario would cause, and he began to warm to the idea. If nothing else, it would bring him a good deal of pleasure to see the looks of horror on his men's faces when he made the order.

"So, yer mum has strong fondness fer cleanliness, does she?"

Ian nodded his head vigorously and hoped he'd soon be allowed to eat. "Aye, she does," he answered. As an afterthought, he added, "And flowers! She loves flowers!"

Malcolm took the last bite of stew and chewed slowly. He had charmed many a woman in his younger days and had even won the heart of a very special lass. Was there a shred of hope that he could win the heart of another?

Maggy was younger than himself by ten years, mayhap more. He knew very little about her other than what she could offer him by means of lands and a title. Aye, he loved being the evil ne'er-do-well that he was, but a little validation wouldn't hurt.

He shook the thought of winning her heart from his mind. He wasn't after the woman's heart. What he truly wanted was the wealth, status, lands, and title that would come with the marriage. A marriage to Maggy would give him the legitimacy he craved.

He decided he would give a try at cleanliness and charm. A lifetime ago his life had been filled with both. The concept was not in the least foreign to him.

If all else failed, he could return to his not-so-old ways, steal off with Maggy, and force her into a marriage. He wasn't above using tactics such as threats and murder. When it was said and done, he hadn't become the chief of his clan through niceties. Niceties, kindness, and compassion were feelings and emotions that left oneself vulnerable. Cairen had broken his heart and ripped his soul away many years ago. He'd not take that chance again.

CHAPTER THIRTEEN

Most of Stirling was fast asleep as Findley and his men—and the woman and boys they had promised to protect—rode its dark streets. The inns, however, were still brightly lit and filled with all manner of travelers and men seeking the comforts of any available bar wench. Loud laughter and conversations spilled out into the streets as Findley and his group quietly passed by on horseback.

They managed to find an inn with three available rooms. As they did in Renfrew, the men shared two rooms with the lads. Findley and Maggy would again pretend to be husband and wife and would share the remaining room.

Maggy wished she were not wearing the cap and veil the boys had given her, so that she could wrap her shawl around her face to better conceal herself. It was a very uncomfortable feeling walking through the inn, her face so exposed. She could feel the many eyes upon her as she walked alongside Findley, his hand holding firmly to hers.

She kept her eyes cast down and prayed no one would recognize her as they trudged through the crowd and up the stairs to their rooms. She had come too far to be found out now.

It wasn't until Findley closed the door behind them that she was able to breathe a sigh of relief. The room was not much bigger than the one they had shared in Renfrew. Utilitarian by nature, the room held a bed, a small table, and two chairs by the fireplace. As she had done in Renfrew, she offered to take the floor while Findley slept in the bed.

"Let us not argue that again, lass," he told her as he started a fire. "Fer ye ken ye'll lose."

Maggy let out a heavy sigh and sat on the edge of the bed, too tired to argue. "Fine then," she told him. "If ye want to be that stubborn, I'll allow it."

He stood and smiled at her. "Ye catch on quick, Maggy. Yer makin' a good wife!"

She rolled her eyes and shook her head, annoyed with his arrogance. She carefully removed the cap and veil and set it on the edge of the bed. "Aye, but ye've far to go as a husband."

He raised an eyebrow and smiled wryly as he sauntered toward her. Her dark red hair spilled over her shoulders, and it was all he could do to keep from reaching out and running his fingers through it. "I do, ye say?"

Her breath caught in her throat as she stared up at him. There was a twinkle in his dark brown eyes, and she knew if she stared into them for too long, they would be her undoing.

"Did ye nae promise to teach me a few things earlier this night?" he asked as he leaned toward her.

Her thoughts flashed back to their earlier conversation. Surely he had not taken her seriously when she spoke of the pleasures she could bring him? A jolt of fear started in her toes and spread through her body, and she found she could not speak. She knew there was not a thing she could teach him when it came to intimacies of a romantic nature.

"I believe ye said I had a duty to perform as a husband," he leaned in closer.

He was close enough that, had she any desire to, she could have simply leaned a mere two inches toward him, and her lips would be firmly planted on his. As wonderful as the thought of kissing him might be, she knew she could not succumb to such a desire. Swallowing hard, she pushed the pleasing thought aside.

"Am I to take yer silence as meanin' ye've no desire to teach me anythin' this night?" he said, feigning confusion.

While she felt warm and tingling sensations wash all over her, she was quite frozen in place. Unable to speak or move, all she could manage was a slight shake of her head. Her mouth had gone horribly dry, and she prayed he could not see her trembling fingers.

"Does me wife reject me after only three days of being married?" he asked, pretending to be offended and hurt. It suddenly occurred to her that if his eyes weren't so dark and sensual and his face weren't so ruggedly handsome, she wouldn't be losing all of her senses. And those broad shoulders and tightly muscled arms weren't helping her either!

He inched closer, so close that Maggy could feel his hot breath on her lips. Did he really plan to kiss her? She closed her eyes, swallowed hard and took in a long, deep breath. What harm could one kiss do?

In the next instant, she heard Findley begin to chuckle. Her eyes flew open in surprise as he stood tall, and his chuckle turned to a full laugh.

"Lass!" he said as he slapped his hand on his thigh. "Ye look absolutely terrified!"

Her nostrils flared as she pursed her lips. The excited anticipation of a kiss was quickly replaced with anger and embarrassment. Maggy stood, placed both hands on his chest and pushed.

"Ye're a despicable man, Findley McKenna!" she said through gritted teeth.

Her anger seemed to amuse him further, and his laughter increased. "Am I despicable because ye thought I meant to kiss ye? Or are ye angry that I did nae?"

She scowled at him and stomped her foot. "I would nae be wantin' any kisses from the likes of ye!" She was angry and frustrated, and she had no clear inclination as to why she felt that way. Frustrated, she pushed against his chest again, but it had no effect on him. He was as firmly planted as a wall made of stone.

The fact that he didn't move, blended with the fact that he looked so positively pleased with himself for making her angry, nearly threw her over the edge of reason. She tried pushing him again, and still he didn't move.

"Lass," he said with laughing eyes, "ye can push on me all the night long, and I am afraid ye'll not get the result ye want!"

His last statement was enough to push her over the edge. She drew her face into a twisted knot of anger, placed both hands on his arms and kicked him square in his knee. The toe of her new boot landed squarely in the soft spot under his kneecap.

His laughter instantly disappeared as he let loose with a grunt. She had caught him off guard. As he leaned forward to grab his injured knee, Maggy placed both palms on his shoulders and pushed hard.

She could not hide her proud and satisfied smile as she watched him tumble backwards onto his rump. "Did I ever mention that I have seven older brothers?" she asked, quite pleased with herself. "I be the only girl and the youngest child. They taught me well to defend meself against all manner of men."

Findley glared at her angrily whilst he rubbed his knee. Under different circumstances he may well have let her be, let her feel as though she had done well to defend herself. *God's teeth, how can I find this woman to be so breathtakingly beautiful, yet she frustrates me to the point of murder at the same time?*

His anger and frustration won over. A low growl escaped his throat as he reached up, grabbed her about her waist and pulled her down to his lap. The look of utter surprise and fear in her eyes brought him a momentary sense of satisfaction.

In the blink of an eye, he decided there were times in life when it was better to ask forgiveness than it was to ask permission. Forcefully, he put one hand at the back of her neck and pulled her closer.

This wasn't happening as he had imagined all these past months. In his daydreams he had imagined their first kiss would have taken place under the moonlit sky while walking along the loch near his castle. Or mayhap on a blanket after sharing a picnic. In those daydreams, Maggy was sweet, demure, and innocent. The kiss would have been tender and soft.

But this was no daydream. He pressed his lips against hers with a firm, hard, and unyielding desire that surprised even himself. He wanted her with a passion he'd never felt before, not with any woman. His want of her increased a thousand-fold when he realized she was returning his kiss with a zealous passion of her own.

Gawter never kissed me like this! Brazen, hard, passionate! I cannot feel me toes or me fingers! I swear there be lightning bolts flashing in me stomach!

It was impossible to think clearly with his lips so firmly pressed against hers. Her body seemed to grow a mind of its own, and for the life of her she could not find the strength to resist. She realized then that she didn't want to resist, she did not want the kiss to end.

After a time, the kiss softened and turned gentle, as did his hold on her. Maggy drew herself closer, wrapping her arms around his waist. She was losing herself, losing her heart, and if she were able to think on it, she was losing her mind.

Just as she was enjoying the way his hands felt as they caressed her back and the way his teeth felt as they nibbled on her bottom lip, a sudden sense of guilt flooded over her.

Ian.

Malcolm Buchannan was still holding him as a prisoner. That is, if he still lived. Her son had to be alive, for she couldn't imagine her life without him.

And where was she? Falling into the arms of a man she had known only a short time, letting passions and desires cloud her judgment.

She reclaimed her good senses and pulled away from Findley's hold.

"Nay!" she said as she tried to catch her breath. "I cannae do this!"

She scurried off his lap and raced to the fireplace. Her heart was pounding, and her breathing was coming in rapid bursts. She was angry with Findley for kissing her and angry with herself for enjoying it.

"I'll nae be yer mistress, Findley McKenna," she said to him over her shoulder. She didn't have the strength to look at him.

Findley stood, mystified by her statement. "I dunnae recall askin' ye to be such, Maggy."

"What difference does it make? The intent was the same. Ye were tryin' to win me over with yer bright smile and yer kisses." She had been won over by both and felt painfully guilty for it.

"It was just a kiss, Maggy, nothin' more. 'Tis nae like we--"

She spun on her heels before he could finish. "But ye would have been glad if I had let ye..." she searched for the right words, "let ye do whatever it was ye were plannin' on doin'!"

He bit the inside of his cheek to keep from laughing, prouder than he ought to be with the realization that the kiss had affected her. She had responded in a very positive manner when his lips touched hers. He had heard her breath hitch and felt her melting into his arms. He hadn't imagined her response.

"I think ye liked me kiss, and ye feel guilty over it."

"Nay!" she said unconvincingly. "'Twas just a kiss as ye said, and I would nae let it go to yer head, Findley McKenna!"

"Go to me head?" he asked as he crossed his arms over his chest.

"Aye! To yer pig-headed head!"

"Pig-headed?" he asked, nonplussed.

"Aye! Ye be a pig-headed lummox to think that one kiss could turn me into a wanton woman, ready to swoon and rip yer clothes off and let me have me way with ye!"

He could not stifle a very proud chuckle. "Do ye nae mean to say fer me to rip yer clothes off and have me own way with ye?"

"That's what I said, ye fool!"

He shook his head. "Nay, ye did nae say that. What ye said was--"

She cut him off again by stomping her foot, her level of frustration growing to unbelievable heights.

"It matters nae what I said, ye eejit! I cannae let me feelings get in the way of things. I cannae think of nothin' else but gettin' Ian back!" Tears clung to her eyelashes as she did her best to fight them back.

There it was: the truth. It wasn't that she had objected to the kiss.

She felt guilty for kissing him while her son remained Malcolm Buchannan's captive. His conscience wouldn't allow him to hold that against her.

He realized a few moments later that he should have simply agreed with her and apologized for his behavior. However, he hadn't much experience with the opposite sex other than the few bar wenches he had purchased on rare occasions. Findley knew nothing about real relationships. He would regret the next words that came from his mouth for a very long time.

"So, ye did like the kiss, and ye did want more, but 'tis yer guilt over yer son that makes ye behave so--" he paused as he searched for an apt description.

Maggy's eyes narrowed with anger. "So *what*, Findley?"

"Like an angry fishwife." His answer was more blunt than he had intended.

Maggy's eyes grew wide, and her mouth flew open, utterly appalled by his choice of words. She began searching the room with her eyes for something to throw at him, when they fell on a silver candlestick that rested on the mantle.

She had moved so quickly that he hadn't the time to brace himself for the impact when it landed in the center of his chest. Her aim was as good with the candlestick as it had been with stones.

The pain took his breath away for a moment as he doubled over, clutching his hand to his chest. As he fought to get his breath back, he saw that she had picked up the small stool that sat near the fireplace.

He held up his free hand, "Maggy!" he shouted. "Put that down!"

She cocked her head slightly as a wicked smile came to her face. Findley barely managed to duck out of the way as the stool hurled past his head, grazing his ear in the process. It hit the wall and fell to the floor.

"Maggy!" he shouted again. "Settle yerself down!" His voice boomed throughout the room.

"Nay! I am just playin' the part of the angry fishwife, Findley!" She looked for something else to throw, but the only things within reach were the chairs standing next to her.

"Fishwife! I would nae marry ye if ye were the last man on God's earth! Ye could ask me a thousand times, and I would give ye the same answer as I gave the Buchannan!"

Findley righted himself, dumbfounded by her statement. He hadn't asked her to marry him, so he could not think where she got that notion. Aye, the thought of marrying her, at least up to this point, had been very pleasant. The angrier she became, the more he questioned his earlier desires.

"I did nae ask ye to marry me," he told her.

"And I would nae if ye did!" she shot back, putting her hands on her hips. She knew that Findley hadn't come anywhere close to a proposal. But the events of the past few years had her suspicious of all men. She assumed it was just a matter of time before Findley proposed.

It was the kiss that had her behaving in such a manner. It had been passionate, deep, warm, moist, and quite disarming. Her thoughts were a jumbled mess, and her heart would not stop its incessant pounding.

"Maggy," he began, but was interrupted by a knock at the door.

The knock told him it was one of his men. Findley and Maggy stared at each other with unmistakable anger alight on their faces and in their eyes.

Findley took a deep breath before going to open the door. Wee William loomed large and held a curious look to his face. He had to duck under the door jam in order to enter the room.

"I have got lads in the next room who are tryin' to sleep. But there be such a loud argument takin' place between the two of ye that sleep is impossible." Wee William cast each of them a chastising look.

"The lads be worried. They dunnae like to see the two of ye goin' at it like a couple of cat-o-mountains." He crossed his arms over his chest.

Maggy was the first to break her silence. "I be sorry, William," she said as she took a deep breath. "I'll go see to the boys. There will be no more fightin' this night." She swept past both men, her lips pursed into a thin line of fury as she left the two of them alone.

Wee William continued to stare at Findley as if he were a father waiting for an explanation of an argument between two of his children.

"And what have ye to say fer yerself?" he asked, crossing his arms over his chest.

Findley took a deep breath and ran his hands through his hair. "I cannae explain it, William. I am doing me best, but no matter what I say or do, she becomes angry with me. And then I feel the need to reciprocate her anger."

"What did ye say or do to anger the lass so?"

The last thing he wanted to do was explain the kiss or what happened after it. "'Tis nothin'. Leave me be."

"Nay, I dunnae think so." Wee William stood firm.

"I dunnae wish to discuss it with ye," Findley told him.

Wee William lifted an eyebrow but remained silent.

Findley was growing impatient with him. "I said I dunnae wish to discuss it with ye." As if Wee William hadn't heard him the first time.

"Lad," Wee William began. "Any fool with half a brain can see how ye feel about the lass." He held his hand up when Findley began to speak.

"Findley, dunnae try to deny it. She is a bonny lass. Smart, strong, and as sweet as the day is long."

Findley snorted at Wee William's last statement. Aye, Maggy could be as sweet as honey. But rile her? Get her mad? Aye, she had a temper that could flare in the time it took for a heart to beat once!

"I think it be time ye told the lass how ye feel."

Findley shook his head and began to pace the room. "I dunnae think that be the best idea ye've ever had, William."

Wee William turned to watch his friend and leader pace the room. He was glad not to have a woman in his life that would make him behave so foolishly. To his way of thinking, there wasn't a woman in all of Scotland, nay, the entire earth who would be worth the trouble. William made a quiet, solemn vow to remain single to his dying day. As much as he wanted children of his own, he didn't believe a wife was worth the trouble. He would remain happy with spending time with other people's children.

As angry as Maggy was with him, Findley doubted she would be willing to listen, let alone warm to the idea of a romance with him. He knew he would love her until the end of time but doubted she would ever return his feelings.

"I'll take that under advisement, William," Findley told him, knowing full well he would not be sharing any of his feelings with Maggy at any time in the near future.

Wee William wasn't fooled but decided to let the matter drop for now.

"Good," he told him. "Now, about the morrow. What time would ye like to take Maggy and the lads to the abbey?"

"I say we leave at first light," Findley answered. "We will nae tell them what we be doin' until we are safely inside the abbey." He imagined it would take a good amount of time to convince Maggy that the abbey was the safest place for her and her sons.

Wee William nodded his head in approval. "And do ye think ye'll be able to get the lass to see the sense of it?"

Findley shook his head and sighed heavily, absentmindedly rubbing his stomach. He could feel the bruise forming. "William, do ye think about these questions before ye ask them?"

Wee William chuckled. "Sorry, I must have lost me head fer a moment."

They stood in quiet contemplation for a moment before Wee William spoke again. "What is yer plan if she refuses to stay with the monks?"

"To lock her away until we are far gone from the place." Although he didn't like the idea, he could not come up with a better plan.

"I feel sorry for the monks."

"Aye," Findley nodded in agreement. "Mayhap we should see they have plenty of armor with which to defend themselves. For We will be unleashing a wrath unlike any mankind has ever seen."

Wee William noticed Findley rubbing his stomach and the candlestick and stool lying haphazardly on the floor near the door. "Which one did she hit ye with?"

"Both."

William nodded his head approvingly. "At least we ken the lass can defend herself!"

"Aye, that she can," Finley agreed.

"She is a strong-willed lass," William offered.

"Aye, that is true as well."

William contemplated the situation for a moment. "A soft answer turns away wrath, but a harsh word stirs up anger."

Findley raised an eyebrow at his friend.

"Proverbs 15:1," William explained. "Me da was fond of referring to it. Ye cannae gentle something without a soft voice, Findley."

Findley sighed heavily and ran a hand through his hair. "What on earth are ye goin' on about?"

A broad smile came to Wee Williams lips. "Lad, if ye want to win that lass over, ye cannae do it with harsh words. If ye want to warm her to ye, use soft words, kindness, and a gentle hand. I imagine 'twould go quite far with a lass like that."

Findley considered the idea for a few moments. Mayhap he could be a bit gentler with her. The trick would be in controlling his own temper. For some strange reason his thoughts turned to the young lad, Robert. Hadn't his opinion of the lad been that if he could get his temper under control, he would someday be a fine warrior? Mayhap Findley would need to take a bit of his own advice, especially when it came to Maggy. In that instant, he made a silent vow that no matter what she might say or do, he would keep his temper and anger in check.

INFURIATED, it was all Maggy could do to keep from storming into the room and beating both men senseless. She had not heard the entire conversation between Findley and Wee William, but she had heard enough.

She was never one to eavesdrop or lurk in the shadows. After settling her sons down for the night, she had returned to her room. Just as she was ready to push the door open, she heard Wee William's voice coming from within, and he was talking about monks.

Maggy wasn't sure which part of the conversation offended her more, the fact that they intended to leave her and the boys with the monks or the arrogance of both men discussing her temperament.

Gentle me? Gentle me? As if I am some kind of wild animal!

She was half tempted to burst into the room and ask them if they intended to use a bit and bridle to temper her spirit.

Far better men than ye have tried, lads, she thought to herself.

Their conversation could only mean that Findley did know her secret. Just like the Buchannan, all that Findley wanted was to increase his purse, power, and lands through Maggy. Apparently, the kiss had meant nothing to him other than a means to soften her heart toward him.

Her mind whirled, and her hands shook with anger as she stood in the hallway listening. They intended to leave her with the monks while they attempted to rescue her son. She'd have none of it.

Her first thought was to get her sons, get to their horses, and hie off without the men. She quickly dismissed that notion. Even if they did make it to the Buchannan keep before Findley and his men, what would she do then? There was no way she could defend herself against all the Buchannans, no matter how many rocks she might have at her disposal.

Being alone with Malcolm Buchannan was a revolting prospect. The only way of surviving that encounter would be to marry the man. Mayhap she could agree to marry him and then slice the ghoulish man's throat while he slept. Nay, there was too great a chance of having to bed him first, before she had the opportunity to put a blade to his throat.

There were two things she was severely lacking at the moment: time and a plan.

A sudden thought came to her. Would it really be all that bad to marry Findley? It was a more palatable alternative to marrying Malcolm Buchannan.

Findley had shown on more than one occasion that he could be a kind and generous man. Had he not brought her lads back to her that past summer? He hadn't been angry and demanded she beat them as punishment as she knew other men might have. Nor had he beaten them himself. He hadn't ranted or raved or stomped his feet demanding payment for the time spent searching for his stolen cattle.

Nay, he had done none of those things. On the contrary, he had been quite pleasant and patient about the entire ordeal. He had even left three cattle behind to feed her people with, a blessing that had, at the time, meant a great deal to her. It had been an act of generosity that brought tears to her eyes every time she thought of it for weeks after. If she were honest with herself, she had thought of him many times since that day.

She was still angry with him, and she could not be certain that his intentions were still as honorable as they had appeared to be that summer. Her life with Gawter had taught her that men would say or do anything to get what they wanted. Findley was no different, was he? He was, after all, a man.

The sound of Patrick's voice broke through her troubled thoughts.

"Maggy?" he asked. "Are ye well?"

Startled, she spun around to face him. "Aye, I am Patrick," she answered softly. 'Twas an out and out lie. She imagined it would be quite some time before she felt well again.

Findley paid to have a bath brought up for Maggy. She had been unusually quiet when she had returned from settling the lads. He reasoned it was the hard days of riding and worrying over Ian, not to mention the argument that had taken place between the two of them.

He left her alone for the better part of an hour while he washed the layers of road dirt from his own skin and hair and changed into clean clothes. He shook out the clothes he had been wearing, getting rid of as much dust and dirt as he could, and carefully folded them and returned them to his pack. He sorely missed the comfort of Castle Gregor, the smell of clean clothes, and Mary's cooking. It would be weeks if not months before he would be back into the friendly folds of his clans.

Patrick had taken the first watch and sat on a stool in the semi-dark hallway. Findley thanked him and told him he would take over in three hours' time.

Maggy was already in the bed and under the covers when he returned. Her back was to the door, the covers pulled up around her ear. He felt sorry for her, exhausted from the journey and the worry over her son. And he'd been a damned fool for kissing her!

Nay, he didn't regret the kiss, just the timing of it. The kiss had been beyond pleasant; he had felt it all the way to his marrow.

And how joyous he had felt when she returned the kiss. There was something there. He hadn't imagined her melting into his arms or the soft sighs of pleasure. Mayhap when this was all over and done with, she might open to the idea of spending the rest of her life with him.

He was disappointed that she was asleep but relieved to know there would be no further arguing this night. Spreading his plaid out in front of the low fire, he lay down and tried to sleep.

But sleep was impossible. Maggy was but a few steps away, and his mind kept wandering to what it might be like to be lying next to her in that warm bed. He took in a deep breath and realized she must have used rose scented soap in her bath. Try as he might to push any thoughts of desire aside, he could not.

Tossing and turning on the hard floor, his mind could not settle. His thoughts ran rampant from images of a rose petal covered Maggy to devising creative ways of torturing Malcolm Buchannan. When he wasn't thinking of clever ways to woo Maggy, he was making mental notes on all they would need to lay siege to the Buchannan keep.

He imagined he'd need at least fifty men, and a floor plan for the keep would be helpful. In between plans of courtship and plans of attack, he prayed.

He prayed that Angus would send the men he so desperately

needed to help him get Ian back. He prayed that Ian was well. He prayed for God's mercy and forgiveness. Forgiveness for letting his family down all those years ago and forgiveness for the wicked thoughts he was having of Maggy.

Just as he was finally drifting off to sleep, there was a knock at the door. Two quick taps followed by three slow told him it was one of his men.

He grabbed his sword just in case and carefully opened the door. Richard stood in the dim light with a very worried look to his face.

"Findley," he said nervously, "Andrew is ill."

Findley's brow creased with worry as he lowered his sword to his side. "Ill?" he responded. "What is wrong?"

"He is thrown up thrice in the past quarter hour," Richard answered as he raked a hand through his hair.

"Does he have a fever?" Findley asked as his worry increased.

"Nay," Richard said. "But the runs have set in as well. We have not enough chamber pots to keep up with the lad."

Findley's stomach tightened with worry. If Andrew were contagious, there was a great risk that the rest of them would become ill. That thought left a great sense of unease in his chest. While the abbey was not far from town, he couldn't very well leave a group of sick people with the monks. And forcing his men to travel whilst throwing up and fighting the runs would make for a less than delightful journey.

Maggy was dressed and standing beside him before he had time to think on it further.

"'Tis Andrew?" she asked, the sound of her voice giving Findley a start. He turned toward her, and he could see the worry and exhaustion etched on her face.

Richard nodded his head. "Aye, I am afraid so, lass."

She gave a quick nod to both men and headed down the hallway with Richard and Findley following close behind.

Maggy hurried to Andrew. He was sitting on one chamber pot whilst he threw up into another.

"Och! Lad!" Maggy said as she felt his forehead with the back of her hand. "Ye've no fever," she said quietly.

The other boys were awake and standing together watching their brother. Maggy looked at each of them. "Are any of ye feeling unwell?"

Each of the boys shook their heads and mumbled a nay. Maggy turned her attention back to Andrew. "Do ye have pains, lad?"

'Twas all he could do to nod his head. "In me guts," he mumbled. "I think this is what it'd feel like to be run through with a dirk."

Maggy felt his cheeks again. He was clammy and pale, and dark circles were beginning to form under his eyes.

As she spoke gentle words of comfort to her son, Findley came and stood beside her and gently rested his hand upon her shoulder. "Lass, tell us what ye need, and We will see to it."

Maggy could see the sincerity and concern in Findley's eyes. For some inexplicable reason, his hand on her shoulder and his genuine concern made her feel better. And for the first time in many years, she did not feel alone.

"Milk thistle would be best if ye can find it. But ginger will work as well," she said. "But where ye'll find either at this hour, I dunnae."

Findley gave her shoulder a gentle squeeze. "Do nae worry over it. We will find it."

Maggy nodded, having no doubt in her mind that they would. "Thank ye, Findley," she told him. "I'll be needed some warm water and compresses as well. And I'll need a kettle to brew the milk thistle tea with."

She turned her attention back to her son. "I am sure ye'll be fine soon enough, Andrew," she said, giving him a reassuring smile. She hoped her worried heart did not belie her words. She was worried but did not want to let Andrew know.

As long as he did not draw a fever, he should be well in a day or two. Maggy hoped that this current bout of illness would pass quickly and prayed that no one else would come down with the ailment.

Within moments, Findley sent Richard and Patrick in search of the items Maggy had requested. He took the other lads to the room next door so they might get some rest and told them not to worry too much over Andrew.

It HAD TAKEN Richard and Patrick less than an hour to find the items that Maggy had requested. They returned to the room to find Andrew still doubled over in pain and vomiting. Neither man could hide their worry.

Like nervous fathers, Findley and his men paced the hallway outside the bedchamber. Findley worried that the other boys and mayhap his men might come down with whatever was plaguing Andrew. This could set their plan back by days, if not weeks. He felt instantly guilty for worrying about the delay instead of worrying about the boy. As a warrior and leader, he not only had to worry about those people he was responsible for, but he must also concern himself with the mission at hand. He wished Angus were there to take over the responsibility of worrying about the mission so that he might concentrate fully on Maggy and the boys.

They'd not been in the hallway long when Maggy stepped out of the room holding a very full and smelly chamber pot. Richard took it from her with the offer to dispose of it properly so that she might stay by Andrew's side.

So it went for the next several hours, Maggy handing filled chamber pots to one man or another in exchange for clean ones. Andrew had vomited to the point that he now had dry heaves, but the diarrhea would not subside.

Maggy sent Patrick off to find large stones. He hesitated for a moment when she made her request.

"Do nae worry, Patrick," she said with a tired smile. "I mean not to pummel ye with them. I want to be warmin' them in the fire for Andrew's stomach."

She had to bite her lip to keep from laughing when Patrick blew out a sigh of relief. He returned a short time later with good-sized stones and helped Maggy set them in the fire. It didn't take long before the stones were hot, and she could wrap them in cloths so that Andrew could hold them against his stomach. As sick as he was, Andrew still apologized repeatedly for delaying their quest.

"Wheest, lad!" she told him more than once. "I'll nae have ye worrin' over it. I think we all could use a day or two of rest. We will have yer brother back before ye ken it, Andrew."

"But had I not gotten ill, we'd be even closer to getting' him back," he retorted weakly.

Maggy didn't have the heart to tell him the truth. Sick or not, the only people who would have been any closer to getting Ian back were Findley and his men. Had Andrew not taken ill, they would, at this very moment be locked away at the monastery.

While Maggy was dreadfully worried over her son, she was glad for the delay. It would give her time to think of a plan, to come up with some way to not be locked away whilst Findley and his men rode on to Aberdeen without her. She tried to think of a means of escape but knew escape would be quite difficult with four young boys in tow, especially if they were all ill. She prayed often that Findley would not abandon her just yet, for if the rest of the boys grew ill, she would need his help.

Dawn had come and gone hours ago, and none of them had slept well. Maggy's back ached from sitting on the small stool next to Andrew. Her legs burned from the constant up and down of tending to her son.

Before she realized it, noon time had come and gone. Andrew was finally able to remove himself from the chamber pot and lie down on the bed. He was weak and exhausted, and his stomach and bum were quite sore.

Maggy knew it would be at least another day or two before they'd be able to resume their trek. That was, unless the others came down with the same ailment. She didn't know which was worse; having all the boys sick at once or having it drag out for days on end with little to no rest for any of them.

She kept a watchful eye on her son while he slept fitfully in the bed. Her body had grown numb, but she could not bring herself to leave his side just yet. Repeatedly, she would reach out to touch his cheeks and forehead and, each time, send a prayer of thanks up to the good Lord for keeping fevers away.

CHAPTER FOURTEEN

"So, lad," Malcolm asked as he placed a hand on Ian's shoulder. "Does me clean face meet with yer approval?"

Ian stared up with eyes wide at his captor. He didn't have the courage to tell the man that no matter if he bathed a hundred times a day or shaved thrice daily, his mum would still not marry him. He nodded his head but remained quiet.

A broad smile came to Malcolm's face before he threw his head back and laughed loudly. Ian could only stand on trembling feet and stare as the man's belly shook with laughter.

After several long moments, Malcolm's laughter subsided, but his smile remained on his face. Ian did his best to keep his legs from shaking, but it was quite difficult. He wasn't sure which terrified him more: an angry Malcolm Buchannan or a happy one.

"Lad," Malcolm said as he turned Ian and began to walk. "I fear yer still mightily afraid of me."

Ian swallowed hard. The last thing he wanted to do was to say something that would anger the Buchannan.

Malcolm chuckled and gave the boy's shoulder a gentle squeeze. "I cannae say that I blame ye, lad. I imagine I would be wettin' me pants with fear as well, were I in yer shoes." He smiled thoughtfully as he led the boy down the stairs to the large gathering room.

"Do ye see how we are cleanin' our keep, lad?" Malcolm asked with a touch of pride to his voice.

Ian looked around the large room and was quite surprised to see the moldy rushes and dog poop had been removed. The room was full of women who were scrubbing floors and washing walls. A young woman, heavy with child, was industriously scrubbing the layers of smoke from the stones of the fireplace.

Though the faint scent of urine still hung in the air, the sight before him was a vast improvement over days past. Still, he knew that no matter how clean the Buchannan or his keep became, his mum would never agree to marry him.

"Do ye think yer mum would be pleased with the improvements, lad?" Malcolm asked hopefully.

"Aye," Ian muttered.

Malcolm nodded his head and led Ian out the large door and down the stairs into the courtyard. In a matter of moments, four large and mangy dogs charged towards them. Ian's eyes grew wide, instantly terrified the animals were going to attack. Reflexively, he jumped behind Malcolm and held on for dear life.

He could hear Malcolm laughing as he reached around and grabbed Ian. "Do nae worry it, lad!" he told him. "I'll nae let them bring ye any harm!"

Ian's eyes were closed tightly, and he braced himself for an attack. He did not trust anything Malcolm Buchannan might say. He could still hear Malcolm laughing as the man bent down.

"There's a good dog!" Malcolm said playfully. "Did ye miss me, lassie?"

Ian held his breath and waited for gnarled teeth to start eating away at his limbs. A short time passed, and nothing happened. His curiosity was piqued, forcing him to chance taking a look. Slowly, he opened one eye.

There before him on the steps of the keep was Malcolm Buchannan lying on his back being licked to death by the four dogs.

Malcolm was petting the animals, talking to them as if they were bairns and laughing loudly.

Ian was astonished to see the man behaving in such a manner. He almost appeared human.

One of the dogs took notice of Ian and came bouncing up the stairs. It was a large, gray, wiry-haired beast whose face was level with Ian's chin. The dog playfully put his front paws on Ian's chest, and when he stood on his hind legs he was a good two heads taller than Ian. The dog began an all-out assault with his tongue. Ian couldn't help but giggle as the dog pushed forward with more force and knocked Ian down.

The remaining three dogs heard Ian's laughter and came to join in the tongue attack. Before Ian realized it, all four dogs were playfully sniffing and licking at him as they stepped all over him. Ian couldn't remember the last time he laughed so much.

For a few short moments, he forgot where he was and why he was there. But when he looked up and saw the smile on Malcolm's face, he remembered. He supposed it would be all right for him to play with the dogs, but he'd do his best not to forget that Malcolm Buchannan could not be trusted.

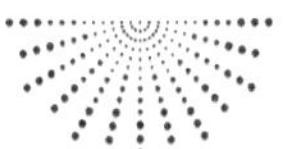

CHAPTER FIFTEEN

Maggy had dozed on and off, refusing to leave Andrew's side until she knew the worst of his ailment was over. When the dark of evening fell, and Andrew said he might like to try eating a bit of bread, she felt very relieved. She continued to keep a watchful eye on her other sons for any sign that they might become ill.

Findley had made several attempts throughout the day to get Maggy to rest and eat. The only time she accepted his offer to sit with Andrew was when she took a few moments to tend to her own necessary needs.

Findley did his best to hold his tongue and not argue with her need to remain at Andrew's side. He admired her devotion to her son but worried that she would exhaust herself to the point of becoming ill as well.

It wasn't until she saw that Andrew could keep the bread and light broth down that she finally agreed to leave his side to rest, much to Findley's relief. He left her alone to tend to her ablutions while he met with his men at the end of the dark corridor.

"I doubt Andrew will be able to sit a saddle for a day or two," Wee William said.

Findley and the others agreed. "Aye, and we dunnae ken if any of us might contract the same illness," Richard whispered.

"'Twould be wrong to leave them at the abbey just yet. I am sure the monks would nae appreciate us leaving them with a group of sick people," Patrick offered.

Findley chewed on the situation at hand for a few moments before finally speaking up. "'Tis agreed, then," he said as he crossed his arms over his chest. "We will wait two days more, and if none of us become ill, we will take them to the abbey."

The men agreed with nods of their heads, and Wee William offered to take the first watch. Findley was beginning to grow fuzzy-headed from lack of sleep. He had been up all night and day in case Maggy or Andrew needed him.

He tapped gently on the door of the chamber he shared with Maggy. When no reply came, he knocked again, a bit louder. He paused for a moment before slowly opening the door in case she was indisposed.

He found her asleep in the bed, still fully dressed. Her long, silky, auburn hair spread over her shoulders and onto the pillows. Her beautiful face rested on her hands, and her legs and feet were curled up under her skirts.

'Twas a sweet and beautiful sight, and it warmed his heart. Careful not to wake her, he quietly closed the door. Taking the blanket from the end of the bed, he covered her with it. Standing quietly in the warm glow of the fireplace, he watched her sleep.

For a moment, he was quite tempted to crawl into the bed and lie down next to her. What he would not give for just a moment to hold her in his arms. A moment would not have been long enough. Nay, he wanted an entire lifetime.

He shook the thought away. Now was not the appropriate time to be thinking such things, no matter how pleasant simply holding her might be. He pulled off his boots and spread his plaid on the floor to face another restless night. If he didn't get to Ian soon, he was going to lose his mind.

WHEN THE COCK crowed at dawn the next morn, Maggy cursed the hapless bird to the bowels of Hades. Grumbling under her breath, she wearily pulled herself from the warm feather bed. Findley was still asleep on the floor in front of the fire.

Maggy rubbed the sleep from her eyes, stretched, and took a deep breath, all the while doing her best not to let her eyes linger on Findley's resting form. He was lying on his back with an arm draped across his forehead, his bare chest rising and falling slowly with each breath he took.

Even in sleep his muscles seemed to be chiseled from stone. His chest, with its mass of soft-looking hair swirling over it, made her breath hitch. She wondered what it would be like to run her fingers through it or to rest her head against it.

Chastising herself for such thoughts, she pulled on her boots, grabbed her shawl, and quietly stepped out of the room. Richard was on watch, dutifully perched on a chair between the two rooms the lads shared. From his vantage point, he could see anyone who might be ascending the stairs.

When he saw Maggy softly closing the door behind her, he jumped to his feet with a questioning look.

"Be there a problem lass?" he asked.

"Nay, Richard. I simply need to use the privy," she told him.

"I cannae let ye go unattended, lass," he said, stopping her in her tracks. "We have chamber pots."

'Twas far too early in the morning to be arguing such nonsense. "I am well aware of that, Richard. But Findley sleeps still, and I will not be using a chamber pot whilst he sleeps but a few steps away." She pursed her lips and stood taller.

Richard stared down at her with a firm look of his own. "Lass, I cannae allow ye to go alone. Me brother would kill me."

She really didn't care one way or another if Findley would be angry. Her bladder was full and begged for relief. "Richard, I am a full-grown woman, and I am perfectly capable of tending to my own needs. I do not need an escort; what I need is the privy. Now, kindly step aside and let me pass."

Richard let out a heavy sigh. "Wait here. I'll have Patrick go with ye."

He held up a hand to stop her protests. "Lass, we dunnae ken if any Buchannans are about. We need to be vigilant."

Although she knew he was right, it did nothing to make her feel better. She would be glad when this ordeal was over, and her life could get back to normal. She shook her head at the notion of normal. Her life had been far from normal for many years.

Patrick appeared after a few moments looking quite tired but untroubled at having been awakened to escort Maggy. "Mornin', Maggy," he said, his voice rough and sleepy.

Padding softly down the stairs with Patrick leading the way, they made their way out of the inn and to the rear of the establishment. 'Twas not yet light out, and not a star could be seen through the early morning fog. Maggy could smell the threat of rain in the distance, as well as the foul-smelling privy that stood a good fifty yards east of the stables

As they drew nearer, she wondered if a tree might not be preferable to the foul-smelling privy. Giving the horizon a quick look for a tree, she realized there were none close enough. She would simply hold her breath and move as quickly as possible.

Her lungs were close to bursting by the time she finished. She pushed through the privy door and ran as fast as she could away from the disgusting smell. Patrick grinned as he quickly fell in behind her.

"Not the best way to start yer mornin', is it lass?" he said with a chuckle.

Maggy stopped halfway between the inn and the privy and rested her hands on her knees. She took deep gulps of air and tried to settle her stomach. Shaking her head, she said, "Nay, 'tis nae, Patrick." But it was still far more appealing than trying to use a chamber pot within ear and eyeshot of Findley.

After a few more breaths of air, she righted herself and looked about her surroundings. The fog muffled the early morning sounds of the awakening world. Birds chirped and tweeted happily as they fluttered from rooftop to rooftop. A pig squealed in the distance, and she heard the whicker of a horse coming from the stables.

"Patrick, do ye think we could walk about for a short while? I would be grateful to work the kinks out of me back and legs and take in some fresh air."

Patrick looked nervously toward the inn and debated the suggestion. 'Twas early yet, and Maggy had been cooped up all of yesterday taking care of Andrew. Surely there could be no harm in a short walk. He was well armed, and as long as they stayed within earshot of the inn, all should be well.

"Aye, but a very short walk, and we will not venture far, lass," he told her.

Maggy's smile lit the morning darkness, and she appeared relieved as well as grateful. Without thinking, she gave Patrick a hug. "Thank ye, Patrick!" she exclaimed before breaking the embrace.

Patrick swallowed hard and took a deep breath. Mayhap Wee William was correct, and women were indeed strange, mysterious creatures best left alone.

Maggy looped her hand through Patrick's arm, and together they walked away from the stables and inn. They kept to the rear of buildings, while Patrick strained to listen for any signs of trouble. He knew Findley would run him through with his broadsword if he let anything happen to his Maggy.

They had not ventured far before the sky let loose with a heavy rain. Large raindrops pelted their heads and shoulders and splattered across the black soil. Maggy gasped as she pulled her shawl over her head and looked up at Patrick.

Patrick gave a quick survey of their surroundings. The blacksmith shop was closer than the inn. Grabbing Maggy's arm again, he ran toward the shop and gave a hard pull on the door. Thankfully, it was not locked and gave way easily. Once they were safely inside, he yanked the door closed enough to keep out most of the rain and still allow him to maintain a watchful eye for any signs of trouble.

Maggy removed her shawl and shook the rain from it. The air in the blacksmith shop was heavy and warm from the embers that remained in the forge. Apparently unaffected by the fact that he was nearly soaked to the bone, Patrick stayed near the door.

Maggy walked to the forge and began waving her shawl over it in hopes of it drying. As she fanned the coals, she apologized to Patrick. "I be terribly sorry, Patrick. I did nae realize 'twould be rainin'."

Patrick did not turn from his post. Over his shoulder he replied, "Dunnae worriy over it, lass." He wondered how angry Findley would be if he learned that he and Maggy had been trapped in the shop. While Patrick and the others enjoyed tormenting Findley over his affections for Maggy, he doubted Findley would see any humor in the matter. Still, the image of Findley grinding his teeth and threatening to disembowel them all if they so much as laid a finger on his Maggy was enough to bring a wry grin to his face.

Maggy was beginning to feel guilty for asking to take a walk. If they weren't back soon, Richard would begin to worry. She was certain he'd wake Findley, and a search would immediately ensue, and she had no doubt that he'd be extremely upset with her.

Her stomach tightened with anger. Why did she care if Findley would be upset? Aye, he was making a sacrifice in order to help her get Ian back. But what did he expect as his reward? Her hand in marriage?

He was a braw, handsome man who was showing great kindness to all of them. Her heart longed to be able to trust him, to believe that he was doing all of this for reasons other than what he could gain from it. Mayhap he did have some sort of affection for her, affections or feelings that he'd been unable to share. After all, he had kissed her, and that had to mean something.

Her mind still warned her heart, however, that men were never moved to do anything if there weren't a gain of some sort in it for them. The only exceptions to that rule had been her father and brothers. Aye, those were the only honorable men she had ever known. Until now. Could she really trust these men? Or more specifically, Findley.

When she thought back to the conversation she had overheard

between Findley and Wee William, the anger began to creep back up. They had talked about her as if she were a filly that needed her temper tamed. Broken was more like it. Findley wanted to crush her spirit and her independence, just like Gawter had done.

It had taken a long time to rebuild the spirit that Gawter had taken from her. Maggy was not ready to give that up, not for Findley nor any other man. She had made a promise to herself that she'd never let another man treat her as Gawter had, with a cold and spiteful heart.

Nay, she'd been alone too long. She had grown to like her independence and not having to answer to anyone but herself. She'd not give that up no matter how much she had enjoyed Findley's kiss or the way she felt when she had been wrapped in his arms.

'Twas merely a physical reaction, or so she tried to convince herself. She was a grown woman for heaven's sake! She wasn't naive enough to believe that only men had physical needs.

As soon as Andrew was better, they'd be leaving for the abbey. Findley would leave her and her sons while he went off to rescue Ian. How many weeks would it be before they returned? How long would she have to remain cosseted behind the abbey walls, waiting?

As if she weren't capable of offering some sort of help in getting her son back. As if she were incapable because she'd been born a woman and therefore couldn't form her own thoughts, ideas, or solutions to problems.

As if I would wait patiently behind like a docile lamb. The more she thought about it, the angrier she became. Escape was not a viable option, for she knew Findley would find her in very little time.

Mayhap Findley's only reason for leaving her behind was so that he could rescue Ian and return as the valiant hero. Did he mean to sweep her off her feet? Did he hope she'd be so impressed with his skills that she'd lose all of her good senses and agree to marry him? And how would he behave afterward if she did agree to such a union? Would he remain the honorable man she was beginning to have feelings for, or would he end up like Gawter: cold, cruel and uncaring?

She could not risk it. There was too much at stake. He couldn't possibly want her or her heart. Nay, it had to be all that she and Liam could give him.

Fuming with anger, she waved the shawl more vigorously over the embers. *He knows the truth yet pretends he does not. 'Tis nae me he wants, but all that Liam and I can give him. 'Tis the land, the title, and the power, nothing more.*

She vowed she would not allow him to leave her at the abbey. There had to be a way out of this, a way to keep her dignity intact and her heart her own.

If only she had a weapon. Armed, she might be able to force him into at least listening to her. Nay, he'd just lie and agree with her until she put the weapon down, then go on with his plans like the pig-headed Highlander that he was.

As she cursed under her breath, her eyes fell to an object that hung on the wall just a few steps away. She cast a quick glance at Patrick, who still stood at the doorway with one hand on the hilt of his sword, his eyes focused on the area surrounding them.

Her pulse quickened as hope began to build. A devious smile came to her lips as a plan began to unfold in her mind. Her prayers had been answered. *Nay, Findley, ye'll not be leaving me so soon after all.*

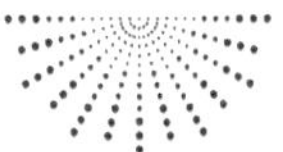

CHAPTER SIXTEEN

Malcolm Buchannan gave an approving nod as he stood in the center of the large gathering room. He could not remember a time it had ever been this clean. Nor could he remember a time that the women of his clan had been this happy. He also could not remember his men ever being this sorely disappointed in him.

"We are warriors, for the sake of Christ!" Almer shouted as he stomped across the room toward Malcolm.

"What be yer problem this fine, beautiful mornin', Almer?" Malcolm asked as he calmly crossed his arms over his chest.

Almer's face was alight with fury. His dark brows furrowed, giving him the appearance of having a large wooly-worm resting above his eyes. He came to an abrupt stop a few steps away from Malcolm and dared not to get too close to his leader, for he no longer trusted the man.

Almer shook his head. "The problem? The problem is ye're lettin' the women folk drag me men away from trainin' in order to clean the keep! The problem is ye've got men scrubbing walls and washing windows! The problem is ye're spending money on draperies and fabrics and nonsense!" He wagged his finger at Malcolm.

Malcolm remained steady. He momentarily debated running his dirk across Almer's throat but decided against it. The floors had just been scrubbed and new rushes laid down. Gertie, the woman he'd put in charge of the keep, would likely beat him with her broom if he bloodied up the newly cleaned gathering room. Malcolm stifled a chuckle and wondered how many years had passed since he worried over angering a woman.

"And yer problem with that is...?"

Almer huffed. "Ye've lost yer mind!" He swallowed hard as fear flickered momentarily in his dark eyes. The moment the words left his mouth, he knew he had crossed the line. Certain that he'd be dead in the span of a few heartbeats, he took a step backward.

Malcolm tilted his head. "Ye think I have lost me mind?" he asked, proud that he was holding his temper in check. "Ye think I have lost me mind because I have got the women folk happily cleanin' the keep?"

"And the men are forced into helpin'," Almer added.

"And what be wrong with the men helpin' to reach places the women folk cannae reach?"

Almer didn't answer. He was too busy trying to figure out a means of escape to save his own life.

"Almer," Malcolm began "I am sure ye ken well why I am doin' what I am doin'."

When Almer remained silent, Malcolm continued. "Do ye worry I have gone soft? Merely because I be preparing the keep fer me future wife?" He studied the silent man standing before him for a moment. More likely than not, the rest of his men were thinking along similar lines.

"I can assure ye, Almer, that I have not lost me mind. Nor have I gone soft. I am merely having the keep prepared for Maggy. She is a fine woman who is used to the finer things in life. I ken ye think I should just drag her here by her long red tresses and plant my seed in her against her will, but I'll nae be doin' that."

Almer noticeably flinched when Malcolm uncrossed his arms and clasped his hands behind his back. Malcolm was pleased to see that he was still capable of evoking fear in a man.

"My plan is to gently win the woman over, for that is the kind of woman she be. Maggy be nae bar wench or scullery maid," he told Almer as he took a step toward him. "Think of battle, Almer. Do ye go against every man in the same fashion? Or do ye adjust yerself for each man ye go up against? Do ye nae look for his strengths as well as his weaknesses and use both against him? Or do ye just go in swingin' yer mace at anythin' that moves?"

Malcolm nodded his head in approval when he saw Almer's expression change from fear to confusion before finally turning to understanding. "That's right, Almer, ye adjust yerself for each battle. Ye get to know yer enemy before ye take him down."

"So, this is all just a ruse?" Almer asked.

"Aye, that it is. Once I have shown the lass what she wants to see and get what I want from her, I assure ye that things will go back to the way they were."

Almer's lips began to curve into a smile. "We will go back to trainin' instead of cleanin'?"

Malcolm nodded his head.

"And we will go back to takin' what we want instead of askin'?"

Another nod from Malcolm caused the man's smile to broaden.

"And no more makin' the men to bathe every other day?"

Malcolm laughed. "Nay, ye will still be made to bathe. I did nae realize just how badly the lot of ye stank!"

IAN WATCHED QUIETLY from the alcove. He had known all along that it was too much to pray for that a man like Malcolm Buchannan would suddenly change into a good and decent man. Ian knew that no matter what Malcolm did to portray himself as a kind and decent person, deep down he was still the same evil man.

Ian had decided days ago to play along. They had moved him out of the small, dank room and into a nicer chamber near Malcolm's own bedchamber. Ian still kept track of the days by scratching marks on the wall. He prayed it would not be much longer before his mum and brothers came to rescue him from this place.

His heart ached with missing his mum and brothers. He had no idea how they would actually go about freeing him from Malcolm, but knowing his family, they would do whatever they could to rescue him.

He would do what he must to convince Malcolm that he was warming to him and believed the lies the man told. By doing so, he would be able to learn more of Malcolm's plans, and in the end it might just help his family.

CHAPTER SEVENTEEN

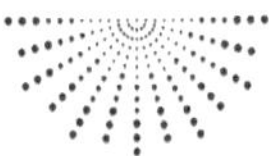

"Y e're a fool!"

Findley took a deep breath as he tried to rein in his anger. If he did not know better, he would think Maggy was intentionally trying to anger him.

"Lass, I am sorry," he told her between clenched teeth.

"Ye can be as sorry as ye want, it does nae change the fact that ye're a fool," she shot back at him.

He took another deep breath. "Lass, ye've been yellin' at me fer nearly a quarter of an hour now, and I still dunnae what I have done to anger ye so."

"Bah!" she said. "I could tell ye and draw ye pictures, and ye still would nae understand anything. Ye're a fool and an eejit!"

Findley sighed heavily and rubbed his palms over his face. He was gaining no ground with her, and he was not getting any closer to finding out what he had done to offend her.

"Lass," he said. He spoke softly in an attempt to calm her.

"Do nae try being kind now!"

"I am merely attempting to make amends with ye," he said quietly.

"Amends? Amends?" Maggy began pacing around the room. This

was not going to be as easy as she had thought. Why must he be so insufferably calm?

"Ye want to make amends? I do nae think that is possible, for ye be a foolish eejit of a man." If he didn't get angry soon, she would have to move on with her second plan, a plan she did not want to use.

Findley stood with his fingertips resting on his narrow hips. It was all Maggy could do to keep from running to him, begging forgiveness, and begging him to kiss her as he had done yesterday. But she knew that one kiss would not be enough, and it would seriously interfere with her plan.

"Maggy," he said, sounding quite tired, "forgive me."

He looked forlorn, lost, and if she didn't know better, quite sorry. Her heart wanted very much to tell him the truth. All of the truth, from her true identity and why Malcolm Buchannan wanted to marry her, to why she was purposely trying to anger him. Reminding herself there was more at stake than Findley's feelings, she pushed further.

"I'll nae forgive ye," she told him, hoping he did not see her trembling fingers. She was about to cross a line she had no true desire to cross. She had to stay her current course, for her second plan of action would throw her own heart into such despair she doubted she'd ever be able to overcome it. It was cowardice that propelled her forward and nothing more.

"I'll nae forgive ye, and ye'll not find yer redemption with me. Ye're a coward, Findley McKenna."

His response was not what she had expected. He was supposed to have yelled back, called her a few choice names, and mayhap thrown a chair or two against the wall. Then he was to have stormed off and not returned until he was well into his cups. That was how Gawter would have responded. She was quickly learning that Findley McKenna was nothing like her dead husband. Findley McKenna was not like any man she had ever known.

Hurting him had not been her intention. But hurt was exactly what she saw when she finally had the courage to turn and look at him. Pain and sorrow were etched in his handsome face, and she'd give anything to take it back.

Before she could find her voice to whisper an apology, Findley shored up his shoulders, pursed his lips together, and cast her a disdainful look as he left the room.

Torn between wanting to run after him and beg his forgiveness and wanting to not lose herself or worst of all Ian, the tears she'd been holding back came bursting forth. She whispered an apology to the closed door before sinking into the chair.

"What have I done?"

FINDLEY SAT ALONE at a table tucked into a dark corner of the inn. He was on his sixth tankard of ale when his brother Richard appeared and sat in the chair opposite his own.

Richard sat quietly, studying his brother. While he had not heard the words spoken between his brother and Maggy, he had heard a good deal of Maggy's shouting through the walls that separated their rooms. Whatever his brother had done, it had definitely upset her. As he looked at his brother, who was tossing back the remainder of his ale and waving at the comely bar wench to bring another, Richard knew his brother was drinking with a purpose.

"What did ye do to anger Maggy so?" Richard finally asked.

Findley huffed and shook his head. "I'll be damned if I ken."

Richard turned in his seat and stretched out his long legs. Getting information from his brother would be like pulling teeth from a bear.

"Ye dunnae what ye've done?" Richard asked as he adjusted his broadsword to rest across his lap. "Did she nae tell ya?"

"Ha!" Findley laughed and thanked the bar wench, who set two tankards of ale on the table. "Keep them comin', lass, and do nae stop until I have slid under the table. And then still bring them and pour them down me throat until my heart no longer beats, and keep bringin' them for a fortnight after they've set me body in the hard, cold earth."

The plump young woman rolled her eyes and walked away. Apparently, she'd seen many men in a similar state as Findley's and was not shocked by the request.

"So?" Richard asked as he took a sip of the ale.

Findley clenched his jaw before taking a long pull from his tankard. His brother apparently had never enjoyed the pleasure of the company of a tetched woman. For had he known what joy that could bring, he'd be tossing ale down his own throat and joining in commiserating with him.

"So what, little brother?"

"So, what did ye do to upset the lass so?"

"Again," Findley said holding his palms up and staring up at the ceiling. "I tell ye I dunnae what I did!"

Richard raised a brow in disbelief. His brother had to have done or said something to have upset Maggy. Elst, he wouldn't be sitting here with the distinct purpose of getting full into his cups.

Findley gave a quick sigh before taking another drink. "I tell ye, Richard, I have done nothing that I am aware of. I returned to the room to ask if she was hungry, and the next thing I ken, she is hurling one insult after another at me. Calling me everything from an eejit to a fool to..." his voice trailed off.

Why did she think him a coward? Was he not doing everything in his power to protect her and her sons? Was he not spending every last coin to his name to clothe her, to put a roof over her head at night so she did not have to sleep out of doors? What more could he do to prove his worth, his bravery, or his love for her?

The sound of Richard's voice repeating a question finally broke through Findley's ale-induced reverie.

"Findley?" Richard raised his voice slightly. "I asked what else did she call ye?"

Findley took another long pull of his ale and looked for the bar wench. "It be nae important."

Richard chuckled. "Apparently it is, elst ye'd not be sittin' here and drowning yer misery in drink." It had to have been something quite damning, for Findley was not normally one to drink himself into a stupor.

"Leave it be, brother," Findley said with a clenched jaw.

"Ye love her." It was a statement, not a question.

Findley threw his head back and laughed. He laughed until his body shook and beads of sweat broke out across his forehead. His laughter began to draw the attention of other patrons, which worried Richard. The last thing they needed was someone remembering the drunken fool and relaying their whereabouts to the Buchannan.

"Findley," Richard lowered his voice and drew himself closer to his brother. "Hold care, lad. Ye dunnae want to draw too much attention to yerself." He hoped his brother wasn't so into his cups that he would not heed his warning.

Findley's laughter stopped abruptly, and he drew his body across the table to whisper to Richard. "At this point, Richard, I dunnae give a care in the world what happens to her. Malcolm Buchannan could walk through that door, march up those stairs, throw Maggy over his shoulder, and march out again. I would do nothing to stop him." He shook his head and slowly slid back into his seat.

It was the ale talking and not his brother's true heart. Something Maggy had said had hurt him deeply. Mayhap he had finally told the beautiful lass how he felt, and she had spurned his advances. Richard shook that thought away. Findley would have looked upon that as a challenge. He wouldn't be drinking himself under the table.

"She drives ye to drink, brother. Only love could do that."

"Bah!" Findley drank down the rest of the ale and scanned the room. He wanted to drink himself to the point of forgetting Maggy Boyle altogether. He'd give her the horses and tell her to hie off on her own and see how much luck she had at getting her son back without having to marry Malcolm Buchannan.

"What do ye ken of love, brother?" Findley spat. "'Tis nae love she shows fer me, that much is certain. The lass is tetched, I tell ye, fer nothin' she does or says makes any sense to me. One minute she is as sweet as a spring day and the next? She is yellin' at me as if I am the one who is tetched."

He was slurring his words and swaying in his seat. The ale was doing very little to numb the hurt and pain of his heart. *Why does she think me a coward?*

When the bar wench did not immediately appear with another ale, Findley took his brother's. Richard said nothing, keeping his palms on the table and his eyes on his brother.

Findley drank half the tankard and slammed it down on the table. "A more beautiful woman ye'll never find in all of Scotland. That much I'll give ye. But ye'll also nae find another as tetched!" He could not shake the images of Maggy from his mind. He loved her, and though he said he cared not what happened to her, it was a lie.

Richard remained mute and allowed the ale to loosen his brother's lips. He'd volunteer more information than Richard could gain from interrupting.

"And she smells like heaven, Richard. Heaven. And her lips? Aye, as soft and warm as none like I have ever touched before. And the way she loves her sons, even though four not be her own. Aye, a mother's love like none I have ever witnessed before." He took a deep breath and silently wished he could find more faults other than her wicked temper. His drunken mind searched for flaws other than temper but came up empty. She was perfect in every way. *I be nae drunk enough if I still think she be perfect.*

He slammed back the rest of the ale as the bar wench brought two more tankards. She set them on the table, took the coin Richard offered, and quietly walked away.

"Ye love her," Richard repeated. "And I am beginnin' to believe she loves ye back." Richard was no fool. He had witnessed on more than one occasion how Maggy looked at his brother when she thought no one could see. When the two of them weren't fighting like a pair of cat-o'mountains, they were busy trying to hide the affection they felt for one another. Richard thought them both fools.

"Bah!" Findley retorted. "A woman who loves a man does nae call him a coward!"

Finally, the truth of the matter. Richard's brow creased with confusion as well as disbelief. Mayhap his brother had misunderstood something she had said; for the life of him he could not imagine Maggy saying such a thing.

"Nay," he said, his voice laced with disbelief. "I dunnae believe ye." He took a drink of ale and shook his head.

"'Tis true," Findley said deflated. "She said she would nae forgive me and called me a coward." He sat back in his seat beginning to wish he'd not drunk so much so fast. The room was beginning to spin.

As he clung to the edges of the table to keep from falling out of his seat, Wee William appeared like an apparition. He stood behind Richard and looked puzzled. He needed only a moment to sum up the situation before him.

"What did ye do now, lad?" he asked as he took a seat and caught the eye of the bar wench.

Findley let out a long breath. "Why must everyone assume 'tis me that's done something?"

"Maggy called him a coward," Richard offered as he took another drink.

"Nay!" Wee William said, surprised. "She would never say such a thing."

"'Tis true," Richard offered. It was the only explanation as to why his brother was drinking. Nothing else made sense.

"What did ye do to make her say such a thing?" Wee William asked, looking at Findley as though he were guilty of some tremendous injustice.

"I dunnae ken!" he seethed.

"He keeps sayin' that," Richard offered. "And I am beginnin' to believe he really does nae ken what angered the lass so."

The bar wench brought three tankards of ale and set them on the table. She eyed Wee William up and down approvingly and stared longer than would have been appropriate in any other setting. Wee William ignored the fact that she brushed her bosom against his arm, for he still could not believe Maggy had called Findley, of all people, a coward.

"Well, ye must have said or done something," Wee William said. He took a drink of the cold brew then shook his head. "I cannae imagine Maggy sayin' such a thing. It makes no sense."

Findley shook his head and immediately wished he'd not done so. The room was spinning again. "I swear, as God is me witness, I dunnae ken what I said or did. And I do nae ken why she called me a coward, but she did."

To be called a coward was perhaps the biggest insult that could be thrown at any man, let alone a Highlander. That or to make fun of the size of his manhood. Either insult would be enough to drive any Highlander to drink.

The men stared at each other for a long moment, each lost in his own thoughts. After a time, they simultaneously took long pulls of ale before slamming the empty tankards on the table.

There had to be a plausible explanation as to why Maggy would fly into a rage and hurl such insults at Findley. Wee William ordered another round.

"I have got it!" Richard shouted as he slammed his fist on the table. A broad smile beamed across his face as if he just discovered the lost Ark of the Covenant. He looked tremendously pleased with himself.

Findley blinked several times and tried to get his bearings. Why must the room continue to spin, and what the hell was his brother going on about?

"I ken why the lass behaves so," Richard announced proudly. Wee William gave him a smile that bade him to continue. Findley increased his hold on the table, his stomach suddenly feeling quite unwell.

"Please, by all means, share yer insights, lad," Wee William said as Findley began to keel in his direction. Wee William held up a hand to keep Findley from falling out of his seat.

Richard ignored his brother's distress and took another long drink of ale before sharing his discovery. "It be her time!" Richard said confidently.

Wee William's brow creased in confusion. "Her time fer what?"

Richard's eyes rolled. "Her time," he said as if repeating himself would bring forth more clarity. Wee William stared at him with great confusion. Findley was working hard to keep his eyes open and focused on his brother. He had suddenly grown quite tired and believed he had lost the use of his tongue and perhaps all feelings from his waist down.

Richard shook his head in frustration and let out a low growl. A foster mum and two foster sisters had raised him. He saw now Maggy's attitude and behavior with perfect clarity.

"Ye fools! It be her time of the month."

Wee William's eyebrows raised with understanding. Findley sat swaying, unable to follow the direction Richard was leading. "Time fer what?" he asked before letting lose with a small belch.

Richard sat watching his brother, who was fighting to maintain his balance. Wee William still held onto Findley's shirt with one hand while taking a drink with the other.

"Think on it, brother," Richard spoke slowly. "Do ye nae remember when we lived with Bree and Bridgett? Each month, they would grow weepy-eyed one moment and as angry as a cat-o'mountain the next," he let the words slowly seep into his brother's ale-addled mind.

Richard and Wee William waited patiently for Findley to catch up. Once the explanation found its way through the alcohol-induced fog, he let out a quiet, "Oh."

"'Tis the only explanation," Richard offered, directing his attention back to Wee William. His brother was so far gone that Richard doubted he could remember his own name.

Wee William thought on it for a brief moment. "Aye, I believe ye're right. Maggy be far too sweet and bonny to say anything for the mere pleasure of hurtin' a man's pride."

Both men sat up straighter, growing excited with believing they had figured out why Maggy had called Findley a coward. "Aye, I agree William. I believe that in another day or two, she will be as right as rain and her bonny self once again."

Wee William grew bored with holding Findley up. He looked carefully at his friend and took a few moments to set him straight in his chair. Seeing that he was able, at least for the time being, to sit upright unaided, he let go and turned his attention back to Richard.

"I remember with me own sisters. Och! The trials beautiful women can bestow on a man! I was always careful to tread softly around them during their monthlies."

Richard smiled up at the giant. "That was very thoughtful of you, as a brother I mean."

Wee William shook his head, grabbed what remained of Findley's ale, and drank his fill. "'Twasn't kindness that caused me to tread softly, Richard. 'Twas fear!"

Richard blinked, unwilling to believe for a moment that anything, least of all a woman, could scare Wee William.

Wee William detected the note of doubt in Richard's face. "'Tis true! Remember, Richard, ye only had two sisters to deal with. I had six!"

Richard involuntarily shuddered at the thought of sharing a small house with so many women. He sent a silent prayer up to the good Lord to please bless him with only sons.

"Aye," Wee William said when he saw the realization hit Richard. "Six. Why do ye think I left home at such an early age? 'Twasn't adventure I sought, nor fame or riches. It was to save me own neck! Fer I was certain if I said the wrong thing at the wrong time, och! They'd cut me throat whilst I slept!" It was Wee William's turn to shudder at the memories of his six sisters. He downed the last of the ale, caught the attention of the bar wench, and held up two fingers.

Both Richard and Wee William turned their thoughts inward as they waited for another round of ale. It was Findley who broke through the quiet that had befallen their table.

"What month is the time?" he asked, listing to his left. Wee William rolled his eyes and sat him upright again.

"We will need to show the lass much kindness on the morrow, Wee William," Richard told him.

"Aye, that we must," Wee William offered. "We must also arm ourselves for battle."

"Do ye think 'tis safe to return Findley to his room?" Richard asked, worried if perhaps his brother's life might be at stake, and he'd not see the morrow.

"He will be fine," Wee William said as together he and Richard watched Findley lean first to the right then back to the left. He paused, held up a finger as if to make some point in the matter, closed his eyes, and fell over. He landed with a dull thud on the floor near Wee William's feet.

"As drunk as he is, I doubt he would feel a dagger cross his throat. I doubt he is in any condition to say anything' to get him further into trouble," Richard offered, apparently untroubled by the fact that his brother was lying in a heap at Wee William's feet.

"Better he be too drunk to feel a dagger piercing his skin!" Wee William chuckled.

The men stared at each other for a moment, shrugged their shoulders and decided that mayhap it would be best to quit the inn's tavern and take their fearless leader up to his room.

MAGGY WAS LYING in bed staring up at the dark ceiling, all the while her heart was pounding from worry and guilt. Findley had been gone for quite some time, and she worried that he hadn't gone below stairs to drink away his troubles. Mayhap he had gone to sleep in one of the other rooms with the lads. If he didn't return soon, and if he didn't return well into his cups, then stealing the item from the blacksmith's shop would have all been for naught. She could only pray that her tactic would work on Findley as it had worked on Gawter.

Her hopes rose as she heard the sounds of heavy footsteps and loud whispers coming from the hall outside her door. After a brief moment, someone knocked the secret knock, and she felt her heart fall to her toes. Sending a silent prayer up to the good Lord, she jumped from the bed and raced to the door.

She took a deep breath before opening it. There stood Richard looking quite solemn and Wee William beside him, with Findley thrown over his shoulder, his rear end presented toward Maggy.

Stifling a giggle with one hand, she rested the other on her stomach. Richard cleared his throat. "Maggy," he said. "Findley seems to have had a bit too much to drink."

"If ye do nae want him in yer room, lass, we can toss him in the stables," Wee William offered, looking as though that was what he'd prefer to do.

Maggy bit her bottom lip and shook her head. "Nay, that will nae be necessary. Ye can put him on the bed."

Wee William raised an eyebrow as if to make doubly sure that was what she wanted. Maggy nodded her head and stepped away to allow the men entry.

Wee William tossed Findley onto the bed with a slight grunt. The bed shook and rattled as Findley let out a groan. "Are we under attack?" Findley mumbled.

"Aye, lad, we are," Wee William chuckled. "An attack on yer good senses!"

"Men the send the walls, William!" Findley whispered, raising a hand. "And for the sake of Christ, quit spinnin' the room."

Wee William rolled his eyes, shook his head, and loosened the belt that held Findley's broadsword. With little effort, he pulled the belt from Findley's waist and turned around.

He was about to hand the sword to Maggy when the memory of a wee lass wielding a broadsword a few months ago flashed in his mind. That lass had killed two dozen Englishmen. He had no desire to have the same fate fall on his friend. He hugged the sword to his chest and quickly left the room.

Maggy thought his reaction quite odd, but then most things men did puzzled her. She turned to Richard for an answer but found none.

"Is there anythin' ye need, lass?" Richard offered quietly.

"Nay," Maggy answered.

Richard looked at her thoughtfully. "Are ye certain? For if there's anything ye need, I can send the innkeeper's wife up to ye."

Maggy's brow creased with confusion. "Nay, Richard. There is nothing I need other than sleep."

Richard nodded his head as if he were in complete understanding. "Well, I am right next door if ye need anything." He nodded toward his sleeping brother. "And if he gets to be too much to handle, just cry out, and we will be here in the blink of an eye."

With a tilt of her head and a chuckle, Maggy said, "He be not the first man in his cups that I have ever dealt with, Richard."

Richard started to say something but thought better of it. With a slight bow, he quit her room, quietly closing the door behind him.

While she was relieved that her plan had worked, she still felt quite guilty over what she had done and was about to do. Her plan was falling into place quite nicely, but she still felt ashamed for having called Findley a coward. She knew he was anything but a coward. Hours ago it had seemed the only course of action.

Maggy quietly stepped toward the bed and stared down at Findley. He was such a large man and took up nearly all the bed. Moonlight streamed in through the window and across this face. Och, but he was handsome!

Her stomach tightened with excitement, making her curse under her breath. If she allowed the feelings she was having for Findley to grow, she knew her heart would end up as broken as her spirit. Under no circumstance could she allow herself to fall in love with Findley McKenna.

She reached into the fur she had placed under the bed earlier and retrieved her stolen item. It felt cold and heavy in her hands. As she stood over Findley she began to have second thoughts on what she was about to do.

Had he been a more reasonable person, she wouldn't be forced to take this course of action, she argued with herself. He had no one but himself to blame for what was about to happen.

Without thinking, she reached out and touched his cheek with her fingertips. What she would not do to change the events of the past weeks. Part of her wished she had never met Findley McKenna, but a deeper part of her was glad for knowing him.

As she struggled with her own conscience, Findley rolled his head and opened his eyes. With a start, she pulled her trembling hand away and hid the item behind her skirts.

A smile came to his lips and he looked at her through sleepy lids. "There ye are, lass," he whispered drunkenly. "The most beautiful woman I have ever laid eyes to."

Maggy straightened herself and felt her heart swell with something she wished she did not feel. She tried to convince herself that it was the drink that made him speak so sweetly. He'd never say such things in the light of day and with a clear mind.

"Maggy Boyle," Findley whispered as he took a deep breath. "The most beautiful woman in all of Scotland." He closed his eyes, but his smile did not fade, instead, seemed to grow as if he were dreaming of something quite wonderful.

"To have ye as me own for all the rest of me days would make me complete," he said in such a soft voice that it brought tears to her eyes. She tried to convince herself that she'd not heard him correctly. No one had ever said such things to her, drunk or sober. Mayhap the drink had loosened his tight rein on his feelings, and he was speaking from his true heart.

Nay! She scolded herself. She swallowed hard and wished fate had dealt her a much different hand. If only she had met Findley years ago, before her life had the chance to change so dramatically.

She choked back more tears and wiped those that had escaped with her fingertips. Convincing herself she had no other choice, she willed herself not to confess all her secrets to him and to move forward with her plan. Everything she was about to do was for Ian.

Maggy rested a knee on the edge of the bed. Through the darkness she whispered softly to Findley. "Please forgive me for what I am about to do."

CHAPTER EIGHTEEN

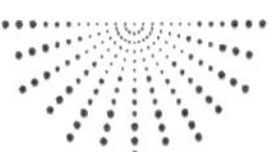

'Twas a dream from which he had no desire to wake. Maggy's plump derrière rested snuggly against his thighs as he had one arm wrapped tightly around her waist. He held onto her as if he was afraid of drowning, and she was the only thing that kept him afloat. She fit into his body as if God had designed her specifically for that delightful purpose.

He was drifting along quite comfortably in that state between dreaming and wakefulness, and he had no desire to leave. Sunbeams broke through the small window, and Findley could feel the warmth on his skin. But nothing warmed his body or his heart as much as the feeling of holding Maggy; 'twas a blissful, heady experience that he wanted never to end.

He pulled her closer, clinging to her as if she were the only reason for breathing. A warm smile curved his lips when he heard a contented sigh come from the woman he loved more than life itself.

Unable to resist the urge and still believing he was adrift in a beautiful dream, he kissed the top of her head. Unsatisfied and needing more, he kissed her temple, then her cheek. He could not resist the urge to kiss her lips, for he knew them to be sweet, full, soft, and warm.

He never wanted to wake, for in his dream he was kissing Maggy, and she was not running away. The kisses brought life to an otherwise dying soul and made him feel alive and loved. Her kisses were his salvation.

"Maggy," his throat was dry and husky from sleep. "Ye fill me heart."

Whether it was the sound of his own voice that broke through the heavy fog of sleep or the sound of Maggy's hitched breath, he did not know. But one of those things crashed through the fog, and soon he realized he did not dream. She really was lying next to him, returning him kiss for kiss.

A small, irritating voice began to rise in the back of his mind, and it gave warning: Ye must guard yer heart as well as hers.

He told the tiny voice to go jump from the tallest cliff, for Maggy was here, next to him. And if her rapid breathing and returned kisses were any indication, she was as happy to be there as he was to have her.

The desperate desire to make her his, to tell her he loved her and wanted to spend the rest of his days with her, filled him to the marrow.

When he brought his left hand down to caress her cheek, her own hand followed. Mayhap he had slept on his hand wrong, for it felt odd and heavy. His bladder felt just as heavy from all the ale he had drunk the night before.

"Findley!" She was struggling for air. "Please."

He was not sure if her pleas bade him to continue or to stop. He opened his eyes only to see hers filled with fright. He was relieved to see that she did not look angry, but her fearful expression told him all that he needed to know. While she, too, might be wanting the same thing he did at the moment, she was afraid. Of him or of what might happen if they did not control themselves – his heart wouldn't allow him to answer the question.

He loved her. He could find no fault with the lass being afraid. She was a widow and a mum of five boys, and he knew she had much to be frightened over.

He swallowed hard before speaking, choosing his words carefully, for the last thing he wanted to do was spoil this moment. "I be sorry Maggy," he began. "Ye seem to bring out the best and the worst of me."

His lips curved upward when he saw the relief in her eyes and her shoulders relax. He lifted his hand to caress her cheek, and as he was about to reveal the secrets of his heart to her, he caught notice of something out of the corner of his eye.

Perplexed and disbelieving what he was seeing, he squeezed his eyes shut, shook his head twice before opening them again. It was still there. He stared for a long moment before looking at Maggy. She was chewing on her bottom lip and attempting to look innocent.

Anger swelled from deep within his stomach as his eyes went from his wrist to her face and back again. He growled before pushing himself upward and rolled out of the bed. Maggy squealed as she was pulled along with him.

"Findley!" she exclaimed. "Please be careful!"

He heard Wee William's voice in the back of his mind warning him to show care and be gentle with the lass. Silently, he told Wee William to jump from the same cliff he had sent his inner voice to minutes ago.

"What in God's teeth have ye done?!" His deep voice boomed and echoed off the walls of the small bedchamber. He towered over Maggy and thrust his hands to his hips. Her right hand followed his left.

He caught the faint flicker of fear in her eyes before she righted herself and stood taller. "If ye'll calm down, I can explain it to ye." She hoped he hadn't detected her fear.

Findley yanked his left arm up to dangle in front of her eyes. Her right arm followed his. There they were, plain as day. Wrist irons. Heavy, black wrist irons shackling the two of them together.

"Where is the key?" He spoke slowly, through clenched teeth.

"Please, Findley," she pleaded. "If ye'll let me explain."

"Maggy, I warn ye, if ye do nae give me the key this verra minute, I'll nae be responsible fer me actions!" His anger threatened to explode like a pot of stew left unattended over the heat of a fire. As did his bladder.

Maggy swallowed hard. An image of Gawter flashed through her mind, and she felt herself shrinking. Giving her head a shake, she remained silent and prayed that Findley would not show his anger in the same manner as Gawter would have.

Findley took a deep breath. "Maggy, I be in no mood for games. Where is the key?" It wasn't a request but a demand.

She swallowed hard again before throwing her shoulders back. "There be no key."

Findley stared at her and did not believe her for even the briefest moment. "Ye lie." He needed to be free of the shackles for many reasons. The most pressing was the need to relieve his bladder.

She was lying, but she wasn't about to admit it. The key was safely secured in a pocket she had sewn into her shift the night before.

"When I took the wrist irons I did nae see a key," she said, lifting her chin and tossing back her shoulders.

Findley began to pace the floor of the small room with his mind racing and his head pounding as a result of far too much ale the night before. Maggy was forced to follow closely as there were not but six inches of iron links separating the two of them.

"If ye'd only listen to reason for a moment," she began before Findley stopped abruptly.

He spun around to his left, which in turn pulled Maggy behind him. For several moments, they went around in circles looking very much like a dog chasing his tail.

Finally, Findley stopped, got his bearings, and turned to loom over her. There was no disguising the fury that flared in his eyes. Maggy began to tremble, feeling a little unsure that he wouldn't lash out at her.

"Reason?" he seethed. "Ye think this—," he held up their joined wrists in front of her face, "—be reasonable?"

"I needed a way to get ye to listen to me!" Maggy stomped her foot.

Findley growled. "Lass, ye've had plenty of opportunity to speak with me. Ye did nae have to resort to wrist irons!"

"Aye, ye'd listen, but then ye'd do whatever ye wanted!"

"And what is that supposed to mean?" he asked, thrusting his hands to his hips, giving Maggy a jolt. She pulled her hand back angrily.

"Ye were plannin' on leavin' us with the monks!"

Findley's brow creased as he tilted his head. "Where did ye hear that?"

"From yer verra lips, Findley McKenna! I heard ye talkin' to Wee William, so do nae deny it."

Findley took a deep breath and wished he were still below stairs drinking ale. Lots of ale. He was not a drinking man, but this lass was quickly driving him to addiction. His aching bladder and pounding head warned against the idea.

"I ken ye would nae listen to me and were going to leave me behind." Maggy's voice softened. "And I have no intentions of being left behind with strangers, in the abbey no less, while ye go and get Ian back. I want to help."

"I leave ye behind fer yer own good, Maggy. 'Tis nae a punishment, 'tis fer yer own safety and the safety of yer other sons." His head was beginning to pound mercilessly.

"Nay," her jaw tightened. "'Tis because ye're a man, and ye think because I be a woman, I be too weak and muddle-headed to help!"

"I be glad ye're able to read me mind and heart on the matter, Maggy! Weak? Nay, I dunnae think ye're weak. But muddle-headed? I am beginnin' to believe that," he said, dangling the evidence before her eyes once again. "Now give me the bloody key!" He raised his voice again, more from the intense pain growing in his side. If he didn't undo the shackles soon, he would burst.

"I'll nae be left behind," she told him, trying to sound determined and strong.

Findley was growing weary with arguing. "Ye be goin' nowhere but the abbey! And ye'll stay there 'til I come back with yer son!"

"I'll do no such thing!" She stomped her foot for added emphasis.

"Ye will!"

"I will no'!"

"Maggy, I need ye to give me the key, and I need it now," he was practically begging. It was his achingly full bladder making him speak softly. He needed the key, and he needed relief.

Tossing her shoulders back and lifting her chin she stared up at him with fierce determination. "I told ye, I do nae have the key."

Findley took a step toward her. "Ye dunnae understand, lass," he spoke through clenched teeth. "I have a need to do somethin' that I do nae need ye witness to."

Her brow furrowed in puzzlement. "Ye're tryin' to trick me," she accused.

"I can assure ye that 'tis no trick," he told her.

She refused to be bullied or tricked into giving up the key. "Nay," she told him firmly.

His bladder ached to be emptied, and his head continued to pound. He was done with arguing or trying to reason with her. "As ye wish, lass." He smiled, gave her a slight bow, and then dragged her along to the corner table. He retrieved the chamber pot, crossed the room in four steps and placed it upon the chair.

Maggy's eyes grew wide with shock. "Ye dunnae mean to-"

Findley cut her off as he undid his belt and loosed the ties on his trews. "Aye, I do!" he said, smiling down at her triumphantly.

"Ye cannae do that whilst I stand here!" she argued and pulled her hand away. She was beginning to question her own thinking. She had not planned on what they might do when natural bodily functions might need addressing.

"I asked ye nicely fer the key, lass," he said jerking his hand back to free his appendage from his trews.

Maggy pulled her hand back, appalled with his lack of good manners and the audacity he had to relieve himself while she stood next to him.

Findley pulled his hand back once again and with a devilish smile, he said, "It takes two hands to hold on to it, lass." He winked, smiled more broadly, and let loose with a happy and relieved sigh.

Maggy stood with mouth agape and eyes wide with shock. How

dare he do something so, so…she searched for an apt word but found none. He was arrogant beyond measure!

She tried keeping her eyes pinned to the fireplace, the ceiling, the floor – anywhere but there. The sound of what he was doing echoed through the small room, and it seemed to be taking an inordinate amount of time for him to finish. She was relieved when she heard him stop, but the relief was short lived, for he started again.

It went on like that for what seemed like an eternity. Stop and go, stop and go, heavy sigh and chuckles. He was enjoying the torment he brought her. He would not feel guilty, for he had asked nicely for the key.

As she stood with her shoulder brushing his arm, she waited impatiently and tapped her foot. She tried looking for something to focus on, but it was impossible. When she glanced up at his face, she saw the devilishly pleased way in which he was staring back at her.

Maggy scowled, pursed her lips together, and turned to look at the wall. Her plan had seemed flawless when it had first popped into her mind. She had been fully prepared to keep the key hidden and Findley shackled to her until they arrived in Aberdeen. How pleased she had been with herself the moment she hid the wrist irons in her pocket. It had been difficult to contain her excitement over the prospect of showing Findley that he wasn't nearly as smart as he believed himself to be.

But not once in all her mental meanderings did the thought of how they would tend to nature's bidding ever enter her mind. She could kick herself for not having thought the plan out more fully.

"Are ye done now with this foolishness?" he asked her.

Maggy looked at him from the corner of her eye to assure herself that he had returned himself to a more decent state of being. Seeing his clothing put back to rights, she turned her gaze to his. While his face looked less pained than it had minutes ago, he still looked quite angry.

"I'll nae let ye leave me here, Findley. I'll find a way out of the abbey. I'll walk all the way to Aberdeen if I must."

None of the events over the past several days gave him any reason to believe otherwise. She was a strong, independent, and determined woman. He shook his head, disgusted with himself for not having left her in Renfrew. He imagined that if there were a way of depositing her on the moon, she would still find a way to Aberdeen.

Maggy Boyle had a secret, mayhap more. She was also very determined. He prayed the combination wouldn't be deadly. He took a deep breath and let it out slowly.

"Fine," he said through gritted teeth. "If ye chose to be unreasonable, then far be it from me to stop ye."

Maggy eyed him for a moment, distrust awash in those deep green eyes. "Ye mean to take us to Aberdeen then?" she asked.

"Aye, I do," he nodded. "Now, please, unlock the shackles."

Maggy shook her head. "Nay, I dunnae believe ye, Findley. Ye mean to trick me, have me undo the shackles, tie me to the bed, and hie off without me."

"While I find that thought pleasin', I would do no such thing." A wry smile came to his face, and his eyes twinkled playfully. Her heart fluttered when he looked at her that way. So devilishly handsome and so sure of himself.

They stood staring at one another for a long while. It was Maggy who broke the silence. "So, ye dunnae believe me, and I dunnae believe ye."

Findley ran his hand across his chin. "Aye. It appears we are at a standstill."

"I'll nae allow ye to leave us behind."

"I said I would take ye to Aberdeen," Findley said, standing a bit taller as if to brace himself for more of her ire.

"I ken what ye said, but I dunnae believe ye."

"Ye've no intention of unlocking the shackles, do ye?"

Maggy thrust her chin upward. "I told ye, I dunnae have the key."

Findley growled, ran his hand through his hair, and let out an exasperated sigh. He had never met a more vexing woman!

"Fine, lass! If ye choose to be unreasonable and difficult, I'll nae deny ye!" Stomping to the bed, pulling her behind him, he sat down and reached for his boots. "Ye'll be at my side, as ye wish, lass. Where I go, ye go, so keep that in mind."

He forcefully tugged on one boot before turning to the other. "And ye'll no be complainin' over it! Ye'll remain quiet at all times and not be interjecting yerself into any conversations I may have with anyone."

He stood up, pulling her along with him. "And if anyone asks what these are all about," he raised his shackled hand as if to remind her they were still bound together, "'tis me who has done the shacklin' and nae the other way around. Do ye understand the way of it?"

Maggy could feel the heat rise to her cheeks, and she wasn't at all certain that she didn't feel the heat of his anger emanating from his body. She wondered if part of his anger wasn't from embarrassment for her outwitting him. Tamping down a bit of pride over that possibility, she stood unwavering in front of him.

Momentarily forgetting she was shackled to him, she tried crossing her arms over her chest. Her cheeks flamed again when his hand brushed against her bosom before she quickly shoved her arms back to her sides.

"I have a few demands of me own, Findley McKenna," she began. "Ye'll be respectful to me at all times, and ye'll nae be dragging and jerkin' me around as if I am a sack of leeks." Her wrist was already beginning to ache from all the yanking, and she knew it would be bruised before the hour was out.

With pursed lips and angry eyes, he remained quiet. It would have taken very little effort on his part to remove the shackles. Instead, he chose to play along with her ridiculous notion. He wondered if the longer they were shackled together, the better would be his chances of winning her heart and learning her secrets.

It angered him that, as vexing and frustrating as she could be at times, he still wanted her. Not just her magnificent body, but her heart as well. Not just for a day but for the rest of his days.

I have lost me mind! He could only hope that once they rescued Ian, she wouldn't always be so trying. Mayhap as a wife, she'd do better to control her tongue and her temper.

Something told him, and most likely it was the harsh scowl she was giving him at that particular moment, that a Maggy Boyle with a controlled tongue and temper was as likely as a man someday walking on the moon. Neither event was ever likely to happen.

WEE WILLIAM MADE no attempt to hide his amusement when Findley began to explain why he was shackled to Maggy. The man laughed so hard that tears came to his eyes, and he grew dizzy. Each time he thought his laughter had settled, he'd take one look at Findley's angry and embarrassed face standing next to the very proud Maggy Boyle, and the laughter would return.

As far as Wee William was concerned, Maggy Boyle was a force to be reckoned with, and Findley should simply surrender. Findley was doomed.

When Richard and Patrick saw the shackles and the proud smile on Maggy's face and the fury on Findley's, more laughter ensued. Nearly a half an hour was given to the men's laughter, followed by another quarter hour of the lads joining in.

Findley had reached the limits of his patience. "To the devil with the lot of ye," he told them calmly. "We leave within the hour."

He abruptly left them, pulling Maggy behind him. She let out a squeal that he pretended to ignore. Once they were back in their room, he ordered her to pack.

There was no choice but for him to observe, for he was bound to it, so to speak. While Maggy carefully folded and packed the few possessions she owned, Findley held open the bag impatiently. His gut told him he wasn't going to survive being shackled to her. Mayhap the best thing would be to ask one of his men to run him through with a sword. It couldn't be more painful than the humiliation of what she'd done.

He was growing to admire her tenacity, and that fact made him angrier. How would he be a good husband to her if he allowed her to rule him as if he were as weak as a lamb? How could he hold his head up around his men, or anyone else for that matter?

He caught a glimpse of the lovely ice-blue gown that lay in the bottom of the bag. "Why do ye nae wear the blue gown?" The question escaped his lips before he had a chance to keep the thought to himself.

Without looking at him, Maggy answered. "'Tis a special gown, and I be savin' it fer a special occasion."

"Such as?" He cursed his tongue for apparently having a mind of its own. He had no desire for small talk, but his tongue would not listen. Whenever he was near her, his good senses seemed to run away.

"I dunnae ken," was her curt response. "I doubt I'll ever have a need to wear it, but I'll treasure it all the same."

His heart swelled with pride over the fact that she would want to keep some treasure, some memento of their time together. He hoped that when their journey was over and mission complete, he might have a chance to see her wear it. Mayhap on their wedding day, he thought briefly before pushing the thought aside. He was furious with her, but for some cursed reason, his thoughts would meander to making her his wife. He cursed his heart and could not wait for this to be over.

While he longed to make her his, something in the back of his head told him that the chances of her accepting a proposal of marriage were right up there with his man on the moon and a tempered Maggy theories. His list of things that would probably never happen seemed to be growing by the hour.

"Where do we head for today, Findley?" she asked as she pulled the strings on her bag, cinching it closed.

"Dundee," he answered softly.

Maggy's spirits lifted. "I have a brother in Dundee," she told him, still fidgeting with the strings on the bag. She didn't want to look into those dark brown eyes, for she knew her legs would quiver at the sight of them. But she took a deep breath and drew herself up. She'd need to be strong if her heart were to survive this ordeal.

"He owns three ships. He is a good man, and I ken he will help us," she told him. That is, if he can overcome the shock of learning I be nae dead. Aye, Roald would be glad to learn she had not perished with the rest of her clan. Though it would be quite a shock, Roald would understand the reasons behind her deception.

Maggy finally glanced up at Findley. Her heart skipped a beat, and her legs felt weak. Those brown eyes would surely be her undoing, for they seemed to burn right into her heart.

Oh, how she wished she could trust him enough to tell him everything. Mayhap after they had Ian back, she could explain the way of things. She prayed Findley was honorable enough to forgive her for keeping so many secrets from him.

BEING SHACKLED to Findley proved harder than she had imagined. She was forced to ride balanced on the saddle in front of him. Far too close for the comfort of her heart or her mind.

It was so very tempting to rest her head against his warm chest, but she denied herself that delight. She did her best to keep their conversations to a minimum. Remaining distant and quiet would help steel her heart against the feelings that were growing with each beat of her heart.

Unwittingly, Findley assisted in her endeavor. He was grouchy and ill-tempered most of the first day. His mood made it nearly impossible for anyone to be fond of him. Even the lads did their best to stay clear of him.

The most difficult thing for Maggy to get used to was answering nature's calls with an audience. Whenever she was tempted to undo the shackles for a bit of privacy, she would think of Ian. Each time she thought of how terrified her son must be and all that he was going through, the images helped strengthen her resolve. *I am doing this for Ian,* she would remind herself.

As much as she hated to admit it, she did enjoy sleeping next to Findley. The warmth from his body and the way he would pull her close while he slept filled her heart with a sense of happiness as well as longing. She felt happy, content, and safe when wrapped in his arms. But she knew it would all end soon. When this was over, they'd each be forced to go their separate ways.

The closer they got to Dundee, the heavier her heart felt. It would not take long for word to spread that she and Liam were still alive. Once her secrets began to unravel, her life would never be the same.

As they rode along the second day, through a heavy, dense fog, she thought of the three people who had helped keep her secrets safe. Her maids, Claire and Kate, and her guard, George. Over the years, they had become her second family. George had been like a father to her and Claire and Kate more like the sisters she never had than the servants they were.

George knew how mean Gawter could be, and there had been a time or two he had intervened to pull Gawter off Maggy. Had George not stepped in, heaven only knew how badly the beating would have ended for her. Had it not been for George's interventions, Maggy felt she would have been dead a long time ago.

The lies that had kept her safe these past years had begun late at night, just hours after Gawter's death. George had come to Maggy's room with worry etched into his auld face. He did not grieve the loss of his earl. Instead, he worried over what would become of Maggy.

"M'lady, ye ken that after ye're mournin', Laird Brockton will have ye married off," he whispered as they sat near the fireplace. "I fear ye may get ye a husband even worse than the one ye already had."

Claire and Kate had voiced their worries as well. 'Twas Kate who fretted over the three boys Maggy had taken in after the deaths of their parents. As she sat on a stool next to Maggy, Kate whispered, her voice full of fear and concern, "Yer new husband could send the lads away, m'lady. A new husband might not care where the poor lads go!" Tears had dripped from Kate's young eyes.

Maggy knew her friends were right. Gawter's uncle would not care about the kind of man he would marry Maggy off to. Laird Brockton would do anything he could to keep his hands on Liam's inheritance. There was no doubt in Maggy's mind that Brockton would marry her off to someone eager to share in the fortune and power left by Gawter's death and all too willing to keep a tight rein on Maggy's spirit.

Their plan was born in the very early morning hours, while the rest of the castle was fast asleep. George, Kate, and Claire would spread word that Maggy and the boys had come down with the pox. They would quarantine them against the rest of the castle.

After so many deaths, no one would question the quarantine. Those people lucky enough to avoid the pox up to that point would be all too happy to stay clear of anyone afflicted with it. After a few days, they would sadly announce to the rest of the castle that Maggy and the boys were dead. Those few days had offered George plenty of time to ready their escape.

After hiding them in a hay cart, George quietly took Maggy and the boys away from the castle. That quiet morning had begun the start of their new lives. It also began Maggy's search for her lost spirit and heart.

Maggy could not find it in her to grieve the loss of her husband, but she did mourn for her people. More than two thirds of her clan had died before she fled into the Highlands. George would visit as often as he was able, bringing them what supplies he could pilfer from the dwindling larders of the castle. Sometimes he brought survivors with him; people with no one left to care for them. They were the very auld, who amazingly enough had survived only to have their grown sons and daughters and grandchildren fall victim to the horrible disease.

On one of those occasions, he brought Collin, who would become her fifth son. During the first six months, Maggy's new little clan had grown to some thirty people. After that, there was no one else for George to bring. The younger and healthier people lucky enough to survive had moved on to other parts of Scotland. As far as Maggy knew, no one ever questioned her death or the deaths of the boys.

Everything had gone well enough in the beginning. Maggy and her clan had built a home a good five days' ride from her former castle. She had planted a large garden and tended to the auld. She helped the boys grieve the loss of their families while building a new one. It had by no means been easy, but living hand-to-mouth was far better than being thrust into another arranged and loveless marriage.

Before Maggy realized it, another day of riding had passed. Findley pulled rein, bringing her out of her quiet reverie. "We will camp here for the night," he told her as he helped her down from the horse before he dismounted.

Maggy looked around their surroundings. They were making camp in a small clearing in the middle of a forest. Riding through the country was beginning to take its toll on her. Every muscle in her body ached. She wondered how many more days they'd be living out of doors.

She also wondered if she'd be able to go back into hiding again. Once word spread that they were alive, would she be able to retreat into the shadows? Run and hide for the rest of her days or allow herself to be married off? She didn't like either option. But living on the run, hiding from the world, was far more palatable than ending up in another loveless marriage to a cruel and heartless man.

Wee William took Robert and Collin to hunt for meat for their dinner. Richard and Patrick worked with starting a fire, sending the other boys off to gather firewood.

"Maggy, would ye like to help me get water?" Findley asked sarcastically.

Maggy rolled her eyes. "Does bein' daft come natural to ye, Findley? Or is it somethin' ye must work at?"

Richard and Patrick chuckled as they pulled packs from their horses. "'Tis like they be already married," Patrick offered.

Richard nodded his head. "Aye, 'tis like gettin' a glimpse into the future."

"Do ye think Findley sees it?"

Richard lowered his voice to a whisper. "Nay, he is too struck by her beauty and nae thinkin' with his head."

Patrick nodded his head. "I believe ye're right," he began. "It has been the downfall of many a good man who thinks with something other than his brain."

Findley shot a scathing look at his men, which in turn brought wry smiles to each man's face. Findley grabbed empty water bladders from the back of his horse. Without warning, he began to stomp away, pulling Maggy behind him.

She'd learned over the last few days not to bother with complaining, for her words would fall on deaf ears. Findley was fond of reminding her that she was in this predicament by her own choosing. She could get out of it at any time by producing the key he knew she had hidden on her person. Maggy was not about to do that.

Findley pulled her along through the trees in search of water. They walked in silence for a good distance before finding a narrow stream that cut through the forest. Findley stomped toward it, ignoring Maggy's grunts and sighs of exasperation.

He knelt down and pulled the stopper from the bladder before thrusting it into the cold water. He was beginning to grow quite weary of the woman attached to his wrist. He made a silent promise that once they reached Dundee, the first thing he'd do would be to find a blacksmith who would be able to break the shackles.

As he silently fumed and cursed his situation, Maggy let out a slow breath and leaned toward the stream. She began splashing the frigid water on her face. The shock of cold water caused her to gasp and shudder.

Findley studied her closely for a moment. Her face was beautiful. Tiny droplets of water hung to her lashes, and more drops fell from her chin. When she was finished, she sat back and drew her knees up to her chest and stared off into the distance.

She was going to be the death of him. No matter how hard he tried to stay angry with her, one look at that beautiful face and those deep green eyes caused him to lose what remained of his common sense and logic. Surmising he had lost his mind completely, he threw all caution to the wind and grabbed her.

He pulled her close, giving her no time to object, and slanted his lips across hers. He growled low in his throat as he kissed her thoroughly and passionately.

There was no resistance on Maggy's part. She let loose with a growl of her own before melting into him, lost in the heat of the moment. She wrapped her free hand around his neck, holding on for fear he would stop. Why on earth did she lose her good senses whenever his lips touched hers? Why did he have this effect on her heart and head?

The longer he kissed her, the more he wanted to make her his wife. He could not fight the feelings that had been building for months. He was falling victim to his own heart.

He knew that if he did not stop kissing her now, he'd not be able to stop.

'Twas quite difficult to think of anything else with her pressed so closely to his chest, her mouth demanding more of his. Before he lost himself into the abyss of passion, he pulled away. He wanted her. All of her. But not like this, not until he knew he'd won her heart and made her his wife.

Keeping his eyes closed, he took long, deep breaths and tried to regain his composure. Resting his forehead against hers, he searched for the right words to express what his heart felt.

"Maggy," he said, his voice husky with desire. "Marry me."

She was certain she had misunderstood him. "What?"

"Marry me," he repeated. He didn't have the courage to open his eyes to see her reaction.

Marry him? Her mind raced, knowing full well it would be impossible to marry him. There were too many reasons why she could not say yes, no matter what her heart begged for.

"Findley," she began, searching desperately for a way explain why she could not give in to the temptation.

When he finally found the courage to open his eyes, disappointment filled his stomach. She needn't say it aloud. He could see her answer simply by looking into her tear-filled green eyes.

"Why?" he asked her.

"Why what?" she whispered, still holding tightly to his tunic. She did not want to let him go, not now, not ever.

"Why will ye nae marry me?" he asked.

She stammered and fought back tears. How could she explain it without breaking his heart? Without revealing all of her secrets?

She took a deep breath and steeled herself. "There are many reasons why I can no', Findley."

There was hope in that statement. She hadn't said she didn't want to marry him, only that she couldn't. "And what might those reasons be?"

As much as she wanted to tell him everything, she couldn't. Remaining silent, she looked away, feeling ashamed as well as angry. Ashamed that she felt she could not confide in him and angry for the lot life had dealt her.

"I ken there's much ye're nae tellin' me Maggy. Why do ye nae trust me enough to allow me to help ye?"

She swallowed hard. "I dunnae trust anyone, Findley."

Her words stung. "Why? Ye trust me enough to get Ian back fer ye, but ye'll nae trust me beyond that. Why?"

She knew if she looked up into those dark brown eyes, she'd be lost in them. "Findley, ye dunnae understand."

"Ye're right," he said as his anger began to return. "I dunnae understand many things. Do ye think I am not intelligent enough to understand? Do ye think I be too daft? Too weak?"

She still couldn't look up at him. "Nay, 'tis nae that."

"Then what?" He was growing exasperated.

"I cannaee tell ye." She swallowed hard.

"Do ye think me too much of a coward?" His jaw tightened.

Her head shot up to look him in the eyes. Guilt washed over her.

"Nay!" she told him. "I only said that to-"

He placed his fingertip on her lips to stop her. The look of guilt blended with sincerity told him she told the truth. Fighting a chuckle, he said, "'Ye angered me on purpose to get me to drink that night."

She couldn't deny it. "Aye, I did," she answered before taking a deep cleansing breath.

"Ye did it so ye could put these on me," he said, dangling the shackles between them.

"Aye. 'Twas that or a sleepin' powder."

He tilted his head, admiring her tenacity as well as her honesty. "Pray tell, where would ye get a sleepin' powder?"

A sly smile came to her lips. "I'll nae divulge that to ye, Findley. I may still have a need fer it."

Findley shook his head and returned her smile. "I see. Ye wilna marry me, but ye've nothin' against getting me drunk or givin' me a sleepin' powder?"

Her eyes widened, and she began to protest. "Now, Findley," she began before he stopped her again with his fingertip.

"Haud yer wheest, lassie," he told her. "If I didnae ken better, I would think ye did want to marry me. After all, ye've shackled yerself to me, literally." He dangled his wrist again.

Her lips drew into a hard line. "I didnae shackle meself to ye, I shackled ye to me so ye could nae get away."

He nodded his head thoughtfully. "'Tis the same thing. Ye did nae want me gettin' away. I think ye shackled me under false pretenses. 'Twas nae to keep me from leavin' ye behind. I think ye love me and do nae want me far from ye."

He smiled down at her, attempting to goad her into an admission she'd die before giving. "Nay!" she protested. "I dunnae love ye!" she hissed. "And ye're daft if ye think it!"

Findley threw his head back and laughed. "Lass, ye can deny it all ye want, but I'll nae believe ye." He touched the tip of her nose with his finger. "Ye love me. And what is there nae to love about me?" He spread his arms out wide. "I be a handsome man with a kind heart and a good disposition. I be strong as well. And I am verra, verra honorable."

"Do nae forget to mention arrogant, pig-headed, foolish, daft, and an eejit!" she retorted.

"So, ye agree that I be handsome?" he teased.

"Nay! I never said that, I won't ever say that about ye!" She might well think it, but she'd never admit it aloud.

"But ye do nae deny it?"

"Deny what?"

"That ye find me handsome?"

She growled at him. "Findley McKenna, ye are the most arrogant, self-centered, egotistical, illogical, foolish man I have ever ken in me life!"

"But ye do nae deny my handsomeness?"

Forgetting they were tethered together, she shot to her feet in an attempt to get away from him, but she was yanked backward. Pulled into Findley's chest, she gasped when his hand wrapped around her waist. He wouldn't relinquish his hold on her.

His hot breath brushed over her ear as he whispered to her. "I think ye're beautiful." He nibbled her earlobe and could not deny the satisfaction he felt when she gasped and sank into his chest.

She could not allow her attraction to Findley to interfere with her plans. It was much easier on her heart when he was angry with her. Moments like these, when he was being sweet and horribly romantic, made her forget her mission and who she was.

"I demand that ye stop," she whispered as she offered him more of her neck.

He nuzzled her neck, and in between soft, warm kisses that sent jolts of excitement coursing through her body, he said, "Nay. I like the way your breath hitches when I kiss ye."

She damned her body and heart for responding so eagerly. *I need to keep me wits about me!* The only time she felt in control of her good senses was when she thought of her sons. Maggy willed her mind in that direction and an image of Ian popped into her mind.

Gathering her strength and resolve, she twisted out of his grasp. "Findley, I said nay!"

She was determined not to allow him to dissuade her or distract her. "Do nae kiss me again."

The anger in her eyes was like a splash of cold water on his lustful thoughts. *Why must she deny her feelings for him?* Findley decided that, one way or another, he'd work all of her secrets out of her. Believing anything was possible and they could overcome whatever obstacles, real or imagined, he took a deep breath and chose his words carefully.

"Ye cannae deny how ye feel when I touch ye, Maggy."

Anger simmered in her eyes. "Do nae tell me how I feel."

"Give me the key," he demanded quietly.

"I dunnae have a key."

Her fingers clutched at her skirts, and Findley knew the key was hidden somewhere among them. Though he was half tempted to wrestle her to the ground, he would not be riffling through her skirts unless she were to invite him to do so.

"Ye're an exasperatin' woman! Ye shackle yerself to me, forcin' me to drag ye to Aberdeen! Ye trust me enough to get yer Ian back, but ye'll no trust me with yer secrets!" He was yelling at her and didn't care at all if he was about to hurt her feelings. "Is this the kind of treatment ye inflicted on yer first husband? Did ye drive him mad as well? Did ye make him beg fer yer affections?" he demanded, dangling the shackles in front of her face again.

Maggy's hand flew up before she could stop and landed a hard smack against his face. She felt instantly guilty but was too furious to apologize. Findley had no idea what kind of marriage she had suffered with Gawter. He couldn't have known, for she had refused to share any of her past with him. But that fact did not stop her from being hurt by his words.

In truth, it had been the other way around. It had been Maggy who begged for her husband's attention, at least in the beginning. After so many years of begging and pleading with him, she finally realized Gawter would never look at her as anything more than the woman who bore his legitimate heir. Gawter would never love her. He barely acknowledged her existence, and he found his comforts in the arms and the heart of another woman.

"Do nae speak to me again, Findley, of things ye ken nothin' about! I would nae marry ye now if ye were the last man on the face of this earth!" She choked back stinging tears.

His cheek stung, as did his pride. "As ye wish, Maggy!" he bellowed before taking a deep breath and lowering his voice. "Ye may keep yer bloody secrets. I formally withdraw my earlier proposal. Ye can do as ye wish. Once we get Ian back, ye can go yer own way and I'll go mine."

The thought of never seeing him again clawed at her heart and made her stomach churn with regret and sadness. Silently, she cursed fate, her dead husband, her parents, and everything else that had brought her to this point in her life.

She looked into Findley's eyes and saw his torment. Oh, how she wished she could take the pain away from his heart by giving him hers. But it was not meant to be, no matter how much she wished and prayed for it to be different. Findley shook his head at her. He picked up the full water bladders and led her back to the camp.

Maggy walked behind him, not wanting him to see the tears that fell down her cheeks. Through no fault of her own, any freedom to choose her own way, her own destiny, had been ripped from her grasp ten years ago. Lies, greed, and betrayals by people she'd never even met had led her to this point in her life. Maggy's heart ached, leaving her feeling empty and desperate.

Those same lies, treacheries, infidelities, and greed seemed to chart her life's course. Wiping tears from her eyes, she knew there wasn't a thing she could do about any of it.

CHAPTER NINETEEN

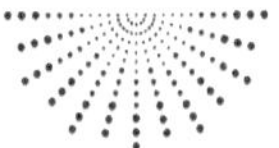

After the argument with Maggy, Findley set a grueling pace. He refused to stop for more than an hour or two at a time and ignored everyone's grievances. They reached Dundee in the very early morning hours. They clopped quietly through the streets shrouded in dense fog, unable to see more than a few feet in front of them.

They obtained rooms at the Crooked Arms Inn near the center of the town. The inn was full, and the only rooms available were on separate floors. Apparently, many people were traveling this time of year, finishing up business or visiting with family before winter set in.

The men and boys would stay on the second floor while Maggy and Findley took a room on the third. 'Twas habit now, each person knowing with whom they'd be sharing a room.

Maggy and Findley collapsed into the small bed after washing off the road grime and dirt. They hadn't said a word to each other in two days. Their stern silence had cast a cloud over the rest of their group, but neither appeared to care.

They had fallen asleep lying on their backs, each lost in lonely heartbreak. Maggy wanted to apologize and confess everything, but she held back. Soon enough, when they reached her brother's home, the truth would begin to unravel. Or at least parts of it. One of her secrets, the biggest of them all, was known only to two living beings; Maggy and one other. That secret, she was sure, would remain hidden for eternity.

Findley wanted to apologize as well, for being so stubborn and pig-headed. As he lay in the dark listening to Maggy's steady breathing, he wanted nothing more than to pull her to his chest and tell her how sorry he was for pushing her too hard. The secrets she held must be large and serious if she felt the need to suffer with them alone and to sacrifice any potential happiness the two of them could find together.

He drifted off to sleep trying to figure out a way to express his regret and his feelings for her. He knew the only way to overcome the barrier between them was to know what these secrets were that she clung to with such vengeance. If he could learn the truth, then he could develop a plan to defeat it. He fell asleep holding to the hope that nothing was insurmountable.

FINDLEY WOKE to a most pleasant feeling. Maggy had snuggled into him, her head resting on his chest, her free hand on his stomach, and her leg tossed over his. Her long auburn tresses were splayed across the pillow, and a bit of it covered her face. She was beautiful, asleep or awake, happy or angry, it mattered not; her beauty oftentimes took his breath away.

He held his breath, not wanting to disturb her or the wonderful sensation of having her so close. *This is where ye belong, lass,* he thought contentedly, *here, with me, like this. Och! How I wish I could bring this kind of peace to ye durin' yer wakin' hours. I wish ye'd believe in me enough to tell me what secrets ye hold.*

Unable to resist the urge, he carefully brushed the strands of hair away from her face. She snuggled in closer and let out a most contented sigh.

While he lay there wishing that she would find contentment with him in other ways than sleeping, a light knock came to the door. A moment later, he could hear Wee William's voice from the other side.

"Findley?" he whispered through the door.

Maggy stirred again and hugged him tighter. He wished they weren't shackled together so that he might allow her more time to sleep. He knew she was exhausted, worn and probably wanting a bath. As his mind wandered to mayhap being forced to share a bath with her, the shackles suddenly seemed more a blessing than a curse. Wee William knocked again.

Findley gently nudged Maggy's shoulder. "Lass, we need to wake now. I need to speak to Wee William."

Maggy mumbled something about cursing Wee William to the devil if he didn't go away. Findley chuckled and thought about searching for the key. Mayhap he could unlock the shackles, talk to Wee William for a moment, and then quietly come back to the bed. The image made him want to remain shackled to the lovely Maggy for a little while longer.

"Findley!" Wee William spoke a little louder. "Ye need to wake now! 'Tis important!"

The seriousness in Wee William's voice caused them both to bolt upright. Maggy wiped sleep from her eyes as Findley climbed over her and headed for the door. One would think that after nearly a week of being shackled together, he would remember the shackles. As he stepped away from the bed, he pulled Maggy off it, and she landed with a thud on the cold floor.

Irritated with his forgetfulness, she let out a heavy sigh as he mumbled an apology and pulled her to her feet. Together they walked to the door to let Wee William in.

Worry was imprinted on his face. He ducked into the room and shut the door behind him. "Findley," he began before stopping himself. He looked down at the shackles and shook his head. "When are the two of ye goin' to quit this nonsense?"

Maggy pursed her lips together and stood taller. "'Tis nae nonsense, Wee William!"

He shook his head and looked at the two of them. "Ye're both fools," he told them. He made no attempt to hide his disgust.

"I am sure ye did nae wake us to insult us, William. What be the matter?" Findley asked, choosing to ignore his friend's insults.

Wee William looked at Maggy before turning to Findley. Seeing there was no way around having a private conversation with Findley at the moment, he began. "There are Buchannan men about. Richard saw them below stairs a few minutes ago. Three of them."

Without thinking, Maggy stepped closer Findley. With a swoop of his arm, he pushed her to stand behind him. Maggy could feel his muscles grow tense with worry.

"Where are they now?" Findley asked.

"Still below stairs. Richard came to tell us, and he is gone back down to keep a close eye on them."

Findley thought on the situation for a moment. "I suppose they be not here alone."

"'Tis my worry as well," Wee William agreed. "We need more men, and we have no time to purchase anyone's fealty."

Findley understood the gravity of the situation far too well. He could only hope that the Buchannan men that were here were not well trained. It was the only hope he could cling to at the moment.

Maggy spoke up. "I have a brother here, Findley. His home is not far from us. There's naught he would nae do fer me."

Findley turned to look at her. Her worry was quite evident, but her eyes glistened with hope as well as determination. "Give me the key, Maggy. We will go to yer brother and ask fer his help."

Maggy's eyes widened with fear. "Nay!"

"Maggy, 'tis no trick!" he pleaded with her. "'Tis only yer safety I have in mind. We have no time to waste on arguin'!"

She shook her head. "Ye dunnae understand! Me brother will nae be believin' ye when ye tell him ye're tryin' to help me."

Findley furrowed his brow in confusion. "Why no'?"

Maggy took a deep breath and let it out slowly. "I canna tell ye," she murmured.

Findley growled at her. "Maggy, this be nae the time fer keepin' yer secrets to yerself! Now give me the key!"

"Nay, I cannae do that Findley. Please, trust me when I say I cannae tell ye-"

Findley cut her off. "Trust ye? Ye want me to trust ye?" The look of disgust on his face was enough to fill her eyes with tears.

Unable to stand the way he was looking at her, the shame she felt loosened the lock she held on her tongue just enough. "Because he thinks I be dead," she murmured.

His frown deepened. "What? Why would he think ye be dead?"

"I cannae tell ye," she said, closing her eyes.

"How many bloody secrets do ye have, woman?" he asked angrily.

Maggy opened her eyes. "Findley, I had good reasons fer lettin' everyone believe I was dead. Please trust me when I say there were no devious reasons behind it. I did it to protect me sons."

He wasn't sure if he believed all of what she told him. He reckoned there was some truth to it, but there was far more she wasn't telling.

They could spend the rest of the day going around in circles. Realizing she wasn't about to divulge anymore than she already had, Findley grunted. "Fine. But if we run into any Buchannans and I have the need to fight, ye'll unlock these bloody shackles or I swear, I'll cut yer hand off!"

Maggy nodded her head. "Aye, I will Findley," she promised him.

Findley barked orders to Wee William as he and Maggy shoved feet into boots. "Ye put all the boys in one room and bar the door. Have Richard stay close to the Buchannans," he said as he reached for his sword and belted it around his waist.

"And what of Patrick?" Wee William asked.

"Patrick will go with us. I want ye to stay here and guard those boys with yer life."

"And if the Buchannans discover us here?" Wee William asked.

Findley could not help but chuckle at the first thought that came to his mind. "Arm the lads with stones!"

A devious smile came to Wee William's face as he absentmindedly rubbed the spot on his head where Maggy had hit him with a stone so many days ago.

"Aye, that'll keep the bloody fools busy fer a time!" Maggy interjected. She blushed when she realized she had said it aloud.

Wee William looked surprised to hear such language coming from Maggy. But surprise quickly turned to pride and adoration. "I would still shave me beard if ye asked me to, lass."

Maggy's cheeks flamed red with embarrassment. Findley's flamed red for entirely different reasons. If Wee William didn't stop offering to shave his beard for Maggy, Findley was ready to send him back to Gregor and fight the Buchannans without him.

Findley eyed the two of them for a moment. "Are the two of ye quite finished with admirin' each other?"

Wee William snorted and smiled. He leaned in close to Findley's ear and whispered. "'Tis yer heart the lass wants, nae mine. But if ye dunnae marry her, I will." And with that, he righted himself and left the room before Findley could think of an appropriate response.

IT HADN'T TAKEN Patrick much time to find a way out of the inn without being seen. When he, Findley and Maggy left through the back door of the kitchen, Richard was still sitting at a table in the corner, surreptitiously watching the three Buchannan men.

Maggy had the hood of her cloak drawn over her head and kept glancing over her shoulders as they made their way through the busy streets of Dundee. She could not shake the sensation that they were being followed. But every time she took a chance and glanced behind her, she saw nothing suspicious. Mayhap it was the worry over the shock she was about to bring to her brother that was keeping her on edge.

They made good time and were soon standing at the back door of her brother's home. Maggy paused and took a deep breath before knocking on the door. As she stood waiting for someone to answer, Findley took her hand in his and gave it a comforting squeeze. She glanced up at him and smiled. She doubted she would have the nerve to do this alone and found she was quite glad to have him there.

It seemed like hours had passed before someone finally opened the door. Maggy took in a quick breath when she saw that it was her sister-in-law who answered the door.

"What is it ye need? We are nae takin' on any new help, so if that be what ye want, ye can leave now," Oribilia told them. She stood in the doorway with one hand on her hip, the other on the door-latch.

"Oribilia," Maggy whispered. Her chest felt constricted, as if it had been bound tightly. How many years had it been since she'd seen her dear sister-in-law? Far too many for her liking.

Oribilia squinted at the cloaked figure before her. She could not see the face, but she thought she recognized the voice.

"May we come in?" Maggy whispered, her throat suddenly feeling quite dry.

"Do I know ye?" the woman asked, puzzled and confused.

"Aye, ye do," Maggy offered. "But I fear tellin' ye from here. May we please come in, Oribilia?"

Oribilia scanned the trio with her eyes. "I be nae alone," she told them as she began to worry.

Maggy finally lifted her face to look into the eyes of her sister-in-law. She pulled back the hood of her cloak, but only enough so that Oribilia could see her face.

It took a moment for Oribilia to recognize her. She stepped backward as her hand flew to her mouth. The cry of shock and disbelief was stuck in her throat as the three people quickly entered her kitchen. She stumbled about, her free hand finding a chair. She clung to the back of it, as if it alone could keep her from falling to the floor with fright.

"Oribilia," Maggy repeated. "Och! How I have missed ye!"

The two women embraced, their tears flowing freely. Findley felt horribly uncomfortable, as he was unable to step away to offer them any privacy. The two women stood holding on to one another for several minutes, neither one able to find her voice.

Maggy cried for many different reasons. Relief, guilt, and longing.

She was relieved that her family would soon learn that she had not perished three years ago. The guilt was for having deceived them and allowing them to believe she was dead. And she longed for the time in her life when she was free, innocent and ignorant of the hard truths of life.

When their tears began to ebb, they pulled away from each other, maintaining their grasps, and studied each other. A warm smile came to Oribilia's face. "Maggy, I cannae believe ye stand before me. Am I dreamin', lass?"

"If 'tis a dream, then we be sharin' it, and I never want to wake," Maggy smiled back at her.

'Twas then that Oribilia noticed the shackles. "Och! Maggy! What is this?" she asked, staring at the chains.

Maggy laughed at her sister-in-law as she wiped tears from her face with her fingertips. "This?" she said, lifting her shackled hand. "'Tis nothing to worry over. I had to do it so he would nae leave me behind."

Oribilia studied the two of them for a moment, unsure what to make of the shackles or the fact that her sister-in-law was truly standing before her.

They finally took chairs and sat facing one another. Patrick stayed near the door, his hand on the hilt of his sword. Findley stepped behind Maggy, keeping his shackled hand on her shoulder.

The women were lost in their reunion and had forgotten both men.

"Maggy, why did they tell us ye were dead, lass?" Oribilia asked as she took Maggy's hands in hers.

"Oribilia, ye canna know how hard it was to let me family think it! But there was no other way around it."

"And what of Liam? How is he?" Oribilia asked, hoping against hope that the boy was still alive.

"He is well," Maggy told her. Oribilia's shoulders shrank with relief.

"Praise God!" she said, "Why, Maggy? Why did they tell us ye were dead?"

Maggy remembered that Findley was standing beside her and chose her words carefully. "Och! Dear sister, there is so much to tell, but I fear we have nae enough time to explain all of it to ye."

Oribilia looked confused. "Lass, ye must tell me! Ye're in trouble, I can sense it."

Maggy let out a short breath. "Aye, that I am," she told her, giving her hands another squeeze. "Is Roald here?"

Oribilia took the ends of her apron and wiped the tears from her face. "Nay, he is at sea. He won't be back for another fortnight."

Maggy's heart sank at the news. She needed her brother, needed his help.

"Do ye ken of Eonon? Be he still livin' in Aberdeen?" Eonon was two years younger than Roald and just as faithful.

"Aye, he is, Maggy. He be married now, to a fine young girl. They be expectin' their first bairn at any time."

Maggy chuckled at the news. Eonon had sworn and be damned he'd never marry. How many times had he said that women were more trouble than they were worth? "She must be somethin' verra special, then, if she convinced him to give up his oath to never marry!"

"Aye, that she is, lass!" Oribilia smiled at her. "She's got a fierce temper, much like yers!"

Patrick and Findley chuckled. Both men doubted there was another female on the planet with a temper like Maggy's.

Maggy chose to ignore the snorting coming from behind her. "Oribilia, we canna tarry here much longer. I fear fer yer safety, sister. Do ye have someone ye can stay with until Roald returns?"

Oribilia leaned back in her chair, surprised and confused. "Why do ye fear fer me safety?"

There was no way easy way to explain it. "Oribilia," she began quietly. "There are men searching for me. Verra bad men. They be here in Dundee. We took a great risk comin' here. Had I ken Roald was nae here, I would nae have come. I am verra sorry for putting ye at risk, sister. But ye must listen to me, please. If these men learn I was here, they'll bring harm to ye and yer babes, I am sure of it."

"Why do these men search for ye? What have ye done?" She cast a glance at the shackles before looking back to Maggy.

A sad smile came to Maggy's face. "I have done nothin', I swear it." She paused to take a deep breath. "Gawter died, Oribilia."

Maggy hoped her sister-by-law would be able to put two and two together and figure it out on her own. A few moments passed before the realization and direness of the situation sank in. Her eyes widened with shock as well as understanding. "Oh, lass! Now I see the right of it! Ye poor thing! 'Tis Laird Brockton's doin', isn't it?"

Findley's brow lifted slightly at the mention of the name Brockton. It sounded familiar to him, but he could not place it. He remained mute, glad for one more piece of information that might help him solve the mystery that surrounded the woman he loved.

Maggy cringed at the mention of Gawter's uncle. "I dunnae ken if he knows we live or not. But ye know what will surely happen once he learns the truth." Maggy swallowed hard and fought back the uneasy feeling creeping into her stomach. "I have four more boys now, Oribilia. Boys I have adopted as me own. Their parents died from the same pox that took Gawter. 'Tis their safety as well as Liam's that I think of now. I cannae let Lord Brockton find us."

So 'tis Lord Brockton she fears. The sudden realization left Findley's stomach tight and uneasy. But why does she fear him?

Oribilia looked pitifully at Maggy. "Ye poor thing. But who are the men that search fer ye?"

"Have ye heard of Malcolm Buchannan?" Maggy asked, sure that anyone who had been in Scotland for more than a day had heard of the man.

Oribilia shivered at the mention of his name. "Aye, I have heard of him. They say he is tetched, and the devil has his soul." Oribilia quickly touched her fingers to her forehead and made the sign of the cross, as if that alone could protect her from the evil man.

"I believe it to be true, Oribilia. 'Tis his men that look for me."

Oribilia looked horrified. "Why?"

"Malcolm Buchannan wants to marry me," Maggy let the words sink in.

"Nay!" Oribilia said, unable to hide her horrification. "Please tell me ye told him nay!"

"Of course I refused!" Maggy looked disgusted by the thought. "Every time he is asked, I have refused. But he has me son, Ian. And I have to get him back, Oribilia!" Tears began to fill her eyes again as she worried for her son.

"Och! Lass, what can I do to help?" Oribilia stood and threw her shoulders back. "I will stab Malcolm Buchannan in his cold, evil heart fer what he is done! I have horses! We can ride to his keep together!"

Oribilia was quite ready to lead the charge against Malcolm Buchannan. Findley and Patrick looked at each other, surprised to find there was yet another woman who apparently had no fear of raising arms against the Buchannan clan.

A sudden image crashed into Findley's mind. In it, he was leading a thousand women and children, all armed with rocks. They charged the Buchannan keep with the same fierceness and determination he and his men held. He shook the thought away, for there was no way on God's earth he'd allow any woman, least of all Maggy, to go up against such an evil group of men.

Finding his voice, he leaned in a bit closer. "Ladies," he began softly, afraid for his own life, for Oribilia was looking at him with bloodlust in her eyes. "While we appreciate ye wantin' to get Ian back, I believe it will take more than just the six of us. We'd be needin' more men to help."

Oribilia looked at him as if he had just fallen from the sky. "Do ye nae think women capable of fightin'?" It was a direct challenge, and he knew there was no way of winning.

"Aye, I do!" he answered quickly. "But I'll need more than two women. The Buchannans are at least one hundred strong. While I am sure ye'd do well against them, I think it would be best for everyone if we had reinforcements." He hoped his answer would placate her. Or at the least get her to remove the look of disgust she wore on her face.

Oribilia turned back to Maggy. "Who be the eejit?" she asked as she nodded her head toward Findley.

Maggy turned her lips in to keep from laughing as she saw Findley stand taller, affronted by Oribilia's insult.

"Sister, be kind. These men have sacrificed much to help me. This be Findley McKenna and his friend Patrick," she introduced them.

Once the introductions were complete, Maggy steered the conversation back toward Oribilia's safety. "Sister," she said with a smile. "I ken ye mean well to help. But I fear that if anything happened to ye or yer children, Roald would never find it in his heart to forgive me. He is a stubborn man, ye ken it as well as I. But he loves ye, that much we ken. Please, will ye nae leave until he returns? Keep yerself and the children safe?"

Oribilia studied Maggy for a moment, turning it over in her mind. After a time, she nodded her head. "I will have word sent to Roald when he returns. The children and I can stay with me sister and her family in Renfrew."

She thrust her hands on her hips. "Are ye sure ye can trust these men of yers?"

Maggy smiled, a full smile that showed her straight white teeth. "Aye, I trust them with me life and the lives of me sons." She resisted looking directly at Findley when she said it. She could only hope he would believe the sincerity of her words.

Findley's heart swelled with pride. He hoped she meant what she said and wasn't merely saying it to appease Oribilia. He was grateful that Maggy felt safe enough with Oribilia to speak openly with her. While he might not have all the answers, he was beginning to put some of the pieces of the puzzle together.

Maggy stood and hugged Oribilia. Neither wanted to let go of the other.

"Maggy, promise me ye'll be safe?"

"Aye, I promise," Maggy whispered into Oribilia's hair. "And ye as well sister. I fear ye must hurry and get to yer sister's home, quickly. Malcolm Buchannan is capable of anything."

Oribilia pulled back and looked into Maggy's eyes. "Lass, I could nae stand to lose ye again. It nearly killed me last time."

Maggy smiled, holding back tears. "I love ye, Oribilia. I be glad to call ye sister."

The women hugged briefly before pulling away. Maggy carefully covered her hair with the hood of the cloak before being led out of the house. As they walked down the pathway, Maggy prayed that God would keep Oribilia and her children safe.

RICHARD HAD REMAINED hidden in the corner of the inn, keeping a close eye on the three Buchannan men who sat huddled on the other side of the room. None of the men looked pleased, but Richard shrugged off their demeanor as being typical for Buchannan men.

Findley, Maggy, and Patrick had been gone for a quarter of an hour. Richard prayed they would not encounter any trouble while they ventured to her brother's home. The hairs on the back of his neck had been standing at full attention for days now, unrelenting, full of warning. He would not rest easy until they were in Aberdeen. And then only if Angus had sent the additional men Findley had pleaded for in his missive.

As he sat in the dark corner, he wondered if any of this would be worth it in the end. He imagined his brother would feel like a fool if, when all was said and done, the fair Maggy would have no interest in him. Richard shook his head at the notion. Two people who argued like Maggy and Findley were meant for each other. Richard imagined that if they could be as passionate about loving one another as they were at arguing, they'd have a long, happy life together.

A short time later the three men stood up from their table. Richard's hand went instinctively to the hilt of his sword. He pretended to stare at the mug of ale, attempting to blend in and go unnoticed.

One of the men tossed a coin on the table before they sauntered toward the door and left. Richard counted to twenty before he stood and left to follow them.

WITH MAGGY IN THE MIDDLE, Findley and Patrick remained vigilant and watchful as they walked back to the inn. Findley stayed as close to Maggy as possible so as not to draw any unwanted attention to the shackles that bound them together.

Patrick spotted them first. Just two blocks from the inn, he saw the two Buchannan men as they rounded a corner. Without missing a step, he spoke quietly and calmly to Findley. "Do ye see them, Findley?"

Findley followed Patrick's gaze. Up ahead and coming toward them were two Buchannan men. Maggy tensed as Findley and Patrick scanned the area for more Buchannans, as well as a quick escape.

Findley knew there had been three that Richard had been watching back at the inn. He had not seen those men, so he could not be sure if the men walking toward them were part of that trio or if they were two more.

"Findley," Maggy whispered as she slowed her pace.

Findley and Patrick knew they'd draw more attention if they stopped abruptly so they pulled her along. "Relax, Maggy. Do nothin' to bring attention to us."

Just a few steps ahead, Findley spied a sign over a shop door indicating it was a dressmaker and haberdashery. "Into the shop, Patrick," Findley said with a nod of his head.

While Patrick led the way, Findley glanced toward the Buchannan men who were rapidly advancing. It didn't appear as though they had been seen, but Findley wouldn't feel any sense of relief until he had Maggy safely back in their room.

Findley guided Maggy to the rear of the shop while Patrick pretended to look at the fine dresses near the window. Pulling Maggy to his side, his hand on the hilt of his sword, he gave a quick survey of their surroundings.

An older man, apparently the shopkeeper, stood behind the long counter and conversed with an older woman. Apparently she was a noblewoman, for she had two maids in her attendance. Both looked bored and solemn as they stood behind and to the side of the older woman.

More people were scattered throughout the large store, looking at the fine fabrics, discussing dresses, shoes, and other mundane things in which Findley had absolutely no interest. Tall shelves that sat in the middle of the shop blocked most of his view.

As he peered through a small opening in the shelves to get a better look at the front of the shop, he heard his name being called. And it was not Maggy who spoke it.

"Findley!"

He whirled around, shoving Maggy behind him for protection. Before he realized it, Patrick was standing beside him with a smile on his face.

"What are ye doin' here?" the woman asked as she wrapped her arms around him and gave him a firm hug.

"Aishlinn?" he asked, puzzled by her presence in the shop. He had said goodbye to her and Duncan more than two sennights ago. Why was she here?

She pulled away from him, her bright smile beaming at him as she hugged Patrick and patted him on the back.

"What are ye doin' in Dundee? I thought ye were goin' to find yer beautiful Maggy and her boys and take them back to Gregor?" Her look was a blend of confusion and disappointment.

Maggy had reflexively drawn into herself, hiding behind Findley and Patrick. She had been terrified to see the Buchannan men moments ago and had been searching the shop for a means of escape. Her fear was momentarily displaced when she saw this strange, beautiful woman hugging Findley.

Yer beautiful Maggy? Who was this woman, Maggy wondered. And how does she know of me? Maggy stood on her tiptoes and tried to get a better look at the woman. But Findley and Patrick were so tall that it was impossible, even on her tiptoes.

"I could ask the same question of ye!" Findley said as he smiled down at Aishlinn. Her belly had grown since last he saw her. He could not fathom why she was so far from home in her condition.

Aishlinn caught Findley's glance at her belly and smiled. "Yer nearly as bad as Duncan and my father!" she said as she placed her hands on her hips. "I be fine! Our babe is not due until springtime."

Maggy's ears perked up. The woman had an English accent. She tried to wriggle in between Findley and Patrick, but both men were like walls of stone! When Findley felt her press her head into his arm, he closed in tighter to Patrick. She fought the urge to kick them both.

"My father insists on new furniture and fabrics for his grandchild," Aishlinn said. "He says nothing is too good for his grandchildren. He wanted to send Isobel for me, but I convinced him she was needed at Gregor and that I could manage quite well. He finally relented, but only if Duncan came with me!" Aishlinn shook her head and smiled. "And we had to bring guards!"

Hope began to throb in Findley's heart. "How many?" he blurted out.

Not knowing the importance of the question, Aishlinn giggled, "Only five and twenty!"

Findley and Patrick looked at each other. 'Twas a good number to start with, and for the first time in days, Findley felt hopeful.

Maggy grew confused. Who was this woman, and why would her father insist on guards to accompany her to buy furniture for her babe? And who was Duncan? She tried to wriggle through the human wall before her, only to be pushed backward again. Enough was enough!

Maggy took her knee and landed a firm blow to the back of Findley's knee. He was caught off guard as he felt his knee give way, and he nearly fell down. Maggy took the opportunity to push her way in between the two men.

The woman standing before her was breathtakingly beautiful. Her golden blonde hair was woven into an intricate braid around her head. An expensive and luxurious length of silk trailed from the top of her head to the hem of her beautiful green damask gown. Maggy thought she was perhaps the most beautiful woman she had ever seen.

"Hello," Aishlinn said with a warm smile.

Maggy had momentarily lost her voice. She looked up at Findley who was scowling down at her, but she did not care. Her curiosity was piqued as to how this woman knew about her.

"Maggy," Findley said. She chose to ignore the tone of warning in his voice.

Maggy turned back to Aishlinn. "M'lady," she said, giving her a curtsey.

Aishlinn shook her head, smiled, and held out her hand. "Please, call me Aishlinn. Ye must be the beautiful Maggy I have heard so much about."

Maggy took her hand, confusion swarming in her head. *But I have heard naught about you.*

Aishlinn read Maggy's confused expression. "Findley could speak of nothing else but ye while he was healing this summer."

"Healing? From what?" Maggy asked, growing more confused.

Aishlinn turned her gaze to Findley. "Did ye not speak of it to her, Findley?"

Was that a blush of embarrassment Maggy saw flashing across Findley's face? And why was Patrick chuckling?

"'Tis a story fer another time," he said to Aishlinn before turning to Maggy. "And time is a luxury we do nae have at the moment."

As Maggy looked to Findley and Patrick for answers, she caught sight of a man approaching them. Fear shot from her toes to the top of her head. He was an imposing figure, tall and broad shouldered, but it was the scowl on his face that frightened her. Without thought, Maggy ducked in behind Findley and Patrick.

"Duncan!" Aishlinn said happily.

"Aishlinn!" Maggy detected more than just a hint of anger in his voice. "I have been lookin' all over fer ye!"

"Och! I have been right here, husband."

Duncan let out an exasperated sigh. "But ye were to stay beside me at all times! Ye sneaked off without tellin' me! I swear ye've scared ten years off me life!"

"I doubt there are any English here, husband," she said teasingly. "And look, Findley and Patrick are here now, as well."

"I can see that, wife." Duncan shook his head and lowered it. "Findley, do ye see what torture she puts me through?"

Findley and Patrick laughed as they shook hands with Duncan. "Aye, we do," Patrick said. "Is she worth the worry and torture?"

Duncan crossed his arms over his chest. "I find meself askin' that same question multiple times a day, Patrick."

Aishlinn raised her eyebrow and pulled on her husband's arm. "And how do ye answer that question, husband?"

A slow smile came to his face as he pretended to ignore his wife. Duncan winked at his friends, "Be smart, lads! If a beautiful and beguiling woman tries to get her talons into ye, run! I swear, the torture, the worry is more than I can bear at times. Marriage be nae for the faint of heart! Nay," he shook his head, "it takes a strong man with the patience of Job just to get through the mornin'!"

Aishlinn glared at him. "Yer torture is nothin' compared to what I have to endure!" She was slipping into a Scottish brogue as she began to chastise him. "And it grows worse with each day! Dunnae lift this, dunnae lift that! Do nae strain yerself. Do nae test me patience, wife! Och and arrrgh!" she said mockingly. "All the day long, like I be somethin' fragile and weak, and I am unable to care for myself!"

Relief washed over Maggy when she realized the large and imposing man was Aishlinn's husband. She was enjoying the back and forth banter taking place between the two people. Even a fool could see that they loved one another. Through a small sliver of space between Findley and Patrick, Maggy could see Duncan had slipped his arm around his wife's shoulder.

"But she does make up fer it at the end of each day," he said with a devious grin.

Aishlinn's face burned red. "Duncan!" she chastised him. "Ye shouldn't speak like that!"

Duncan chuckled. "I dunnae where yer mind is, wife. I was speakin' of the fine meals ye prepare me each eve!"

Maggy felt laughter bubbling up, and she had to put her hand to her lips to keep it from escaping. But the look in the man's eyes as he stared down as his very tiny wife brought a sense of sadness and longing to Maggy.

She wished she could someday have that kind of playful relationship with a man, but those wishes would not be granted, and her prayers would go unanswered. She knew all too well the kind of life that waited for her at the end of this ordeal, and it would resemble nothing like what the two young people before her shared.

"Duncan, ye have scared Maggy! She hides behind Findley and Patrick!" Aishlinn reached in between the two men, found Maggy's arm and pulled her through.

"Maggy, this is my husband, Duncan McEwan," she said with a nod of her head. "Duncan, this is Findley's lass, Maggy."

It was Maggy's turn to burn red. What on earth did she mean by Findley's lass? Mayhap the young woman was confused, had taken a blow to her head at some point. There was no relationship between her and Findley. He was merely helping her get her son back and nothing more.

Duncan bowed slightly and smiled at Findley. "She's just as bonny as ye described her, Findley."

Maggy looked up at Findley. The muscles in his jaw were clenching, and she detected a twitch forming in his eye. What on earth had Findley told these two people?

"Findley," Maggy whispered, but she could not think of how to form the question burning in her mind.

Duncan and Aishlinn hadn't a clue as to why Maggy looked at Findley with such a perplexed expression. They cast each other looks of confusion, shrugged their shoulders, and turned their attention back to Findley.

"Have ye eaten yet?" Aishlinn asked the three of them. "I realize it is not quite time for an evening meal, but I find myself quite hungry," she said as she patted her belly with her hand.

At the moment, Maggy had no appetite. There were unanswered questions hanging in the air. Findley was purposely ignoring her even as she tugged on his arm.

"I am afraid we have no time, Aishlinn. I have a need to speak with

Duncan if ye dunnae mind. 'Tis verra important." Findley was unsuccessful in hiding his worry. He now had two women to worry over. There was no telling what the Buchannan men would do to any of the people he might come in contact with.

Aishlinn sensed the seriousness in his tone. She had learned there were times when the men in her life wanted nothing more than to protect her and those they loved. Eventually she'd drag the problem out of her husband. Too hungry at the moment to beg for more information, she stepped toward Maggy.

"We might as well give the men the privacy they need at the moment, Maggy. We can go back to our inn and eat while the men talk." Looping her arm through Maggy's she began to pull her away from the men.

Maggy was too flummoxed to argue and began to walk with Aishlinn. She had only taken a few steps when she was abruptly reminded that she could not leave Findley's side. She let out a slight grunt when the shackles pulled her back toward Findley.

Aishlinn turned to see what had stopped Maggy from following. Her eyes grew as large as saucers when she saw the shackles holding the two of them together.

"Findley McKenna! What on earth have ye done!" she exclaimed.

Findley rolled his eyes and shook his head. "I have done nothin', lass," he tried to explain further but was interrupted by Aishlinn.

"Dunnae lie to me, Findley McKenna!" Aishlinn said angrily. "Ye've got the poor lass shackled to ye like a prisoner! Is that any way to treat the woman ye lo-"

Findley cut her off sharply, his voice loud. "Aishlinn!" he boomed. "I assure ye that these shackles aren't here by my doin', but by Maggy's!"

Aishlinn looked at him disbelievingly. "Nay! I dunnae believe that! Why would she do such a thing?" She turned to Maggy with her hands on her hips and waited for an explanation.

Maggy let out a quick sigh. "I had to, or he would have left me and me sons with the monks, m'lady. I had no other choice in the matter, I assure ye." She cast a look of dismay up at Findley. He still would not look at her.

"The monks?" Aishlinn asked. She shook her head as if doing so would somehow bring clarification to the burgeoning questions. "Why would ye leave them with the monks?" she asked Findley. When no answer was immediately forthcoming, she looked to Patrick. Apparently both men had taken a vow of silence, for neither would answer.

"Ye were supposed to bring them all back to Gregor," Aishlinn said. "And now the poor lass has to shackle herself to ye in order that ye won't desert her," she said to no one in particular.

"'Tis a verra long story, m'lady," Maggy offered. "And I am afraid it be nae a pleasant one."

"I think," Duncan interjected, "that there is much we dunnae ken about it, Aishlinn. I think mayhap we should find a quiet place to discuss the matter?" He looked to Findley for affirmation.

"Aye, we should," Findley pulled Maggy closer and nodded his head toward Aishlinn. "Duncan, there be Buchannans lookin' fer us. Ye best find yer men and meet us back at our rooms at the Crooked Arms."

At the mention of Buchannans, Duncan's hand reflexively went to his sword as he pulled Aishlinn into his free arm. "Buchannans?"

"Aye," Findley said with a nod of his head. "Patrick, will ye see if there be a back door we can use?"

Patrick nodded his head and disappeared through a door at the rear of the shop.

"Buchannans," Aishlinn murmured as fear flashed into her eyes. "What do the Buchannans want?" she asked, growing more confused and fearful.

Findley answered her question. "They want me Maggy."

THERE WASN'T MUCH that escaped the dark stranger's eyes. He had seen them arrive late last night and had been watching them ever since. Last night he had thanked whatever intervening forces had brought them to this place. He wouldn't thank God, for he had long ago given up believing in a kind or gracious God. The hell he had endured all those years as a prisoner had destroyed his faith.

It really didn't matter how she got here, only that she was. Soon, he would be able to exact his revenge on the man who had destroyed his life. He'd do that by taking something near and dear to the betrayer's heart: his woman and his son.

While he was quite tempted to walk up to her and run a dagger through her heart, he knew that he'd be dead before her corpse hit the ground. Nay, he wanted to kill them both, especially the boy. The boy was the key.

Years of training had taught him how to study people without being noticed. From what he just witnessed from the other side of the street, he could tell Maggy and the men she was with were hiding from Buchannan men. What he hadn't figured out yet was why.

Instinct and experience told him they'd probably leave the shop through a back entrance. Knowing the alley behind the wall of shops led in only two directions, he slowly crossed the street. As he walked by the shop, he could see them standing and speaking with a young woman.

He made his way to the corner, stopping occasionally to look into a shop window before making his way around the corner. Pausing nonchalantly at the entrance of the alley, he waited. The wait wasn't long before he saw them flood out of the rear of the shop. Seeing they were heading away from him, he went back the way he came and was able to follow at a good distance.

He had to find out why they were hiding from the Buchannans. Surmising the best way to do that would be out of the mouths of Buchannans, he decided on his next course of action. He'd go back to the inn and learn what he could from those men.

Night had descended by the time Findley had recounted to Duncan and Aishlinn all that had transpired. Duncan had readily agreed to giving half his men over to aid Findley and his quest for the kidnapped Ian.

Had Aishlinn not been with him, Duncan would have joined in the quest himself. But his wife and unborn child were his primary concern. He would take her back to Gregor at first light and then meet with Findley and the others in Aberdeen.

Aishlinn and Duncan had done their best to convince Maggy to return with them to Gregor. Their pleas fell on deaf ears, for Maggy would have none of it. She would not admit to having a key, though everyone around her believed that she did.

Maggy did agree to send her sons back with Duncan and Aishlinn. She knew the boys would be angry with her decision, but their safety was her main priority, and she refused to take any further chances of them ending up in the hands of the Buchannans. As she had suspected, the news did not settle well with them.

"I will nae go run and hide like a bairn!" Robert said, appalled and angry that his mother apparently had no faith in him.

"'Tis nae hidin' ye're doin', Robert. I need ye to help protect yer other brothers. Liam and Collin be far too young to go against the Buchannans. I need ye and Andrew to protect them and help see them safely to Gregor." She could only hope that he would believe her. She would feel better knowing Robert was with the younger boys, especially Liam.

"I be nae fool, mum! Ye hope to build up me pride and make me think that is what ye want. But I ken better! Ye worry I be too young, too inexperienced to help get Ian back!" he was pacing around the room.

Aye, she did worry over him, and she did believe he was too young to battle against the Buchannans. It was a fine line a mother sometimes had to walk between helping her children to believe in themselves and keeping them safe. There were times when a mother had to step back and allow their children to learn by their own mistakes. This, however, was not one of those times.

"Robert," she said sternly. "Ye're a good and smart lad. Ye will go to

Gregor and get the trainin' ye need to become a fine warrior. Ye will nae be goin to Aberdeen, and that is the end of it!" She didn't want to yell, but there would be no way she'd allow him to go anywhere but back to Gregor.

"I need ye to protect yer brothers, Robert," she said, her voice softening. "I need ye with them." Her voice cracked as she looked at her eldest son. For the first time since this ordeal began, she was not sure if she'd come out of it alive. There was a very real chance that she would end up dead. Death didn't frighten her nearly as much as the thought of no one being there to raise her sons.

Aishlinn had made a promise to Maggy not more than an hour earlier. If anything happened to Maggy, then Duncan and Aishlinn would take the four boys in as their own. It was a tremendous pledge that Aishlinn made, and though Maggy hadn't known her but for a few hours, Maggy knew in her heart Aishlinn would keep her word.

"Promise me, Robert, that ye'll take care of yer brothers for me," Maggy said as she wiped a tear from her cheek.

Robert kept his back to her, his fists clenching at his sides. *I am nae a bairn. We are warriors and we take care of our own.* How many times had he said that to his brothers? How would he ever be able to look any of them in the eye again if he ran and hid like a frightened lamb? His mother was asking him to make a promise, one he did not think he could keep.

She asked me to take care of me brothers, he thought to himself. *She didnae say how I was to do it.*

Robert stood taller, pushed his shoulders back, and turned around to look at his mum. Her face bore an expression he'd seen far too much of lately: fear, dread, and worry. Findley's didn't look much better.

"Aye," he finally said. "I promise ye I'll take care of me brothers."

Maggy's shoulders sagged with relief. For a minute she thought she'd have to tie him up in order to get him to listen to reason. She held back a laugh when she realized this must be what Findley feels like.

Maggy walked to her son and held him in a tight embrace. She whispered into his ear, "I love ye, son. I have faith in ye to always do what's right. I be verra proud of ye." She gave him a kiss on the side of his head and a pat on his back.

He may be on the verge of becoming a young man, but he was still her son. No matter how tall he became, no matter how old he grew, he would always be her son.

Robert wiggled from her embrace and left the room, leaving his mother and Findley behind.

A LONG, silent moment passed before Findley spoke. "Too bad his mother won't listen to the same good sense and reason."

"Tis nae the same, Findley. I be a full-grown woman. He is just a boy."

"Nay, he be a young man, Maggy. And a proud one."

Maggy let out a long breath. "Would ye have him go with us then?"

Findley shook his head and lifted a hand to her shoulder. "Nay, Maggy. I would prefer ye went with them back to Gregor."

"Ye ken I cannae do that, Findley!"

"I ken no such thing," he said softly. He knew it was killing her inside to be sending her boys away. But he knew she had only their safety and well-being at heart. "If ye had any sense in that beautiful head of yers, ye would go back with them, instead of pretending ye do nae have the key to these," he said as he lifted his wrist and dangled the shackles between them.

Maggy remained mute. She had grown weary of having the same argument over and over again. Changing the subject, she headed toward the bed. "I am tired, Findley. I wish to sleep now."

Findley tugged on the shackles and pulled her back to him. Wrapping an arm around her waist, he pressed his stomach to her back. She tried wiggling her way out, but his hold on her was too strong.

"Maggy," he whispered into her ear. "Why do ye insist on staying shackled to me? Why will ye nae share yer secrets with me?"

There was a sensuality to his voice that caused her stomach to bubble with excitement. She didn't think she'd ever understand how one man could have such an effect on her! She wanted him with a desperation that frightened her. Oh, how she wished things could be different for them. In moments like this, when she was ready to tell him everything and beg for his forgiveness, she felt at her weakest. Moments when she wished she could agree to marry him and pretend they could live out the rest of their days together in quiet, blissful peace.

But it was not to be. Laird Brockton would never agree to a marriage between Maggy and Findley. Had Findley been a man of wealth with no spine, then Laird Brockton would, more likely than not, allow such a union.

A poor Findley might be welcomed in her uncle's home. Poor men could sometimes be bought for the right price. Brockton would have been able to keep a poor man in line with threats of pulling funds or the enticement of bribery.

But it would be Findley's strong moral character and honor that Brockton would see first, and those would be reasons enough to deny a marriage. Within five minutes of meeting him, Brockton would see that no amount of money or threats would bend Findley McKenna's will or honor.

His strong sense of honor and duty would be the things she needed most to help get her son back. They would also be the things that would keep them apart.

Findley laid a gentle kiss on the side of her neck and breathed in her scent. She smelled like earth, warmth, and fresh air, and he found it took his good senses away.

"Maggy, tell me yer secrets. Let me help ye," he whispered as he pressed another kiss to her neck, right below her ear. It sent flutters of delight from her stomach to her toes.

"Findley," she said breathlessly. He made it quite difficult for her concentrate. She suddenly felt beyond tired, beyond exhausted. The fight in her was quickly fading.

"Maggy," he whispered. She was melting into him, the last of her defenses falling slowly away.

"Why will ye nae marry me?" he asked as he left another kiss on her neck. He could make no sense of it. "Is it because ye still mourn fer yer husband?" He'd been chewing on that idea for a few days. Mayhap her resistance came because she felt honor-bound to her dead husband.

Maggy turned to face him, tears pooled in her eyes, the candlelight making them glisten. "Nay, I dunnae mourn me husband," she told him as a strong need to purge herself of Gawter's memory overcame her. "I never mourned his death." She couldn't believe she had said it out loud.

Findley's expression changed to one of confusion. "Ye did nae mourn his death?"

She choked back tears. "Nay, Findley. He was nae a good man, not like ye."

Then there was something else holding her back. Something that frightened her to the point that she would continue to deny her feelings for Findley.

"Ye can confide in me, lass," he told her as he pressed a kiss to her forehead. "I promise I will nae judge ye or think ill of ye."

Maggy swallowed hard and took a deep breath. Would it be so wrong to tell him some of the truth, if not all of it? Mayhap if she told him, then he'd understand why they couldn't be together.

"Ye say that now, but ye dunnae ken the truth yet, Findley. I be afraid ye'll change yer mind once ye learn it."

He pulled her close, and she buried her head in his chest. "Nay, lass, I swear nothin' ye could say could ever change how I feel about ye."

The dam burst, and a torrent of tears came flooding through. Tears she'd been holding onto for many years welled up and spilled out, unstoppable. By the time she was done crying, Findley's tunic was damp from her tears.

Her resistance was gone. She knew that once the word spread that she was in fact alive, there'd be no turning back. There'd be no way on God's earth that Laird Brockton would allow her another chance at escape, for he had far too much at stake to lose her again. She was trapped: a prisoner of a destiny not of her own choosing.

Maggy wished she could turn back time and go back to the day before her mother had announced that she would marry the Ninth Earl of Kerse. She would always remember that day as the last care-free and innocent day of her life. There had not been another since.

Findley held her close, rubbing her back and whispered words of encouragement. His heart broke for her because he could see the pain and fear that she'd been holding on to for quite some time.

"Wheest, lass," he murmured as he kissed the top of Maggy's head. "It canna be as bad as what ye think."

"Ye dunnae understand! It's worse than that!" she sobbed into his chest.

"Tell me, then. Tell me so I can understand it and help ye better."

Maggy's breath stuttered as she tried to find the right words and a good place to begin. "I canna marry ye because Gawter's uncle will nae allow it."

Findley's brow furrowed slightly as he listened. He wondered what on earth Gawter's uncle had to do with it. "And why would he have a problem with ye marryin' me?"

"Please, Findley, promise me ye'll nae hate me," she pleaded with him.

"I do so promise," he said as he led her to the bed and set her down carefully. He pulled a chair from beside the bed, sat down, and faced her.

She couldn't look him in the eye for fear she'd see either disgust or greed fill his. "My real name isn't Maggy Boyle," she said as she looked at her fingers on her lap. "I mean, at one time it was, but nae anymore."

Findley cocked an eyebrow at this puzzling bit of news. She wasn't making much sense. He remained quiet and allowed her to continue.

She took a deep breath and blurted it all out. "My real name is Lady Margaret de Menteith, widow of Laird Gawter de Menteith, the Ninth Earl of Kerse!" She steeled herself and waited.

Findley was dumbstruck. What did her title have to do with

anything? He waited for more information, but when he realized none was forthcoming, he took her chin in his hand and lifted her face up. "And?"

"Think of it, Findley. The Ninth Earl of Kerse." She hoped her words would sink it. But by the confused look on his face, she could tell that he truly didn't understand. "My late husband, Findley, is King David's fourth cousin." Maggy let out a frustrated sigh and continued. "That means me son Liam is royalty."

It began to make sense to Findley then. If Liam was of royal descent that meant his mother wasn't just another poor peasant girl.

Maggy went on. "Liam is a descendant of Scottish royalty. With that comes titles, lands, and earldoms. Gawter's uncle, Laird Brockton, will nae allow me to marry anyone who does nae come with a title and money. Gawter made him promise, on his deathbed, that he would nae allow me to marry anyone who could take Liam's heritage away from him."

Findley's heart sank. He had no money, no lands, and no title. Laird Brockton was responsible for not just his nephew, but for Maggy as well. There'd be no way on earth the man would allow Maggy to marry Findley.

"Laird Brockton is a cruel man, Findley. He never liked me. He was against the marriage from the start, but for whatever reason, he allowed the marriage to take place. I never understood why, and I never understood how my mother managed to arrange the marriage. I was just the daughter of a farmer, the youngest child of Blaine and Lila Boyle. Me da was a farmer; he had no titles, no lands, and I had no dowry," she sighed and shuddered, suddenly felt quite cold.

"Findley, if it were different, if I had a choice in the matter, I would marry ye." He barely heard her, for she had spoken so softly.

He looked into her beautiful eyes and cursed the fates that had brought them together only to pull them apart. There had to be a way around it. There must be something he could do that would allow him to marry Maggy.

A strong tug pulled at his heart. He could not deny how he felt about her, and he could not keep it secret from her any longer. He slowly knelt on the floor in front of Maggy and took her hands in his.

"I dunnae care about what Laird Brockton thinks or wants. Ye're a grown woman, free to choose yer own husband, Maggy. Laird Brockton can go to the devil, for all I care. I want ye as me wife." He lifted her chin so that he could look into her eyes. He needed her to know what was in his heart. He loved her. No matter how stubborn a woman she was, no matter what obstacles life threw at them, he loved her.

"Please, Findley, dunnae say anything that my heart will nae be able to bear." She pressed her trembling fingers to his lips. "Whisper no words that my heart will nae be able to hear every day for the rest of my days, because 'twill leave it empty and dead, and I can nae bear it!"

Tears welled in her eyes again. If he said aloud what was truly in his heart, if she heard the words, then the rest of her days would be spent filled with longing and sorrow. Once this ordeal was over and she had her son back, there would be no future with Findley at her side. Her life was predestined to be spent as someone else's wife, not his. No matter how desperately she wanted to be his wife and spend the rest of her days by his side, she knew it would not be allowed to happen.

If he uttered the words, she would lose herself in them. She would tumble over a precipice and into a chasm she would never be able to pull herself from. Maggy could not bear the thought of hearing those words this night, only to have him taken from her and never hear them again.

He didn't have the strength to stop himself. He loved her with all that he was or would ever hope to be. It was much more than just a physical desire; he needed her as a drowning man needs air. As a tree needs the sun and water to live, he needed her. Without Maggy in his life, there would be no reason for him to take his next breath.

She was everything to him, and he wasn't prepared to give her up.

If he had to spend every day of the rest of his life trying to find a way for them to be together, he would.

"I love ye, Maggy," he said softly, touching his forehead to hers.

More tears came to her eyes. Her chest tightened, and her heart shattered into a thousand pieces, for she knew nothing could come of it. It mattered not how much they loved each other, for powers stronger than their feelings would see to it that they would never be together. Taking in a slow breath, she fumbled with her skirt, found the key and handed it to him.

Findley gave her a devilish smile and tossed the key over his shoulder. "Nay, I'll nae be lettin' ye go, lass. Ye're mine now. Now and forever," he whispered, his voice husky and filled with desire.

When his lips claimed hers, slanting across her mouth, the last of her resistance faded as quickly as a falling star. "I'll never let ye go, lass."

CHAPTER TWENTY

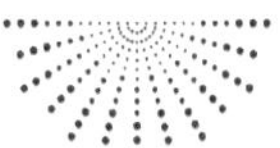

As Maggy slept peacefully beside him, her head resting on his chest, Findley made plans. No matter how dire she thought her situation might be, he would somehow find a way for them to be together. If he had to go to the king and beg for a special license, he would. They were destined to be together, and he'd not let anyone or anything stand in their way.

There was no way he could let her go. Not now, not ever. As he drifted off to sleep, he felt at peace for the first time since he was a child. Completely and utterly at peace. Little did he know that sense of peace would be short-lived.

CHAPTER TWENTY-ONE

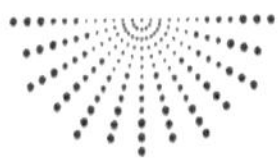

They woke to the sound of a knock at the door. Maggy pulled the sheet up to cover her naked body while Findley slipped on his trews before going to the door. Wee William burst through without waiting for an invitation. He looked worried.

"What is it, William?" Findley asked

"Robert and Andrew," he said before realizing Maggy and Findley were no longer shackled. He glanced at Maggy before turning to Findley.

"What of them?" Findley ignored the surprised look Wee William held and was positive he was not going to like the answer.

"They be gone!" Wee William's expression changed from surprise to anger.

"What do ye mean they be gone?" Maggy said as she sat up in the bed. Worry flooded her heart as guilt set in. If she hadn't been with Findley last night, then…then what? The boys would still be missing.

"When I went to wake them to break their fast, they were gone. I have looked everywhere, but I canna find them," he told her.

"And Liam and Collin?" Maggy asked as Findley brought her clothes to her.

"They be well," Wee William told her. "Patrick is with them. They say they know nae where Robert and Andrew went."

Maggy knew her boys. One didn't make a move without the other four knowing about it. Aye, Liam and Collin probably knew exactly where their brothers were.

She cast a perturbed look at Wee William and twirled her finger in the air by way of ordering him to turn around. Wee William blushed, blinked, and turned to face the door. He couldn't resist smiling. He was glad that Findley and Maggy had finally come to their good senses.

"Where is Richard?" Findley asked as he pulled his tunic over his head.

"He still searches for the lads, hoping they went to find a privy and may have gotten lost," Wee William told him. "The fog be as thick as soup right now. It's quite possible they've lost their way in it."

Maggy was standing by the bed now, pulling on her dress. "Wait until I get me hands on them!" Maggy said as she thrust her arms into the sleeves.

"I am sure they be well, lass," Findley offered as he strapped on his belt and sword. "I am sure they've not gone far." He cast a look at Wee William. Findley was worried but was trying to keep Maggy calm.

"I pray for their sakes that ye're right, Findley," she huffed as she tied the laces on the front of her dress. She slipped on her boots and headed toward the door. "I will question Liam and Collin," she said as she walked by them, and they quickly followed her.

As they walked down the hallway, Wee William whispered down at Findley. "Am I to gather by yer lack of shackles that the lass has released ye?" he couldn't stop the smile from forming.

"Nay," Findley said as he bounded down the stairs. "Shackles or nae, I still be shackled to her, and she to me."

Wee William smiled broadly. "Then she has agreed to marry ye?"

Maggy was but a few steps ahead of them as they walked to the end of the hallway.

"Nae exactly," Findley told him. "There is much to tell ye, Wee William, but it will have to wait. We need to find the boys."

Wee William let the subject drop as they followed Maggy into the room. From the two terrified sets of eyes that stared up at the fiery lass, Wee William was glad for a moment that Maggy wasn't his mum. If there were a secret to be kept, he doubted he would have been able to hold on to it for more than a minute before her penetrating and angry eyes broke his spirit.

"Collin! Liam!" she said as she thrust her hands on her hips. "Tell me now, and dunnae think of lyin' to me, for I swear there will be nae skin left on yer hides if ye do!"

The boys shot to their feet, eyes as large as saucers as their mum loomed over them. Normally she was a very patient mother, kind and as generous as she could be. Both boys could tell that now was not the time to test her patience.

"Where are Robert and Andrew?" she asked, using a tone of voice that only a mother was capable of using.

Their eyes were wide and filled with fear. Whenever their mum used that tone of voice, they knew they were in jeopardy of being skinned alive. The boys answered in unison. "They have gone to get Ian back!"

Wee William stared at them, dumbfounded. He had asked the boys repeatedly if they knew where their brothers had gone. And the answer had been the same each time: "We dunnae."

Their mum walks in and has her answer after asking the question but once. She was a fierce thing!

Maggy didn't blink. She didn't come apart or fall into a weeping heap or melt into histrionics. She pursed her lips and spoke to her sons. "Get yerselves dressed now," she ordered before turning to Wee William and Findley. "As soon as they get dressed, we will take them to Aishlinn and Duncan. I will nae allow more of me sons get lost to the Buchannans this day." She pushed past the two men and raced back to her room. Findley ordered Wee William to stay with the boys and try to find out what else they knew before he raced after Maggy.

She was throwing garments into her bag and mumbling under her breath.

"Maggy," he began softly. "I am sure they cannae have gotten far."

Maggy spun on her heals to face him, her hands balled into fists. "Findley, I swear to you, if I have lost more of me sons to Malcolm Buchannan, I shall kill the bloody fool with me bare hands!"

Findley went to her and wrapped his arms around her. "Wheest, lass," he whispered. "We will find the boys."

"What if the Buchannans have them?" She fought back tears of anguish as well as anger. She knew she could not survive losing more sons.

"We will get them back, Maggy, I swear it," his lips mumbled into her hair, then planted a kiss on the top of her head. His love for her seemed to be growing with each beat of his heart. There was nothing that he would not do for her, nothing he wouldn't give in order to bring back her beautiful smile and the sparkle of her eyes.

"Maggy," he said as he pulled her away. Lifting her chin so that he could look into those beautiful eyes, he felt his heart seize when he saw the pain in them. "Please, will ye now agree to go back with Duncan and Aishlinn?"

How many days had she been fiercely determined and relentless about getting her son back? How many years had she spent being independent, taking care of her small clan? How many nights had she lay awake and prayed for someone just like Findley to walk in to her life, sweep her off her feet, and tell her all would be well? A man who would love her and adore her but still allow her be herself.

Aye, she loved being independent, but with it came more responsibility than one person could bear. She'd shouldered it all alone, with no one to talk to, no one to share her dreams or with which to build a life.

She felt as though she had failed and failed miserably. She had let them all down, her people that were killed protecting her and now her sons.

"I have let them all down, Findley," she wept in his arms. "My people are all dead because of me. My son has been kidnapped by a madman, and now possibly two more have fallen into his hands. I was so determined to take care of them all, to be independent, and to do it all alone, but I failed them. I failed them all!"

"Lass, ye did what ye had to do." He kissed the top of her head again and drew her closer. "I dunnae ken another who could have done what ye've done and not gone mad from it."

"Had I just agreed to marry Malcolm," she began before he stopped her by pulling her away.

"Nay! Do nae ever say it! Had ye married Malcolm, then ye could never have loved me or I you!"

Her green eyes glistened as the tears fell from them down her cheeks and chin. She loved him, wholly and passionately. She shuddered at the thought of being bound to Malcolm Buchannan. The image of the nasty, repugnant man made her stomach roil and lurch. Nay, she could never have been with a man like that.

"But my decision cost my people their lives, Findley! They all be dead because of me!"

He shook his head. "Nay, lass, they be dead at the hands of a mad man. Do ye nae think that once he got whatever it is he wanted from ye that he would have no thought to killin' ye or yer sons? Think on it, Maggy! Ye may not have saved them all, but ye did save yer sons."

Maggy choked on tears and tried to speak, but the words were stuck in her throat. There was more he did not know, much more, but she could not get the words out.

"Maggy, ye ken I am right." He pressed a kiss to her forehead. "Maggy, please, if ye love me at all, ye'll go back to Gregor with Duncan and Aishlinn." He kissed her cheeks and wiped the tears away with his thumbs. "Maggy, I'll nae be able to go into battle if I must worry over yer safety. I canna fight like I must if I worry ye'll be injured or worse. Please, Maggy, I beg of ye. Go to Gregor."

The only things she had left in the world to fight for were her sons. Could she hold onto a glimmer of hope that she now had more to fight for? Another reason to live besides her boys?

In the deepest recess of her heart, she knew that she and Findley would never be allowed to be together. There were too many forces, all more powerful than the two of them, that would keep them apart.

The thought of Findley wounded or killed as he tried to free her son from Malcolm Buchannan twisted her stomach into knots. After all these years, there was finally someone who worried over her. As she looked into his dark brown eyes that pleaded with her to listen to reason, she knew he was right. If she insisted on going to Aberdeen with him, he would not be able to concentrate as he would need to. He'd be far too worried about her to do what he must.

"Aye, I will go back with them." She nodded her head as more tears trickled down her cheeks. At least she could keep her other two sons out of the reach of the Buchannans, and she could delay any marriage that Laird Brockton might try to force on her.

A big swoosh of air escaped Findley's lungs as his shoulders relaxed with relief, and he embraced her so tightly she could barely breathe. "Och! Thank ye, lass!" he said as he began kissing the top of her head. "I will get our Ian back, I promise ye! And when I return to Gregor, we will be married."

Our Ian. He hadn't simply claimed her, he was claiming her sons. Maggy took in a deep breath as she pushed away from him. She knew that a battle against Malcolm Buchannan, the most reviled and hated man in all of Scotland, would be far easier than trying to gain permission for her and Findley to marry.

"Aye, I'll marry ye, Findley," she said as she forced a smile. She couldn't have him go into battle thinking anything else. If he knew that she at least wanted to marry him, he could carry that with him. She would let him take that hope with him. She loved him too much to deny him that.

———

THEY DIDN'T BOTHER SITTING to break their fast. Patrick had gotten them bannocks, dried beef, and fresh apples to eat along the way.

Wee William led them out of the inn. He held Collin's hand while Patrick and Findley walked on either side of Maggy and Liam. She held on tightly to her son's hand as he munched on a hunk of bread.

The sun had not yet begun to rise as they stepped out onto the street and into the dense, heavy fog. The men were glad for the cover of darkness and the protection the fog afforded them. If they could not see more than a few feet in front of them, then no one would be able to see them.

Duncan and Aishlinn were staying at an inn just three blocks from their own. Findley felt confident as they made their way down the dark streets heading north that in a matter of a few minutes, Maggy and the boys would finally be heading toward freedom and safety.

"Findley," Wee William's deep voice came from a few steps ahead. "If ye take Collin, then I'll go ready our horses."

Findley thought it made good sense. "Aye," he said. "The sooner we are away from this place, the better I'll feel."

They stopped for a brief moment so that Wee William could put Collin's small hand into Findley's. He bent down to one knee to speak to the boy. "We are goin' to go get all yer brothers and bring them back to ye. Now, can ye take good care of yer mum, lad?"

Collin nodded his head. "Aye, I will if ye promise me ye'll bring Malcolm Buchannan's head in a basket to me."

The men chuckled, and Wee William rubbed the top of the boy's head. "I am glad ye're on my side in this!"

Next, he said goodbye to Liam and Maggy, giving the small boy a hug and the same instructions to guard and protect his mum. He stood and put a hand on Maggy's shoulder. "If Findley does nae marry ye, then I will, lassie!" he said with a smile and a wink.

Maggy laughed, gave him a hug, and prayed for his safe return. Moments later, Wee William disappeared into the fog.

Liam was pleading with Maggy to allow him to walk with Findley and Collin. Because she could not shake the sense that they were being watched, she believed the boys would be better protected with Findley. She gave a nod of her head and gave him over to Findley.

They walked another two blocks with relative ease considering the thick blanket of fog that surrounded them. As they stopped to cross at the corner, Findley stepped out onto the street with the boys. Maggy was about to follow when she heard the sound of a wagon coming toward them. Patrick pulled her back to stand beside him, and they paused to allow it to pass.

When she realized there was more than one wagon, she called to Findley, who was by now safely on the other side of the street.

"Findley, we are here! There be wagons comin'!"

Findley called back to stay close to Patrick, and he waited with his nerves on edge for the wagons to pass. They moved far too slowly for his liking.

Four wagons passed by, all moving slowly because of the dense fog. Findley could barely see the wagons, let alone Maggy or Patrick. He cursed the wagons and the fog as he kept his eyes and ears peeled for any sign of trouble.

When the last wagon passed, and it appeared no more were coming, he let out a sigh of relief. He waited for Patrick to bring Maggy across.

Long moments ticked by without a sign of them. After several moments he realized he was holding his breath again. Surely, they should be crossing by now.

"Patrick!" he called out into the foggy early morning.

When no answer came, fear and dread seized his heart. He ran across the street, pulling the boys with him as he shouted for Patrick. He received no answer.

When he reached the other side, he found Patrick lying on the ground moaning. As he knelt beside him, Findley saw blood trickling down the side of Patrick's head. Findley noticed his sword was still in its scabbard, indicating he had been caught unaware.

"Patrick! Patrick, wake up!" he said as he shook Patrick's shoulders. Patrick moaned and mumbled incoherently.

He called Maggy's name once then waited, hoping to hear her voice call back to him. He could hear nothing but the sound of his own heartbeat as it rushed in his ears.

Liam and Collin stood just a step away, holding each other's hand. Tears were welling in their eyes. "Where's our mum?" Liam asked, visibly shaken.

From the ground, Patrick moved and tried to sit, but was unable. The pain in his head was intense. He grabbed Findley's sleeve and pulled him closer.

His words were slurred, his voice hoarse. "They got her, Findley. I am sorry!"

———

MAGGY HAD BEEN STANDING on the corner waiting for the wagons to pass as she clung to Patrick's arm. Suddenly she heard a dull thud, then she felt Patrick's grip loosen as he fell to the ground beside her. Before she could move to help him, she was grabbed tightly around her waist and lifted into the air before she felt the cold blade of a dagger as it pressed against her throat.

"Do nae call out, or I'll slit ye throat, I swear it, Maggy." She could feel his hot breath as he spoke into her ear, and she was sure she recognized the voice.

"That's a good lass," the man whispered again.

'Twas then that she knew who held the blade to her throat, but it could not be! He had died in battle more than four years ago! "Traig?" she whispered. "I thought ye dead! We were told ye died in battle," she whispered as she grabbed the arm holding the dagger. She knew this man and many years ago had called him friend. Much like Maggy, he was back from the dead. But why was he holding a blade to her throat?

"Dead? Nay, lass, but I have been to hell," he spoke again, his voice nearly drowned out by the wagons. "I warn ye to remain quiet, and I'll nae harm ye." He began to pull her down the street.

"Where are ye takin' me?" she stammered as he lifted her up higher so that her feet no longer touched the ground. She knew it would be no use to struggle or fight with him, for he was much taller and stronger.

"Why, to yer betrothed. Where else?" he chuckled, but it wasn't the same warm, soft chuckle she remembered from years ago. Nay, this was the laugh of a mad man.

"Me betrothed? I have nae been betrothed to anyone, Traig!" she was confused as well as frightened.

"Well, then ye best be tellin' Malcolm Buchannan that, fer he is offered a reward fer yer safe return."

ANGER, fear, trepidation, loss, fury, and grief flooded over him in the span of one heartbeat. *I have lost her again!*

Findley still knelt next to Patrick, who was struggling to remain conscious. Patrick felt a wave of nausea roil up in his belly as the pain in his head seemed to get worse.

"Did ye see them, Patrick? How many were there?" Findley struggled between needing information and needing help for his friend.

"One, but I did nae see his face," Patrick answered as he struggled for air. "But I dunnae think he's a Buchannan," he said, suddenly growing quite cold.

Findley looked at his friend with confusion and worry etched on his face.

"She knew him, Findley," Patrick said as he tried in vain to steady his breathing. "She called him Traig. I heard her say she thought he had died in battle." The world around Patrick began to spin, and he suddenly felt like he was on ship at sea. There was a terrible and violent storm taking place all around him. He was cold, sick, and in a tremendous amount of pain.

"Patrick, are ye sure?" Findley asked as he held his friend's hand. He tried to hide the worry on his face; the worry that said Patrick was not long for this world.

To nod his head would have caused him more pain. He could only whisper that yes, he was certain. *I am goin' to die soon, but I must help Maggy.*

"Findley," Patrick said as he struggled to remain awake. He had to tell Findley what he knew before he could submit to the sweet release of sleep or death.

"He is takin' her to Malcolm," he sputtered out. "I heard him say he was takin' her to Malcolm." He took a few more deep breaths and tried to hold on. "She was scared, Findley, and I could nae help her." His mouth was horribly dry, and his tongue felt swollen and thick.

"I could nae help her," were Patrick's last words.

FINDLEY'S HEART ached for the death of his good friend as much as it ached for Maggy. Malcolm Buchannan was as good as dead; he just didn't know it yet. And so was the man who had killed Patrick and taken Maggy.

Findley had raced back to the stables as fast as he could with two little boys in tow. Wee William had most of the horses saddled and ready by the time Findley reached him.

Telling Wee William that Patrick lay dead on the street corner was one of the hardest things he had ever had to do. The grief in Wee William's face was too much to bear. Wee William remained silent, his anger masked behind a stony expression. He saddled up the last horse and raced down the street to retrieve his friend's body.

The sun was just beginning to break when he reached Patrick. As he knelt on the ground and cradled the lifeless form in his arms, he made a silent vow to kill the man responsible.

"Ye take the lads to Duncan. I'll see to Patrick," Wee William said as he lifted his friend in his arms. "I'll catch up with ye verra soon."

Findley looked up at Wee William, the man's eyes filled with sadness and grief. "William," he began, not sure what he could say that would make either of them feel any better.

"Go, Findley! Take the boys and hurry. We are wastin' time, lad. We have evil men to kill!" The deep timbre of Wee William's voice broke through the quiet morning. Findley knew he was right, that the longer they stood and mourned the loss of their friend, the greater the distance between them and Maggy.

With a nod of his head, Findley grabbed the reins of their horses and hurried the boys to Duncan and Aishlinn.

Wee William looked down to Patrick and spoke softly. "As God is me witness, lad, I'll avenge yer death if it's the last thing I do."

As soon as he had settled the boys in with Aishlinn and Duncan, Findley met up with Richard and Wee William. Richard had been keeping a close eye on the Buchannans. Shocked and sadden by the loss of their friend, Richard also made a silent vow to avenge the death of his friend.

Wee William had left Patrick's body with the local healer. He gave him five and twenty groats and the promise that he'd return in a month's time to take the young man's body back to his parents.

They didn't have time to waste waiting for Duncan's men to ready themselves to ride out, so they departed immediately in search of the missing trio. They rode like banshees from hell toward Aberdeen, pushing themselves and their horses to near exhaustion. There was much on their minds, and they worried over Robert and Andrew as well as Maggy. They could only hope that they'd catch up with the boys before the Buchannans did. Findley was so angry with the two of them that he worried he'd be unable to control his temper and not beat the lads senseless once they caught up with them.

They figured the lads were heading to Aberdeen in some brazen attempt to rescue Ian alone. Wee William had found the lads' horses and saddles missing earlier and knew there could be no other explanation.

Dozens of tracks from horses, oxen, and wagons led out of town, making it next to impossible to track anyone. Findley wasn't sure if he hoped the boys' sense of direction had improved since last spring or not. If it remained as bad as it had been, then they were likely roaming the countryside, and God only knew how long it would take to find them. If it had improved, then the fools might make it to Aberdeen before they did. Neither thought was comforting.

The fog had finally lifted near midday, but the day brought very little relief or warmth. It was a cold day in late autumn, and the skies threatened rain.

They headed north over hills and through valleys without speaking, each man lost in his own thoughts. Richard and Wee William prayed that Angus would send enough men to help and hoped they'd be waiting for them in Aberdeen.

Wee William worried over Patrick's parents. He and Patrick had been very good friends for many years, and Wee William knew his parents well. The pain it brought to his heart when he thought of how he would have to tell them that their son was dead was insufferable. The only thing that kept him going was the thought of avenging his friend's death. Aye, whoever this Traig man was, there'd be nothing left of his body to send to his family when this was over.

Findley's heartache over Maggy's kidnapping threatened to tear him apart. This feeling was worse than when he'd come across their burned home those many days ago. 'Twas far worse now, because he knew he loved her. Just as importantly, she loved him. They were planning a future together, and now she was gone. Anger burned at his insides.

He rolled Patrick's last words over and over in his mind. *She was scared. I couldn't help her. She was scared.* She hadn't gone willingly, he knew it in his heart. She'd been taken by one mad man who apparently wanted to give her to another. The thought tore at his heart, at his soul, and burned through his stomach. He had to get to her before she was turned over to Malcolm Buchannan.

Whoever this Traig was, Findley was completely prepared to hunt him to the ends of the earth. He'd kill the man with his bare hands if he laid a hand on Maggy.

Earlier, Findley's only concern had been trying to find a way for him and Maggy and the boys to be a family. Now he was forced to worry over Robert and Andrew as well as getting Maggy back. And now this Traig was thrown into the pot.

Fate had stuck its nasty hand in to interfere again. Either that, or God was testing his mettle and courage. Either way it didn't matter, for he'd get them back, and come hell or high water, they'd be a family. No matter what happened, he'd have his Maggy.

Please, God, let her be safe.

CHAPTER TWENTY-TWO

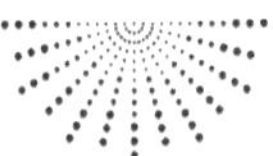

"Robert, I am c-cold! Are ye sure we c-can't start just a w-wee fire?" Andrew's teeth were chattering. The rain had started more than an hour ago, and now the two boys were soaked to the bone. They had taken refuge under a small clump of trees, but the nearly bare branches did little to keep out the rain or the cold.

"Nay," Robert told him through his own chattering teeth. "I told ye, a f-fire will draw attention." A fire, even if he could find wood dry enough to burn, might draw unwanted attention, and that was the last thing they needed at the moment.

"How long d-do ye think th-the rain will last?" Andrew asked. He hadn't thought about rain or hunger last night when Robert came to him with his plan. All he had thought about was the adventure and rescuing his little brother. This afternoon, however, he was beginning to question his decision.

Robert was growing frustrated with him. They were on a mission, a mission to rescue Ian. If they let a little rain dampen their spirits, then what kind of warriors would they make? "I dunnae ken, Andrew," he told him. "But w-warriors never c-complain of the rain or c-cold or hunger."

Andrew pulled his cloak a bit tighter around his body. He had always looked up to Robert. Robert was always the brave one, the serious one, and he took his duty as eldest brother very seriously.

Andrew suddenly wondered how Robert knew so much about great clans and warriors. They'd lost their families more than three years ago. Robert was only nine or ten at the time. They'd lived in relative seclusion ever since. Maybe all of Robert's stories were just that: stories he had made up in order to keep his younger brothers in check.

Someday we will have a clan of our own. One filled with many fighters, warriors. We will be the biggest and most honorable clan in all of Scotland. We will live in a grand keep, with plenty of land to grow food to feed our people. We will have the best and fastest horses, the best weapons, and the best men. We will fight for those who are less fortunate as well as our freedom. How many times had he heard Robert say those things?

Andrew knew it wasn't greed that pushed Robert. Nay, 'twas honor. It was some deep-seated sense of wanting to provide and protect his mum and brothers that drove him.

Once Andrew thought it through, he realized it didn't matter if Robert's stories were true or not. What mattered was that Robert would do everything and anything he could to make their dream of someday having a great clan, and enough to eat, a reality.

That realization did little, however, to warm his cold fingers or toes.

"How mad do ye think Mum will be?" Andrew asked quietly.

Robert looked over at his brother and shuddered before a small smile slowly appeared on his face. "I think we need to fear her more than the Buchannans."

Andrew couldn't help but laugh. "Aye," he said. "But think how proud she will be of us when we rescue Ian."

Robert nodded his head in agreement. Aye, their mum would be angry as well as proud. And very relieved to have their Ian back. They'd prove to her once and for all that they were men, not just wee boys. They'd prove that they could take care of their own.

"We might want to take whatever armor we can from the Buchannans we will slay," Andrew chuckled. "We will need it."

Robert's eyebrows knitted together. "I will nae wear any Buchannan cast-offs," he said. The thought of wearing anything that had touched a Buchannan was revolting. "Someday we will be rich enough to purchase our own armor."

"Nay, not fer future battles," Andrew said with a serious and thoughtful tone. "We will need it now to protect us from the skelpin' Mum is goin' to give us!"

The ever-serious Robert couldn't help but laugh! Aye, the battle they'd face with their mum was going to be far worse than any battle with the Buchannans. Somehow, fighting against the evil man who took his brother seemed far less perilous than when they'd be forced to face their mum.

Robert estimated the rain had kept them in the trees for at least three hours. Once it had finally let up, he and Andrew climbed their horses and trudged on.

They could not go as fast as they would have liked, for the ground was too sodden and muddy. He cursed the rain, the mud, and the cold. He cursed Malcolm Buchannan and the men who followed him. Why men chose to follow someone evil instead of doing what was right, he could not fathom. Mayhap it was fear that forced them to follow, or mayhap there were far more evil men in this world than he cared to admit.

When he was older, he'd inspire his men by always being valiant, honest, and strong. He'd have very strict rules in his clan; there would be no beating of wives or children, for starters. There'd be no lying, no cheating, or stealing.

They were covered with mud from head to toe. Their clothes were soaked and clung to their bodies. Robert couldn't remember a time he'd been this wet or this cold. He could remember, however, being this hungry. He had taken enough bread and cheese to last them at least a week. Guilt from having stolen it chewed at his conscience.

When he had taken it from the kitchen of the inn, he had reasoned that he was taking it for a good reason. He would need his strength to for the journey to Aberdeen. Leaving a note for the innkeeper, with his vow to return someday very soon to repay him, made taking the bread and cheese feel a lot less like stealing and more like borrowing.

It amazed him what the fear of starvation would get a person to do. Robert knew that when all was said and done, he was an honest person. Someday, he told himself, he would never have to steal again in order to survive.

They rode for another hour or two before darkness began to descend upon them. He had learned that past summer not to travel after dark in unfamiliar territory. That had been a huge mistake, and that was how they had ended up so many days from their home and on MacDougall lands.

Not wanting to risk ending up on lands belonging to people far less kind than Findley and his men, Robert searched for a place to make camp. They settled into a small, dense forest, tied their horses to low hanging branches, and removed the saddles and tack.

Weary, exhausted, and soaked to the bone, they each ate a slice of bread and a hunk of cheese before lying down and succumbing to sleep. As he drifted off, Robert prayed for God's speed and mercy to help in getting Ian back. He knew he couldn't do it alone.

THEY HAD BEEN PULLED from their cold slumber by hands grabbing their clothes and pulling them to their feet. Fear enveloped each boy, and they felt it clear to their toes.

"Ye little heathens!" Wee William's voice boomed through the early morning air. He was holding Robert up by the scruff of his tunic, anger ablaze in his eyes.

Richard held onto Andrew, who shook and trembled with fear. Findley stood in front of them, his hands balled into fists, his anger quite evident in his scowl and piercing eyes.

"Do ye realize how badly ye scared yer mum?" Wee William boomed at Robert before turning to the still-trembling Andrew.

The boys remained mute. While Andrew was visibly frightened,

Robert kept his cool demeanor. He'd not show fear, no matter what the consequences.

Findley remained where he was. He knew if he took one step closer to them, he would be sorely tempted to skin their idiotic hides.

"Mum was goin' to send us hidin' like cowards!" Robert said through gritted teeth. "We are nae cowards!"

"Nay! Ye're worse than cowards!" Findley finally spoke. "Ye're fools."

Robert turned to look at him. "Nay!" he shot back. "We are men, and we take care of our own!"

In three strides Findley was standing in front of him, his face just inches from the lad's. "Nay, ye're not men, ye're boys. Boys who aren't smart enough to realize they cannae fight a hundred plus men with only a *sgian dubh* and a handful of rocks! And ye're fools if ye think differently!" He was doing his best not to knock the boy's head off his shoulders.

Robert's eyes darted from one man to the other before realizing his mum and Patrick weren't there. Had she sent the men to deal with them? To give them a good skelping before handing them over to Duncan and forcing them to go hide like frightened children?

It was Richard who spoke next. "Lads, we ken ye wanted to help, but ye were foolish to run off like that." His voice was calm and belied the anger he truly felt.

"What are ye goin' to do to us?" Andrew squeaked, still trembling.

Findley eyed both boys for a moment before shaking his head. "Ye'll be punished, that much I ken. But we have no time fer it now," he said calmly. He'd let them worry over it for a time, let them stew in their own juices. Once he got them back to Gregor, they'd be cleaning privies for the next six months.

"Mount up," Findley told them as he walked toward his own steed.

Richard and Wee William let loose the boys and walked toward their own horses. Robert and Andrew looked warily at each other. Robert was sure it must be some kind of trick to get them to let down their defenses. He shook the rain from his cloak. Andrew followed him as they walked toward their horses.

"Where is Mum?" Andrew whispered as they saddled their horses.

Robert's expression remained calm and resolute. "I dunnae ken," he whispered back. "But she must not be far."

A very panicked look came over Andrew's face as he tossed the saddle to the back of his horse. "We did nae get to rescue Ian, Robert!" His hands shook from the cold and the fear that washed over him.

"Now she won't be proud. She will just be angry!" He didn't like the thought of a very angry mother. The plan had been to rescue Ian. With Ian safe and sound, their mum would be far less likely to skin them alive. Without Ian, the chances of surviving their mother's wrath were nil. Suddenly, he didn't feel well. Not well at all.

<hr>

ROBERT AND ANDREW listened somberly to the events that had unfolded after they'd run away. A tremendous amount of guilt fell on their shoulders.

"Do ye ken the name, lads? Do ye ken who this Traig might be?" Richard asked the boys as they rode north to Aberdeen.

Robert's brow furrowed in contemplation. "Nay," he said after thinking on it for a few moments. "The only Traig I remember was Ian's da. But he died when Ian was a wean, so it could nae be him."

"How did he die?" Findley asked. Maggy wasn't the only one in history to play dead for a time.

"I am nae sure, but I think I heard Maggy speak on it once. English soldiers attacked Traig and Liam's da when they were travelin' to Dundee. But I canna be sure of it. 'Twas a long time ago."

Robert didn't care who the man was that took his mum and had killed Patrick. It changed nothing. Patrick was still dead and his mum missing.

"'Tis all me fault," he said, his voice barely audible over the sounds of the horses trudging through muck and mud.

For a moment Findley thought of letting Robert believe just that. But he knew what guilt could do to a boy. It would eat him alive.

"Nay," Findley told him as he cast a glance toward Robert. His shoulders were slumped, and his face had gone horribly pale. "Either way, he would have found a way of takin' yer mum."

Robert's eyes were glued to his horse's mane. He was certain Findley was only trying to make him feel better. "Nay, had I been there, I could have stopped him," he mumbled.

Findley reached over and pulled Robert's horse to a stop along side his own. "Aye, had ye been there and done somethin' foolish, it could be ye layin' dead instead of Patrick."

Robert finally looked up. The grief and guilt in Robert's eyes was enough to tell Findley the boy was truly remorseful. He had to remind himself that Robert was just that: a boy. Aye, he had turned three and ten more than a month ago, but he was still a boy.

"And how do ye think yer mum would respond to losin' ye?" Findley asked him.

It mattered not. Mayhap had he not talked Andrew into running off with him, Patrick might still be alive, and their mum would be safe.

"Robert," Findley began. "Ye're a fine young lad. I see great potential in ye and a good future fer ye."

Robert cast him a disbelieving look and turned his face away.

"I am not just blowin' air up yer plaid, lad. I mean what I say, and I say what I mean. None of us is perfect, and we all make mistakes. The trick is to learn from them."

Robert nodded his head, only half listening. His mind was elsewhere, worrying about his mother and brother.

Findley let out a heavy sigh, shook his head, and thumped the boy upside his head. "Listen to me, ye fool!"

Robert rubbed the side of his head, his face twisted into frustration and a bit of anger as he finally looked at Findley.

"Ye made a mistake and used poor judgment. 'Tis no because ye're stupid, 'tis because ye're young and inexperienced," Findley told him.

If Findley was trying to make him feel better, he was doing a poor job of it.

"If ye really want to be a fine warrior someday, then ye must first learn to listen to yer leader, listen to those with more experience and wisdom."

Robert stared at Findley. "How am I to be a fine warrior if I keep gettin' left behind any time there's trouble?" he asked him sullenly.

Findley sighed again. The boy was a stubborn fool. "Ye'll keep getting left behind with that attitude, lad. Ye can't just go into a fight with swords drawn and vengeance on yer mind. Ye must have a plan of action!"

"I did have a plan of action, and it did nae involve drawn swords or fightin'."

A look of surprise and confusion came to Findley's face. "What do ye mean?"

Robert let out a short breath. "We'd planned on just going up to the gates and askin' to be let in."

Findley looked at him as if he lost his mind. Robert explained further. "Who would be suspicious of two lost boys? Surely, they'd give us shelter for at least a night or two, until our equally lost fathers found us," he smiled up at Findley.

'Twas as if a light suddenly came to a dark room. Findley quickly followed Robert's train of thought. "And ye'd be able to find Ian and keep him safe until we got there." 'Twas more of a statement than a question.

"Aye," Robert nodded, looking quite proud of his plan. "And then we'd draw swords and fight!"

Findley rolled his eyes and ran his hand across the top of Robert's head. It was indeed a good plan. He wasn't sure, but it might just work. "Ye've a devious side to ye, lad," he said with a smile. "A very devious side."

"I would nae call it devious. I would call it intelligent." He looked wounded. He never wanted anyone to think him devious.

"Do nae take it so personally, lad. 'Tis a good trait to own, Robert."

It was just like adults to have both a positive as well as negative meaning to the same word. He shook his head slightly and touched the flanks of his horse, moving it forward. They were wasting precious time talking. They had a woman and child to rescue.

"I'LL ASK YE AGAIN, Maggy. Where is my son?"

He was squeezing her arms so tightly she thought they'd snap in two! She was still reeling from the shock of seeing Traig alive and well. Then again, perhaps 'well' wasn't the right word, for he was far from well in the mental sense. He had lost his mind.

"I told ye, Malcolm Buchannan has him! He took him days ago!" She was pleading with him to listen and prayed he would realize she spoke the truth.

"Why would Malcolm do that?" Traig's voice thundered through the afternoon air. They'd ridden all day and well into last night. They had slept out of doors with no fire, and Maggy was frozen to the marrow. He had pulled her up from a sound sleep and thrown her up onto his horse before daybreak. They had stopped only once so that she could relieve herself before setting off again.

She was cold, tired, sore, and very hungry. But above all that, she was terrified.

"I told ye before, Traig! He is mad, and he took him to force me to marry him."

The anger in Traig's eyes sent a shiver down her spine. His grip on her arms tightened. "But why?" he demanded as he shook her.

Traig only knew that Malcolm Buchannan was offering a very substantial reward for anyone who brought Maggy to him. He had overheard the Buchannan men's conversation at the inn a few nights past. Seeing that he could seek some amount of revenge for his friend's betrayal five years ago, along with the potential of earning enough coin to start his life anew with his son at his side, taking Maggy had made perfectly good sense. But nothing else did.

"Tell me, Maggy! Tell me the truth, or I swear, if I think ye be lyin', I'll no hesitate to kill ye!"

Maggy took a deep breath and tried to sound far calmer than she felt at the moment. There was no doubt in her mind that Traig would keep his word.

"Traig, please, you're hurtin' me!" she pleaded with him to loosen his grip. "I'll tell ye everythin', I swear it. But please, loosen yer hold."

He tilted his head slightly and looked as if he were trying to read her mind. His expression was filled with hatred and mistrust and doubt. Maggy could not begin to understand why her once good friend now looked at her with such disgust.

He loosened his grip and sat her down rather harshly onto a fallen tree trunk. Maggy rubbed her arms where he had held them so tightly. She took a deep breath before speaking.

"Gawter is dead, Traig," she said bluntly. At one time, Gawter and Traig had been the best of friends. It was a friendship that had always confused Maggy. They were as opposite as night and day, but somehow the two men had forged a friendship.

She was fully prepared to see Traig become grief-stricken. Instead, he looked angry, very angry, not at all like a man who had just learned of his best friend's death.

"I am sorry, Traig. I ken ye loved him like a brother," she said softly. She realized that this was not the same man she knew from years ago. No, the man standing before her was filled with hate and anger. Gone was the ready smile, the kind word, or the playful teasing. She didn't know this stranger.

"How?" he spat at her.

"How what?" she asked, unsure what exactly he wanted from her.

"How did he die?" his voice thundered as he towered over her.

Her blood went cold. Something had happened; something horrible had taken place that changed Traig into this cold, angry monster.

"The pox," her voice was shaky. "It wiped out nearly all our clan, Traig."

His face went pale. He began to pace back and forth in front of her, demanding answers to his questions.

"Nearly everyone?"

Maggy nodded her head. "Aye," she said softly. "I am sorry, Traig, but Helena did nae survive either." She trembled and waited; ready to comfort him as the sadness of learning of his wife's death sank in.

Mayhap the news of Helena's death would bring back at least a little part of the Traig she knew and loved like a brother.

"Dead? Helena's dead?" he asked, more shocked than saddened by the news.

Maggy could only nod her head and dig her fingers into the tree trunk for balance.

He stopped pacing and turned his angry glare toward her. His reaction surprised her more than seeing him alive for the first time. He smiled down at her. 'Twas a happy smile that blended with an evilness she'd only ever seen on one other man before him. "Then she is dancin' in hell with yer husband."

Maggy's eyebrows knitted together. She was growing more and more confused by his reactions. "Traig, she was yer wife! And Gawter, as much as he was a hard, unkind man, was yer friend!"

"My friend?" he laughed at her, and his laughter sent another chill down her spine. "My friend?! Nay, he was a lyin', cheatin' cur who deserved to die at me own hands instead of by a disease!" his voice rose angrily.

Maggy shook her head and tried to make sense of his reaction. "Traig, I dunnae ken what happened to ye! Why do ye say such things?"

"I speak the truth, Maggy! Gawter was a liar, a cheat. A man with no scruples."

She stared up at him, her confusion written all over her face. Traig threw his head back and laughed for a moment before he began pacing again. "Ye truly are a bonny lass, even if ye're a bit dimwitted."

Normally she would have been quite insulted by his remark and would have argued back at him. He was too terrifying at the moment to do anything but sit and tremble.

"How did Gawter react after my supposed death?"

Maggy thought on it for a few moments and searched her mind for memories of that time. While she had cried nearly nonstop for many days after learning of Traig's death, Gawter had remained apparently unmoved by it. Maggy had simply believed it was Gawter being his typically cold and callous self. But she had wondered at that time why he didn't seem more moved or more saddened by his friend's death. He and Traig had been like brothers. But Gawter hadn't shed one tear over Traig's death.

"Aye, I can see ye thinkin' on it, lass!" Traig seemed to become more energized as the moments passed. "I would bet gold to bannocks that he did nae shed one tear, did nae act at all like a grievin' friend. Am I right?"

Maggy could only nod her head in agreement.

"And have ye asked yerself why?"

'Twas because he was a cold, cruel man who only cared of himself. Maggy couldn't speak the words aloud. For some strange reason, she felt she needed to help Traig hold on to the good memories he had of their friendship.

"Ye're not that dim, Maggy. Ask yerself, why?"

She shuddered when it suddenly occurred to her that Gawter had somehow had a hand in Traig's supposed death. While Gawter had made more than one attempt on Maggy's life, she would never have thought him evil enough to kill his best friend. How wrong could she have been?

"Tell me Traig, what happened?" she asked with a scratchy voice.

"I think ye've already begun to piece things together. But I am sure by the shocked look on yer face that ye dunnae ken all of it, do ye lass?"

Maggy remained quiet and still as she braced herself mentally for the news he was about to give her.

"As ye can see, I be not dead as Gawter told ye. I did nae die on the battlefield, as I am sure he told ye. Nay, Maggy, 'twas a fate far worse than death, that I can assure ye."

He resumed his pacing, his hands waving in the air as he spoke. He looked as insane as he sounded. "Aye, there was an attack, but nae from foes. The attack came at Gawter's own hands. He could nae kill me outright, he was too much a coward for that. Nay, he did nae have the guts to do it himself. Instead, he handed me over to English soldiers."

Maggy's hand flew to her mouth. Her husband was far more evil than she had ever known.

"Aye, that he did, lassie," Traig said coldly. "I ken the man to be cruel, but to betray me like that? To betray his best friend? Nay, lassie, not even I thought him that cruel and evil. But betray me he did. He had hired English soldiers to kill me. I was beaten, near death after fighting Gawter. It had been a surprise I hadn't seen comin', and I was fully unprepared fer it," he shook his head in disgust at the memory of that day.

"So, he handed me over to the English soldiers that he hired to finish what he had started. I had broken bones and was near death. My only savin' grace was that the soldiers were even more cruel than Gawter!" He chuckled softly and clasped his hands behind his back. "So, they made me a prisoner. They used me to help build towers and walls and fortresses against me own people. For more than five years I languished, Maggy, beaten nearly every day and forced to work like an animal. Starved if we did nae work hard enough or fast enough. They fed their dogs better than us."

He stopped suddenly and looked down at her. His lips curved upward into a dastardly smile. "Would ye like to ken why?"

Did it really matter why? Somehow she knew he'd tell her.

"He did it fer Helena."

Helena. Maggy felt like she had just been kicked in the chest. Helena had been her best friend, her confident, and the keeper of one of Maggy's deepest secrets. Aye, Maggy had known that Gawter strayed and strayed often. She had heard the stories of the loose women and wenches he enjoyed while far from home. She also knew of the occasional servant and maid. But Helena? Nay!

"Aye, Maggy, I speak the truth!" he seemed utterly pleased to be bringing such heartache to her.

"Nay! She was me friend!" Maggy could not wrap her head around it. She suddenly felt dizzy and out of breath.

"Maggy, I would nae tell ye lies. She and Gawter had been carryin' on fer quite some time. I did nae ken it meself, though, until the day he tried to kill me." He started pacing again, like an animal in a cage.

"As I lay on the ground bleedin' to death, he confessed. He told me he had to kill me so that he and Helena could be together."

He stopped suddenly and turned to her again. "I must say I was quite surprised to find ye still breathin'."

She didn't bother asking why. Nothing he could say from this point on would surprise her.

"Ye see, lass, after he was to have me killed, he was goin' to take yer life as well."

No, that did not surprise her in the least, she snorted disgustedly. Gawter had, on two separate occasions, poisoned her tea. Both times —and only by the grace of God, she was certain—she had been found by Claire and Kate. The first attempt on her life had led her to make one of the most difficult decisions of her life. The second attempt had reassured her that she had done the right thing.

"Ye do nae look surprised, Maggy." Traig studied her closely for a long moment.

"Nay, I am nae surprised, Traig. He had tried twice to poison me. Once when I was heavy with child and then again when Liam was a wean," she told him. Her head was beginning to pound. How could Helena, of all people, have betrayed her.

Traig nodded his head thoughtfully for a moment. "But the news of Helena's betrayal, that surprises ye?"

Her shock was beginning to be replaced by anger boiling up in her stomach. "Aye, that it does. I canna believe she would do such a thing! I was her friend, and I thought she was mine!" Maggy stood and began to pace, her mind running in a thousand different directions. "How? How could she do that? How could she, after everything, after all she knew?"

The two of them paced and mumbled aloud, neither of them paying any attention to what the other was saying. They were lost in their own grief and shock.

Traig stopped suddenly and grabbed Maggy by the arms again. "Ye still haven't told me why Malcolm has me son."

Maggy forced a breath through her nostrils. "I took Ian to raise as me own after Helena's death. We went into hidin'. I did nae want

Laird Brockton to marry me off. With me parents both dead and me the mother of Liam, who is the heir to all of Gawter's fortune, Laird Brockton would have wanted me married off within a year's time! I could nae do that again. While Gawter was cold and cruel, I knew there were worse men than he! So, I went into hidin', and that's where I have been these past three years." She choked back tears of sorrow, regret, and fear.

"A few months ago, Malcolm Buchannan stumbled upon our camp. He recognized me from years ago. I tried to deny it, but he refused to believe I was just a peasant. He asked me three times to marry him, and each time I refused. The last time he came, I was nae there. I was in the forest looking for herbs to help Ian's fever." The memory of that day would haunt her for the rest of her life.

Traig squeezed her arms more tightly. "Then what happened?"

"They killed everyone in the camp! All the auld, the sick. They took Ian and hold him now as hostage." She was speaking rapidly, the fear rising in her again.

"And how did ye happen to be in Dundee?"

"Me friends, Findley McKenna and his men, they were helpin' me to get to Aberdeen, to Malcolm's keep so that we could get Ian back!"

He twisted her around so that her back was to him as he wound an arm around her waist and the other around her neck. "Ye better pray we reach them before yer friends do, Maggy!"

"Why? What are ye plannin' Traig? Mayhap I can help, we can help each other get Ian back."

His laughter was haunting, filed with callousness and spite. "Help each other? Nay, lass, we will nae be helpin' each other."

Maggy swallowed hard before asking her next question. "What are ye plannin' on doin', Traig?"

"I plan on givin' ye to Malcolm. He is offerin' a good deal of coin to any man that brings ye to him." His breath felt hot as he spoke into her ear and squeezed her tighter.

"Traig, ye dunnae have to do that! We can take Ian. Ye can come live with us, and together we can raise him!" She was pleading with him and praying that he would listen to reason. The thought of Traig taking her son away and never seeing him again was heart wrenching.

"Raise him together? Why? So he can learn to be a fool and trust people? Nay! I'll raise him to learn to trust no one. I'll nae allow anyone to betray him as his mum and Gawter betrayed me."

"Please, Traig, ye dunnae have to do this!"

Disgusted with her pleas he pushed her away from him with enough force that she fell to her knees. She landed in the mud and muck.

"Nay! I'll have enough money from handin' ye over that Ian and I can start our lives over. We will live far away from the likes of ye and Gawter and Malcolm Buchannan. We will have each other, and that's all we will ever need!"

Her entire world was falling apart. She lay in a heap on the cold ground, her heart breaking, tears wracking her body. After everything she had fought for, everything she had done, the sacrifices they had all made to remain free were all for naught.

She was surrounded by more evil than anyone should ever have to be. Traig was going to take her to Malcolm. Her boys would be taken from her, all but Liam. And then, when Malcolm had what he wanted, she'd no longer be of any value to him. She would end up dead and, more likely than not, Liam as well. And Ian? He'd be raised by a man who had lost his mind. The other boys? She could only pray that they would be able to seek refuge with Findley's clan.

Findley. Every fiber of her body hurt with knowing she'd probably never see him again. Nay, she could not think that! He loved her, she knew it down to her marrow. He would come for her and rescue her along with Ian!

Hope rapidly rose from her belly, but she couldn't allow Traig to see it. Nay, she had to appear fearful of him and of Malcolm. No matter what happened when they reached the Buchannan keep, she knew that Findley would come for her. He loved her and would do anything to protect her.

CHAPTER TWENTY-THREE

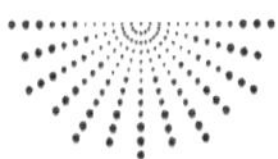

She had lost track of how long she'd been away from Findley and the boys. Somewhere along their trek, she had passed the states of exhaustion and hunger. Now, she was shattered, depressed, and starved. Add freezing and ill to the mix, and one would have described her perfectly.

Rain had fallen off and on since Traig had taken her. It seemed that the moment her clothes began to dry, another drizzle or downpour would start up again. The rain didn't matter, for her only thoughts were of Findley and her boys. No matter how weary she became, she had to hold on to the hope that they would get out of this alive and in one piece.

She had been happily dreaming of a warm bed and a full stomach when the sound of Traig's voice broke through, shattering the comforting dream to a million tiny pieces.

"Welcome to yer new home, Maggy," Traig whispered in her ear.

She shot upright and stared ahead. They were at the Buchannan keep. It sat atop a hill surrounded by tall spiked walls. The gray sky that threatened still more rain added to the sense of foreboding that tugged at her stomach.

"Traig, there is still time to change yer mind," she whispered, as a gust of wind swooped over them, chilling her further. She knew her words fell on deaf ears, but she couldn't give up hope that some part of her old friend, the one who had once been an honorable man, still existed in the shell of the man who sat behind her.

"Och, Maggy! Ye might as well get used to the new life that lies ahead of ye. Fer I imagine ye'll be Malcolm's bride before this day is out."

His laughter mingled with the wind and added more heaviness to her heart. In a matter of moments, she'd be facing another mad man and had no idea how to get herself out of this mess.

***

TRAIG HAD VERY UNCEREMONIOUSLY TOSSED Maggy over his shoulder and carried her into the large gathering room of the keep. Once there, he dropped her into a chair that sat near the end of a long table before sitting himself opposite her.

Maggy's breaths came in rapid succession as she sat and tried to gain some semblance of control. She was dirty, tired, hungry, and terrified out of her wits, but she wasn't about to let anyone see her fear.

The keep looked nothing like what she had expected. It was clean and in good repair, though she did detect the faint scent of old urine. Even Malcolm's men appeared different, for they had apparently recently bathed and wore clean clothing.

They hadn't sat long before Malcolm Buchannan came bounding down the stairs.

"Maggy!" He cried out as if she were a long-lost friend. He came racing into the room and around the table, then pulled her to her feet.

"Let me look at ye, lass!" he said gleefully as he held her at arms length and studied her. "My! Ye're a sight!"

She knew that she was. The hems of her dress and cloak had been torn more than once, and she was covered nearly head to toe in mud. Her hair was plastered to her face from the rain. Her boots squished whenever she walked and how she had not succumbed to the ague or fever from the cold and rain, she didn't know. It had to be sheer determination and utter will on her part, as well as a little divine intervention.

Maggy couldn't hide her surprise. This was not the same man who just a month ago rushed into her camp and killed so many people. He had shaved, wore clean clothes, had brushed his teeth, and no longer stunk to the high heavens. But Maggy was no fool. She knew that underneath this clean façade lay an unpredictable and dangerous man.

"It has been a long journey fer ye, lass! I'll have a warm bath readied fer ye. And a nice soft bed," he said as he gave her arms a gentle squeeze.

Maggy wasn't sure what frightened her more; the man who now stood before her or the true man she knew him to be. Malcolm's smile sent chills down her spine.

"Och! Even in yer current state, ye're still the bonniest woman I have ever laid eyes to!" He motioned for her to sit, and he took the chair beside her. "Ye must be hungry, lass. I'll have the cook bring ye somethin' to eat."

He had paid no attention to Traig who sat quietly with his arms crossed over his chest. Traig cleared his throat loudly, forcing Malcolm to acknowledge him.

Malcolm wasn't happy with the interruption and turned an angry eye toward Traig. "Ye're the man who brought me Maggy to me?"

"Aye," Traig answered.

"Go see me man, Almer. He will see to it that ye get yer reward."

Traig shook his head and twisted his lips inward. "Aye, I'll get me reward, Malcolm, but there is more here that I want."

Malcolm eyed him suspiciously. "What do ye mean?"

"Apparently ye've stolen me son." His words were straight and to the point.

Malcolm pulled his head back and looked verily surprised. "Yer son? Me? Kidnap a boy?"

Traig could see through his mock surprise. "Aye, me son Ian. Ye have him, and I want him."

Malcolm turned his gaze to Maggy. "Ian is his?"

Maggy could only nod her head. As she watched the back and forth between the two men, she felt as if she were having some macabre dream wherein she was surrounded by insane men. It all made her stomach feel quite uneasy.

"He is a very good boy, Maggy," Malcolm complimented her. "Ye've done a good job with him," he said before turning back to Traig. "But I am afraid I have grown quite attached to the lad. I am not sure I am ready to give him up just yet."

Traig was about to pull Malcolm from his seat and run him through with the dirk he had hidden in his boot. But a shout came from the floor above. The sound of the small boy's happy voice gave him pause.

"Mum!" Ian screamed as he raced down the stairs and ran into his mother's arms.

The relief Maggy felt in that moment was indescribable. She stood and scooped him up and held him tightly. He was alive! She held on to him, squeezing him, and planting kisses on his cheeks.

"Och, Ian! I have been so worried, son!" Maggy said, as tears of relief fell down her cheeks. "Are ye well? Have ye eaten? Have they harmed ye?"

Ian pulled back and looked at Malcolm before turning to his mum. "Aye, they've fed me! They've been very nice to me, Mum! And Malcolm gave me a puppy!"

As if he heard them talk of him, the puppy, a fat bundle of brown fur, came bouncing down the stairs and into the gathering room. His tail wagged happily as he ran to Malcolm, who bent and picked him up and held him to his chest. "Aye, I did," he said as he looked at Ian and smiled, running his hand along the back of the pup.

None of this is real, Maggy told herself. Malcolm, his men, and the keep were clean. Malcolm was behaving as if he'd never tortured or killed, and apparently Ian had grown fond of the mad man. Mayhap it was she who had lost her mind and was now hallucinating.

"Mum, his name is Dingle," Ian announced as he held his hands out for his puppy.

Malcolm handed the pup over very gently, the warm smile still on his face. "Malcolm thought his name should be somethin' fierce, but I like the name Dingle better," Ian explained.

The pup licked Maggy's face before turning to bathe her son in slobber. Maggy felt lightheaded from the surreal atmosphere.

She set Ian on the floor and slowly sat back into the chair. Ian had always been a good judge of character. How had Malcolm duped him?

Ian gave his puppy a hug and his mother a bright smile. "Do ye like him?"

Maggy could only nod her head as she placed a hand over her heart. It pounded pitilessly against her breastbone.

"Ian," Traig finally spoke. He'd been standing off to the side and observing. The boy definitely loved Maggy as much as a son could love a mother. The bond between them was quite evident.

When he had first raced into the room, Traig's heart stopped beating for several moments. After all these years, he was finally in the same room with his son. The boy had changed dramatically. No longer was he a chubby little wean with light brown hair. Nay, he had grown into a wiry young boy with bright green eyes and dark, unruly hair.

Traig swallowed several times as doubt began to creep into his soul. Traig was fair-haired and blue eyed, as Helena had been. Ian could have passed for Gawter's son. Traig slowly began to realize he'd been an even bigger fool.

He collapsed into the chair. "Ian," he whispered again.

The little boy stared at him, a puzzled look on his face. "Aye, I am Ian," he said as he gave his pup another hug. "Who are ye?"

Maggy answered before anyone else could. "This man was a friend of yer father's, Ian. He brought me to ye."

Ian tilted his head and smiled at Traig. "Thank ye! I have missed me mum something fierce!"

Traig could only sit and stare at the lad. For more than five years he had imagined this moment, when he would return and claim his son again. But in his dreams, the boy was fair-haired and blue eyed like him. In his dreams, his son would have remembered him and known instantly that Traig was his da. He would have run into his arms and said how glad he was he had returned.

Anger began to boil in his stomach. Helena had lied to him as had Gawter! Gawter had proudly admitted to his affair with Helena, right before turning him over to the English. He had said the affair had been going on for less than a year. The evidence of that lie stood before him. It had gone on much longer than Gawter had admitted. But why would Gawter have lied? He had thought Traig as good as dead. Why not admit the truth?

UNLESS HELENA HAD SPREAD her legs for someone else who looked much like Gawter. What else could it be? He was either Gawter's or someone who looked very much like Gawter. My God! How many men had my wife slept with?

He wanted to scream, to throw up, to kill everyone in the room. But he knew the moment he drew a sword he'd be signing his own death warrant. Malcolm's men would kill him. Mumbling to himself, he stood up and left the gathering room. It was all too much to deal with at the moment.

"Ian," Malcolm said quietly, sounding very much like a doting father. It made Maggy's skin crawl. "Take yer pup outside. We do nae want him messin' on the clean floors."

Ian smiled up at him and walked over to his mum. He reached up and pulled her down to his level so that he could hug her. "I am so glad ye're here, Mum!" he said happily, as if nothing in the world was the matter.

Very softly he whispered into her ear. "Dunnae believe anythin' ye see or hear, Mum," he told her, his breath tickling her ear. "Malcolm is insane, so I must play along like nothin's wrong."

He gave her a peck on her cheek and hurried out of the room.

Her hope was renewed. Her son had not been duped, and she had not lost her mind. Malcolm Buchannan was still the insane, mad man that she despised.

"So," Malcolm said once Ian was out of the room, "ye've changed ye're mind, and now ye're here," he rubbed his hands together excitedly. "Ye make me heart fill with joy, lass, that ye've decided to accept me proposal."

"I have done no such thing," Maggy said before turning to look at him. "My answer remains the same. I'll nae marry ye. Nae now, nae ever."

Malcolm tilted his head and looked at her with disbelief. "I believe ye're merely tired and hungry, lass. Once ye've had a hot bath and a warm meal, ye'll feel better. Once ye've gotten to know me, ye'll change yer mind."

"I do ken ye Malcolm, more than I would like to. And no matter how many baths ye take, no matter how ye try to present yerself as a kind, decent man, I ken better." She stared him straight in the eye as she sat taller in the chair.

His jaw clenched as he stared back at her. Maggy could see his ire rising and could tell that he was fighting his inner self. The real Malcolm, the one that was cruel, mean and vindictive would soon make his presence known. She didn't care how angry he became; she'd not agree to marry him.

Malcolm took a deep breath and let it out very slowly. He came and stood in front of her and studied her closely. Slowly, he bent at the waist and placed a hand on either arm of her chair, leveling his eyes to hers. "How much do ye love yer sons?"

Maggy reminded herself that getting him angry was just as dangerous for her as it was for Ian. "Ye ken how I feel, Malcolm. Ye ken I love me boys, that's why ye took Ian."

"Aye, I do. So if ye wish to keep the lad alive, well, and happy, ye'll rethink ye're refusal," he said before leaning in close to her ear. "Aye, I may be attached to the little bugger, but I am not so attached that I would think twice about running a blade across his throat."

He stood up but kept his eyes glued to hers. "Now, would ye care to take some time to think on it, lass?"

He could give her a hundred years to think on it, and her answer would remain the same. She remained mute and squeezed the arms of the chair so that he couldn't see her hands tremble.

Malcolm watched her for several long moments. He would give her time to think, all right, but he wouldn't give her much.

The old Malcolm, the one who bore no patience, began to creep to the surface. He was growing tired of her refusals and tired of the pitiful looks his men had been giving him for weeks now.

"Almer!" he shouted before turning away from her. He went to stand beside the fire and waited silently.

Moments later a very tall, dark man appeared in the doorway next to the fire. Malcolm didn't bother looking up at him. "Take the wench upstairs to the room we prepared for her. Keep her under constant guard."

A wicked smile appeared on Almer's face, one that said he'd be all too happy to oblige Malcolm. Maggy shrunk back in her chair, terrified yet resolute.

In just a few strides, Almer was standing in front of Maggy and pulling her out of the chair by one arm. Maggy resisted and tried to free herself from his tight grasp. The look he gave her made her skin crawl.

As Almer pulled her toward the stairs, Malcolm spoke. "Almer, if ye touch one hair on her head, I will kill ye."

Almer's smile left his face. Maggy knew the only reason Malcolm warned the man was because he wanted her all to himself.

CHAPTER TWENTY-FOUR

Driving themselves to the point of exhaustion, and in grave danger of killing their mounts, Findley and his small band of warriors rode silently and with purpose. They had to, for the sake of Maggy and Ian.

The terrain, for the most part was flat compared to many other parts of Scotland. Still, there were many hills to climb and forests to trudge through. They rested very little as they rode like the devil to reach Aberdeen.

As the days and nights flew by, the boys never once complained of hunger or need of sleep. The sacrifices were necessary in order to free their mum and brother from the bonds of a mad man. Too much was at stake to complain.

As the horses began to slow and the boys began to fall asleep in their saddles, Findley decided they needed to stop. They found refuge at the home of a farmer who allowed them the use of his barn. They slept but a few hours and set out before dawn.

The farmer had informed them they were but a day's ride from Aberdeen. If they pushed, they could reach it before nightfall.

So, they pushed. Through forests and over hills, across streams and around lochs, they pushed onward.

Hours later, and still many miles from Aberdeen, they spilled out of a dense forest onto the edge of a vale. Findley pulled his horse to a quick halt. The sight before him nearly caused his heart to seize.

HOW MANY DAYS had she been locked in this room? Maggy had no way of knowing. There were no windows; no way for her to tell how much time had passed.

Occasionally, Malcolm would enter the room and offer another less than heartfelt proposal. And each time she would decline it and beg to see her son. Malcolm was relentless, just as she remembered him to be, and each time he would deny her her one request.

Her room consisted of a small bed, a chair and a chamber pot. She paced around the room for hours at a time, thinking, trying to figure a way out of this mess.

And she prayed. She prayed for Liam and Collin, Duncan and Aishlinn and their unborn babe, to all arrive safely at Gregor. She prayed for Robert and Andrew, that they'd either get lost and end up far away from here, or that no one other than Findley and his men would find them and take them to safety.

Findley. Her heart ached whenever her thoughts turned to him. *He will come for me and Ian. Please Father, let him be safe.* She needed to remain strong for Findley, for her boys. She knew she could not succumb to the fear that jolted through her body every time the latch on the door moved.

No matter what torture Malcolm might put her through, she'd not agree to marry him. He could keep her locked in this room forever and her answer would remain the same.

"You'll nae see yer son again, or any of yer sons fer that matter, until ye say yes," he said, standing in the doorway again. She hadn't heard the latch, lift for she was lost in her thoughts of Findley and her sons.

She guessed it was nighttime only for the fact that the torches were lit in the hallway outside her room. Malcolm stood in silhouette against the yellow light of the torches. Maggy could barely see his face, but he appeared to have not shaved today. Dark shadows fell on his cheeks, leaving him with an eerie and sinister look about him.

Every muscle in her body ached and burned. He had not let her bathe, hadn't let her eat more than a slice of bread and a small chunk of cheese when they remembered to bring her food. They kept her hungry as well as thirsty, offering her only a small cup of water with her meals.

"Where is Ian?" her voice was scratchy and dry from lack of water.

"Ian is fine, Maggy. He is below stairs with his pup," his voice was low and stern.

"Please, Malcolm, do nae do this. Please," she was not above begging. "Please let me see him!"

Malcolm remained standing in the doorway. "I like how ye beg, Maggy." He sounded amused. "If ye were me wife, ye'd be beggin' fer other things, I assure ye."

Bile rose in her throat. Righting her shoulders, trying to appear as if she hadn't heard him, she pressed further. "I demand to see me son."

"Ye are in no position to demand anythin'," he said as he took a step into the room. "Ye'll nae see him until ye agree to marry me."

For a brief moment, she thought again of agreeing to marry him. Once she had him alone she could kill him…

"Nay," she said firmly.

He was across the room and pressing her against the wall before she had a chance to blink. Grabbing her wrists, he pinned her to the wall and thrust a knee between her legs.

Fear shot through her veins, and she knew she had pushed him too far.

Malcolm watched as her bosom rose and fell with each rapid breath she took. He felt the old Malcolm fighting for control with the new man he was trying to be. His old self would have stripped her bare, tossed her on the bed, and taken what he wanted.

His new self, the one that struggled minute by minute to remain strong and somewhat kind, refused to succumb to his baser needs and wants. Nay, he wouldn't take her, not yet. He'd give her more time to think it over. A few more days locked in here without any comforts would get her to come around. He'd take her then. With her spirit broken and no fight left in her, he would take her.

Maggy stared angrily into his eyes, refusing to look away or allow him to see her fear. Her green eyes flashed with fury, hatred, and disgust.

The next moment, his lips were upon hers. Hard and demanding he kissed her. Pressing her wrists harder against the wall, she gagged and coughed, repulsed by his touch.

He drew his head back a few inches and glared at her. She wanted to wash her mouth out and be rid of the taste he left behind.

"Gunnar!" he shouted without taking his eyes from Maggy's.

Oh God, what is he going to do to me? A new fear flashed over her. She had pushed him over the edge of reason, she was sure of it. She was certain that he called for his man to come in and help hold her down while he had his way with her. If she had had any food in her belly, she would have wretched on his feet.

A moment later a man appeared beside them. "Aye, m'laird?"

"Help me put her in the chains."

FINDLEY'S HEART nearly leapt from his chest with joy. At least two hundred men and horses covered the field below Findley and his men. What a beautiful sight it was to see the MacDougall flags flapping and waving in the wind alongside those belonging to the McDunnah and McKee clans. It was perhaps the most glorious sight Findley had ever seen.

He and his men let out a war cry and raced down the small incline and into the center of the camp. Relief, joyous, glorious relief swept over him, and for a moment he felt like he could cry from it.

They dismounted quickly as men surrounded them. Rowan and

Black Richard had made their way through the thick crowd of men. Findley was very glad to see them.

There was much backslapping and hand shaking taking place as Findley searched the crowd for Angus. In a matter of moments, the crowd parted like the Red Sea to allow Angus McKenna to emerge.

Chief Angus McKenna was taller than Findley by a few inches. Broad in the shoulders and chest, he was also as strong as an ox. He was dressed in a tunic and plaid this cold, rainy day. Soft leather boots hugged his substantial thighs. Long blond braids framed both sides of his face.

"Ye're a sight fer sore eyes, Angus!" Findley said with a broad smile.

Angus eyed him seriously for a moment. Just as Findley's smile began to fade, Angus wrapped him in a huge bear hug.

"I just hope the lass is worth it!" he said as he slapped him on his back.

When their embrace broke, Findley looked around at the sea of men.

"Angus, I only asked fer fifty men! It appears ye've brought far more than that!" He wasn't complaining, he was grateful and happy to see so many men here to help.

"Well, now," a voice came from the crowd. "When we heard ye was goin' up agin the Buchannan, we could nae let ye have all the fun."

Two very tall men stepped aside, and Caelen McDunnah stepped forward. "Malcolm Buchannan is a festerin' boil on me arse," Caelen said. He stood next to Angus, with his arms crossed over his chest, feet spread apart. Caelen McDunnah was a fierce looking man with long black hair and muddy brown eyes. A long scar ran from his forehead down the left side of his face before disappearing somewhere on his chest.

Though he wasn't one of Findley's favorite allies, he was an ally nonetheless. No matter his reasons for being here, Findley was grateful.

"Caelen," Findley said as he extended his arm. Caelen grasped Findley's arm for a moment before righting himself.

"So, Findley," Caelen said as he looked at the crowd of men. "Is she as beautiful as we have heard?"

Laughter erupted from the crowd. Jealousy tried to rear its ugly head. Findley knew Caelen was merely trying to inflame him; it was one of the sick pleasures the man drew from life. Caelen liked to fight, and where there typically would be no reason to come to blows, Caelen would sometimes find one just for the sake of starting a fight.

"Aye, she is Caelen," Findley said as he rested his fingertips on his hips.

Wee William chimed in. "Beauty so fair it will take yer breath away," he told them with a nod of his head. "I would have shaved me beard fer that one."

A stunned silence fell over the men. Those who knew Wee William knew he had sworn there wasn't a woman in all of Scotland worth shaving his beard for. To hear him announce to everyone within earshot that the woman they were all here to help was bonny enough to tempt Wee William into shaving was quite a surprise. She must be one bonny woman.

Caelen nodded his head approvingly. "And I hear Malcolm Buchannan has killed her people and taken one of her wee ones?"

Findley chewed on the inside of his cheek. "Aye, 'tis true."

"And I hear that Malcolm wishes to marry the bonny lass?"

Findley's jaw clenched tightly with thinking of it. "Aye, that is true as well."

A devilish smile came to Caelen's face. "And are we to assume that ye'd like to make sure the nuptials dunnae take place?"

"Aye," Findley answered with a wry smile slowly coming to his lips. "That be our goal."

Caelen lifted his head and searched the crowd. "And where be the bonny woman that tempts Wee William into shavin'?"

Findley crossed his arms over his chest. "She was taken several days ago. We believe Malcolm now has her."

Caelen and Angus cast a glance at each other.

"Well, then," Angus said as he rubbed his hands together. "I reckon we should go rescue the lass."

Angus put a hand on Findley's shoulder and began to lead him toward a campfire. "Ye look like ye could use a drink, Findley," he said as they walked side by side.

"Aye, Angus, I could."

Moments later they sat around the fire while food and drink were brought to Findley, his men, and the boys. The boys looked around in awe at all the warriors around them. All the men, horses, and armor especially impressed Robert, and he remained silent while he listened to the men talk.

While they ate venison and bread, another tall man appeared and stood before Findley.

"I see we have to save yer sorry arse again," the man said bluntly. Robert and Andrew looked at each other. The man looked angry as he stood in front of Findley. Both boys rose to their feet, fully prepared to assist Findley should he need it. For the thousandth time in the past weeks, Robert wished he had a sword.

'Twas Nial McKee, chief of the Clan McKee, who stood before him. While not as tall as some of the other men, he was an imposing figure all the same. He wore his brown hair cut close to his scalp and he had penetrating gray-blue eyes.

"Nial," Findley said as he stood. Findley had known Nial for years. Nial had fostered with the MacDougalls as a young boy.

"I am growin' weary of havin' to pull yer arse from the flames. I have got much better things to do with me time."

Findley sat his trencher of food on the ground at his feet, stood upright and shook his head at Nial.

Robert nudged Andrew, and the two boys went to stand beside Findley. They crossed their arms over their chests and looked up at the man who was insulting Findley.

"How do yer dance lessons go?" Nial asked. His expression remained unchanged.

"How goes yer needlework?" Findley asked.

"Have ye quit wettin' the bed?"

"Do ye still like wearin' dresses and prancing around like a faerie?"

A smile finally broke across Nial's face. "Aye! And when I do, I dream of ye dancin' with me!"

The men broke into a fit of laughter and hugged each other while Robert and Andrew looked at each other. 'Twas a confusing hello, to say the least.

"Nial McKee, ye bloody cur! How long has it been?"

"Far too long, ye scurvy dog!"

Findley looked down at Robert and Andrew. "Lads, I want ye to meet someone who is even more insane than Malcolm Buchannan," he said as he cast a wry smile to Nial.

Nial looked down at the boys with a menacing expression. "Aye, I am. And you'd be smart to remember that, lads." He winked at each of the boys, raised his eyebrows, and sat down on the ground near the fire.

Findley laughed as he sat back down and retrieved his trencher. "Robert and Andrew, this is Nial McKee. He fancies himself chief of the Clan McKee. But he is really more the chatelaine of their castle." He winked at both the boys, who had now returned to their seats.

Nial ignored the insult as he stretched his legs out and crossed his arms over his chest. "Aye, I may be the chatelaine, but I am still here to pull yer arse from the fire. Again."

Findley ate and began to feel better. With so many men here to help, he no longer doubted the success of the mission at hand. With the combined forces of the MacDougalls, McDunnahs and McKees, they'd have Maggy and Ian out of harm's way in no time. At least, that was his sincerest hope and prayer.

When they finished eating and washed off the mud and sweat, they gathered around the fire and began to plan their assault. If everything went as planned, Findley would have his arms wrapped around Maggy before the sun rose the next day.

LIGHTNING RIPPED VIOLENTLY and dangerously through the night sky.

Thunder rattled and shook Lady Judith Kinleigh's carriage, causing a squeal of fright to escape her maid's lips.

"Kate!" Lady Judith hissed. "Please, do not squeal so!" Aye, she too was frightened of the storm that had descended upon them as they crossed Scotland from Inverness to Aberdeen. Lady Judith, however, remained graceful and dignified.

But Kate trembled and shook with each flash of lightning and rumble of thunder. She sat across from her lady, a death grip on the velvet seat. "I am sorry, m'lady," her voice more than a bit shaky. "I have never liked storms."

Lady Judith let out a sigh and rolled her eyes. "'Tis just a storm, Kate. There is nothing to be frightened over." She lied, of course, but she didn't want her maid to know that she, too, was quite unsettled by the storm.

Lady Judith hated traveling by carriage, especially on these rough and uneven roads. She would have much preferred to have ridden her mare, but her husband, Lord Kinleigh, wouldn't allow it. She was, after all, a lady. And ladies, he insisted, didn't ride by horseback all the way from Inverness to Aberdeen. What would people think?

Truth be told, Lady Judith didn't care much what other people thought. But she did love her husband, a highly unusual thing that was, and his opinion did matter. She knew he lied when he said he worried over what society might think of his wife riding horseback for such a long distance. But the truth of the matter was he worried over her safety. There were ne'er-do-wells and highwaymen galore in many parts of Scotland. He couldn't stand the thought of some blackguard taking her for ransom. Or worse.

If it gave her husband's heart some measure of security to have her travel by carriage, then so be it, even if the bone-jarring ride made her feel as though she were on a ship at sea, being tossed about in a horrific storm.

They traveled with two carriages and fifteen soldiers. One carriage held Lady Judith and her maid, and the other held their luggage. Lady Judith could barely wait to return home to her husband and three children. She missed them terribly, so she had insisted that they keep pushing onward even after the sun had set. She hadn't been prepared for such a threatening storm as the one they now rode through. She was beginning to wish she had listened to Forbes earlier when he suggested they stop and take comfort at an inn. But Lady Judith had been far too anxious to return home and insisted they stay their course.

As they rode down the severely rutted road, being tossed about like loose potatoes inside a large bowl, Lady Judith fought her queasy stomach. It amazed her how one could get seasick without so much as a toe set upon a ship. Her stomach, however, proved such a thing was possible. She swore that if they didn't stop soon, her late dinner would soon be splattered all over the floor of the fine carriage.

She didn't think it possible for the road to get worse, but it soon did. The carriage hit a very large hole that sent both Lady Judith and her maid flying from their seats. When they landed with a great thud, the carriage listed heavily to one side and slammed both women into the wall.

"Oh! This can't be good, m'lady!" Kate cried when the carriage finally stopped swaying to and fro. It remained precariously perched to one side, forcing both women to sit on the wall instead of the bench. They heard voices shouting outside the carriage, and for a moment Lady Judith feared they might be under attack.

The carriage was practically lying on its side. Lady Judith reached for Kate's trembling hand and gave it a reassuring squeeze. "We will be well soon enough, Kate," she told her, more to reassure her own mind than her maid's.

Only a short moment passed before the door to the carriage flew open, and her man Forbes poked his head through. "Are ye well, m'lady?" he asked with much worry in his voice.

"Aye, we are, Forbes. A bit shaken, but I do nae believe anythin' is broken," she answered, unable to hide the relief in her voice at seeing him.

"Are we under attack?" Kate asked fearfully.

Forbes laughed. "Aye, we are, miss! But not from blackguards or robbers! 'Tis Mother Nature herself that's doin' the attackin'!"

Kate shot him a furious look, angry that he was making fun of her plight. Lady Judith, however, laughed along with him.

Forbes reached in and hauled the women out one at a time, handing each off to one of his soldiers. Forbes was the personal bodyguard of Lady Judith. He had proudly served her for ten years now and would protect her to his own death if necessary.

First, he handed Kate into the arms of a waiting soldier. She clung to him for dear life as the rain beat down in long sheets. With each flash of lightning, she would jump and bury herself deeper into the man's arms.

Forbes had never seen the young Kate so terrified. Of course, they'd never been stuck out in the middle of nowhere during a violent thunderstorm before. Normally Kate was a strong-minded, sharp-tongued lass who held her own. That was probably one of the reasons Forbes had grown quite fond of her, though the lass hadn't an inkling of his feelings.

Forbes pulled Lady Judith from the carriage and handed her down as gracefully as possible considering the circumstances. They stood huddled together in the driving rain.

"M'lady." One of the mounted scouts came bounding up to them. He called out to Judith as he pulled his horse to a stop near the small group. "We found a castle nae far from here," he bowed slightly to both women from atop his horse. He appeared unbothered by the rain that beat down and splattered his face.

"Might I be so bold as to suggest we seek shelter fer ye and Miss Kate? At least until the storm passes, and we can dislodge the carriage and fix the broken wheel?"

Lady Judith could not help but smile at the man. In his own polite way, he was trying to appear unbothered by the storm, as well as make it look as though the whole thing was Lady Judith's idea.

She didn't need to think twice over it. "I believe that to be a splendid idea, John!"

Kate let out the breath she'd been holding but didn't let loose her hold on the soldier. Forbes felt a rush of jealousy rise up, not liking at all the pleased look on the man's face. Kate was a beauty, to be sure, and she could melt the heart of many a man.

Forbes wanted to reach out and offer Kate his hand, but Lady Judith was his primary responsibility.

"Forbes," Lady Judith said, her voice barely audible over the sound of the thunder and driving rain. "Will ye be so kind as to escort Kate and me to the castle?"

Forbes nodded his head and went to retrieve his mount. When he returned and ordered a man to help Lady Judith up on his horse, Lady Judith declined.

"Please, Forbes, my maid is trembling like a leaf. Please allow her to ride with you. I shall be perfectly content riding with John."

She gave him no time to argue, and within a blink of an eye, the soldier Kate had clung to was lifting her up to Forbes. He couldn't be more delighted to have her sitting atop his lap, but he sent a silent prayer up to the good Lord to help him keep his wits about him. It wouldn't do to be distracted by the lass.

Kate wrapped her arms around Forbes' chest and clung to him tightly. "I hate storms," she whispered.

Forbes was no longer cursing the storm. In fact, he was quite glad for it.

"M'LAIRD," Almer was trying to get Malcolm's attention and had repeated his title three times.

Malcolm was staring into the soft embers that crackled in the stone fireplace. He sat quietly, a dram of whiskey in his hand and quite lost in his own thoughts.

Why won't she marry me? He wondered to himself. *I have done everything I could think of to get her to say aye, but still she refuses me.* He took a sip of the fine whiskey and continued to ignore the man standing next to him.

Anger boiled deep within Malcolm's gut. It was her own fault she was locked in the room, chained to the wall. He felt no pity for her, just burning anger. He had decided that he'd not give her another chance to deny him. She'd eventually crack, agree to his proposal, and soon he would be the laird of a vast estate, married to a titled lady, and a very wealthy man.

Then they'd no longer whisper about him behind his back. Aye, people would still cower in fear in his presence, but the rumors that he'd lost his mind would stop. They would admire his tenacity and intelligence. They would still fear him, but no longer would they make fun of his appearance when they thought he could not hear.

A scarred man, a crazy man would not have been able to win the heart of one so lovely as the Lady Margaret. A marriage to her would prove to the naysayers and gossips that his face was not so scarred and his mind not so bent as they had previously thought. With Maggy on his arm, at his side, nothing could stop Malcolm from amassing thousands of soldiers, more power and more land. The laughing would soon stop.

"M'laird!" Almer raised his voice again to gain Malcolm's attention.

"What is it?!" Malcolm shouted. He didn't like being disturbed when he was in his private chambers. He'd gut the fool if whatever he was interrupting him for turned out to be unimportant.

Almer's expression remained stoic. Although Malcolm terrified the hell out of him, he was still his chief, his leader, and he would afford the man the respect he deserved -- even if his laird had gone completely mad.

"We have visitors. People seekin' shelter from the storm," Almer explained. "A lady and her maid."

Malcolm looked confused. No one sought shelter here. At least not the titled or wealthy. He wondered for a moment if it wasn't some kind of trap.

"Just one woman and her maid?"

Almer shook his head slightly. "Nay, m'laird. She has five men with her. She says her name is Lady Kinleigh."

Malcolm searched his memory. The name sounded familiar. "Lady Kinleigh?" he repeated the name as if doing so would help him to remember.

"They say they be traveling from Inverness to Aberdeen. They say their carriage broke a wheel a few miles away," Almer explained further. "They are soaked to the bone, m'laird, and have asked to stay while the carriage is fixed."

Malcolm thought on it for a moment. No one would send a lady and her maid as a distraction. Deciding it would do no harm to allow them shelter, he gave an approving nod. He knocked back the rest of his whiskey and placed the empty goblet on the table by his chair before standing.

"Well, let's go welcome our guests, shall we?" he said as he slapped Almer on the back. Malcolm figured that soon enough, he'd be opening his doors to the estate that came with marrying Maggy, so he might as well get used to such intrusions.

Lady Judith didn't bat so much as a lash when Malcolm appeared before her. She'd seen scarred men before, so Malcolm's appearance didn't startle her. While she appeared stoic and all manners on the outside, her insides were quite another story.

She knew the moment he came walking down the stairs exactly who he was; he was currently one of the most feared and dangerous men in all of Scotland.

"M'laird," she said. She gave a low curtsy and extended her hand when he approached.

Malcolm blinked, apparently not used to such gesticulations. Most people cowered in fear in his presence. Or worse yet, fainted at the sight of his face.

He politely took her hand and kissed her gloved knuckles. How many years had it been since he'd been in the presence of a noble lady or kissed a delicate hand?

"M'lady," he said with a slight smile. "I hear you're in some distress this night?"

Lady Judith stood and smiled at him. "Aye, 'tis true, m'laird. I am afraid the treacherous road has claimed my carriage as hostage," she said jestingly, and cringed inwardly at her poor choices of words. If the stories of Malcolm Buchannan were true, she'd be his hostage before daybreak.

Malcolm threw back his head and laughed. "Aye, I am afraid these roads are treacherous at times! I am glad that I could offer ye some comfort from them." He bowed slightly at the waist before turning to look at the men who stood around her.

"At least ye've brave men to help ye battle these roads that rob fine ladies of their carriages!"

Forbes and his men stood at the ready, guarding their lady. Forbes knew who Malcolm was, but he followed his lady's example and feigned ignorance. He cursed himself for having brought Judith and Kate here. There would be no way for him and four men to defend themselves against Malcolm Buchannan and all of his men. Though that didn't mean he wouldn't enjoy the fight!

Judith's mind was a whirl as she continued with her coy charms. "Aye, they are a brave lot! My husband refuses to allow me to travel these roads without escort," she said quietly.

Kate had remained quiet and shivering as she stood behind her lady. She had been standing as close to Forbes as she could and wished they'd hurry up with the pleasantries so they might sit by a warm fire and dry their drenched clothing. She hadn't been able to see the man her lady was speaking to.

Kate let loose with a very unladylike sneeze. Judith glanced at her over her shoulder and gave her a look. Kate knew that look well. It held a warning that something was afoot, and Kate needed to be on her toes.

"Och! Ye've a wee lass there! Excuse me fer being remiss in me duties!" he bowed again and turned away. He called for Nettie, his cook, before turning his attention back to Judith.

"Almer," Malcolm said, looking happy and quite the gentleman. "Please see the lady and her men to rooms on the third floor."

To Judith he said, "We do nae get many guests here, m'lady," he said sweetly. "I do hope ye'll be comfortable."

"I can assure ye, sir-" Judith stopped suddenly. "Please forgive me, but I do nae know yer name!" She fluttered her eyes and flashed a brilliant smile.

Malcolm bent at the waist again and returned her smile. "Malcolm, dear lady. Laird Malcolm."

Judith continued to smile. "Laird Malcolm," she said with a nod of her head. "I cannae thank ye enough fer yer kind hospitality. I can assure ye, we shan't dwell long here. I am afraid me husband is verra, verra ill, and I must return to him in Aberdeen as soon as possible." She painted a very sad and grievous look on her face.

Kate was glad she stood behind her lady, for her expression could not have been seen by anyone. Forbes, however, had noticed it, and he gave her hand a slight squeeze. She could feel in her bones that something was wrong, and for a moment, she wished she were back in the blasted carriage.

"Almer," Malcolm said as he introduced his man to the lady and her entourage, "will see ye to yer rooms, m'lady."

Judith gave a nod of her head and flashed another dazzling smile. "Thank ye kindly, Laird Malcolm." She then turned to face Forbes.

"Forbes, we are in good hands here," she told him with a wink that only he could see. "Please go back to the carriage, and see to it that yer men repair it quickly. I truly wish to reach my husband as soon as possible."

"But, m'lady, if I leave ye here unattended, yer husband, no matter how sick he is, will have me head!" he pleaded through gritted teeth, hoping she'd not continue to insist he leave. He should have known better.

"Never ye mind about Alfred! I want ye to see to the carriage. If it makes ye feel any better, ye can leave two of yer men with us," she said before grabbing one of the other soldiers and putting her hand on his elbow.

She turned her attention once again to Malcolm. "I am positive Laird Malcolm is an honest and kind gentleman!" She flashed him another smile. "I am sure we are in good hands here, Forbes. See to yer duties!"

Malcolm laughed and called for Nettie again. "I'll have a meal brought up to yer room, m'lady. Nettie is a fine cook, even if she be a bit slow."

"I would be glad fer anythin' in my stomach right now, m'laird! And again, I thank ye fer yer kindness."

Forbes shook his head as he watched his lady ascend the stairs with her hand on one of his soldier's arms. Kate followed right behind her, keeping her eyes on the floor. Forbes nodded to John. "Ye stay with them," he said. John quickly fell in behind the others as Forbes looked on.

As the lady followed Malcolm's man up the stairs, a sense of dread fell over Forbes. He could only pray his lady knew what she was doing.

CHAPTER TWENTY-FIVE

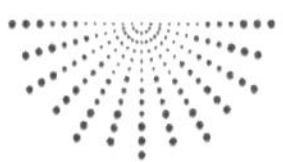

"Could ye nae have picked a better night to lay siege to a mad man's castle?" Nial asked as he rode alongside Findley.

Findley looked ahead, appearing not at all bothered by his friend's badgering and complaining. "I think ye'd complain if it were a bonny spring day in June with the sun shinin' and birds singing, Nial."

Nial snorted and kept his eyes focused, looking for any signs of trouble.

After a moment, Findley spoke again. "Ye ken, there's still time fer ye to go home and wait with the women and children if the storm frightens ye so, Nial."

"I be no more afraid of the storm than ye, ye heathen," Nial retorted.

Andrew and Robert rode as close to Wee William as they could. Somehow they felt safer near him, certain they were that even the lightning was afraid of the man.

"How much longer do ye think we have, Wee William?" Robert asked.

"Nae long," Wee William answered. He worried over bringing the lads with them. But he knew that they'd have had to tie the boys to trees and keep a guard of twenty men on them in order to stop them both from doing something even more remarkably stupid than what they'd already done.

Robert adjusted himself in his saddle, and for the hundredth time in the past two hours, he rested his hand on the hilt of his sword. 'Twas a fine sword to boot! Nial had given it to him. Nial had said if Robert was dumb enough to steal cattle from Angus McKenna, dumb enough to pelt rocks at Wee William, and still dumber yet to have run away to fight the Buchannans on his own, then aye, the lad was dumb enough to carry a sword. Robert took it as a compliment.

While the lightning had decreased, the rain still fell in sheets. The closer the group of Highlanders got to the Buchannan keep, the quieter they became. Scouts had been sent ahead in three different directions and had not yet returned.

Nearly two hundred mounted men, divided into three groups, spread across the countryside. Had it been daylight, it would have been an intimidating sight to behold.

Not much time had passed before the scouts returned with news.

"The Buchannan keep be less than an hour from here, Findley," one of the scouts said excitedly.

Findley sat taller in his saddle as he began to mentally prepare for the battle that lay ahead. Their plan was simple. They would come at the keep from three sides and lay siege to it with no warning. A group of men would be sent over the walls in search of Maggy and her son. It was to be a simple in-and-out mission with the only priority being to rescue Maggy and Ian.

***

"M'LADY!" Kate whispered as she helped Judith out of her cloak. "What in God's bones is happenin'?"

That was one of the things Judith loved most about her maid. She was not afraid to speak her mind. Nor was she above using a colorful word every now and then.

"Wheest, Kate!" Judith hissed. "I am nae sure yet if the walls have ears. Go about as ye would under normal circumstances," she told her.

Kate pursed her lips and draped their cloaks over a chair. Almer had built them a fire, and it was quickly helping to warm the room.

Judith made the soldiers stand guard outside so that she and Kate could remove their gowns and dry themselves by the fire. In a matter of minutes, both women stood in their chemises with warm, dry blankets wrapped around their shoulders. Kate had draped their wet clothing on hooks that were fastened to the mantle.

They'd not brought any dry clothes with them, for it had been perilous enough in the horrible storm without worrying over trunks and such things. Escaping the storm had been far more important. As they sat huddled together by the fire, they spoke in very hushed tones.

"Kate," Judith whispered. "Did ye happen to catch a glance at Laird Malcolm?"

"Nay, m'lady," Kate answered. "I was too busy shiverin' and wishin' fer a warm fire. Why?"

Judith leaned in closer and whispered in Kate's ear. "Dunnae react in any fashion, young lady, to what I am about to tell ye."

Kate nodded her head slightly as a chill of foreboding ran over her skin.

"The man who acts as our gentleman host is none other than Malcolm Buchannan."

Kate was paralyzed for a moment, positive her heart had stopped beating. "Nae *the* Malcolm Buchannan, m'lady?" she whispered. She prayed her lady was mistaken.

"Aye," Judith said. "The Malcolm Buchannan," she let the words settle into her maid's mind for a time before going on.

"Kate, I dunnae ken if he will let us leave or no'," she said quietly. "If he has realized who I am, he may not. He may try to hold us for ransom, and Kate, I do nae wish for that to happen."

Judith had been held for ransom once before, and it was an experience she didn't care to repeat. For five long months she was hidden away in a cold, damp castle in the far north. 'Twas her husband who had rescued her. Of course, he wasn't her husband at the time. But they did marry some three months after meeting.

"What is yer plan, m'lady?" Kate asked quietly. She had been Lady

Judith's personal maid for two and a half years. If she'd learned anything in that time, it was that no one dared cross Lady Judith. The woman was as sweet and kind as the day was long. But she had a streak of strength and determination that ran deeper than the sea. Kate felt safer around Lady Judith than she did around most men. Well, save for Forbes.

"I have been thinking on it, Kate. I sent Forbes back on purpose. I feel better knowing that if we are held fer ransom, Forbes is on the outside to help us instead of held captive with us."

"Aye," Kate said thoughtfully, even though she would have preferred to be held captive with Forbes at their side. Still, it made better sense to have him on the outside to help.

A few moments had passed as each woman thought over their current predicament. It was Judith who finally broke the silence when an idea suddenly hatched in her more than devious mind.

"Kate, dear," she began with a wry smile on her lips. "How long has it been since ye used yer talents as a spy or yer feminine wiles?"

Kate smiled coyly as if she had no idea what her mistress meant.

FINDLEY and his men were not far from the Buchannan keep when they came across a small band of men and carriages stuck in the mud.

Angus held up his hand to bring his band of warriors to a halt. He took a moment to study the scene before him. How many times did reivers use the ruse of a carriage accident before pouncing on unsuspecting travelers? Thankfully, Angus had eighty men beside him. He doubted seriously any reivers would take the chance of attacking such a large number of men.

He sent one of his men ahead to get a better idea of what was happening. The man rode ahead, spoke for a few minutes to whoever was in charge and returned to Angus in short order.

"'Tis Lady Judith Kinleigh's carriage, m'laird!" the warrior exclaimed. "One of the wheels broke and got stuck in the mud, and they be doin' their best to repair it."

"Is Lady Kinleigh well?" Angus asked. He had met Lady Kinleigh on more than one occasion, but it had been some time since he'd last seen her. He remembered she had a most beguiling smile and a temper just as dangerous.

"Nay," his warrior told him. "They've taken her to seek refuge-" his sentence was broken by the sound of men on horseback rapidly approaching the carriage.

Angus and his men watched, and moments later the mounted men rode toward them.

"I am Forbes Stewart," the middle rider announced as he approached Angus. "I am guard to Lady Kinleigh," he said as he eyed Angus and his men closely. "Who might ye be?"

"I be Angus McKenna, chief of the Clan MacDougall. Is Lady Kinleigh well?"

The relief in Forbes face and body was quite evident. "Thank God! I thought ye might be more of them."

"More of who?" Angus asked.

"More of Malcolm Buchannan's men! We had to find refuge for Lady Judith and her maid. The storm was somethin' fierce, I tell ye! We did nae know it, but the keep we sought is Malcolm Buchannan's."

Angus sat up taller in his saddle as Findley, Wee William, and Richard appeared beside him.

"Findley, this is Forbes Stewart, Lady Kinleigh's guard," Angus said as means of an introduction.

Forbes gave Findley a nod and continued. "Lady Kinleigh and her maid are now inside the Buchannan keep," he said with more than a hint of anger and distress in his voice.

"What?" Findley asked.

"We did nae know it was the Buchannan keep," Forbes explained. "We had to get the lady and her maid out of the storm. We sought refuge at the nearest keep."

Findley's chest constricted. How many more people was he going to have to rescue from the hands of Malcolm Buchannan?

"Is Malcolm holding them hostage then?" Angus asked.

Forbes shook his head. "Nay, at least nae yet! I am certain Lady

Kinleigh knows just who he is, that's why she insisted I leave under the guise of fixin' her carriage. But she did allow two of my best men to stay behind with her."

Angus and Findley looked at each other for a long moment before turning back to Forbes.

"Do ye think Malcolm will allow her to leave?" Angus asked.

"I am canna be sure. But," Forbes stopped to think on the events that had taken place at the castle.

"But what?" Angus asked.

Forbes pursed his lips together before letting out a quick sigh. "He did nae appear like the Malcolm Buchannan I hear so much about."

"What do ye mean?" Findley asked.

"Well, he did have the horrible scar and the milky eye. But he was clean-shaven, well kempt, and his keep was immaculate. It goes against all the stories that I have heard. He did nae appear tetched, filthy, or deranged. In fact," he stopped to think on it for a moment, running the events through his mind. Angus cast him a look that bade him to continue.

"Well, I canna think of any other way to put it. But Malcolm acted like a fine gentleman."

Angus and Findley cast surprised looks at Forbes and then to each other. Malcolm Buchannan a fine gentleman? Nay, 'twas impossible.

"Are ye sure 'twas him?" Angus asked, unable to believe what he had just been told.

"Aye, as sure as I am of anythin'. 'Twas him, but he said he was Laird Malcolm, and did nae use his last name."

"Well that puts a knot in things, doesn't it?" Wee William said as he pulled his horse to the front and turned to face Angus.

Forbes and his men did not hide their surprise when Wee William rode to the front of the group. They'd never seen such a large man before.

The group discussed their options. Forbes' main concern was for his mistress and a certain young maid. The possibility that there was a wee lad and another woman held captive made things even worse.

As they talked, Robert and Andrew grew curious. They pulled

their horses up and quietly walked to the front to see what was happening. Robert listened intently as they men discussed the different ways of gaining access to the keep and what to do to protect the women and child behind its walls.

As the men talked, and Robert listened carefully, Findley's eyes fell upon the lad. After a few moments, a smile came to Findley's face along with a twinkle in his eye.

"Gentlemen," he said as he turned to look at the men before him. "I believe I have found our way in."

Curious eyes fell to Findley who was smiling at Robert. Their gazes followed his, and soon all eyes were fixed on Robert.

Robert's dream of becoming a warrior was going to become a reality far sooner than he had hoped for.

KATE WALKED the deathly quiet halls of the Buchannan keep in her bare feet, her silk chemise, and a blanket draped around her. She walked as stealthily as a king's spy, hiding in shadows, nooks and crannies. This wasn't the first time she had done such a thing, and not the first lady she'd ever crept about in the dark gathering information for.

Kate was very good at this, had done it dozens of times for dozens of different reasons. Still, she knew that overconfidence could lead to her death. She'd tempted fate once before and didn't want to do it again.

Her search of the third floor led to nothing but mostly to unoccupied rooms save for the one she and her lady had been given. One that she had to assume was the laird's for it was decorated very handsomely, and a third where a small child slept. She thought little of it and assumed the child might belong to Malcolm. From what she could see, he slept in a very nice bed and an appropriately appointed room. A small pup slept curled up against the child's back. They looked so peaceful that no alarm warnings went off for her.

She did manage to find a set of servants' stairs that allowed her access to the other floors of the keep.

Ever so quietly, she tiptoed down the back staircase and into a long corridor on the second floor. She was able to use the keyholes to peer in without having to open any doors and taking the risk that a rusty hinge would give her away. Some of the rooms were empty while others were filled with big, snoring men.

She searched for only one thing: information. She needed to find out if the Buchannan planned on holding Lady Judith for ransom. With her ears straining to hear any little sound, she crept down the hallway, keeping her back to the cold walls.

When she came to the end of the corridor, she noticed it spilled out into a wide and open walkway. She could see straight into the grand gathering room, which fortunately for her was now empty. The fire had died down and only low-burning embers remained.

She muttered a curse, quickly made her way to the other end of the corridor and turned right. There was another long hallway that she reckoned led back toward the servants' staircase.

Keeping her eyes on where she was going and her ears on sharp alert, she peeked into one room after another with no luck. Not even a wee mouse could be found in any of these rooms.

As she bent to peer into the last room on the left, she was surprised to find a key in the lock. Where none of the other rooms she had found thus far appeared locked, this one had a key on the outside.

Kate pressed her ear to the door and listened, her heart pounding. She had stumbled upon something, but what, she did not know. Instinct told her that whatever lay hidden on the other side of the door was important.

Her heart pounded so loudly that she could no longer hear anything but the rushing of blood in her ears. She cast a quick glance down the empty hallway and noticed there were no torches at this end. She could risk opening the door only to listen. Her keen hearing and her instincts would guide her the rest of the way.

As quietly as she could, she slowly turned the key. A moment later, she heard the quiet click as the door unlocked. Taking a deep breath, Kate very slowly pushed the door in and listened.

MAGGY'S THIRST and hunger was so great that she would have agreed to nearly anything for just one swallow of water and half a slice of bread. Every muscled burned and ached, and she would have done nearly anything to have the shackles removed so that she could collapse onto the cold floor.

How many hours had she been hanging on the wall with the tips of her toes barely touching the floor? She could not begin to guess. Her arms had gone numb so long ago that she wondered if she'd ever regain the use of them.

She had cried until she had no more tears left. She was breaking, she could feel it, and she prayed that Findley would forgive her. She simply could bear no more.

Maggy hadn't heard the door unlock, but she had felt a rush of warm air come across her feet when the door opened. *He is back*, she thought to herself. *I canna take anymore*. Profound dread flooded her veins. She was going to give in, agree to marry him only so he'd let her down, let her drink, eat, and bathe. Her limit, she reckoned, had been reached.

Taking a deep breath, she used what little energy she had left to lift her head and look up, fully expecting to see Malcolm standing in the doorway with that sick and sinister smile on his face. He'd take one look at her, and he would know that he had won.

"Maggy!" came the sound of a very shocked and surprised voice from the doorway. It wasn't Malcolm.

The shock and surprise was overwhelming. Kate had recognized her the moment Maggy had lifted her head. She stood in stunned silence for several more moments with her hand to her lips.

Kate whispered her name before stepping into the room and closing the door behind her. She raced to Maggy, reaching out and touching the shackles.

"Kate?" Maggy asked, her throat was so dry, it was all she could do just to whisper.

"Maggy!" Kate cried, trying to keep her voice low. "What on earth is going on? Why do they have ye chained like this? Och! Maggy!"

Maggy could not speak. She was in shock, and for a moment she wondered if she weren't dreaming or had finally succumbed to madness.

"Maggy!" Kate exclaimed again. "Where is the key?"

Maggy shook her head and tried to explain. Kate had to lean in close in order to hear her. "Malcolm has it," Maggy managed to scratch out.

Kate muttered a slew of curses that would have made even the most hardened of men blush like maidens. "Why? Why do they have ye chained?"

Maggy couldn't answer; she didn't have the strength to. "Water," she begged.

Kate looked around the room and found a pitcher of water on the floor by the bed. She grabbed it and raced back to Maggy, holding the pitcher up to her lips.

Maggy drank greedily, not caring how long the water had been there. It ran down her chin, her neck, and down the front of her dress. It didn't matter.

When she had finally had her fill, she still felt like death warmed over, but at least she could speak. Seeing Kate here was like a breath of fresh air, and her presence began to energize her.

"Kate, is it really you?" she asked, her voice still rough and her throat still quite sore.

"Aye, Maggy, 'tis me," she said as she wiped Maggy's face and neck with the hem of her blanket. "What are ye doin' chained to the wall?"

Kate could hardly believe that Lady Margaret was here! The last time she had seen her was more than three years ago, right before Maggy was carried away in the back of a hay cart. Kate had been her maid then, her friend and companion as well. It had nearly broken Kate's heart in two to have to say goodbye.

"Malcolm Buchannan," Maggy said. "He is mad! He chained me here when I refused his offer of marriage!"

Kate's eyes grew wide with that bit of news. "Nay!" She couldn't blame Maggy for refusing the man, for she'd have answered in similar fashion.

"He has me son, Kate! He has Ian."

Kate's eyebrows knitted into an angry glare. "The cur!"

"Aye, Kate, please, ye must get help!"

Kate's mind raced for a plausible solution. It would take them a few days to reach Aberdeen with all the mud the rain had left behind. She could insist that some of their soldiers ride ahead and get help from Laird Kinleigh, but it would take days to accomplish that.

"Kate, there is a man, a good man," Maggy began speaking so quickly it was hard for Kate to keep up. "His name is Findley McKenna. He is of the Clan MacDougall. He was helping me when Traig took me and brought me here. Ye must find Findley, tell him I am well and haven't married Malcolm yet! Please Kate, promise ye'll find him!"

The desperation in Maggy's voice was enough to bring tears to Kate's eyes. She was doing her best to keep up and remember everything Maggy was telling her. But the mention of Traig's name caused her to pause. "Traig?" she asked, uncertain she had heard correctly.

"Aye, our Traig! He is nae dead. There's no time to explain! Ye must hurry, Kate, before they discover ye here. Please Kate, remember Findley McKenna! Go, lass, hurry!"

Kate did not want to leave her, but she knew she could not risk staying any longer. She had to get back to Lady Judith and let her know what she had found.

Kate quickly embraced Maggy and kissed her forehead. "Maggy, I swear to ye I'll get help. I'll find yer Findley, and we will come back. I promise!"

Maggy forced a smile to her lips before shooing the young woman out of the room. As soon as the door closed behind her, Maggy hung her head and cried.

"ARE YE CERTAIN?" Lady Judith asked, still unable to believe that one floor below her, Lady Margaret de Menteith was chained to a wall.

"Aye, m'lady, as certain as ye're standing before me now! He has her chained because she has refused to marry him."

Judith shook her head in disbelief and paced in front of the fireplace. Her mind raced between a way to rescue Lady Margaret and a way to kill Malcolm Buchannan.

Judith stopped pacing and felt the dresses and petticoats that hung near the fire. They were still damp, but not so damp that she couldn't wear them.

"Quickly Kate, help me to dress," she whispered as she lifted the petticoats and stepped into them.

Kate stood behind her and quickly tied the long string into a bow. As she helped her lady to dress, she filled her in on the rest. Kate told her of Maggy's son Ian and of Traig, but she could not answer Judith's question on how or why he was alive nor why he had brought Maggy to this God-forsaken place.

"What are ye plannin' on doin'?" she asked as she reached for the kirtle.

"I do nae ken just yet," Judith told her. Her mind searched rapidly for a plan of action. "Do nae tie it too tightly, Kate," Judith told her. "If I need to run a man through, I don't want any constraints."

Kate giggled, knowing full well her lady was not being anything but honest. Lady Judith was not your typical genteel lady in that she didn't wile away her hours with needlework and painting. Lady Judith, who would soon be turning forty, liked to spend her days practicing archery, fencing, and riding.

Kate lifted the dress over Judith's head and began lacing up the back. When she was finished, Judith helped Kate with her own dress and laces.

Just as they were putting on their slippers, a knock came at their door. They cast fearful glances at each other. For the second time tonight, Kate felt her heart slip to her toes.

"Heaven help us," whispered Judith.

"Aye," Kate said, "Heaven help us."

Judith sat in the chair by the fire, steeling her nerves for whatever might be about to happen next. She had a *sgian dubh* attached to each of her thighs, one tucked into the pocket of her kirtle, and yet another tucked carefully in the sleeve of her left arm. No one could say she was ever ill prepared.

Kate herself was just as well armed. As a woman, she knew men might have the upper hand when it came to brute strength. Being a woman often afforded her the appearance of innocence. Nothing could be further from the truth.

Judith gave Kate a nod of her head signaling her to open the door. Kate took a deep breath and pulled the door open. Standing before her was a lad of no more than fourteen, and he was wearing one of her soldier's uniforms. She recognized the young boy, though he had grown several inches since last she'd seen him.

"Miss Kate," Robert said with as steady a voice as he could manage. When Forbes had told him the maid's name was Kate, Robert had not thought for a moment that it would have been Maggy's Kate. He was beyond surprised to see her here, as well as grateful. Kate had helped them once before and would, more likely than not, help them again.

He looked into the room and spotted the woman he needed to talk to. "Lady Kinleigh," he said as he bowed at the waist.

Judith smiled and hoped her look of surprise didn't bring any unwarranted attention from the very large Buchannan warrior who stood next to the young man.

"Forbes sent me, m'lady, with a message on the carriage," the young man swallowed hard as he stared at her. His eyes were pleading and a tad frightened.

"Why yes, boy!" Judith said as she waved her hand and bade him to enter. "Ye must be frozen to the bone! Come in and warm yerself by the fire."

The Buchannan guard looked quite tired and put out. He simply nodded his head and quit the room. Kate carefully closed the door.

Robert started to speak, but Lady Judith held a fingertip to her lips and her palm up to stop him. Her eyes were glued to Kate who stood at the door with her ear against it. After several long moments, Kate felt certain no one but their own guards remained on the other side and ran to join Judith and Robert.

"Who are ye, lad?" Judith asked with a curious expression across her face.

Robert leaned in closer to speak as well as to warm his hands in front of the fire. He wasn't cold as much as he was terrified. Terrified that he'd slip up and make a mistake. Mistakes could get people hurt, and that was the last thing he wanted.

He lowered his voice and whispered. "I dunnae have much time, Lady Kinleigh, but me name is Robert. I am the son of Maggy Boyle." He held his hands to his mouth and blew on them before holding them in front of the fire again. "Ye might ken her as Lady Margaret." He looked up at the woman before him.

"Ye're one of the boys she adopted."

Robert asked how Lady Judith knew Maggy had adopted him.

"Lady Judith is above reproach, Robert," Kate whispered. "Lady Judith will take me secrets to her grave, just as I will take hers."

It was too late now to worry over Maggy's secret. If word had not yet spread that she was alive, it would be only a matter of time now. "Aye, m'lady, I be the oldest. We met yer men on the road. Forbes says to tell ye yer carriage will be fixed soon, but he asks fer yer patience."

"Were those his exact words, young man?" Judith knew better. Forbes would have had a far more colorful message for her.

Robert glanced at Kate who stood beside Lady Judith with one hand on her shoulder. He wasn't sure how to answer the question.

"Ye can tell me his exact words, lad," Judith's smile encouraged him.

Robert cleared his throat before speaking. "He says fer ye to hold yer horses, and for the sake of all that is holy, do nae kill anyone just yet!"

Robert looked away and stared nervously at the fire. Certainly, a lady as refined as the one before him would be insulted by the use of such harsh language. He finally got up the nerve to cast a glance at her and was quite surprised to find her smiling up at her maid.

"That would be Forbes, fer ye!" she chuckled. "What else does he say?"

"He canna come fer ye right away, m'lady. Ye see, we are also here to rescue me mum. We are nae certain, but we think Maggy be somewhere in this castle. Me brother is here as well. Malcolm Buchannan holds them both hostage." He looked down at the fire, his jaw clenching as he thought about everything that his mum and brother must be going through. He couldn't even be sure they were both still alive.

"Well, ye can go back and tell Forbes he can come straight away," Judith told the boy. Slowly she leaned closer and placed a warm hand on his. "Yer mother and brother are well, lad. We know exactly where each of them is."

Robert could not conceal his joy at the news. His face lit up with a wide, relieved smile. "Nay! Ye're certain, m'lady?"

"Aye," Kate said. "I have seen them both this night. Yer brother is on this floor not far from us, just down the hall and around the corner." She could not help smiling back at the lad, for he looked like the weight of the world had been lifted off his shoulders.

"And me mum?"

Kate's smile faded. "She is alive, but they've got her in chains, lad. She is in a room below us, at the very end of the corridor."

Robert shot to his feet and began to shake with anger. Lady Judith stood and put both hands on his shoulders. "Lad, ye need to keep yer head about ye," she whispered soothingly to him. "Ye've come this far. Yer mum and brother are alive." She gave his shoulders a gentle squeeze. "We have far to go this night before 'tis all said and done. Now, are there any other messages?"

Robert stared into Lady Judith's eyes and found comfort in them. For some odd reason, he felt a strength emanating from her, much like the strength he would sometimes feel when his mum would put her own hand on his shoulder.

"He says there will be a surprise waitin' fer ye in the carriage when we return with it. The carriage has been repaired. Now that we know where me mum and brother are, it should nae be long before we return fer ye," Robert told her.

Judith gave his shoulders another squeeze before releasing them. "Ye've done verra well this night, lad. Yer mum will be verra proud of ye," she smiled down at him. "Now be off with ye! Ye must tell Forbes we are well, and I promise I will nae kill anyone unless I have to."

Robert looked back and forth between the two women before his eyes settled on Lady Kinleigh again. There was something in the woman's hazel eyes that told him she spoke the truth.

CHAPTER TWENTY-SIX

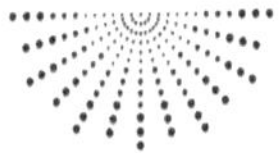

Robert rode as hard and as fast as he could. The news that his mum and brother were still alive left him feeling giddy with excitement and joy. It brought a new surge of energy to him as he raced into the group of waiting men. He was proud of himself for many reasons, the biggest being he hadn't gotten lost on the way to or from the Buchannan keep.

He didn't wait for his horse to come to a complete stop before he slid down from it to give the good news to Findley and the rest of the men. Findley looked down at the boy with such a tremendous amount of pride in his eyes that Robert was on the verge of tears.

"Ye did well, lad, verra well!" Findley told him as he slapped him on the back.

Robert returned Findley's smile, anxiously ready to press on with the next step of their plan. At Angus' signal the men mounted, and within minutes they were headed for the Buchannan keep.

Thankfully the lightning had let up, but the rain and clouds had not. This allowed the Highlanders to approach the keep under the cloak of darkness. Every lantern available was lit and hung on the outside of the carriages. This was meant to draw attention to the carriages and away from the two hundred men waiting to lay siege to the keep.

ALMER HAD BEEN MADE aware that Lady Kinleigh's carriages would soon be returning, the broken wheel having been repaired. Almer thought nothing of opening the gates and allowing the expensive carriages entry into the courtyard. He mumbled curses under his breath, angry that his chief refused to hold the lady and her entourage hostage. They would have been worth a small fortune in ransom.

Two months ago, Malcolm would have done just that very thing. Now, however, the man had refused. Malcolm had it in his mind that once he married the wench Maggy Boyle, they'd no longer be living as rogues and ne'er-do-wells. They were going to be gentlemen, living on Maggy's vast estate near Dundee. Malcolm explained that there was no better time than the present to begin behaving as such. Almer could only shake his head and do Malcolm's bidding.

Most of the keep was fast asleep, save for the men on watch, Almer, and that strange man who had brought Maggy to the keep days ago. Traig appeared to be crazier than Malcolm. The man paced the grounds day and night, muttering unintelligible words to no one in particular.

Almer was ready to gut the tetched man and be done with him. He worried, however, that if he killed the stranger, then whatever demons were possessing him would take up residence in Almer's body. 'Twas a risk he wasn't willing to take. Even if the man were a nuisance, Almer had no desire to tempt the devil.

Almer also wanted to be rid of Malcolm and the wench who was chained to the wall. And he looked forward to being rid of the brat that had somehow convinced Malcolm that all he needed to do to win Maggy's heart was to bathe and clean the keep. It was utter nonsense as far as Almer was concerned. He wanted to go back to the way things had been before Malcolm had lost his mind. Back to the days of taking what they wanted instead of asking for it.

He'd sent a man in to let Lady Judith know that her carriages approached. As the gates were lifted, the lady, her maid, and two guards descended the stairs of the great room and walked through the large doors and down the steps that led to the courtyard.

The carriages pulled up in front of the steps that led up to the keep. One of the drivers stepped down from the carriage, bowed to his lady and took her hand. The sight of all the genteelness sickened Almer.

He waited for the lady and her maid to be assisted into the carriage before turning his back on them. He was thankful they were leaving and only wished that they'd be taking the wench and the brat with them.

Just as the carriage door closed on the lady and her pretty maid, a war cry pierced through the quiet night air. The sound of it made Almer's blood run cold as he turned around to see what the bloody hell was happening.

His last thought before the arrow pierced his heart was that he had been right all along; no good could come of taking the boy or the wench. In the matter of time it took for one heartbeat, perhaps two, the Buchannan keep was besieged.

***

FINDLEY, along with Wee William, Richard, and Angus led the assault wave that poured in through the open gates. He and his men were dressed in chain mail, hauberks and helmets. Broadswords hung at their sides or were strapped to their backs. Daggers were hidden in boots and sleeves, and there wasn't a man there not fully prepared to bring down Malcolm Buchannan and his men.

Nial and his men attacked from the rear of the keep while Caelen's men climbed the walls on the east and west. Lady Judith's men rode with Findley so they could surround her carriage and whisk her away and out of danger.

They had meant for the carriage carrying Lady Judith, her maid, and the lads to be safely on the other side of the gates before the attack began. However, one of the Buchannan men had somehow spotted something or someone and let out a war cry. There had been no time to spare, and the order was given to attack.

Once the breach was made, several of Findley's men took to the walls to keep the gates open. Atop their mounts, swords drawn and targes at the ready, Findley and his men poured through the gates and began attacking any Buchannan who stood in the way of their reaching the steps of the keep.

Lady Judith's men headed straight for her carriage. Three Buchannan men were trying to gain control of it. One had run his sword through one of her drivers, whilst the other two tried to open the doors.

Lady Judith would have none of it! With a *sgian dubh* in each hand, she and her maid began thrusting through the open windows, much to the surprise of Robert and Andrew. They didn't think another woman like their mum existed: one who would fight tooth and nail for survival!

More men began swarming the carriage while the lady and Kate thrust and twisted their small daggers into the bellies and chests of the Buchannan men. Robert finally found the courage to draw his sword, and he too began thrusting through the open windows at anything that moved.

The sound of metal thrashing against metal, bones crushing, and skin being torn open was enough to make Andrew's stomach want to wretch. He could not move, could not offer any assistance. He was frozen with fear.

Two more of the lady's men fell to the ground as they tried to keep her out of harm's way. Over the din of the battle, Forbes' voice could be heard shouting orders. "Get that bloody carriage out of here!"

Without any forethought, Robert flung open the carriage door, shimmied up the side, and jumped into the driver's seat. Grabbing the reins, he yelled and snapped the reins hard to get them moving. His only thought was to get the lady, her maid, and his brother out of there!

Snapping the reins again, shouting and whistling at the horses,

Robert crashed through the increasing number of Buchannan men! He dared not stop as he drove the carriage like a Roman chariot, yelling and screaming at the horses to go faster.

The remainder of the lady's soldiers followed Robert out of the courtyard and into the night. Once they were clear of the gates and heading for safety, Robert yelled for the lanterns to be doused. Seeing they were free of the keep, Andrew finally managed to find his courage.

Though he shook like a leaf in the wind, he held on for dear life as he leaned through the open windows to extinguish the flames. They were riding at breakneck speed over rutted and gnarly roads. The lanterns were swinging to and fro, making it nearly impossible to get a grip. Having had enough of trying to fumble with the flames, he began tearing the lanterns off and throwing them to the ground.

Robert did not let up on the horses until he saw Forbes riding beside him and heard him call out.

"Slow down lad!" he yelled. "Ye'll do us no favors if ye tip the carriage over!"

Robert's heart was pumping quickly, and his hands and feet trembled. He pulled up on the reins and slowed the horses just enough so that one of the lady's soldiers could climb onto the carriage. Robert gladly handed the reins over to the man.

As they dashed along the open road, the soldier sitting next to Robert cast a smile his way. "Was that excitin' enough fer ye, lad?" he asked.

Robert was taking deep breaths of air into his lungs as he tried to steady his shaking hands. He shook his head and gripped the edge of the seat. "Aye, 'twas," he answered.

He had not felt any fear when he had jumped out of the carriage and into the driver's seat. 'Twas instinct that had kicked in, or madness, he wasn't sure which. But as they rode along, the realization of what he'd done began to settle into his bones. He was no longer certain he wanted to live the life of a warrior when he grew up.

WHILE ROBERT WAS DRIVING the carriage to safety, Findley and the rest of his men were in a full-out attack in the courtyard. The resounding ring of metal clashing against metal and the coppery scent of blood that spilled from those slain assaulted the senses.

Findley and Richard made their way through the courtyard with relative ease. Their real fight, however, began as they made their way up the stairs and into the keep. Buchannan men had begun to pour out from all directions like bugs escaping from under a rotted log.

As they stepped through the door of the keep, three men came at Findley from his right, and two more were on Richard's left. Richard thrust his sword upward into the gut of one man, while using his dagger to slice through the throat of the second.

Findley plunged his broadsword into the chest of one of his attackers as another swung his sword directly at Findley's head. In one fluid motion, Findley ducked low and spun the dying man's body that still hung on his sword and pushed hard against him with his shoulder. The man was thrust into one of his comrades, and the two tumbled down the stairs back into the keep.

As Findley rose, he swung his sword across the belly of his third attacker, who fell forward against him. Findley shoved the man away, tossing him on the pile of men at the bottom of the stairs.

Together, he and Richard raced down the steps, swords slicing, and daggers thrusting as they fought their way into the grand gathering room. Nial and a group of his men soon appeared to help fend off dozens of Buchannan men.

The MacDougall and McKee men fought their way through the throng of Buchannan men, slashing, plunging, and hitting their way toward the stairs. Findley knew that Maggy was on the second floor and Ian on the third. The plan was to have himself and Richard make their way to Maggy while Nial and his men made their way up to get Ian.

As he fought with a frenzied hatred, Findley made his way up the stairs to the second floor. Just as he stepped onto the landing of the second floor, a Buchannan man jumped from the shadows. Findley had been thinking of Maggy and how close he was to reaching her now and had been caught off guard.

The Buchannan man's sword was coming straight for his head! Findley tried to duck, but not before the tip of the man's sword found its way through the gap in his hauberk and managed to inflict a good cut under his right arm. A sharp pain shot up Findley's arm, and for a moment the pain took his breath away.

The man raised his sword in both hands, preparing to smash Findley's skull with the hilt of the sword. Findley feinted left, then right, before thrusting his dagger up into the chin of the man before him. Blood splattered in all directions and speckled Findley's face and torso.

More Buchannan men, most without armor, began pouring down the stairs from the third floor. Richard, Rowan, and Nial helped Findley to fend off their attacks, allowing Findley to make his way down the corridor in search of Maggy.

He found the last door on the left and bothered not with trying to unlock it. With two good kicks of his foot, he was inside the room in good time.

His heart did not beat, not so much as a flutter, when he saw Maggy chained to the wall and the look of sheer terror on her face and in her eyes.

A man with dirty blonde hair and even dirtier clothes stood beside her. In one of his large hands, he held Maggy by her hair, pulling her head up and against the wall.

In his other, he held a long dagger against her throat. The man paid no attention to Findley or to Rowan, who now stood behind him in the doorway of the room. Findley was afraid to startle the man, for fear he would twitch and cut Maggy's throat.

Covered in sweat and blood, Findley stood almost motionless as he tried to keep his anger in check. His chest heaved as he tried to steady his breathing. He watched, waiting to make his move.

The man was shouting at Maggy, his words slurred as if he had suffered some form of apoplexy.

"Ye lied! Ye lied to me, Maggy!"

"Traig," Maggy said, her voice trembling with fear. "I am sorry! I had no other choice! I did it fer Ian's sake!"

"Aye, 'tis what ye keep sayin', and I want to ken why! Why did ye lie? Ye had to ken Ian was Gawter's! Ye can tell by lookin' at the lad that he isn't mine! Yet, ye pretended nae to ken that Gawter and Helena were sharin' a bed when I told ye!"

"I did nae ken, I swear it!" She hadn't known. Aye, she'd known Gawter had bedded many women during their marriage, but she had no clue that Helena, the woman she loved as a sister, was one of them. She felt more than just betrayed by her friend; Maggy felt like a fool.

"Lass, nae even ye can be that stupid! It had to be goin' on fer years. How could ye nae see it by just lookin' at the boy?"

Maggy's head was spinning. Traig was going to kill her; she could see it in his glassy, angry eyes. Mayhap if she kept him talking, explained the truth of it, she could get him to change his mind.

"Traig, ye're right, Ian is nae yers," she swallowed, her throat dry, her voice hoarse from crying, pleading for her life, and lack of water. "But he is nae Helena's either."

Traig looked at her as if she was the one who had lost her mind. "That makes no sense!" he shouted. "I have had enough of yer lies, Maggy!"

Findley had taken a step into the room, but Maggy's words stopped him in his tracks. What on earth did she mean that Ian was neither Traig's nor Helena's?

"Traig, listen to me, please!" Tears flowed down her cheeks as she fought to spill the secret she'd been holding onto for more than eight years. "Do ye remember when I was pregnant with Liam, months before I had him, I grew ill and nearly died?"

Traig studied her closely as if he were waiting for the slightest hint of a lie or trick. He did remember it. Everyone but Gawter had been terribly worried over Maggy. She had become violently ill and was abed for a week. Everyone in the clan thought she would lose her babe, or worse yet that she would die. And that would have been a horrible loss for everyone. Everyone, but Gawter.

He nodded his head. "Aye, I remember."

"'Everyone thought 'twas food poisonin', but they were only half right. My food was bad, but it was done on purpose. Gawter tried to kill me, Traig. He poisoned my tea."

Traig remained suspicious, but Maggy could tell he was thinking over what she was telling him.

"I ken it was Gawter. I heard him talkin' to someone not long after I recovered. He was quite angry that I hadn't died! I could nae see who he was speakin' to, but he admitted that he should have used more poison. He wanted out of our marriage, and he did nae care if our babe lived or died. He hated me, Traig!"

The more she told him, the more he loosened his grip on her hair. But the dagger still remained pressed to her throat.

Maggy took another breath. "Ye and Gawter left not long after. Ye were gone fer months and still gone when I gave birth," she said. Tears were rolling down her cheeks and neck, and they began to pool along the edge of the blade.

"When ye returned, ye learned that Helena had given birth to yer son," she paused, choking on tears and guilt. "Ye remember, Traig, ye were so surprised because ye did nae ken she was with child when ye left."

He remembered that as well. Helena had explained that she hadn't realized she was with child until after he had left. He had been so glad to have a son that he hadn't bothered to question her explanations. The look of suspicion remained etched on his face as Maggy spilled forth with the truth. With his brow furrowed, he nodded for her to continue.

"Helena was my friend, Traig. I trusted her more than I trusted another living soul," she said, taking another deep breath. The pain of Helena's betrayal was still very fresh.

"How is Ian nae hers?" Traig asked, believing he already knew the answer.

"Because he is mine," she whispered. "Ian is mine!" She swallowed hard. The guilt was building in her stomach, the bile rising in her throat. "I gave birth to Liam and Ian!"

The words hung in the air like heavy smoke. Findley was frozen in place as he tried to make sense of what Maggy was telling Traig.

"I ken Gawter would try to kill me again, and I worried he would try to kill me sons! If he would poison me whilst I was carryin' them, I kent he would try again! I wanted me boys to live, Traig! I had to keep them safe! If I could nae save them both, then I could at least save one! 'Twas Helena who came up with the notion. She said she'd love him as if he were her own!" she began to sob as the truth spilled out.

"Helena said she would take one of them and raise him as her own. I would nae have to send one of them away. I would be able to see him every day because ye lived in the keep with us! I did nae ken what else to do, Traig! I was terrified of Gawter! And I had every right to be! Months later, he tried again to poison me. But we were better prepared, we were expectin' it. Helena kept several antidotes ready, fer nearly any kind of poison he might use." Her voice was nearly gone, and if she hadn't been chained to the wall, she would have collapsed to the floor in utter exhaustion and heartache.

Giving up Ian had been the single most difficult decision she had ever had to make. Although she had been able to see him nearly every day those first few months, it was not the same. When Traig had learned he was a father and insisted he and Helena move into one of the cottages nearby, it had nearly done Maggy in. Every day, she had to remind herself that she had made the right decision. If Gawter succeeded in killing her and, God forbid, Liam, then at least one of her sons would live. At the time, it had made perfectly good sense and it was the only thing that had given her hope.

Findley was shocked to hear Maggy's confession. He was certain that Maggy spoke the truth. If Gawter had not already been dead, Findley would have been tempted to gut the coward. Not just for the attempts he made to kill Maggy, but because she had been forced to give up one of her sons in order to ensure he had some future and lived beyond his first year!

"So, ye let me believe I was the boy's father?" Traig whispered. His eyes were glazed over as he stared across the room. His mind reeled. Aye, he'd known the moment he laid eyes on Ian that the boy did not belong to him. Deep down, however, he had been holding on to one last thread of hope that the boy was his. Maggy had destroyed that. After a long moment he looked back to her.

"Ye lied, Maggy! Ye let me believe he was mine!"

Fear enveloped Maggy's heart, and her stomach tightened. She had hoped her confession would bring back the man she had once called her friend. She had hoped he would realize why she had done what she had done and would be able to forgive her for it. "Traig, I be sorry! I did nae ken what else to do!"

Traig tightened his hold on her hair and slammed her head back and against the wall. His voice seethed with hatred and anger. "Ye could have told me! I could have helped ye! But instead, ye chose to lie like the wench I married!"

Findley knew that Traig had finally toppled over the edge. He knew time had run out, and there was no hope that Traig would come to his senses and let Maggy go free.

In the length of two heartbeats, Findley pulled a dagger from his boot and flung it across the room. It landed in the back of the man's neck with a sickening thud. The man jerked around, still holding to Maggy's hair.

"Who the bloody..." his words trailed away. A look of confusion painted on his face as death took him in that moment, and he fell to the floor.

Maggy sobbed as large tears streamed down her cheeks. Her eyes were tightly closed, and her body shook uncontrollably. She was unaware of anything going on in the room around her.

"Maggy," Findley uttered her name as he crossed the room to come to her aid. Rowan sheathed his sword and pulled the dead man away so that Findley might have better access to her.

"Maggy," he repeated as he took her face in his hands, unable to control his own tears of relief.

Was she actually hearing Findley's voice, or was she imagining it again? Long moments passed before she could open her eyes and several more before she could convince herself that he was really there. When recognition finally set in, her tears increased, and it was very difficult for her to speak. "Findley," she whispered.

"I hurried, as fast as I could," he told her as he brushed a kiss against her forehead. Though he was relieved to see her alive, the vision of the woman he loved chained to the wall tore at his gut. Had he tarried any longer, she would be dead. The man who lay dead at his feet would have killed her.

Bile rose in his throat at thinking he had been only a heartbeat away from losing her forever. He pushed those thoughts aside as he pulled her head to his chest.

"Please, Findley, I want to leave," she choked. Her emotions ran from relief to terror to anger and back again. She wanted her son and she wanted to get as far away from this place as she could.

"Aye! We will be gettin' ye out of here now, lass!" Findley said. "Do ye ken where the key to the shackles are?"

Maggy shook her head. "Malcolm. I think he has it," she choked. Desperation and panic began to set in. "Ian! Where is Ian?"

"Me friend Nial and his men are gettin' him, lass," he told her. For now, he would pretend that he hadn't heard Maggy's confession to Traig. They would have time to discuss that later. For now, he had to get her and Ian out of the keep.

He studied the chains that bound her to the wall. They were too thick to cut through with his sword, and the hooks that held them into the wall were just as sturdy. He tried pulling on the hooks in hopes they would magically pull from the wall. He'd need a hammer and chisel or the bloody key!

Rowan pulled on the chains with the same fervent hope, but to no avail. "We need the key, Findley," he whispered. "Ye go find Malcolm. I'll stay here with yer lass."

Findley did not want to leave Maggy. He'd tear the room down stone by stone if he had to, to get her out of the shackles. He was torn between wanting to stay to protect her and wanting to get her out of the keep and back to Gregor. The best thing would be to find the key.

"Maggy," Findley whispered as his trembling fingers held her face gently. "This is Rowan, a good friend of mine. He is going to stay here and guard ye while I go find Malcolm and get the key."

"Nay! Do nae leave me, please!" she cried, pulling on the chains, as she had done dozens of times over the past few days. Fire burned in her wrists and sent shocks of pain up to her shoulders.

"Maggy, I promise, I'll come back with the key," he told her before giving her forehead another kiss. "I promise!" He knew the longer he stayed, the longer it would be until he found the key.

He turned to Rowan. "Ye guard her as if she is the queen herself, Rowan."

"Aye, I will," Rowan said. "Now go!"

Findley reluctantly quit the room to go search for the key. He could hear Maggy crying and Rowan trying to console her as he stepped into the hallway. Her sobs wrenched his heart and tore at his soul, causing the anger to build with each step he took away from the room, away from the love of his life.

He muttered under his breath as he raced down the long corridor. *Malcolm Buchannan, if ye be nae dead yet, ye soon will be.*

CHAPTER TWENTY-SEVEN

He'd rather die than let the MacDougalls or anyone else get Maggy or the boy out of this castle alive.

When he'd awoken to the sound of the warning alarms, Malcolm knew instinctively that the doors to hell had just opened. As he threw on a tunic and trews, one of his men appeared at his door to let him know that hundreds of MacDougalls, McKees and McDunnahs were attacking.

No one needed to explain to him why they were here. The reports he'd received from the men he had posted in Stirling had told him that Maggy was seen in the company of MacDougall men. It was enough information for him to put two and two together.

He cared not what the reasons were behind Maggy being with the MacDougalls. All that mattered was the fact that his plan was not working out as he had hoped. His future as an earl with vast holdings, power, and coin was rapidly slipping away from his grasp. He felt very much like a man who had just lost his footing and was now holding perilously to a thin vine at the precipice of a large chasm. At any moment, he'd slip and fall to his death.

Malcolm pulled on his boots and donned his scabbard and sword as his mind raced in a thousand different directions at once. "Get me ten men!" he shouted to the man who stood in the doorway. "I want horses readied immediately."

He grabbed the key to Maggy's shackles from the table by his bed, draped the leather tie around his neck, and headed out of his room, pushing the man aside.

"But m'laird!" the young man called after him. "There are hundreds of them!"

"I do nae care if there are thousands!" Malcolm called over his shoulder as he headed toward Ian's room. "Get me ten men, ready my horse, and meet me in the wench's room!"

The young man's brow creased as he watched Malcolm stomp toward the boy's room. The orders his laird had just given him confirmed the rumors that had been going around the castle of late; their laird, their leader had lost his mind.

There were hundreds of men storming the keep and all Malcolm cared about was the woman and child. The young man tamped down the anger he was feeling toward his leader. Instead of defending their keep, as a good leader would do, his laird was planning his escape.

The young man wouldn't have it. Malcolm could ready his own horses and gather his own men.

As the alarm bells rang out, piercing the quiet night, Ian awoke with a jarring sense of fear. When he heard the sounds of battle carried in through the cracks in the window of his room, his fear immediately turned to relief. He was certain that someone had finally come to rescue him and his mum.

Ian leapt from his bed and fumbled around in the dark for his clothes. If he was getting rescued tonight, he'd want to be wearing his clothes and not a nightshirt. Dingle didn't budge from his spot on the warm bed; he looked up only once, gave Ian a disinterested glance, yawned, and laid his head back on his paws.

"Ye're nae much of a guard dog, ye flea-ridden beast!" Ian mumbled.

Just as he was pulling on his second boot, Ian heard heavy footsteps coming down the hall outside his door. Quickly, he grabbed Dingle, who yelped in protest at having his sleep disturbed. Ian's intent had been to hide in a dark corner or under his bed, but the door flew open before he could do any such thing.

Ian spun around to see Malcolm standing in his doorway. Light from the torches spilled into the room. Ian swallowed, the fear rising with bitter bile that burned at the back of his throat.

"Son!" Malcolm nearly shouted. "We are under attack! I am here to take ye and yer mum to safety," he said as he held out his hand.

Ian hated it when Malcolm called him "son"; he'd rather have his eyes plucked from their sockets by scavengers than to be Malcolm Buchannan's son, real or otherwise.

Ian knew instinctively that Malcolm wasn't there to help. Something deep within his heart warned him not to leave with this man. They weren't under attack by someone wanting to harm either him or his mum, that much he was sure of. Whoever was swarming over the walls and fighting with the Buchannans was here to help.

"Come, lad! We must hurry! We have to protect yer mum!" Malcolm said as he extended his hand further.

He couldn't move; his feet were firmly planted, not from a stubbornness but from sheer, unadulterated fear. Nay, Malcolm no more wanted to protect Ian and his mum than he wanted to jump from the nearest cliff.

Having enough of the child's nonsense, Malcolm rushed into the room and scooped the quivering boy into one arm. He grabbed Dingle by the back of his neck and tossed him on to Ian's bed.

"Ye're fearful, 'tis to be expected," Malcolm said as they walked out of the room and into the corridor. "We will be out of harm's way in short order, lad. Ye, yer mum, and me will be ridin' away this night."

There was something sinister in Malcolm's voice, a menacing tone that made the hair on the back of Ian's neck stand up. Chills ran down his spine, and he had the sudden urge to pee. Fear kept him stiff and made his fingers tremble.

Malcolm drew his sword with his free hand as they sprang down the stairs. Ian could see dozens of men in the great room below, dozens of swords clashing against swords, maces flinging through the air, and fists crashing against jaws. The smell of blood and sweat filled the air and made his stomach churn uneasily.

As they rounded the corner, Malcolm came to a dead stop.

"Just the man I wanted to see."

Ian knew this man! 'Twas one of the men who had taken him back to his mum that summer!

"Who the hell are ye?" Malcolm asked.

"I am the man whose here to send yer sorry soul to hell," Findley said calmly. He was relieved to see that Ian was still alive and apparently well, though the child did look terrified. He hoped the boy remembered him.

A flood of relief washed over Ian. Anyone that wanted to send Malcolm Buchannan's soul to the devil was a good man and a friend.

"Lad, 'tis me, Findley," he said as he took a small step toward them. "Do ye remember me?"

Ian nodded his head and took note of the blood splattered on the man's face, mail, sword, and hauberk. Finding courage, Ian began to wiggle against the tight hold Malcolm had on him.

"Be still!" Malcolm warned, not taking his eyes from Findley.

"Let me go!" Ian cried out. "I will nae go with ye!"

"Put the lad down, Malcolm," Findley said as he took one step closer. He hoped Malcolm would be distracted so that he could get close enough to run him through without harming the boy.

Malcolm tilted his head as he turned to look at Ian. "Shut up, ye brat!"

Ian struggled against Malcolm but that only angered him further. "Be still, or I'll feed yer carcass to me dogs!"

There was no doubt in Ian's mind that, given the chance, Malcolm would do just that. Mustering up more courage than he knew he had, Ian balled his hand into a fist and swung at Malcolm's face. His blow, though admittedly it wasn't a mighty one, landed between Malcolm's eye and nose. It was enough to send him into a fit of rage.

When the boy's fist landed on Malcolm's face, Findley's stomach lurched. He didn't need the boy angering Malcolm to the point of murder, but the look on Malcolm's face was a good indicator that he was to that point.

"Ye little fool!" Malcolm shouted as he let loose his grip. Ian began to fall from Malcolm's arm, but Malcolm caught him by the back of his tunic. In one swift motion, he lifted him into the air and stepped closer to the short railing.

"Ye've a death wish, lad?" his voice dripped with menace and seething anger as he lifted Ian up and over the railing. If he let go, Ian would surely fall to his death!

"Nay!" Findley yelled as he stepped toward Malcolm.

Malcolm grinned maliciously at Findley. "Stop!" he shouted. "Come closer, and I'll drop him!"

Rage simmered just under the surface. Findley hadn't come this far only to have the boy die now. His jaw clenched as he gripped his sword tighter. He looked at Ian, whose eyes and mouth were agape with fear. Even from where he stood, some good eight to ten feet away, he could see the boy tremble, his face turn pale with fear.

"If ye drop that child, ye'll be dead before he hits the floor below." It was a promise he fully intended to keep.

Findley could see a few of his men making their way quietly up the stairs, but the fighting below did not cease. He shot them a look and a slight shake of his head, fearing they'd do something to either startle or anger Malcolm that would cause him to let loose of Ian. The men held their positions.

"If ye want the boy to live," Malcolm said, as a thin sheen of sweat began to break out over his face, "ye'll step aside."

"There be no way out fer ye, Malcolm," Findley warned.

Malcolm was growing quite impatient. With a tilt of his head, he said, "Do ye think I fear ye?"

Findley shook his head. "Nay. But I think ye fear death."

Fury exploded over Malcolm's face. "Fear death?!" he shouted. "I fear nothin'! I merely want that which is mine! Let me pass now!"

"Nay," Findley said, shaking his head, again attempting to keep his voice level and calm. His insides, however, were anything but calm.

He wanted nothing more than to run his sword through Malcolm's heart.

"I cannae do that, Malcolm. Give me the boy, and we shall let ye live this day, that I do promise." He'd hang the bloody dog tomorrow, so 'twasn't a full-out lie.

Though the lad was small, holding him by his tunic and dangling him out over the railing was a strain on Malcolm's muscles. His arm began to shake slightly, and he knew he couldn't hold on to the boy forever.

Malcolm turned his head to look at Ian. The boy had grabbed Malcolm's forearm in a death grip, holding on with both hands. He could feel his sweaty little palms and fingers and could see the panic in his eyes.

It angered Malcolm to no end. 'Twas the brat's fault he was in this predicament. Had the little heathen not fainted at the sight of his scarred face all those many days ago, had he not awakened long-buried feelings of compassion and kindness, then Malcolm would have proceeded in a far different manner.

He would have hunted Maggy down and forced her to marry him. His seed, he was certain, would have already been firmly planted in her belly, and his dreams of a title, lands, and power would well be on their way to fruition.

But nay! The brat had to faint! He had opened old wounds, old feelings and turned Malcolm's life upside down. Admittedly, he had begun to grow fond of the lad. And that, he realized, had been his downfall. The beginning of the end.

There was no way out. He'd not be marrying Maggy. He'd not gain a title, lands, or respectability. All because of the lad who now dangled precariously from his hand.

Malcolm turned, very slowly, to face Findley, and Findley did not like the look he saw in the man's face. 'Twasn't anger or fury or rage but something far worse; 'twas the look of a man resigning himself to death.

"Give me the boy," Findley pleaded as he held out his shaky hand

and prayed that God would somehow intervene and change Malcolm's mind.

"I will see ye in hell," Malcolm said quietly before he closed his eyes and let go of Ian's tunic.

Ian gasped and tried to hold on to Malcolm's arm, but his hands were too damp with sweat! He tried digging in with his fingernails but to no avail.

The world seemed to slow down, everything moved in slow motion as Ian slipped from Malcolm's grasp. Findley shouted, a gut wrenching, "Nay!" He could not reach him in time to grab him! As Ian fell through the air, he took Findley's very soul with him.

———

FINDLEY FROZE with gut-wrenching grief as the cruelty of the situation set in. This was going to kill Maggy! 'Twould be an anguish she would never recover from.

His grief was quickly replaced with fury, rage, and hatred as he lunged toward Malcolm, a low, guttural growl coming from deep in his belly. Grabbing Malcolm by the shoulder with one hand, Findley thrust his sword into the man's chest, tearing through bone, muscle, and flesh until the hilt of his sword was buried to Malcolm's breastbone!

The sound of death gurgled in Malcolm's throat a few moments before blood spilled out of his mouth. Malcolm's body grew limp as his life quickly faded away.

Using his shoulder for ballast, Findley shoved hard, pulling his sword from Malcolm's chest. The force of it hurled Malcolm head first over the railing. Findley heard the sickening sound of bones crushing when the body hit the stone floor below. Findley had made good on his promise; Malcolm was dead before he hit the floor.

His stomach churned and the sour taste of bile rose in his throat. 'Twasn't the death of Malcolm that made him feel this way. 'Twas the thought of Ian lying dead on the floor below and what this news would do to Maggy.

His head began to spin, and his heart pounded mercilessly in his chest. His hands shook, and his legs were beginning to give out. Everything sounded muffled and disjointed as he stooped over and put his hands on his knees. Taking in great gulps of air in hopes of settling his stomach, he felt the world rapidly coming undone around him.

There was a hand on his back, and someone was speaking to him. It was difficult, however, to hear what was being said, and it took several moments to clear his thoughts. Maggy was still chained to the wall, and there were still men fighting to free her. He needed to get his wits about him before one of Malcolm's men ran him through or, worse yet, any harm came to Maggy.

"Findley!" Nial was shouting at him and trying to shake some sense into him. "Findley! Get yerself together, ye eejit!"

Now was not the time for his friend to act like his normal foolish self! Findley took another deep, steadying breath and righted himself. "Nial, I would advise ye to hold yer tongue," Findley warned, his voice shaky and filled with anger.

"And I would advise ye to take a look below!" Nial was smiling at him, and it made no sense to Findley how the man could find anything to smile about at this particular moment.

"Wipe that smile from yer face, or I'll run ye through, Nial!"

"Just look!" Nial said as he guided Findley toward the railing.

The sight below him nearly made him faint!

WEE WILLIAM HAD no doubt that it was an act of divine intervention that had just taken place. He had fought his way into the keep with nary a scratch to his own person. Aye, the Buchannan men might be a fearless lot of the devil's own, but most had taken one look at Wee William and had run in the other direction.

There had been several, however, who had tried—albeit unsuccessfully and to their own detriment—to slay him with sword, dagger, or kill him with a mace. As Wee William made his way into the keep, he had paused long enough to see that Malcolm held a wee lad over the railing! Knowing Malcolm to be tetched, Wee William had no doubt that the man would drop the lad. His pulse quickened as he looked up and saw the expression on Malcolm's face – one of disgust and anger. It was the flicker of fear in Findley's eyes that warned this night would not turn out as they'd planned if anything happened to the boy.

A sigh of relief escaped Wee William when saw that Richard was standing under the walkway, ready to catch the lad. The relief was short-lived, however, when he saw a Buchannan man running toward Richard with his sword drawn. Richard was too focused on the child dangling in the air and could not see the man coming toward him.

Wee William grabbed a knife from his belt and flung it through the air as he raced toward Richard. The knife hit its intended target, in the middle of the man's back. The shock from being stabbed knocked the man forward and into Richard! The two fell to the ground and slid a few feet, coming to a stop under the walkway.

Known for his size, girth, and strength, but not at all for speed, Wee William practically flew through the great room to stand where Richard had been just a moment earlier. He reached the spot under the walkway in time to catch Ian in both hands just moments after Malcolm dropped him!

Wee William could not stop his forward momentum. Wrapping his arms around the boy, he spun in the air and landed on top of Richard and the now dead Buchannan man, crushing them both under his great weight and causing them to slide into the far wall.

As they slid into the wall, Wee William saw a body fall through the air and land where they'd just been standing. The sound of crushing bones and tearing flesh made Wee William's stomach lurch.

Wee William felt his heart quit beating for several moments, as he lay in the heap and fought to catch his breath. The little boy was clinging to him, trembling and quaking with fear. Wee William finally caught his breath, willed his heart to beat, and rolled to his side to stand. He whispered soothing words to the boy as he patted his back.

"Och!" Richard said as he rolled from under the dead man. "How many stone do ye weigh, Wee William?" he groaned as he kicked away the body that draped over his leg.

Wee William smiled down at Richard, who was covered in blood and sweat. "All of 'em!" he said as he tried to shift the lad around so that he might extend a hand to Richard. The little boy had a death grip around Wee William's neck and torso and would not let go. Letting out a sigh, Wee William let go of the boy, shook his head, and smiled for the boy still clinging to him like a leech! Wee William reached his hand out to help Richard to his feet.

"Lad, ye can let go now," Wee William encouraged him.

Ian shook his head quickly, increasing his grip instead of loosening it. There was no way he'd let go! If he let go, he would die, and his mother would be sorely disappointed in him.

When the trio stepped from under the walkway, Wee William felt an intense sense of joy fill him to the core. The dead man was Malcolm Buchannan.

Wee William smoothed the boy's hair with the palm of his hand and continued to speak soothingly to him. "Ye must be the Ian we have come for?" he asked, hoping to calm the boy's fears.

Ian nodded his head as the tears began to flow. He could still hear the fighting taking place all around them, and he wanted nothing more than to find his mum and leave.

Wee William looked around at the death and destruction and decided it was probably best that the lad keep his eyes shut.

"Wee William! Richard!" Findley was shouting from the floor above.

They turned and looked up to see a very happy and relieved Findley staring down at them. Though he looked a bit green, his relief was quite evident. "Search Malcolm fer a key!"

Richard gave a nod of his head and bent to one knee. Around Malcolm's neck was a thin leather necklace holding one key. Using his knife, he cut the strip of leather and pulled the key from it. He rose and threw the key up to Findley who shot back his thanks.

"Get the lad out of here!" he called down to his brother and friend.

Wee William and Richard gave quick nods of their heads and raced out of the great room. Findley stood at the railing and watched as Wee William and Richard safely made their way out of the keep. His gaze then set upon the dead body of Malcolm Buchannan.

The man lay on his back, his body twisted and broken, his dead eyes staring back up at Findley. From his vantage point, Findley could see a dark pool of blood as it oozed from Malcolm's head. One of Malcolm's legs was bent in an unnatural fashion, the calf bone poking through the flesh.

Relieved as he was that the evil cur was now dead, Findley sent a silent prayer of thanks up to the good Lord. He reached inside his tunic and pulled out the bit of bloodied fabric that he'd been carrying around for all these days.

He tossed it over the railing and watched as it slowly fell through the air. It flittered slightly in the breeze that blew through the open doors, before landing across Malcolm's dead, milky eye. It rested there briefly before the breeze lifted it ever so slightly, tossing it into the pool of Malcolm Buchannan's blood -- the blood of innocents now avenged with the blood of the evil and guilty.

RICHARD FLUNG open the door of the waiting carriage as arrows flew through the air. Wee William lunged in through the open door with Ian still clinging to him for dear life. When he landed, he nearly toppled the carriage over from the force of his landing. Richard didn't bother with trying to shut the door as Wee William's legs were dangling out of it.

Swiftly, Richard climbed up and into the driver's seat, grabbed the reins, and snapped the horses into action. Soon they were racing away from the keep and making their way through the gates. No one gave chase as they flew through the dark night to safety, all the while Wee William was half in and half out of the carriage.

With key in hand, Findley raced back to the room where Maggy was shackled. Rowan looked very relieved to see Findley approaching with the key. Nial and three of his men were not far behind.

"Maggy!" Findley said as he rushed into the room. "I have the key!"

Moments ago, she had been convinced that she had no more tears to cry, but seeing Findley return unharmed with the key brought a torrent of them spilling from her eyes.

With shaking fingers, Findley managed to unlock the first shackle. Weak from thirst, hunger, and being hung on the wall like a banner for far too long, Maggy groaned. Sharp jolts of pain shot through her arms and feet as she began to fall away from the wall. Findley caught her with his arm as he handed the key to Rowan.

When she was finally free of the shackles, Findley scooped her up in his arms. "Och! Maggy, love!" he whispered into her ear. "I have missed ye!"

She wanted very much to wrap her arms around his neck, but the pain was too much. She could only fold her arms over her chest and grab onto his tunic. Between sobs she asked if they'd found Ian.

"Aye, Wee William and Richard have him," Findley said as they made their way out of the room. He decided it best to leave out the part where Ian was dangled over the railing and dropped. "He is safe and well, Maggy, and ye will be as well."

With Maggy in his arms, Findley hurried down the hallway with Nial and his men leading the way and Rowan bringing up the rear. Swiftly but cautiously, they made their way down the stairs as the fighting appeared to have died down considerably.

Findley took note of the dead and dying men all around him. He allowed a sense of pride to wash over him as he saw that his men, along with Caelen's and Nial's, had things well under control. In short order they were out of the keep and heading toward waiting horses.

Rowan held Maggy long enough for Findley to mount his steed. He handed her up to Findley who settled her on his lap, wrapped an arm around her waist, and kicked the flanks of his horse. In no time, they were all riding through the gates of the keep at breakneck speed.

Mud flew up from the pounding hooves, the damp air cool against their skin.

With her head pushed against his chest, Maggy could hear his heart beating, even over the din of the racing horses. The sound of it soothed her as if she were a babe in her mother's arms. The only way she knew she was not dreaming was from the pain shooting through her muscles as they sprinted through the night. She didn't care where they were going as long as it was as far away from the Buchannan keep and its men as possible.

'Twas then that she thought of Andrew and Robert, and another sense of dread came over her. They weren't out of the woods yet.

"Findley!" she managed to squeak out. "We still need to find Robert and Andrew!" She'd not be able to rest or even breathe until she had all of her sons safe and in her arms.

"They be safe, lass," he told her as he dug into the flanks of his horse again. "We came across them on our way to get ye." He hugged her closer, glad to have her in his arms again.

Now she could breathe. They were safe, at least for now, but she knew tomorrow would hold a different story. She didn't want to think about tomorrow or all the morrows that would follow it. The only thing that mattered now was that their ordeal was over, and they were all safe.

But she knew that tomorrow would eventually come, and she'd be forced to face her new reality; the life she'd fought so hard to keep was no more.

Turning her face into Findley's chest, she wept bittersweet tears. Though relieved and happy to be wrapped in his arms and away from the Buchannan, she knew it would not last. As soon as Brockton learned she was alive, her life as she'd known it for three years would be over. In its place would be a life she had no desire to live, for there would be no place in it for Findley.

CHAPTER TWENTY-EIGHT

A low fire crackled in the massive fireplace in her room at Laird and Lady Kinleigh's castle. Maggy and her boys had arrived a sennight ago and were more than grateful for the refuge and safety the Kinleighs had so graciously offered.

Maggy still clung to her secret that she was more than just Ian's adopted mother. Until she knew what the future held for her, she would not feel safe telling anyone the truth. Guilt followed her every moment of every day.

Some might ask how she could have chosen which child to keep and which to give away. The truth of the matter was that Maggy hadn't possessed the strength at that time to make that decision. She had instead allowed Helena to make it for her.

Kate had been there during the birth of the boys. She was the only other living soul, as far as Maggy was aware, that knew the truth. Kate would take her secret to the grave as apparently Helena had done.

The more Maggy had thought about it over the past days, the more she realized that while Helena may have slept with Gawter, she had kept their secret safe. It didn't matter to Maggy why Helena had kept the secret, nor why or how she had ended up sharing a bed with

Gawter. All that truly mattered was the fact she had, at the least, not betrayed Ian.

She had not seen Findley since the night he rescued her and Ian from the Buchannan keep. He had reluctantly left her in the care of Wee William, Rowan, and some fifty MacDougall men whilst he went back to the Buchannan keep to help with the dead and wounded. Findley had promised he would return as soon as he was able. She had been too tired to argue with him and too heartbroken to do anything but agree. Maggy knew the longer they were together, the harder it would be to say goodbye.

And say goodbye she must, for news spreads quickly in the Highlands. She had received word from Laird Brockton just that morn that her presence was expected at Castle Maldreigh within three days.

Maggy sat in a comfortable chair by the fire, reading for the twentieth time Laird Brockton's missive. She looked every bit the lovely Lady de Menteith, dressed as she was in an elegant gown of yellow silk and matching damask slippers. Surrounded by beautiful furnishings, a maid standing nearby to do whatever bidding Maggy might give, opulent and luxurious fabrics spread upon her bed and dripping from the windows, one would think there could be no sorrow in such a fine room.

But Maggy's heart was filled with sorrow. She missed Findley beyond measure, and nothing anyone could say or do could break her melancholy. Lord knows that Wee William and Rowan had tried over the days to lift her spirits, as had her sons. The only thing that made her feel better was the knowledge that Liam and Collin had arrived safely at Castle Gregor. But as soon as Laird Brockton learned of Liam's whereabouts, he would send for him as well.

She had slept nearly non-stop the first three days after arriving at the Kinleigh's home, yet somehow she still felt tired and weary. She ate little and declined Lady Judith's invitations to dine with them or to join her in their grand solar to embroider, sew, or otherwise pass the time.

Maggy had no desire for small talk and definitely no desire to start living the life of a lady again. She longed for the days when she and her boys were all together. She missed fishing with them and seeing their excited faces when they'd caught a rabbit or pheasant for their supper. She missed the evenings they'd spent around the fire where she told stories of Beowulf and Grendel. It was the simple life, free from men making demands of her or bargains to gain her hand in marriage. Och! What she would not do to go back to those days.

And if not those particular days, then she wished for a simple life that she could spend with Findley. With each memory of him, her heart broke a bit more. When she thought of the number of days that lay ahead of her, thousands of them and none of them with Findley at her side, her heart broke even more. Unbelievable sadness filled her, knowing she could no more go back to her old life than she could change the future that lay ahead of her.

There came a gentle rapping at her door, which Maggy ignored. She told her maid to send whoever it was away, for she had no desire to see anyone. She wanted to keep to herself, remain alone and private in her misery.

Lost as she was in her own thoughts, she did not realize it was Lady Judith until the woman sat in the chair in front of her.

"Lady Judith," she whispered with a slight nod of her head. "I am sorry, but I am not feeling well this day. I do nae make good company."

Lady Judith studied Maggy closely for a moment. She knew it wasn't the ague or other disease that paled Maggy's skin or put the dark circles under her eyes. 'Twas a broken heart.

"Lady Margaret," she began.

Maggy held her hand up. "Please, do nae call me that. I do nae wish to be referred to as Lady de Menteith or any other title, for that matter. I wish to simply be Maggy again."

Judith lifted an eyebrow and pursed her lips. She took a deep breath in through her nostrils and chose her words very carefully. "You're being a selfish twit," she said bluntly.

Maggy's eyes widened, quite astonished with Lady Judith's insult. "Selfish? Me?" she shook her head in disbelief. "What do ye ken of me heart or why I feel the way I do?"

Judith shook her head slightly and rolled her eyes. "Do ye think ye're the only woman ever to have a broken heart? Do ye think ye're the only woman ever to curse being born a female or never having a say in her own future?"

Maggy's brow creased as she took a deep breath. "Nay, I ken I am not the first, nor shall I be the last. But it still does nothin' to make me feel better."

"Maggy," Judith folded her hands in her lap. "Ye have five sons ye're blessed with. 'Tis time ye started thinking of them."

Maggy stood abruptly and went to stand before the tall window. "I do think of me sons! I think of them all the time and I worry what will happen to them! Laird Brockton will surely send all but Liam away, and then what? What happens to Robert, Andrew, Collin, and Ian?" she choked back the tears and tried to tamp down her worry over them. Her only prayer was that Findley would take them in, for she knew Laird Brockton or any future husband he might bargain for her would not be willing to take in all of her sons. The thought of never seeing them again made her stomach ache.

"Laird Brockton will nae let me keep them," she said as she wiped away an errant tear. "No doubt he is already found a man for me to marry, and it would nae be any man of my choosing! I'll lose them, all of them."

She stared out at the rolling hills of the Kinleigh's lands. The trees had lost most of their leaves. The nearly bare branches, black from yesterday's rains, stood straight and tall against a lead-gray sky and seemed to match Maggy's dark mood.

Her biggest worry out of all of this was Liam. What kind of man would he grow up to be if she were forced to marry some weak, sniveling fool or worse yet, another cruel and unkind man like Gawter? Would he not have any positive men in his life, men like Findley, who would show him how to be strong, brave, and honorable?

Judith remained seated by the fire as she watched and listened to Maggy. She knew Maggy's heart was breaking, and she felt like she had no control over her own life. Judith remembered feeling much that same way some twenty years ago when she had fallen in love.

"Maggy," Judith said quietly. "I ken ye worry over yer sons, but hear my words now. 'Tis them ye must concentrate on. Do whatever ye can to ensure they grow up to be good men. Ye might not be able to control every facet of yer world, lass, that much I'll give ye. But ye can control how yer lads are raised."

Maggy spun around, anger etched across her face and burned in her eyes. "How can I do that if they all are sent away?" she seethed.

"Ye can choose where they go and what influences anyone might have on Liam. Ye especially can show him."

"How, Lady Judith?" Maggy asked, her voice laced with confusion and desperation. She couldn't fathom at the moment how she could have any positive influence on any of her sons if she weren't with them or if she were forced to marry some vile or despicable man.

"By example!" Judith said as she stood up and came to stand by Maggy. "Ye show yer lads that ye're strong, lass! Ye show Liam how a woman can be dutiful yet strong. Ye show him that his first duty is to his family, then his people. Show the lad how to be strong, kind, and loving by being strong, kind, and loving for him. Ye lead by yer own example."

Maggy understood what Judith meant, but it did nothing to ease her broken heart. There were more than just five young boys counting on her. There were people at Castle Maldreigh who would depend upon her, as well as the farmers and tenants that were spread across the vast holdings that Liam had inherited. Aye, they would all look to her as an example.

"But what if the husband Laird Brockton chooses does nae allow me to have a say in anythin'?" Maggy murmured. 'Twas a very distinct possibility that Brockton would choose someone who would not allow Maggy any say in the running of her own life or that of her son, and that angered her to no end.

"Och! Maggy, ye're a woman fer the sake of Christ!" Judith said as she took hold of Maggy's arms. She was fully prepared to shake some sense into her if she must. "Ye're a woman, and 'tis time ye started actin' like it!"

Maggy stared back at Judith, quite surprised at her tone and choice of words. While Maggy had only met her on a few brief occasions some years ago, she could not have considered her a friend until this very moment.

"Maggy, 'tis time ye went home," Judith told her. "And ye do what ye must to move forward. Ye find a way to be an example to yer lads, and the rest will fall into place."

"Judith, I miss him," Maggy said as the tears began to flow freely. "I miss him so much that me heart feels as if it's been torn in two, and it will never mend!"

Judith drew Maggy into her arms. "Aye, I know that feeling all too well, lass," she whispered. And she did know, for years ago she herself had fallen in love with a braw, strong man. A man she loved more than her next breath. The memory of when she had to say goodbye to him was as fresh and vivid as if it had happened only this morn. Her father had done everything in his power to ensure the two of them could never be together. But Judith also knew that sometimes fate intervenes. And nothing man does can stop it.

"Are ye ready, Maggy, to give yer lads a home now?" Judith asked as she rubbed Maggy's back.

Maggy wiped her tears on her sleeve and sniffed knowing what Judith referred to. Though she firmly believed that home was wherever your family was, there was so much more that she could give her boys. Mayhap Judith had been right to call her selfish.

All these years she'd been so worried about being forced into another loveless marriage that she hadn't thought about the hardships she'd put her sons through. Aye, she knew the sacrifices she had been making, but what sacrifices had she asked of her sons?

Aye, they'd been loved and she had given them everything she possibly could, but there was more she could have done. How many nights had she lain in bed wishing she could give them a warm home, one where the walls kept out the bitter winter winds or the pounding summer rains but hadn't? How many times had she had to send them to bed with nothing more in their stomachs than warm broth and dry bread when she had the power to give them so much food they'd have grown fat?

How many times had she patched torn tunics or given them clothes far too big, when they could have had clothes made from the softest lawn or cotton?

And what of the responsibilities thrust upon Robert to act as the man of the house when he should have been playing at the carefree games of childhood?

She'd robbed them all, and for what reason? To keep herself free and from being thrust into another loveless marriage. She was a thief, robbing Liam of his heritage and birthright and the other boys from having a far better life than she had given them.

Guilt consumed her then, and it made her stomach twist.

And what of Findley? She'd agreed to marry him knowing full well that Laird Brockton would never allow it. Another act of selfishness on her part just so that she might have one night of feeling loved, desired, and cherished. And what good would come of it? How badly would Findley's heart break when he returned and learned that they could not ever be together? She was a liar and a thief. She'd stolen her sons' childhoods and their futures right along with Findley's heart.

Maggy knew what she must do. She'd take her sons and return to Maldreigh. She might not have too much say in her own future, but she would do what she could for her sons.

And Findley? There was nothing to be done about that, other than beg his forgiveness and promise him that no other man would own her heart. It would forever belong to him.

———

WEE WILLIAM, Rowan, and the other MacDougall men, along with a contingent of Kinleigh soldiers, had acted as escort for Maggy and her sons on their journey back to Maldreigh. The boys were each dressed in fine tunics, breeches, and warm cloaks. Much to Ian's dismay, he was forced to ride in the carriage with Maggy, while Robert and Andrew were allowed to ride atop fine horses with the other men.

Only a few short months ago, Ian would have been allowed to ride with the men, but everything was different now, and it was very difficult for him to understand why. His mum refused to explain it and instead had given an answer that many parents give their young when they don't believe the child capable of handling the truth of a matter: We will discuss it when ye're old enough to understand.

He pouted most of the first day of their journey, refusing to speak to his mother on those rare occasions when she wasn't looking out the window. Ian knew there was something serious happening, but he couldn't begin to guess just how serious a matter it was. He supposed that in the end it really didn't matter, for he was no longer in Malcolm Buchannan's keep, and he and his brothers would soon have a grand home in which to live.

None of the boys appreciated the new clothing they'd been given. Aye, 'twas nice to be warm, but the clothes were far too fancy for their liking. They would have much preferred a simple tunic, leather trews, and cloaks like the men around them wore. Robert mumbled that when he was older, he'd not wear such frilly and frivolous clothes, to which both Andrew and Ian wholeheartedly agreed.

They finally arrived at Castle Maldreigh. It was an imposing sight to behold. Four stories tall and made from gray, black, blue, and red stones, it was very impressive, to say the least. Turrets and towers were abundant, as the castle seemed to stretch on forever. They entered through a large stone wall, crossed over a long stone bridge before spilling into the cobblestone courtyard.

The older boys dismounted and stared up at the castle. Ian nearly tripped over his own two feet in his mad scramble to be out of the infernal carriage. He stood beside his brothers, staring up at the magnificent building before them.

Wee William and Rowan dismounted and handed their horses off to one of their men. The men, coming to stand beside the boys, were also impressed with the castle and lands spread out before them.

"Ye must remember yer manners at all times, lads, in a place like this," Wee William said as he ran his hand across Ian's head.

"Aye," was all Ian could manage to utter at the moment, as something niggled at the back of his mind. He felt as though he had been here before, but surely he'd remember a place like this.

"I pray they treat us better than the last time we were here," Robert muttered. He was far from glad to be returning, for his memories of the place were not fond ones. He remembered Gawter and Laird Brockton far too well, and he hadn't cared for either of them.

"Aye," Andrew agreed. While he had lived not far from here and hadn't spent as much time in the castle as Robert, Liam, and Ian had, he had heard enough stories about Laird Brockton to give him the willies.

Rowan helped Maggy from the carriage and took note of her red-rimmed eyes and still damp cheeks. He gave her hand a reassuring squeeze. "Ye'll be all right, lass," he told her. He could only hope that he was right.

Wee William had filled Rowan in as much as he was able on the story of how Lady Margaret de Menteith became Maggy Boyle. Admittedly, Wee William didn't know all the facts and was sure there was much more of it to be told. But he had sworn an oath to Findley that he'd not leave Maggy's side until he returned.

A tall, gray-haired man with a stooped back opened the enormous wood doors and slowly walked down the stairs to stand before Maggy.

"Lady de Menteith, I presume?" he said with a scratchy voice and a slight bow at the waist.

"Aye," Maggy said, not recognizing the man.

"I am Daniel," he said with another bow. "Laird Brockton put me in place here after your..." He had almost said death but thought better of it. "Departure."

"'Tis good to meet ye, Daniel," Maggy said. Wee William detected a slight note of something close to disgust in Maggy's voice. "I am sure ye've done a good job at keeping things in good repair in our absence," she said before giving him a nod and heading up the stairs.

Everyone scrambled to follow Maggy into the castle. They stood in a grand foyer that opened up to a grand gathering room. Several large doors and doorways led from the room, which was open to the third story. The floor was bathed in a myriad of colors from the afternoon sun that streamed in through the stained-glass windows.

"I think ye could fit two, mayhap three of Castle Gregor in this place," Wee William said under his breath to no one in particular. Rowan agreed as he looked around the room.

Maggy didn't bother with stopping to look. The worst years of her life were spent inside these walls. A flood of memories came crashing in, and she wanted nothing more than to go to her room, but first she needed to see that her sons were settled.

"Daniel," she said as she headed toward the spiral staircase. "See to it that my sons have the room next to mine."

Daniel cleared his throat. "Do ye mean Laird Gawter's old chambers?"

Maggy stopped on the stairs and turned to look down at him. He was one of Brockton's men, and she knew he was not one who could be trusted. "Nay, I mean the other room next to my chambers. I also want Rowan and Wee William to have rooms on that floor as well. Ye're to afford them every comfort and every luxury while they be here," she instructed him with a firm voice. She was the lady of this castle, and he would learn soon enough that she'd brook no impertinence from him.

"Aye, m'lady," Daniel said with a bow. "Would ye like to inspect the servants now?"

The way he said it made her skin crawl. They were people, not livestock. She was tempted to ask if he expected her to examine their teeth or hindquarters but decided it would do no good; the humor would fall on deaf ears.

"Nay, I shall meet with them later. For now, I would like baths drawn for all of us. And see to our things, Daniel."

He gave a quick bow and shuffled off to do as she asked. Maggy lifted her skirts and headed up the stairs and into her room. Rowan, Wee William, and the boys followed.

Robert and Andrew came to stand beside her. "Mum," Robert began, "Daniel?"

Maggy knew what Robert meant. "Nay, he canna be trusted if he is one of Brockton's men. Auld or no', do nae trust him."

"I doubt there is anyone here we can trust besides those of us in this room," Andrew said as he looked at the people surrounding him. "How long will we stay before we leave again?"

Maggy looked at him with a peculiar expression. "What do ye mean?"

"We won't be stayin' long, right? We will be leavin' soon, back to the way things used to be. Away from liars, cheats, and people who wish us no good will."

His words saddened her. As much as she would love to escape again, she knew she would not be able to keep her boys safe this time. A person could fake death only so many times in one lifetime.

"Boys, come here," Maggy said as she held out her arms. The boys came to her. She folded them into her arms and held on for quite some time.

"We will nae be leavin'. Not like we did last time," she told them when she finally stepped away.

The boys erupted into protests. "Nay!" Robert said as he balled his hands into fists. "We canna stay here, mum! We do nae want to stay here!"

"Do ye nae think I ken that?" Maggy said through gritted teeth. "I have no choice right now! I canna hide again, fer Brockton will nae allow it." She pulled a handkerchief from her sleeve and dabbed at her eyes. "I want to give ye a good life, boys. Warm walls and a sound roof over yer heads. I wish nae to see ye go hungry again or without warm clothes or decent food!"

Robert understood that she wanted to give them a better life but that didn't mean he had to agree with her decision. "Mum, we'd rather go without all of that than to live here. They did nae like us before, what makes ye think that's changed? They were so mean to ye and to us. I would rather go hungry than be under a roof with no freedom or worry over who I might anger enough that they take a belt to me hide!"

Wee William interrupted before the argument could get out of hand. "Lads, I think yer mum has had to make some decisions that she would rather she did nae have to make. Remember, this is no easier for her than ye." He gave an understanding look to Maggy.

"I think we are road weary and have been through much these past weeks. I say we get ye out of those silly clothes and out of doors for a bit," Rowan offered.

Maggy looked at him with thanks in her eyes. Mayhap between the three of them, they could get the boys to see the right of things. Rowan took the boys from the room and left Wee William alone with Maggy.

"Lass, I canna pretend to ken what's best fer ye or yer lads," Wee William said as he stood near the doorway. "I ken it could nae have been an easy decision to return."

"It wasn't, William!" she said as she sat in a tall chair by the cold fireplace. "If I would had any other choice in the matter, I would have taken it."

Wee William walked to her and sat in the chair opposite Maggy. "I would be hard pressed to offer advice on somethin' when I dunnae the all of it," he said as he raised his eyebrows and winked at her. "What say ye start at the beginnin', and we will see where we might end?"

Maggy doubted that there would be anything Wee William could do to help. It would be good to get the entire truth out, and mayhap if Wee William knew everything then he would be able to help Findley mend the broken heart he was sure to have when he realized they could not be together.

Two hours later, Wee William, normally one who is not easily surprised, sat across from Maggy, his mouth agape as he shook his head. Aye, there was more to this Maggy Boyle lass than met the eye.

He stood and walked to stand next to her, where he rested a big hand on her shoulder. "Well now, I think I'll need some time to ponder all this, lassie. Give me a day or so, and I think we can find a resolution to yer troubles."

Maggy patted his hand thoughtfully. "Ye could take all the rest of yer days, William, and ye'll nae find one where Findley and I can be together."

He gave her shoulder another squeeze before stepping away. "Now, lass, I thought ye'd have more faith in me than that," he pretended to be hurt, but the twinkle in his eye gave him away.

"Aye, I do have faith in ye, William. But I have more fear of Laird Brockton than anything else."

Wee William shook his head and smiled at her. "Don't give him that power over ye, lass. 'Tis when ye succumb to yer fears that yer adversary wins, no matter what kind of battle yer in." He nodded at her and then quit the room.

He left Maggy to think on what he'd just said.

Laird Brockton made his presence known the following morning. Without knocking, he entered Maggy's room with a flourish. He was every bit the domineering and egotistical man she remembered.

Thankfully she had risen early and was dressed when he came into her room unannounced and uninvited. Maggy thought on Wee William's words to her the night before and decided she'd not let the man see her fear.

"Laird Brockton," Maggy said as she rose from the seat at her dressing table and gave him her most elegant curtsey. She didn't bother dismissing her mousy little maid.

"Lady Margaret," he said.

He wore a cream-colored waistcoat and crimson pantaloons and looked more a member of the English court than he did a Scot. Maggy pushed back the urge to laugh at the sight of him, standing all proud while looking as though he had stepped in something foul smelling.

"'Tis good to see ye alive," he said, though the expression on his face belied his true feelings. Maggy knew too well how the man felt about her. She did not doubt for one moment that he was in truth quite angry to learn she had lived.

Maggy remained silent and pretended she hadn't heard him. Lifting the skirt of her green dress ever so slightly, she took a seat in the chair by her fire. With a wave of her hand, she invited Laird Brockton to join her.

"Imagine my surprise at learning ye and Liam were alive and well," Brockton said as he took the chair across from her. "Pray tell, Lady Margaret," he said as he crossed one leg over the other, "why the ruse?"

She was very glad he was being blunt and to the point. "Certainly, ye can understand the why of it, Laird Brockton."

"Nay, I am afraid that I can't," he said with a clenched jaw.

"I ken that it would nae be long after Gawter's death before ye arranged a marriage for me," she told him.

His dark brow furrowed. "Ye ran away, pretended to be dead, because ye feared I would arrange a marriage for ye?"

"Aye," Maggy answered. "I feared ye'd marry me to another man like yer nephew, and that was something I could nae tolerate." She also feared for her own safety and the safety of her son. Gawter had tried to poison her twice, and Maggy was certain his uncle had had some hand in those attempts. She trusted Laird Brockton about as much as she had trusted Malcolm Buchannan. Both were cruel men intent on lining their own purses and increasing their own wealth and status in life. The only real difference between the two was that Brockton had been born to a life of privilege while Malcolm had not.

Brockton looked surprised by her answer. "Was being married to my nephew that intolerable?"

Maggy resisted the urge to snort. "Aye, 'twas. And I have no desire to be married off again, Laird Brockton. I choose to remain a widow, all the rest of me days, rather than marry anyone ye might choose fer me."

Brockton shifted uneasily in his chair, his lips drawn into a hard, thin line. "Ye'll marry whomever I choose for ye, Lady Margaret. Elst

I'll be left with no other choice but to send ye to live at the nearest convent."

A convent? How many women had she known or heard of who, once widowed, had no other choice but the convent? With no lands, no coin, and no prospects at a husband, women were often forced to choose that way of life.

A convent meant she would be away from her boys permanently. She would have absolutely no say in how or where they were raised. Maggy's heart wouldn't allow her to take that risk.

"So, which shall it be, Lady Margaret? Cooperate or begin your packing now and ready yourself for the convent?" He really did not care which she chose for he held all the power.

Digging her fingers into the arms of the chair, more to keep from strangling Brockton than anything else, Maggy lifted her chin and sat taller. The only things she had left were her sons and her dignity. She refused to relinquish either of them to this man. "Ye may choose a husband fer me, Laird Brockton," she said demurely. Aye, he may choose, but it didn't mean Maggy would go willingly.

"I knew ye would be agreeable," Laird Brockton smiled. "Now, on the matter of these urchins ye call your sons."

Maggy had known this day would eventually come and had thought she had prepared herself for it. Nonetheless, her heart shattered; she was losing everything. Findley, her sons, her independence, and her life. All because one man, this pale, selfish man sitting before her, loved power and things more than people.

Any pleas for mercy on behalf of her sons would fall on deaf ears. She could not allow Brockton to choose where her boys might go. If he wanted, he could simply throw them out of the castle to fend for themselves. Or he might send them to another castle to work as servants, stable boys, or farmers.

Though she'd not be allowed to keep them here with her, she could give them something that Brockton could not take away: a future.

"I have made arrangements for them, m'laird," Maggy said as she fought back the resentment and tears. "They'll be goin' with the MacDougalls. They've graciously agreed to foster them fer me."

Maggy knew that under the love, guidance, and care of Findley and his men, her four sons would grow up to be fine men. Someday, years from now when they were older, she might even be able to see them again. It was painful to let them go, just as painful as letting Findley go, but she knew she had no other choice in the matter.

"I really don't care what happens to them, Lady Margaret," he said as he scratched the end of his long nose. "But I want them out of this castle today."

Maggy stood up as anger shot through her veins. "M'laird, I am not yet married off, and I am still lady of this castle. The boys will be stayin' inside the castle until Liam has returned." He might be able to broker a husband for her, but until that time, she still held some power over who could stay inside the castle walls and who could not.

Brockton studied her closely for a moment, and his face still held a look of disdain. "Very well, Lady Margaret. But I warn you: I'll not suffer any insolence or trouble from them."

Maggy knew all too well the man's ill temper, especially when it came to people of lesser stations in life. Robert and Andrew remembered it as well. She would keep them close by and out of trouble.

Brockton stood and quit the room without saying another word. Maggy fell back into her chair and buried her face in her hands. This was not going to be as easy as she had tried to convince herself. Her maid, who had stood quietly in the corner during the conversation with Brockton, rushed to Maggy's side.

"Wheest, m'lady," she whispered as she rubbed Maggy's back. "I ken yer heart breaks fer yer boys, m'lady."

Maggy wiped away her tears with the backs of her hands and sat up to look at the maid. What Maggy saw in the woman's eyes surprised her; she saw compassion. Until this moment, Maggy had never trusted anyone inside these walls, for they'd all been Brockton's people.

The maid smiled thoughtfully at Maggy and brushed away more of Maggy's tears. "Me name's Beatrice," she told her. "I am Claire's sister."

Hope began to grow in Maggy's spirit. Claire had been her maid and friend years ago. If Beatrice were half the woman her sister had been, Maggy would be able to suffer through this ordeal.

"Aye, ye remember Claire, don' ye, lass?" Beatrice smiled when she saw the recognition in Maggy's face. "She's well and livin' in Edinburgh, and I ken all about ye, m'lady. And I ken all about Brockton. We will get ye through this, m'lady. Ye'll see, 'twill nae be so bad as ye think!"

As much as Maggy would have loved to have believed the woman, deep down she knew better. It would be just as bad, for she'd not be with Findley, and her boys were being torn away from her. How on earth could she survive it?

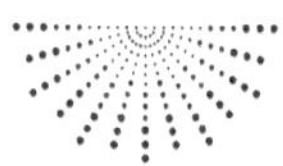

CHAPTER TWENTY-NINE

The days with her sons passed far too quickly for her liking. They spent their days indoors, hidden away in Maggy's room where she would read to them, tell them stories, and make plans for the time when they could all be together again.

They had not taken the news of being sent away very well. Ian cried inconsolably when she had told him he'd be going away. Robert and Andrew had fared only slightly better, each admitting they'd rather go live with the MacDougalls than to stay here and be subjected to Laird Brockton's cruelty.

Still, the boys held on to the hope that somehow they'd all be allowed to remain together as a family. Mayhap, they spoke hopefully, any man that Brockton might choose as Maggy's next husband, would be a good and kind man who would allow them to stay together. Maggy held no such hope.

While the daylight hours flew by, 'twas the nights the nearly did Maggy in. Their passage was agonizingly slow. She missed Findley, missed him so much that at times it hurt to breathe. She wanted nothing more than to hear the sound of his voice whispering in her ear and the feel of his arms wrapped around her. For the first time in a very long while, she felt *safe* with him.

Weeks had passed since she'd last seen Findley. Neither Wee William nor Rowan had heard from him, but they told her not to worry over it much. Winter was not far around the corner, and who knew what kind of treachery the autumn rains brought to the roads. They remained hopeful that he would soon come for her and the boys.

Aye, he might soon appear and want to take them all away, but such a life as that was not meant to be. Maggy was not in charge of her future; Brockton was.

The sun refused to shine for days on end, a harbinger, Maggy supposed, for things to come. The boys were growing quite restless and did not like being cooped up indoors. Maggy longed for the days where they could roam free in all types of weather, but she still felt the need to protect them from Laird Brockton. Keeping them in their rooms seemed to be the safest and most practical way to do that.

On this particular morning, however, the boys seemed more restless than usual. Rowan offered to take the lads riding, away from the castle and Brockton's ever-watchful servants. Maggy reluctantly agreed with the belief that since Malcolm Buchannan was now dead, there were no other threats to any of them, save for the ones inside the castle walls.

It was not long after breaking her fast that Laird Brockton came to her room. He looked positively pleased with himself, and Maggy knew his pleasant mood would not bode well for her future.

"I have tremendously good news for ye, Lady Margaret!" he said as he took a chair in front of the fire.

Maggy swallowed hard and remained seated near the window, her heart lodging itself in her throat. This would not be good.

"I have managed to find ye a husband!" Brockton said quite excitedly as he fussed with the lace cuffs on his waistcoat.

Maggy hoped he was far enough away that he didn't hear her gasp at his news. She sat frozen, her mind reeling, imagining the worst.

Brockton turned in his chair and stared at her. "Well? Are ye the least bit curious as to whom I have chosen?"

Nay, she wasn't. It mattered not who it was. He wasn't Findley.

"Your sullen mood bores me, Lady Margaret. I have worked very hard at finding a suitable man for ye."

Maggy finally found her voice. "I am sure ye have, m'laird," she said quietly. 'Tis no doubt that he is perfectly suited to ye."

"Aye, he is! I dare say, he is quite an amiable man. He is paying a decent enough bride price for ye, and he is allowing me to keep complete control of Liam's birthright until the boy comes of age!"

Maggy wished for a moment that she were a man so that she could wipe the smug smile from his face with her fist.

"His name is Philippe de Roth Montague."

Maggy swallowed hard and fought back the urge to throw something at Brockton. She had heard of Montague and his reputation for the perverse.

"Ye'll never want for anything, Lady Margaret, and neither shall I. He is quite anxious to wed ye. He is heard of your fine beauty but knows nothing of your bold personality. I daresay he will husband ye with a very firm hand," he told her as he picked imaginary lint from the sleeves of his coat.

Maggy knew that Brockton was deriving great pleasure from her discomfort and fear. De Roth Montague had been married three times before. Each of his wives had died suddenly. Rumors had it that he had beaten one of them to death when she refused to sleep with one of his cohorts while he watched.

"I have called for your maid. The wedding takes place after the noon day meal today, and you'll be heading to France immediately thereafter."

Maggy shot to her feet, her hands balled into fists. "France? Nay! What of Liam?"

"Well, Liam will stay here with me, of course. He will remain under my tutelage and care," Brockton told her, still holding the same smug smile. "I am sure that if you're good to your new husband, he will allow ye to visit on occasion."

Maggy began to pace in front of the window. After everything she had done to keep her sons together, Brockton was tearing it all apart. And for what? Coin? Power? Simply because he could? It had absolutely nothing to do with what was best for Maggy or her sons, and it had everything to do with Brockton being nothing more than a cruel, sadistic, and greedy man.

Her mind raced as it tried to find a way out of this. Rowan was out riding with the boys, and Wee William was in the hallway guarding her door. She could call for Wee William and ask him to break Brockton's neck or throw him from the window. But within moments, Brockton's men would descend upon her room and take them both prisoner for Brockton's murder.

Think, Maggy, think, she scolded herself. *Do nae let fear get in the way of doing what must be done!*

But try as she might, she could not come up with anything to persuade Brockton to delay the wedding. There was simply no way out of it. Her heart filled with dread and disgust. Findley, she thought to herself. She'd not get the chance to tell him how sorry she was, how thankful she was for all he'd done for her and for their time together. She would not be afforded a chance to say goodbye to him!

Beatrice knocked gently and entered the room at Brockton's command.

"There ye are! Please, help yer lady to ready herself for her wedding. And pack her things up, for she will be leaving this afternoon." Brockton told the maid without so much as another glance in her direction.

Beatrice had just learned of the plans for Lady Margaret to marry the Frenchman. She'd come to her room immediately, knowing the news would be another blow to her spirits. In the hallway, she had relayed the news to the giant called Wee William.

The look that had come to his face was enough to make her knees knock together in fear. He had her run back down the stairs to send someone to find Rowan and have him return to the castle immediately. By the time she returned to Maggy's room, Beatrice was out of breath and shaking with trepidation.

She flitted about in the large dressing room and waited for Brockton to leave. Poor Lady Margaret! Why must Laird Brockton be so cruel?

"To the devil with ye!" she shouted as she picked up a book from the ledge by the window and threw it at him. The book landed against his shoulder with a thud and fell to the floor. Brockton shot to his feet, anger ablaze across his face.

"Ye stupid wench! 'Tis that very attitude that brings ye nothing but trouble! Montague will break that high-spiritedness out of ye soon enough!"

"Nay!" Maggy shot back. "I'll nae marry him, and I'll nae go to France!" Her hands trembled, and her legs shook. There had to be a way out of this. She couldn't give up her sons!

In a few strides, Brockton was standing in front of her. "Ye will!" he pointed his finger at her. "I'll not have ye being insolent. Ye will marry Montague this very day, or I'll have ye tied and drug to the convent!"

Wee William heard the shouting and entered the room without knocking. He stood with one hand on the hilt of his sword, the other balled into a fist, waiting for Brockton to make a fatal mistake. If he touched one hair on Maggy's head, Wee William would think nothing of breaking the man's neck.

"Are ye well, Maggy?" Wee William asked quietly.

Maggy turned to look at him. "Aye." She choked back tears. "Laird Brockton was just leaving."

Brockton might be cruel and unjust, but he wasn't stupid. He knew there was no sense in raising the giant's ire, for they'd all be out of his hair before the day was out. He nodded at Maggy and quit the room in short order.

As soon as he shut the door, Maggy collapsed into the chair by the window. Wee William and Beatrice came to her side and offered words of consolation.

"Nay! All will not be well!" Maggy stammered. "He is forcing me to marry Montague, and I'll never see me boys or Findley again!"

"Wheest, lass," Wee William said as he placed an arm on her shoulder. "I have sent for Rowan and the boys. We will think of some way out of this."

Maggy swallowed hard and looked up at him. "What? By runnin'?

Nay, William, I canna run for the rest of me life! Me boys need a home. They need nae to be lookin' over their shoulders every day of their lives!"

"But lass, what other option is there? We can hide ye at Gregor, keep ye out of harm's way until we can figure out a way to be rid of Brockton," Wee William offered.

"And bring the wrath of the king upon all yer heads? What good would that do, William?" she wiped away the tears from her cheeks. Nay, she'd not ask anyone to give up their lives for her sake. She'd not put her sons in danger again.

"Ye don' mean to marry the Frenchman, do ye lady?" Beatrice asked, appalled at such a notion.

"What other option do I have that will keep all of ye safe? What other option do I have to give me boys a future?" Maggy twisted her fingers in her hands.

"Surely, there must be somethin' we can do!" Beatrice pleaded.

Maggy huffed. "Unless both Brockton and Montague drop dead before the noon day meal, then I am afraid there are no other options."

The heaviness of the situation hung in the room like a thick and heavy fog. Each of them were lost in their own thoughts for quite some time.

Maggy worried over her boys and what Findley would think of her marrying the Frenchman. Beatrice worried over the boys and wondered how long Maggy would survive being married to Montague.

Wee William worried that Findley would not arrive in time to stop this madness.

As her only way of protesting the marriage, Maggy chose to wear a simple gown of near black silk. She refused to have her hair done in any form of fashion and chose instead to wear a simple braid that hung down her back.

Wee William had begged her to try to delay the wedding, at least for a few hours until he and Rowan could come up with an alternative. She refused, resolving to go through with the marriage in order to ensure a safe future for her sons.

Downing a stiff shot of good whiskey, she steeled her nerves to face her impending doom. Her only request was that the boys be kept away from the ceremony. Beatrice had volunteered to keep the boys quiet and in Maggy's room while Rowan and Wee William stood guard over Maggy. Both believed she was making a dire mistake, and they had made a promise to Findley to keep watch over her. No matter how much they begged her to reconsider and wait for Findley, she could not be moved to change her mind.

Rowan and Wee William led Maggy to the gathering room. Before entering, she paused at the arched doorway and gave each of them a warm hug. "I thank ye both, fer all ye've done," she whispered. "I'll never ferget either of ye."

Rowan and Wee William had the rest of their men spread throughout the gathering room. Both sent up silent prayers for God to somehow intervene and stop this sham of a marriage. The numbers of MacDougall men was matched by Brockton's guards as well as Montague's. Of course, the MacDougalls were better trained and armed and could have easily taken charge of the situation. But out of respect for Maggy, Wee William and Rowan kept their tempers in check. Maggy was a stubborn lass, and there was very little that Wee William or Rowan could do to stop the wedding.

Maggy solemnly entered the gathering room and walked toward the dais where the priest stood. Brockton and Montague stood side by side in front of the priest, waiting rather impatiently for Maggy to join them.

The expression on Montague's face when he saw her for the first time sickened her. He was shorter than she by a good two inches. His dark hair, slick with grease, was combed back and allowed full view of his repugnant face. Thin lips sat under a thin nose, and his gray-green eyes appeared bloodshot.

'Twas lust she saw in those eyes, lust and the look of a man who'd just won some prize that he couldn't wait to get his hands on. A shiver ran down her spine as she walked with her held high toward the two men who held not only her future but her sons' futures in the palms of their greedy hands.

Montague whispered something in Brockton's ear, which brought forth a loud laugh. Maggy didn't even want to guess what they spoke of. Without the usual pomp and circumstance of a traditional wedding, she marched resolutely to the dais, arms at her sides and her shoulders thrown back.

With a nod to both men, she turned to the priest and curtsied.

"You're even more lovely than Brockton promised," Montague whispered as they turned to look at the priest.

Had the circumstances been different, she would have told him that he was even more hideous than she imagined. She decided the best thing was to remain quiet.

The priest began the ceremony to which Maggy didn't listen. Her mind was elsewhere, far from here. She was somewhere safe, in Findley's arms, while the boys played and laughed out of doors. The sun was shining in her daydream, and they hadn't a care in the world.

Lost as she was in her dreams, she didn't hear the priest direct Montague to take her hand in his. It wasn't until she felt his icy, claw-like hands take hers that she was jolted her from her happy daydream.

She gasped when she felt his fingers wrap around hers. She turned to look at Montague. That disgustingly haughty smile on his face repelled her even more than his touch. How could she come to him willingly, as a wife, when she couldn't stand the sight of him? She would be dead before dawn.

The priest had asked her a question that she had not heard. "Lady Margaret," he repeated himself. "Do ye take this man?"

It was in that moment that she realized she simply could not go through with it. How could she promise to love, honor, and obey Montague? Reaching inside her own heart, she finally found the strength to protest.

"Nay," she said, her throat dry and barely audible.

She felt Montague stiffen beside her and heard Brockton take in a deep breath. The priest looked very puzzled and repeated his question a third time.

"I said nay. I do no', I can nae and I will nae marry him!" Maggy cried as she twisted her hand from Montague's grasp and fled the room.

"Laird Brockton! Ye promised me the woman was ready and willing to do this!"

"I thought she was, monsieur," Brockton said as he gritted his teeth and watched Maggy running away. "Give me five minutes, and I guarantee the wench will be more than willing to proceed!" he nodded at Montague and went after Maggy.

Wee William and Rowan had been standing across the room, watching, praying and hoping that Maggy would change her mind. Seeing the sheer anger on Brockton's face, Wee William smiled. "Rowan, I think we better gather our men and prepare fer a fight!"

Rowan returned Wee William's smile and headed to give orders to their men while Wee William went to find Maggy and Brockton.

***

"YE STUPID, UNGRATEFUL WENCH!" Brockton yelled as he slammed the door behind him. He had found Maggy hiding in the solar where she paced back and forth in front of the fire.

"I canna do it! I will nae marry that man!" she screamed back at him. "Send me to the convent, I dunnae care anymore, but I swear I will nae marry that vile man!"

Brockton locked the door and headed toward Maggy. "Are ye sure of that? Are ye sure ye want to go to the convent and never see any of yer sons again?" he asked, standing just a step away from her.

"Aye, I am sure!" A life in the convent was preferable to marrying Montague. Anything would be better than that. Either way, she would never see her sons again.

Brockton was seething, working his weak jaw back and forth. She was ruining everything! He had worked hard to broker this deal with Montague. The man had paid a small fortune for Maggy's hand, a fortune that Brockton could ill afford to lose. With Maggy married and out of the country, Liam's fortune and birthright would be in his complete control. And if anything unfortunate happened to the boy, he would get back everything Maggy had taken away these past few weeks by returning. She was supposed to have been dead!

Unable to rein in his anger, he drew back his hand and slapped her across the face. The force of it knocked her to her knees.

The room spun, and bright sparks of light flittered in front of her eyes. Her face burned, and her eyes watered, not from fear or pain, but from the bubbling anger that was fast turning to a boil. She looked up at him defiantly. "Ye bloody coward!"

As she was scurrying to her feet, he bent over and yelled at her. "I gave ye more chances than I should! I should have tripled yer poison the last time I had a chance!"

So, he was behind those attempts on her life! Silently she cursed him to Hades. As she tried to crawl away, a loud crash came from the other side of the room just as Brockton hit her again, throwing her back against the floor.

When Wee William discovered the door was locked, he knew he couldn't wait for someone to bring him a key, and he knew Brockton wouldn't open it voluntarily. There was no time to waste. He kicked it down with one hard blow, slamming it against the wall where it broke into several pieces.

He hadn't seen Brockton hit her the first time, but he had witnessed the second hard blow to her face. Instantly furious, Wee William thundered through the broken door, reaching Brockton in just a few long strides. Wee William grabbed him by the collar of his coat and flung him across the room as if he weighed no more than a piece of paper.

Brockton landed on a chair, the force of it breaking the chair into pieces and knocking the wind out of him. Utter surprise filled his face, which quickly turned to fear when he saw Wee William approaching him again.

Wee William picked him up by the front of his jacket and threw him against the wall. Framed paintings rattled and fell to the floor, as Brockton slid down, his head lolling from side to side.

Wee William picked him up again, but this time, instead of tossing him about like a sack of leeks, he doubled his hand into a fist and slammed it across the man's face.

Blood poured from Brockton's nose and lips and a cut on his cheek as Wee William hit him again and again and again.

"William!" Maggy was screaming at him. "William, stop!" 'Twasn't that she really wanted him to stop the pounding he was giving Brockton. Nay, if she'd had her preference, she'd let William kill him! But she knew Wee William could be charged with his death, and that was something she could not bear to have happen.

Maggy was pulling at Wee William, grabbing his tunic and trying to pull him away from Brockton. "Please, William! Stop it! Ye're goin' to kill him!"

Wee William held back the punch he'd been prepared to send crashing into Brockton's face and glanced over his shoulder at Maggy. "And what be yer point, lass?"

She didn't know if she should laugh or cry! "William! They'll throw ye in the dungeon, then ye'll hang! I canna have ye hanged for killin' him!"

"And I'll nae have him thinkin' he can treat ye so harshly!" he turned back to Brockton who was limp, bloody, and probably wishing he was dead.

"He is nae man! He is a bloody cur who needs to learn his manners!" Wee William spat on the floor and prepared to send another hard blow to the man's face.

Maggy grabbed his arm with both hands, and he lifted her off the ground.

"Lassie, I warn ye to let go! Let me finish the bugger off!"

"Nay, William!" she was breathing heavily and hanging on for dear life. "I'll nae let ye go to the gallows! Leave him! Please, get me boys, and leave before they discover him like this!"

Wee William thought on the situation for a moment. Shaking his head and sighing heavily, he let go of Brockton as he lowered Maggy to the floor. Brockton groaned and slid down the wall slowly. He was unconscious and bleeding heavily from his face.

"Lass," Wee William said as he turned to face Maggy, "We need to get ye away from this place."

Maggy shook her head and stepped away from him. "Nay, just take me boys and be gone from here, William. When they discover him like this, ye'll hang fer certain," she pleaded with him.

"I made a promise to Findley, lass, to keep ye safe until he returns fer ye," Wee William took a step toward her. "I canna break that promise."

Tears welled in her eyes at the mention of Findley's name. "William, I ken ye made that promise, and I ken ye mean well. But I have told ye before that Findley and I can nae be together!" She swiped the tears away with the back of her hand. "As long as Brockton lives, there'll be no peace fer us."

A low growl escaped Wee William's throat. "Then why did ye nae let me kill him?" She was an exasperating woman!

"Because I canna let ye go to the gallows! He is nae worth it!"

Wee William growled again, realizing she was indeed stuck between the proverbial rock and a hard place. As long as Brockton lived, he would make her life a living hell. But if Wee William killed him, he definitely would be sent to the gallows. And with the kind of friends Brockton had, Maggy would probably be sent as well.

Maggy turned away from William and felt weak for crying so much of late. She was not a weak woman, but these ups and downs her emotions were going through were beginning to take their toll.

"Lass, please, let us take ye to Gregor! Marry Findley, and let the chips fall where they may!"

"Do ye nae think I haven't thought of that? Do ye nae think that I dunnae lie awake each night trying to find a way to be with him?" She took a deep breath and tried to settle her nerves. "'Tis all I do each night, William! I miss him so much that it hurts to breathe! And where is he? Why have we nae heard from him? If truly he loved me..." she let her words trail off, not wanting to admit that that had been one of her fears lately.

If he truly loved her, would he not have returned by now? Why the long weeks of silence without a word from him? Why had he not at least sent a messenger to let them know where he was or what he was doing?

"He does truly love ye, with all his heart."

Her heart sank to her toes and bounced up again! Was the voice she just heard real or a figment of her own desperate imagination? She took a deep breath and turned around.

"Findley," she nearly fainted at the sight of him! But there he stood, tall, braw, and smiling!

"Aye, lass, 'tis me," he whispered.

Maggy stood, unable to move, her throat feeling as though she'd just swallowed a handful of dust and walnuts.

"What took ye so long?" she finally stammered.

Findley smiled and ran to her, wrapping her in his arms and holding her close. He pressed kisses all over her face, which she returned with her own. "Findley! Where have ye been?" she asked between kissing his eyes and his cheeks.

"I have been busy, lass," he said, not wanting to put her down, not now, not ever. Playfully, he said, "I had to shine me boots then me sword. And there were bar wenches to woo-"

Maggy pulled away, a fine line creasing her brow. "Findley!" she began as she struggled to free herself from his grasp.

Findley threw his head back and laughed loudly. "Wheest, lass! Surely ye ken that I jest?"

"I ken no such thing, Findley McKenna!" she said as she hit his chest with her fists and kicked him with her feet.

Findley smiled as he planted a firm kiss on her lips to quiet her. It did no good for her to struggle, for the moment his lips touched hers, she melted into him, her heart swelling with joy and love for this man.

When he finally pulled away, he looked down into her eyes with a twinkle in his own. "Tell me something, lass," he said. "Are ye ready to admit yet that ye find me handsome?"

Surely, he was going to be the death of her! "Ye're insufferable!" she was frustrated beyond measure. This was not the time for his intolerable ego. "Ye're the most egotistical man I have ever met!"

"Aye, but ye always deny me handsomeness." He smiled down at her whilst giving her another squeeze. "Why is that?"

"Findley, this be nae the time to be yer normal pig-headed self, ye daft lummox! Ye need to see Wee William and me boys safely away!" She did not want to let him go, but she worried that Brockton's guards would soon appear. And when they saw what had happened to their laird, there would be hell to pay.

"I am afraid we can nae go just yet, lass," Findley's tone had changed to a more serious note.

"But ye must, Findley! 'Tis fer yer own good!" Why would he not listen to reason? And why wasn't he kissing her again?

"We have a wedding to see to."

Maggy's eyes flew open along with her jaw. "Nay! There'll be nae weddin' here today, Findley!"

He tilted his head slightly as he pursed his lips together. "No weddin'?"

Maggy bit her bottom lip to keep from crying. "Nay, there'll be no weddin'," she told him. How could he even think it? She'd die before she married Montague or anyone else of his ilk.

Findley set her down and turned away from her. He cast a wry smile and a wink toward Wee William. There was a flutter of a conspiratorial gleam in Wee William's eyes before he cast it aside to hold a most serious and solemn expression.

"But Maggy," Findley said as he pulled a sheaf of parchment from the folds of his tunic. "I have worked so hard to get a special license," he pretended to be deflated.

Maggy's brow knitted into a knot of confusion. "Special license?" He wasn't making any sense. How could she have fallen in love with a tetched man?

"Aye," he said quietly, glad that she could not see the gleam of mischief in his eyes. "And Laird Kinleigh, he helped me to obtain it. He will be hard pressed to understand how we could have spent all this time traveling to Stirling then waiting days to see the king and plead our case to him, only to have ye turn me down."

Maggy shook her head in disbelief and confusion. "Findley, what on earth are ye talkin' about?"

Findley wiped the smile from his face, took a deep breath to keep from laughing, and turned to face her. He held the parchment out for her. "'Tis a special license from the king, Maggy. Fer ye and me to marry." He handed the parchment to her. "But if ye've changed yer mind..."

Maggy sucked in a deep breath of air. It could not be! Certainly, he jested; certainly, he had scribbled the license with his own hand, for he was tetched after all. The king? How could Findley have received an audience with King David?

With trembling fingers, she took the folded bit of parchment and studied the seal closely. It did appear to be the royal seal, but since she'd never actually laid eyes upon one before, she couldn't be sure. Her heart was pounding as if it were an angry bear trying to escape a trap.

In her entire life she had never once felt like swooning. But with her spinning head and pounding heart, 'twas a very distinct possibility that could happen this very moment. As if blinded by what she held in her hand, she mindlessly searched for a chair with her free hand. Apparently thinking she'd found one, she began to sit. Or rather fall. Or would have, had Findley not stepped forward and caught her in time.

"Lass, ye dunnae look well," Findley said. Guilt for having teased her began to creep into his heart.

"Findley," she said breathlessly, "how...when?" she was unable to find the appropriate words.

He smiled then, realizing she was in shock and mayhap unable to understand fully what was happening.

"Ye see, lass, Laird Kinleigh was so pleased to hear that we had helped his wife to escape Malcolm's keep without so much as a scratch on her head that he was verra grateful!" Findley guided her across the room and helped her to sit down in a chair. He knelt before her and took her hand in his.

Her eyes were glued to the parchment, as if she could read whatever was written on it without opening it.

"I arrived at Laird Kinleigh's home just three days after ye left to return here. He was still away in Inverness, but Lady Judith, it seems, was very insistent on helpin' ye and me. I think she was mightily impressed with me battle skills as well as me handsome face," he said playfully. Maggy ignored him and continued to stare at the parchment.

"Laird and Lady Kinleigh be good people and friends of Angus's. When Laird Kinleigh returned and learned what had transpired, he insisted on helpin'. 'Twas he who obtained the audience with King David. Kinleigh, it seems, is a long-time friend of his. Something about helping King David leave France some years ago, but I digress," he said as he lifted Maggy's chin so that he could see her eyes. They glistened with tears, and he wasn't sure for a moment if she understood the magnitude of the situation.

"Maggy, King David granted us a special license to marry."

Mayhap 'twas all a dream, and any moment she'd wake from it to discover she had already married Montague and had lost her own mind because of it. To be certain it was real, she reached out and pinched Findley on his arm as hard as she could.

"Ow!" he said, looking quite perplexed. "Why did ye pinch me?"

"To see if I was dreamin'," she explained.

Findley threw his head back and laughed. "Lass, yer supposed to pinch yerself," he told her.

"Nay, I bruise easily," she told him as her lips formed into a hard line.

Findley saw the flicker of fire begin to creep into those green eyes. He'd missed that, her quick temper, as much as he missed the way he felt when she was in his arms. He had missed the way she smiled too, and her scent and the sound of her voice and the sparkle of those bright green eyes. He'd missed everything about her.

Maggy pushed him away and stood up. "And ye could nae think to send word to me?" she said as she began pacing back and forth. "Ye could nae send word to let me ken that ye were well and that ye were workin' to find a way fer us to be together?" her voice was growing stronger and louder.

"All these weeks!" she said as her pace quickened. "All these weeks I cried myself to sleep thinkin' I would never see ye again! Weeks of worryin' over what would become of me boys! Weeks of worryin' if ye'd ever forgive me if I was forced to marry someone he chose!" She motioned toward Brockton, who was still slumped on the floor.

"Maggy," Findley tried to speak, but she wasn't through with him yet.

"Nay!" she said as she turned away from him. Aye, she'd marry him without hesitation or reservation. But first he must know that he couldn't make her suffer as he had done these past weeks.

"Ye, Findley McKenna, are the most pig-headed, tetched, arrogant —" she paused for only a moment while she chose the most apropos expression she could think. "Ye're a pain in me arse, is what ye are!" She stomped her foot for good measure.

Why he found her anger so arousing and humorous at the same time, he couldn't begin to fathom. He couldn't have held back the laughter that escaped him if someone had held a sword to his head.

"And handsome!" he laughed. "Dunnae forget how handsome ye find me!"

He'd seen that look in her eyes before, and it warned that she was searching for something to throw at him. He'd not be caught off guard again. Quickly, he reached her before she could pick up the chair or anything else within reach, scooped her up into his arms and kissed her thoroughly.

She didn't resist, couldn't have even if she wanted to. While he was a pain in her side, she loved him more than she ever thought would be possible. The moment his lips touched hers, her anger melted away, along with her good senses. If she married him, she'd have to remind herself not to be swayed by his good looks or knee-bending kisses he seemed to enjoy bestowing on her.

'Twas the sound of Wee William clearing his throat that broke their kiss.

"If the two of ye are quite finished with yer arguin'," he said as he rocked back and forth on his feet, "mayhap ye'd like to share yer good news with the lads, get yerselves married, and—" he paused for a moment as a blush rose to his cheeks. "Well, ye get my meanin'."

Maggy smiled at Wee William then threw a hard look at Findley. "I haven't agreed to marry ye yet!"

"Aye, ye'll marry me," Findley said.

"How can ye be so certain?" Maggy challenged him.

Findley put her down, and with a smile, he pulled a set of shackles from under his jacket. He dangled them in front of her face and smiled when the look of surprise came to Maggy's face.

"I'll keep ye shackled to me until ye say yes," he said with a wink and a smile.

Maggy went red from head to toe. The last time she wore those had been a most pleasurable experience. She swallowed as she looked into his dark brown eyes. "Ye would nae dare," she said weakly.

"Aye, I would," he said as he lifted her wrist. "And lass, I dunnae have the key."

"Ye jest!"

His smile broadened. "I might have it hidden somewhere upon me person," he told her as he seductively ran the shackle up and down her arm. "Mayhap ye'd enjoy tryin' to find it?"

Her mouth suddenly felt dry, and her legs grew weak. Why on earth did he have such an effect upon her person and her senses?

"Wee William," Maggy said with a shaky voice. "Will ye take Laird Brockton to his room?" She could not remove the smile from her face as she looked into Findley's eyes. "And could ye see to it we are nae disturbed for a time?"

Wee William rolled his eyes and shook his head. *Women,* he thought to himself, *they be nae worth the trouble!* With little effort, he pulled Brockton to his feet and slung his limp body over his shoulder and left the room.

As soon as Wee William quit the room, Findley pulled Maggy to his chest. His kiss was soft, gentle, and very sensual as he claimed her mouth.

When he finally pulled away to look at her, he made a promise. "Lass, I promise to love ye all the days of me life. I'll make ye a good husband."

Maggy's heart swelled with love, joy, and more happiness than she felt a human ought to feel. "I love ye, Findley, with all that I am," she said as she kissed him tenderly. "And I make a promise to ye this day as well,"

"Aye?" he asked, looking every bit a man who had just had a dream come true. "What be that promise?"

A wry smile came to Maggy's lips. "I'll never throw another rock at yer hard head ever again."

Findley threw his head back again and laughed heartily. "Aye! But what of chairs and candlesticks?"

"Those I reserve fer when ye'll be actin' like a pig-headed lummox," she told him. "Fer ye are a man, and 'tis to be expected that ye'll be actin' a fool on occasion and will need me to remind ye of it!"

"Will ye ever admit ye find me handsome?" he asked as he kissed the tip of her nose.

"Mayhap, someday. If yer sick and near death," she answered.

"Ye do find me handsome then?"

"Mayhap," she said. "Mayhap, just a wee bit. But I'll never admit it aloud."

CHAPTER THIRTY

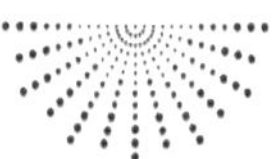

It was a brilliant, crisp autumn day with a vivid blue sky. The sun shone through Castle Maldreigh's tall windows, casting dappled shadows across those gathered to witness the wedding between Findley and Maggy. The bride and groom had decided to wait until all seven of Maggy's brothers, along with their spouses and children, were able to arrive in order that they could all share in the blessed day.

Wee William, Rowan, and Richard stood as witnesses for Findley, while Oribilia, along with Lady Judith and Kate, stood for Maggy.

There was not an empty chair or bench in the grand gathering room. The walls were lined with fierce looking MacDougall, McKee, and McDunnah warriors, some of them still wearing bandages over wounds received in the fight against the Buchannans.

Findley and his men wore their finest tunics and best MacDougall plaids. With broad shoulders, firm chests, and well-muscled legs encased in leather boots, they resembled statues chiseled from stone. The sunlight that poured in bounced off highly polished swords, sending shimmering prisms of light flittering around the room.

The boys proudly wore the MacDougall plaids of blue, green, and goldenrod draped over their shoulders, affixed with a MacDougall cairngorm brooch. Their *sgian dubhs* were openly displayed, tucked into their belts. Maggy had decided that each boy had proved himself to be a fine warrior in the making. After all they'd been through, the courage and bravery each had displayed during the past months were all the evidence she needed that her boys were responsible enough to own such a weapon. She drew the line there, however, and refused Liam the sword he so badly wanted.

Quiet murmurs of awe swelled across the room as Maggy finally appeared in the doorway. Wee William let out a soft, low whistle. Richard elbowed him in the ribs as a reminder that this was a sacred occasion. Others in attendance let out audible gasps as she stood in the doorway looking quite beautiful.

Much to her sons' delight, Maggy wore the ice-blue damask gown. Her auburn tresses cascaded down her back in soft curls, her smile brighter than Findley had ever seen it. Across her shoulder she proudly wore the MacDougall plaid and the cairngorm brooch Findley had given to her the night before.

Much had happened since Findley had returned with the special license from the king. Brockton was currently being held at Stirling Castle for his past attempts on Maggy's life. As far as the king was concerned, attempted murder was attempted murder. He had stripped Brockton of all his titles, lands, and holdings but had not decided yet what other punishment would be imposed upon the man.

Findley had told Maggy that he had overheard the conversation between her and Traig and that he knew the truth – that Ian and Liam were twins. Together they had decided to wait until the boys were a bit older, and the memories of Malcolm Buchannan were no longer so fresh in their minds, before telling Liam and Ian they were, in truth, twins. Findley and Maggy knew it wouldn't matter either way, as the boys didn't care about bloodlines or lineage; they were brothers in every sense of the word.

The sight of Maggy standing in the doorway, with streams of bright sunlight falling all around her, took Findley's breath away. He thought she looked like an angel as she smiled down the aisle at him. With her eyes glistening with tears of joy and a smile on her lips, she was a stunning sight to behold. Findley's legs began to shake, and his hands trembled; he could not believe this day had finally arrived. In a short time, they'd make their promise to love, honor, and cherish each other for all the rest of their days. Finally, she would be his.

Slowly, she made her way down the aisle. Findley's heart was pounding in his chest, and he could barely wait to have her utter the words he'd been longing to hear for months now.

Maggy stopped long enough to give each of her sons a hug before stepping forward and placing her hand in Findley's. As she looked up at him, so handsome and braw, she had to bite her lip to keep from laughing at him. The smile he wore, showing his straight white teeth, gave him the look of a proud, blissfully happy man.

After repeating the vows and promises as the priest instructed, Findley removed his sword and bent to one knee. With one hand on his heart, the other on the hilt of his sword with the tip touching the stone floor, he looked into Maggy's eyes and made his own pledge.

"As long as there is breath left in me, I shall love ye, Maggy. I pledge my love, my troth to ye. I pledge to protect ye. I'll lay down me own life fer ye." Tears began to fill in both their eyes. Findley choked slightly, the muscles of his jaw tightening, and he swallowed hard as Maggy wiped away the tears from her cheeks.

"I pledge to raise yer sons as if they were me own. I will always honor ye, respect and cherish ye, all the rest of me days. I love ye Maggy, more than I love the next breath that I take."

Clearing his throat, Findley stood and returned his sword to its scabbard. He did not wait for further direction from the priest. Placing his hand on the small of Maggy's back, he pulled her to his chest. With gentle fingertips, he lifted her chin, whispered "I love ye" and kissed her firmly on her lips.

A roar of cheers erupted throughout the room. Maggy wrapped her hands around his neck as she returned his passionate kiss. Her heart skipped several beats as he tipped her back, kissing her deeply until they were both out of breath.

When Findley finally broke the kiss, she nearly keeled over from lack of air and the excitement thrumming through her veins. He can kiss me anytime he wishes if he kisses me like that! Her legs wobbled as her face lit with a bright smile.

As they turned to face the well-wishers, Findley bent down and whispered in her ear. "Are ye ready to admit yet that ye find me handsome?"

Maggy couldn't remove the smile from her face. "Aye, as far as pig-headed lummoxes go, ye be handsome enough."

Findley quirked an eyebrow and gave her a wink. "'Tis a step in the right direction."

"And if ye kiss me like that again, husband, I am apt to admit to anything," she teased him and gave his hand a squeeze.

In a matter of moments, they were swarmed and pulled apart by their families and friends and nearly suffocated with hugs and well wishes. As Maggy and Findley stood in the middle of the crowd, they found each other with their eyes.

They smiled at each other from a distance. Findley gave her a wink before mouthing the words, "I love ye." Maggy blushed and returned his words.

It would be a good many hours before the celebration died down so they could slip quietly away to their room. At the moment neither really cared, for they knew they had the rest of their lives to spend loving each other. And that's just as it should be.

EPILOGUE

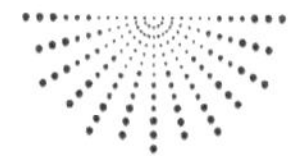

'Twas a few weeks before Christmastide when Maggy fell ill. Morning, noon, and night, she was throwing up, and when she wasn't throwing up, she was sleeping. None of the herbs or teas that Beatrice brought to her had helped to calm her stomach. Dark circles had formed under her eyes and her color had gone deathly pale.

The healer had been called to tend to her, and now they were locked away in Findley and Maggy's bedchamber. 'Twas the eve of Christmas, and Findley and his boys were pacing the halls awaiting news of Maggy. Findley was on the verge of breaking the door down if someone did not allow him entry very soon.

Ian and Liam were huddled together at the end of the hallway. Robert and Andrew paced opposite each other, while Collin traced his new da's footsteps and followed close behind.

After a time, Ian came racing up to Findley, his eyes filled with tears. "Da!" he said as he grabbed Findley about the leg and refused to let go. "Liam says if mum dies, ye will nae be our da anymore, and ye will send us away!"

Findley's heart felt lodged in this throat. He didn't want to think of losing Maggy. They'd gone through too much to have it all simply ripped away.

He scooped Ian up and hugged him close to his chest. "Ian, yer mum will be fine, dunnae worry it," he whispered, hoping if he said it enough times it might turn out to be true.

But Maggy had been so ill! She couldn't keep even a plain broth down, and it seemed as if the life was slowly draining from her. She did her best to maintain her spirits and tried not to have them worry over her. When she had asked Findley to summon the healer, he nearly keeled over from the fright. She must be seriously ill to call someone away from a family Christmas celebration. He couldn't lose her. She was his whole world.

When Findley opened his eyes, he noticed all the boys were looking up to him. He hadn't answered Ian's burning question.

"Lads, do nae worry over yer mum, she will be well and fine in no time. And no matter what happens, I'll always be yer da. I would never send a one of ye away."

"Do ye promise?" Ian sniffed and wiped away his tears with the palms of his hands.

"Aye, I do so promise!" Findley gave him a hug before setting him to his feet.

His thoughts turned back to Maggy. Please Lord, keep me wife safe and let her be well, Findley prayed silently as he resumed his pacing. He needed Maggy like he needed air. Without her, he was nothing.

Findley paused in front of a tall window that looked out onto the rolling lands of Maldreigh Castle. Together, he and Maggy and the boys were making this their home.

Together, Maggy and Findley made plans on how they could bring Maldreigh back to the glorious place it had been long ago. Come spring, they'd plant crops, invest in cattle and sheep, and in a few years, they felt they'd be on their way to having a productive castle and plenty of wealth to feed their growing boys.

But then Maggy had suddenly taken ill. And now she was sequestered behind the chamber door with the healer, and no one was telling Findley a damned thing! He paced and worried, his heart growing heavier with each passing moment. Findley had grown tired of waiting. If they wouldn't allow him entry, he'd bust down the door!

Just as he was raising his hand to pound on the door, it opened slowly. The healer, a woman nearly as auld as dirt, with long gray hair and more wrinkles than teeth, looked up at him with an irritated scowl.

"Och! Ye nearly scared me to death, m'laird! Ye shouldn't do that to an auld woman!"

Findley was irritated and about to tell her to get out of his way so that he could go be with his dying wife when the auld woman shook her head and clucked her tongue at him. "Ye can go see her now," she said. "But mind ye! Do nae upset her!"

Findley swallowed, suddenly frozen with fear. "How is she? Will she live?"

The auld woman shook her head again. With all the wrinkles and missing teeth, it was rather difficult to tell if she was scowling, frowning, or smiling.

"Och! She has news fer ye. She wanted to tell ye herself." The old woman shook her head again. "I warn ye, lad, do nae upset her none! She is in a verra fragile state, and she needs her rest."

Findley felt his heart fall to his toes. Nay! She couldn't be dying! He needed her, didn't she know that? Anger, grief, and sadness blended together and brought tears to his eyes.

The auld woman stepped aside, and he raced to Maggy's side. He knelt by the bed as he took her hands in his. The boys appeared, looking heartbroken, solemn, and very afraid for their mum.

"Maggy," Findley spoke, choking back tears.

"Husband!" Maggy smiled up at him until she saw his eyes brimming with tears and sorrow. "What be the matter?" she asked as she tried to sit. Were they under attack? Had someone died?

"Maggy, I love ye," Findley said as he squeezed her hands. "The healer didna—," he cleared his throat. "Should I make the boys wait in the hall while ye speak with me?"

Maggy tilted her head, a bit confused by the look on Findley's face. "Nay! Husband, tell me, what be wrong?"

"I dunnae! The healer said ye wanted to speak with me." He swallowed again, never before feeling this weak or befuddled.

"Aye, I do, but ye look so sad! Are ye nae happy?"

Findley shook his head. Mayhap she had little time left and was growing delirious. The thought nearly did him in.

"Happy? What have I to be happy about if yer dyin'?" he whispered as he buried his head in her hands.

"Dyin'?" Maggy asked. "Who said I be dyin'?" Had the healer told Findley something she did not share with Maggy? Was Findley here to tell her she was not long for this world? She certainly felt that way, with her queasy stomach and spinning head.

Findley looked very puzzled. "She did nae say it outright, but Maggy, ye've been so ill for weeks now! Tell me," he said, bracing himself for the worst. "What did the healer say?"

Maggy bit her lip to keep from laughing. Now she understood. They were all worried because she'd been so sick, and the healer hadn't told them what was the matter.

"Well, I be nae dyin'," she said as she tried to sit up. She looked at her boys and could tell that Ian had been crying. They all looked very worried about her, and that warmed her heart to no end.

"Lads! Please, yer sorry faces do me no good! And Findley," she said with a warm smile, "ye worry over nothin' that won't be solved come summer."

He wasn't sure if he felt relieved, angry, or sad. He supposed it was all of those things. She had only until summer bloomed across the valley! Aye, he should be very glad for having a few more months with his beloved wife, but his heart ached with realizing it was nowhere near enough time. He hoped her illness would not leave her suffering and lingering. That was no way for a beautiful lass to die!

Maggy rolled her eyes and punched Findley in the shoulder. "Husband! Please! Ye look like ye've lost yer best friend!"

Tears welled in his eyes and streamed down his cheeks. His lovely, sweet, optimistic Maggy! Even with the news she'd received, she still held her good humor. Och! He'd miss her!

"Findley," she said plainly. "I be nae dyin'. I be nae goin' anywhere for a verra long time. I have no illness, ye fool!"

He wiped away the tears and smiled thoughtfully at her. "Maggy, I love ye. Tell me true, lass!"

She let out a long, heavy sigh. "Ye are a fool. And a pig-headed lummox to boot! I be nae dyin! I be carryin' yer child!"

His face went blank, and he sat taller. He looked as though someone had just punched him in the stomach. "What?"

"I am with child, ye eejit! Yer child. Our child!" She let the words sink into his thick skull. Och, she had married a tetched man.

Had he not been sitting, he surely would have fainted from the shock. His hands shook as a new wave of emotions came over him. Aye, he was a father to five boys by adoption, but now? Now he'd be a father to his own flesh and blood.

The boys erupted into shouts of joy, while Findley paled further.

"Ye won't have a girl, will ye?" Liam asked, his face twisted into a look of disgust.

Maggy laughed at him. "We will have whatever the good Lord deems we should have," she said as she held out her hands for a hug.

The boys came to her one by one, giving her hugs and kisses and words of encouragement. She took note that Findley remained seated, looking nearly as ill as she felt. With a smile, she ordered the boys to go and enjoy the celebration below stairs.

She waited until the door closed behind them before turning her attention to her husband. He was staring at something on the wall, muttering under his breath, and appeared visibly shaken by the news. It wasn't the response she had expected.

"Husband?" she whispered as she took his hand in hers. "Are ye nae happy?"

Findley's mind had been racing for several minutes. How could she remain so calm at a time like this? He had resigned himself to the fact that she was dying, only to learn she was carrying his babe. He wasn't sure which one shocked his senses more.

He was stumbling over his own tongue and the only word he could manage to utter was "How?" He meant to ask how she could be so calm at a time like this. How could she be so relaxed and content when she was so ill? How on earth was he going to be a father? Suddenly he felt very weak and ill prepared for the task.

Maggy raised an eyebrow at him. "Findley, are ye serious?" she asked. "Surely ye understand how this happened! We cannae be lovin' each other mornin', noon, and night like we have and nae expect a child to be the result!" Not only was he tetched, he was a bit slow as well! How, indeed!

Findley couldn't resist the smile that came to his lips. "Lass, I ken the how of it! I meant, how can ye be so calm?"

Men. "Husband, I have been pregnant before. Although, I must admit I was never this sick with Liam. I suppose I am this ill because I carry your child, and he is sure to be just as stubborn as his father. But I'll nae allow him to grow to be as pig-headed."

Findley chuckled and squeezed her hand. "And if it be a girl child ye carry, I'll nae let her be as hot-tempered as her mum!"

"Hot tempered? Me? I ken not what ye speak of!" Maggy chortled. "When a man grows angry and speaks his mind, he is considered strong and intelligent. Let a woman act the same way, and she is hot-tempered. I dunnae see the equality in that!"

Suddenly he felt quite fearful. A daughter? If she were half as beautiful as her mother, he'd have to spend most of his time fending off the lads. He'd need more swords. He'd need to build a moat around their castle to keep potential ne'er-do-wells and defilers of her virtue away. He'd need more men who would swear their fealty and allegiance to protect her honor.

He would need more men like Wee William! Aye, if he had a few dozen men as tall, big, strong, and honorable as Wee William, he'd not have to worry about the countless fools who would be tripping over their tongues to get to his precious, innocent daughter!

Eunuchs. Dozens of them, and all as big as Wee William. 'Twould be the only way to protect his beautiful daughter's virtue.

"Findley?" Maggy was trying to gain his attention.

"Aye," he mumbled before looking down into her green eyes. Och! Those eyes! If his daughter had those same eyes, he knew he was doomed. He'd never be able to deny those eyes anything. He was going to make a most miserable father!

"Findley!" she repeated. "Ye look ill!"

"I am perfectly fine, wife!" He shook his head at her. Didn't she realize they had much to do to prepare for their daughter's arrival?

"Och! I swear ye'll be the death of me!"

"Hold yer temper, wife! I have much to do!"

Maggy looked up at him. He could tell she was confused. Women.

"And what do ye have to do? I am the one who has to carry this babe, then birth him, then there's the feedin', the changin', the bathin'-"

Findley touched her lips with his finger. "Aye, but I be her da! I have moats to have dug, more men to bring in to protect her, weapons to amass! 'Tis a great responsibility you're puttin' on me, wife!"

Aye, she'd married a tetched, pig-headed man. Her heart swelled with love and pride. He may be tetched and pig-headed, but she loved him. He was strong, braw, loyal, and very honorable. He was already a wonderful father to her boys, so she felt confident that he'd do well with all of the children they would have. And they would have many, many children.

He was going on about how he needed to protect their daughter from men who would want to steal away her virtue and her heart, but she wasn't listening too closely. She was studying his face and marveled at how handsome he was, even when he was angry as he was now, already worrying over the safety of a daughter that had yet to be born!

She had to bite her tongue to keep from laughing out loud. Aye, he was going to make a wonderful father, even if he was a pig-headed fool. A verra handsome, pig-headed fool.

PROLOGUE FOR NORA

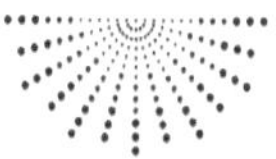

England
Late Winter 1345

Winter was unrelenting. It held on to the land as fiercely as a Highland warrior grasped his sword, refusing to let loose its grip and allow spring its turn.

The cold night air bit at the men who sat silently atop their steeds. Watching, waiting, looking for any movement, any sign of life that might stir in the cottage that lay below them. Gray smoke rising slowly from the chimney before disappearing into the moonlit night was the only sign of life coming from within the cottage.

Puffs of white mist blew from the horses' nostrils like steam from a boiling kettle. The nine were draped in heavy furs, with broadswords strapped to their backs, swords at their sides, and daggers hidden in various places across their bodies. If by chance anyone was awake at this ungodly hour, the sight of these fierce men would bring a chill of fear to even the bravest man.

Each man had been handpicked by his chief for the special quali-ties he held, whether it was his fealty, his fierceness, or his ability to enter a place unheard and unseen. 'Twas a simple task they'd been given: sneak in under the cloak of darkness and retrieve hidden treasures so they could be returned to their rightful owner.

The first inkling that things might not go as planned came from the fact that the night was not bathed in darkness as had been hoped. A full moon shone brilliantly, casting the earth in shades of blues, whites, and grays. Had they not been delayed two days by a snowstorm of near biblical proportions, they would have arrived two nights ago when it was certain to have been pitch black.

No worries, the leader of the nine had assured his men. The inhabitants of the cottage were more likely than not fast asleep at this hour. They would proceed with their mission, moon or no.

After studying the land and the cottage a while longer, the leader gave a nod of his head. He and his men proceeded toward the little farm, taking their positions around the perimeter. Two of his stealthiest men headed towards the barn where they dismounted, and with the grace and silence of a cat, they entered.

The leader stood with two of his men not far from the entrance of the cottage. They waited patiently, keeping a close eye on the barn as well as the cottage. Everything seemed to be going as planned. But the leader of the band of retrievers would not breathe a sigh of relief until they were far away from these God-forsaken English lands. The longer he remained on English soil, the dirtier he felt and the more eager he was to return to his homeland.

He wished he could break down the door of the cottage and slit the throats of the three bastards inside. His chief had shot that idea down, but not before thinking on it for a long moment. The chief had admitted nothing would have brought him greater pleasure than knowing the bastards would not live to see the light of another day. But he could not allow his men to take the chance of being found and taken to the gallows.

Nay, their mission was simple, and if all went well, no blood would be shed this night. In a matter of days, should the weather hold, the treasures would be returned and the men handsomely rewarded for their efforts.

Uneasiness began to creep under the leader's skin. The men in the barn were taking too long. Concern began to well in his belly. If the treasures weren't where they should be, he'd have no problem then in busting down the door to the cottage and killing the men inside. He shuddered when he thought of returning empty handed. 'Twas a possibility he did not enjoy. He swore under his breath he'd tear this farm apart until he found what he had come for.

God's teeth! What was taking them so long? He exchanged a look of concern with the two men who sat on horses beside him. Something was wrong. He could feel it in his bones.

After what seemed like hours, his men appeared from the barn and looked across the yard. They held up empty hands as they shrugged their shoulders. Damnation! This was not good, not good at all. He let out a heavy sigh and hung his head.

'Twasn't exactly how he had planned it, but at least now he had the opportunity to bash in the skulls of the three men inside the cottage. The idea of giving those sons of whores their due brought a pleasant tingling sensation to his belly. The night would not be wasted after all.

LIFE

"*Life is inherently risky. There is only one big risk you should avoid at all costs, and that is the risk of doing nothing.*"
– Denis Waitley

Isle of the Blessed

Forever Her Champion

The Edge of Forever

Arriving 2018

The MacAllens and Randalls Series:

Secrets of the Heart

Arriving in 2019:

Black Richard's Heart

Kiss of the Red Scorpion

The Daughters of Moirra Dundotter Series:

Mariote

Esa

Muriale

Orabilis

The Brides of the Clan MacDougall

(A Sweet Series)

Aishlinn

Maggy

Nora

ABOUT THE AUTHOR

USA Today Bestselling Author, storyteller and cheeky wench, SUZAN TISDALE lives in the Midwest with her verra handsome carpenter husband. All but one of her children have left the nest. Her pets consist of dust bunnies and a dozen poodle-sized, backyard-dwelling groundhogs – all of which run as free and unrestrained as the voices in her head. And she doesn't own a single pair of yoga pants, much to the shock and horror of her fellow authors. She prefers to write in her pajamas.

Suzan writes Scottish historical romance/fiction, with honorable and perfectly imperfect heroes and strong, feisty heroines. And bad guys she kills off in delightfully wicked ways.

She published her first novel, Laiden's Daughter, in December, 2011, as a gift for her mother. That one book started a journey which has led to fifteen published titles, with two more being released in the spring of 2017. To date, she has sold more than 350,000 copies of her books around the world. They have been translated into four foreign languages (Italian, French, German, and Spanish.)

You will find her books in digital, paperback, and audiobook formats.

Stay up to date with Suzan's App for Readers! Available for iOS, Android, and other smart devices.

Apple Store
GooglePlay

Stay Up To Date

www.suzantisdale.com
Email: suzan@suzantisdale.com

Tap any of the icons below to follow me at Facebook, BookBub, Instagram, Twitter, Goodreads, and Amazon.